Prai

'Emma Cowell is a masterful storyteller of sun-drenched, heartfelt, glorious stories . . . Delicious. Luscious. The perfect summer read!'
Adriana Trigiani, author of *The View from Lake Como*

'Beautiful, emotional and uplifting escapism with an exquisitely vivid Greek island setting. Utter bliss.'
Alex Brown, author of *Bring Me Sunshine*

'I was engrossed, hanging on to every word, and so impressed by *Under the Lemon Tree* that I will be recommending it to all my friends.'
Patricia Wilson, author of *Greek Island Escape*

'Greece is evocatively brought to life through a life-affirming and captivating story. A delightful read.'
Kate Frost, author of *One Greek Summer*

'A compelling journey of healing and family secrets.'
Francesca Catlow, author of *The Little Blue Door*

'A beautiful uplifting love story, full of secrets, emotion and hope, set against the backdrop of a gorgeous Greek island.'
Jan Baynham, author of *The Greek Island Secret*

'Absolutely enchanting. I could feel the Greek sun kissing my skin as tenderly as the story warmed my heart.'
Kate Glanville, author of *The Peacock House*

More praise for Emma Cowell

'The brilliant Emma Cowell creates worlds of warmth, laughter, healing and hope in her delicious novels'
Adriana Trigiani

'Beautifully written. Emma Cowell writes with warm assurance and brings the Greek setting to life'
Sue Moorcroft

'Such an emotive tale of love and loss'
Rosanna Ley

'A delicious slice of Greek life. A beautiful love story'
Jo Thomas

'A beauty'
Peter Andre

'Breathtaking world building, stunning imagery and genuine emotion cooked into every page. I adored it'
Helen Fields

'A sweeping novel about sisterhood, courage and new beginnings that will inspire and delight'
Tessa Harris

'When you look up from your train seat/sofa/garden sun bed this summer, you'll be genuinely confused you're not in a taverna knocking back an ouzo'
Caroline Corcoran

'An enchanting treat of a book. Sunshine and friendship, broken hearts and secrets. Cowell's exquisite writing is as delicious as the food she describes. Five honey-smothered stars from me'
Jenni Keer

'A Grecian journey with a culinary twist, female solidarity, friendship, and romance. What more does one need for a perfect summer read?'
Nadia Marks

'I adored *The House in the Olive Grove*. It is a hymn to friendship and love, and is utterly perfect'
Liz Fenwick

'Exploring the power of friendship and love through delicious writing and Greek food, *The House in the Olive Grove* is evocative, compelling and moving. A glorious story'
Kate Frost

'A compelling and tender story, beautifully told by an exciting new voice'
Santa Montefiore

'A sweeping epic Grecian romance about grief, healing, and the unpredictable ways they can drive our stories, *One Last Letter From Greece* is a Jojo Moyes-esque saga that I inhaled'
Laura Jane Williams

Emma Cowell lives between Cornwall and Greece and has worked in philanthropy fundraising for more than fifteen years. A former actress and BBC presenter, Emma is a devoted angler and once held a Cornish record. Also a keen linguist, Emma is still learning Greek and has discovered her language skills excel in tavernas and bakeries. *Under the Lemon Tree* is Emma's fourth novel.

For more info, visit www.emmacowell.com. You can follow Emma on Instagram @emmacowellauthor, on X @emmacowellbooks or on Facebook at EmmaCowellAuthor.

By the same author:

One Last Letter from Greece
The House in the Olive Grove
The Island Love Song

Under the Lemon Tree

EMMA COWELL

avon.

Published by AVON
A division of HarperCollins*Publishers* Ltd
1 London Bridge Street
London SE1 9GF

www.harpercollins.co.uk

HarperCollins*Publishers*
Macken House, 39/40 Mayor Street Upper
Dublin 1, D01 C9W8, Ireland

A Paperback Original 2025
4
First published in Great Britain by HarperCollins*Publishers* 2025

Copyright © Emma Cowell 2025

Emma Cowell asserts the moral right to be identified as the author of this work.

A catalogue copy of this book is available from the British Library.

ISBN: 978-0-00-86245-3-8

This novel is entirely a work of fiction. The names, characters and incidents portrayed in it are the work of the author's imagination. Any resemblance to actual persons, living or dead, events or localities is entirely coincidental.

Set in Sabon LT Std by HarperCollins*Publishers* India

Printed and bound in the United States

All rights reserved. No part of this text may be reproduced, transmitted, down-loaded, decompiled, reverse engineered, or stored in or introduced into any information storage and retrieval system, in any form or by any means, whether electronic or mechanical, without the express written permission of the publishers.

Without limiting the author's and publisher's exclusive rights, any unauthorised use of this publication to train generative artificial intelligence (AI) technologies is expressly prohibited. HarperCollins also exercise their rights under Article 4(3) of the Digital Single Market Directive 2019/790 and expressly reserve this publication from the text and data mining exception.

For my brother David

Artemis & Apollo

Artemis leapt from her mother's womb to attend to her twin brother's birth. Both were born as fully formed adults. Despite being the eldest, Artemis innately knew she would always look to Apollo for answers. His word would be her command, and she would follow him to the end of the ancient world if he so desired. He was half of her, and one couldn't exist without the other.

Prologue

London, October, 6 months ago

'Morning, sunshine,' Kat said to her brother, Nik, as she buckled her seatbelt.

'*Young hearts . . . run free . . .*' he sang at the top of his voice, greeting her with a wink. The words he didn't know, he made up, which made Kat clutch at her stomach with laughter.

'Every single time, Nikólaos, you get it wrong!' She used his full name to chide him.

'It makes perfect sense in my head, Kitty Kat.'

He tried to rev the engine in time to the music until it became a scream and Kat playfully slapped him on the arm.

'Get on with it – the traffic will be hideous,' she said and her twin ceased his silliness and put the car in gear. They set off for the upmarket gallery that was hosting Nik's latest photography exhibition entitled 'A Study of Man'.

Kat thought it a good excuse for her brother to stare at muscular naked models and call it 'work', but she was only too willing to come along in support.

'It's about sinew and shape, not just floppy bits and buttocks,' he'd explained years before, urging her to understand his craft.

His talent was undeniable, and she was incredibly proud: Nik's art would leave a lasting legacy. Her own creativity manifested in journalism, though Kat often wondered what she was hoping to achieve from her life by writing about home design. She loved giving magazine readers advice on interiors, and sharing the latest trends, but it wasn't the fiction she really longed to write.

'Are Mum and Dad coming to the show?' she asked.

Nik replied with his infectious giggle.

'I've tried to warn them about the more explicit pics, but they'll be totally unprepared, of course. Mum will be pointlessly begging Saint Michael to save my soul.' Kat pictured their mother, Mína, energetically crossing herself, and gripped her knees in anticipation of their parents' wrath. 'Leave them to me. And don't worry so much about everyone. We were all born naked!'

She pulled the visor down to shield her eyes from the autumn sunlight and to briefly check her reflection in the little mirror.

'Sorry we haven't caught up properly since you got back from Greece,' she said, fiddling with her cuticles guiltily. 'And before you say it, I know I've been impossible to get hold of and totally snowed under with work. But today I'm all yours!'

'As you should be! God, Kitty Kat, Greece is already a distant memory, as are the beautiful men. It's so cold here I think my tan has frozen off.' Nik sighed for dramatic effect. 'You know I actually wept putting my summer clothes away. I was beginning to think you didn't love me anymore.'

He was teasing but Kat caught his sentiment beneath the barb.

'Nothing in the world could stop me loving you, sunshine.' She flicked his earlobe, and he swatted her hand away. It was something they'd always done in the spirit of irritating one another since they were children. Kat returned to her mass of curls in the mirror, trying out a shorter length by rolling up the ends.

'Would you stop fiddling with your hair!' said Nik. 'It's incredibly distracting.'

'I wonder if I should have it cut short. What do you think?'

He stopped at a junction, then turned to face her. 'You always look fabulous.' He reached out and tucked a stray curl behind her ear. 'But it's only 'cause you look just like me!' His dark green eyes traced her face before he spoke again. 'Little Kitty Kat. I wish you'd follow your heart and be happy. I love you . . .'

With an almighty crash, the world went black.

Chapter 1

London, April, present day

Kat added the final piece of the jigsaw, pressing it firmly into place. She sat back on her heels, exhaling in satisfaction. Now it was finished, she couldn't stand the thought of breaking it up again. Not yet.

The image depicted a moment she didn't remember, but she was there, immortalised in time at five years old beside her twin, Nik, both beaming beneath the bright Athenian sky. Her mother had made an old photograph into a six-hundred-bit puzzle for Kat's birthday; a tradition that endured with no sign of abating, even though Kat was no longer a child. She was thirty-seven today.

It felt strange to think of their precious family image being cut up and mangled to make a jigsaw. Art had unwelcomely imitated life. Kat hesitantly reached out her fingertips and traced Nik's tanned arms, which were spread out wide in front of the iconic structure of the Parthenon. She smiled at the triumphant expression on his face, like he had constructed the monument himself. Beside him, Kat had assumed a copycat pose, looking to him while he faced forwards – always following where he led. Their identical features were in sharp focus tinged with inimitable golden Greek light: dark green eyes, nut-brown skin, heart-shaped faces and sun-streaked brunette curls. The colourful shapes of tourists massed beneath the classical columns towering overhead. Kat's eyes tracked the distinguishable figures in the background: children in profile, the man in red with his back to the camera who was mirroring the twins' stance while crowds of others clustered to gaze in awe at ancient Greek history. As her attention swept back to Nik, the weight of her heavy heart tugged harder at her body.

She looked around the living room. Her mother, Mína, favoured chintzy décor. There was a chaotic comfort to the mismatched patterns and textures though it jarred with Kat's own taste. Mína had stitched tassels onto every available textile: cushions, chairs and the edge of the sofa all trimmed with dangling gold. The sideboard was crammed with photographs of cherished family memories, random distant relatives, and Greek Orthodox religious icons. A group photograph taken at her wedding sat at the fore, which Kat moved to the back row every day, but somehow always found its way to the front.

Her parents had almost succeeded in concealing their disappointment at her looming divorce, having known Kat's soon-to-be ex-husband, Jamie, her entire adult life. He'd been a constant through the ups and the very many downs, held them all as they'd grieved after the accident, nursed her broken bones as they healed and scooped her up when she was unable to function. But it wasn't the sweeping love affair she and Jamie had hoped it would be and if they were honest with each other, which they were, it never had been. The shock of sudden bereavement had cleared the clouds from Kat's eyes and, overnight, life became far too precious to squander. It was the friendliest of unfriendly circumstances, as kind and loving a separation as was possible, and they remained great friends. But living back at her childhood home was becoming intolerable. She was being smothered with food and love, treated like a child again. Her father, Giórgios, had even suggested she take a break from writing for the magazine and join the family business.

'It is what we do, Katerína,' he had said. 'We are family, and this is the most important lesson you will ever learn: no matter who comes and goes from your life, your family will remain as constant as the Peloponnese mountains.'

He was an amateur philosopher, as most of her male relatives seemed to be. Giórgios regularly held court behind the counter of the family eatery. Customers who frequented Zorba's Kitchen knew that whenever he slung a tea towel over his shoulder and uttered the words: 'You see, the problem with young people these days . . .' he'd either embark upon a tale about the glory days of Greece, dismantle the state of British politics or educate his audience on the role of Ancient Greeks in forming society. All while Mína attended to her sizzling saucepans in the back kitchen, shaking her head in amusement at yet another of Giórgios' famed monologues while tending to his grill out front.

Her parents were an exceptional team, having been married more than forty years. It was a relationship Kat aspired to, striking the balance between teamwork and tenderness. But they too were shrouded in grief. Especially this particular Saturday, another 'first'. The first Christmas without Nik was awful, but today was Nik and Kat's birthday. Except it wasn't 'their' birthday anymore. Now, it only belonged to her with the ghost of his memory beside her.

The doorbell chimed, pulling her away from the jigsaw. Opening the front door, Kat accepted a stack of mail from the postman. Then, she signed for a thick package addressed to her mother, which bore an official notary mark from Athens. She'd take it to the restaurant at lunch. It was time to get ready for a day she wasn't ready for at all.

* * *

Through the window, Kat saw Zorba's Kitchen was already packed with people. Slowly soaking in the persistent April shower on the street seemed preferable to the onslaught of questions, congratulations and commiserations she was about to endure.

The twins' annual birthday gathering had been organised regardless of the fact it would be a solo pity party no one wished to participate in. But for the sake of tradition, Kat had reluctantly agreed to it. Not that she had any real choice in the matter. Her parents held customs – family or religious – in the highest regard. Today already felt hollow and pointless; there was little to celebrate.

She took a deep breath, and in her pocket, clutched at the little evil eye that Nik had always carried with him. It was unusual because it was red rather than the familiar blue *máti*. Kat kept it with her as a talisman. She needed its strength to endure the party. As she opened the door, a wall of sound rushed outwards, beginning with the tinkling bell overhead, followed by exuberant chatter. All heads turned towards her, and the noise suddenly quietened as if someone had pressed a mute button.

'*Chrónia pollá, Katerína!*' came the collective shout of 'happy birthday' in Greek as various relatives rushed to greet her. Kat felt numb as she was jostled from one embrace to another, receiving kisses and pretend spits in her hair to ward off bad spirits. But the worst had already happened, and for all their faux spitting, nobody had managed to protect Nik. Their forced merriment collided with how she felt inside, like a limb was missing. She automatically looked to her left, but he wasn't there. Her beautiful, fantastically funny brother whom everyone adored would have been revelling in the attention. Kat was the quieter twin, happier for him to take centre stage, now wishing she possessed a slice of his confidence. There was no buffer between her and the pinching fingers or soggy lips of distant cousins.

She plastered on a smile as her mother stepped towards her to kiss both her cheeks.

'Thank you, *Mána*, for the party,' Kat said using the Greek term for Mum. She lowered her voice. 'I know it's a hard day for you too.'

'*Agápi mou*, my love, is what your brother would have wanted. He was the life and soul of us all, our beating hearts . . .' Mína broke off, wrapping Kat in her arms. The scent of hairspray was overpowering. Her mother's hair had been set rigid with what smelled like half a can of spray. Kat was grateful for any amusement to stymie the survivor's guilt that plagued her days, though her nightmares were even worse.

'Katerína! Come, eat, we have been waiting for the guest of honour to begin our feast!' shouted Giórgios from across the room. It wasn't true. Most people were already gorging on *souvláki* meat skewers straight from her father's grill or plunging pittas into bulging bowls of tzatziki. Kat summoned the bravest face she could muster, side-stepping and bumping her way slowly through the crowd. On the walls she noticed lengths of blue and white Greek flags lettered with *'Happy Birthday'*, which covered framed pictures of the Cyclades islands. The bunting was also draped over plaster busts of mythical gods mounted on plinths.

'*Chrónia pollá, angheloúthi mou*, my angel,' Giórgios said proudly. He thrust a plate at her, which was laden with perfectly charred meat. 'We make all your favourites for this day. Now, will you have a glass of wine?'

Kat vehemently shook her head.

'No, *Babá*, Dad. You know I don't drink anymore.'

'*Endáxi*, OK, OK,' he said in resignation, raising his palms to the air before clapping them together loudly, garnering everyone's attention. Kat felt her cheeks heat: a lengthy speech was imminent. She stuffed a piece of chicken into her mouth, finding it hard to swallow as the penetrating glare of her entire family bored into the back of her head. As she rested her fork on her plate, which she gripped to her chest, oil dribbled onto her green silk vest.

'Dammit. Every. Single. Time,' Kat muttered to herself but did nothing. She felt a hand in hers and looked up from her sullied top to find it was Jamie, her almost ex-husband, who had grasped her fingers.

'Thank God you're here,' she whispered to him as she spotted her boss and friend, Amelia, over his shoulder and then her other best friend Lizzie. She had her 'village', and they physically Rállied around her, forming as much of a protective barrier as possible. Kat absorbed their comfort as they turned to hear what her father had to say.

'We are here to celebrate our dear, sweet Katerína. Her name comes from *katharós* which means *pure* in Greek.

This is for those among you who do not speak our most beautiful of languages as fluently as you should.' His eyes fixed briefly on Katerína, making his point. 'This family is united in the purity of this happy day that of course also has a deep sadness for us all. But we are sent such trials to test our hearts and souls. My people are from Thessaloniki, the place that is named for the victory of the Thessalians. *Niki* is the victory, so you young ones would do well to remember this when you put on your Nike sneakers. You are walking in Greek history with every step.'

'I love your dad – total fucking legend.' Lizzie cackled in Kat's ear as Giórgios continued.

'And our darling Nikólaos which of course means victorious in Greek, has beaten us all to the kingdom of God. He has won and the rest of us have lost. But there is a victory to find beneath the word of God: our Katerína is here with us to see her thirty-seventh birthday. And she has been saved for a purpose yet to be revealed . . .'

Kat felt her bottom lip begin to tremble and she squeezed Jamie's hand tighter as Lizzie's fingers rested on her shoulder and Amelia's on her arm. If Nik was there, he would have swiftly heckled their father, and the silence without his interruption rang in her ears. She admired her father's bravery, but his sentiment jarred: she didn't feel like she had a purpose anymore. Her ambition to write a novel had been swallowed up in the mundanity of life, the relentless routine of work consumed her as she strived to be the best she could. And she hadn't indulged in her decorating passion since she and Jamie had bought their home, which was now sold. There were too many itches she hadn't had the opportunity to scratch. But now she felt adrift with no focus. Nik had anchored her, and she didn't know who she was without him; her zest for life had dissolved into grief. Thankfully, her mother, Mína, stepped in.

'Yes, yes, Giórgios, and *my* people are from the island of Agístri, which means "fishing hook", so please in your vast wisdom, do tell me what we take from that?!'

Laughter filled the room, and Kat couldn't help but join in. The relief was palpable. Eventually a hush descended as Giórgios calmed the noise with his hands. His eyes, identical in colour to Kat's, twinkled with mischief.

'It means that from the moment I saw you, Mína *mou*, my Mína, I was *hooked* by you and utterly helpless. *You* had victory over my heart. And together we have these two beautiful children . . .'

Mína gasped and Giórgios put a hand over his mouth, unable to believe he had fallen into the trap they were all snared within. For occasional half-seconds, they all forgot Nik was gone. He had always seemed so alive; it was impossible to think the opposite. Only six months had passed since he was killed by a drunk driver and it was still so new, so raw, so horribly unreal. Kat's eyes brimmed with tears. They would never have their silly sibling exchanges again. Her morning call or message to him always began '*Morning, sunshine,*' and his at the end of the day to her: '*Night, night, moonlight.*' It had been their thing and now it was nobody's.

'Shall I say a few words?' whispered Jamie in her ear. He meant well, but it wasn't his place anymore. It was down to Kat to spare her parents' embarrassment. She found courage and turned to face her entire extended family, as her friends' faces spurred her onwards.

'In summary, my father just compared himself to a fish and my mother to some kind of angling warrior temptress,' she said, and a few guests tittered politely. They weren't used to hearing her make speeches – that's her brother's job. *Was*. 'So, I want to thank you all for coming, and even though Nik isn't here, he is. He will always be half of me. Please don't ever forget him, and that can be his victory over us all.' Hums of agreement rippled around the room. Kat longed to escape, but drew her brief speech to a conclusion as she caught an encouraging nod from Jamie.

'I'm out of analogies and my chicken has gone cold after that whistle-stop tour of *Babá*'s family geography, so raise your glasses in a happy birthday to me and to Nik. Now, let's all eat!'

Chapter 2

After several hours of feasting and dancing late into the evening, everyone finally left, and Kat felt quite wrung out. She was grateful her friends had turned up in support. They were due to have dinner later in the week to celebrate her birthday in their own way – without the scrutiny of relatives unpicking her relationship with Jamie. Though Jamie's presence at family occasions confused everyone, to them it made a perfect sense.

She was noisily tackling the pile of dishes in the back kitchen with her mother while her father wiped down his prized grill out by the counter.

'Did you see how well Cousin Eléni looks?' Mína whispered conspiratorially, though there was nobody left to overhear. 'She has given up eating *bougátsa* and finds her clothes fit much better. You know she has the most terrible problems with her bowels.'

Kat tutted at her mother's indiscretion. '*Mána*, please! You're obsessed with everyone's health and shape. Is anyone ever just right?'

Mína dried her hands on a dishcloth. 'Yes, *angheloúthi*

mou, my angel. You are, though you need to eat more,' Mína said looking her up and down.

Kat couldn't help but snort in disagreement, waving a large dish around in one hand as she spoke. '*Mána*, there's very little for you to be proud of. I'm thirty-seven, living back at home with you, doing the same job I always have for the same magazine, about to get divorced . . . not exactly a catalogue of reasons to celebrate. Or much to show for my life so far.'

Mína gently prised the platter from Kat's hands then guided her from the pile of crockery to sit at a little wooden table in the corner. Kat had accidentally smashed three plates so far and knew her mother would prefer her away from the breakables.

'Katerína, we have all been through so much, but you must know how very proud I am of you – and your father is too. You make many monies on your home with Jamie because of the brilliance of your design. You get this flair from me, of course. And even though you and Jamie are to be . . .' she inhaled deeply, wincing as if she were in pain, before continuing '. . . divorced, never close your heart to love. Perhaps it is almost time for you to meet someone new. Take your mind off things. We would be very happy if the next was a nice Greek boy.'

Kat summoned any remaining energy to prevent an eye roll of despair. From the moment she announced her separation, she had known the gossip would spread, and it was only a matter of time before she was paired off with someone from the local Orthodox church.

'I think that's the last thing I need. Not just a Greek boy but any boy. I should sort myself out first before entertaining the idea of romance or love.' Kat's voice snagged in her throat as it dawned on her that any reliable counsel about relationships had been from her twin. His advice was now gone. 'I keep expecting Nik to walk through the door.'

Mína's eyes watered and Kat felt ashamed she'd mentioned her brother, but she couldn't keep her grief hidden all the time. She still needed them to be her parents while she came to terms with her own loss. But she was mindful that they too were in immense pain. Swiftly shifting the subject, she said, 'I finished my birthday jigsaw this morning. It's still on the table if you want to see it later. It's lovely, *Mána*.'

Her mother smiled sadly, brushing a spindle of her dark blonde fringe to the side, which pinged back to its original place immediately, having been coiffed to the consistency of concrete.

'I chose that photograph to make the puzzle because it is a very special memory in Athens thirty-two years ago. You were both so little. We were stopped everywhere we went – it is so lucky to see twins. It took us hours to reach the Parthenon. People wanted to bless you both and shake your hands or mine – a mother of twins is most auspicious. Nikólaos of course loved the attention, and you were so timid, always hiding behind his shoulder like a little mouse. But you were both very excited to be on your first trip to Greece and meet—' She stopped abruptly and walked over to drain the sink. Kat frowned as the water gurgled noisily down the plughole.

'Meet who? You took us to Agístri, but I thought you didn't have any family left on the island or in Greece. I don't really remember any of it; I wish I did.'

Mína gripped the edge of the countertop. Kat couldn't see her face, but she noticed her mother's knuckles had blanched as she held on to the side.

'No, I have no family there. I meant meet your heritage in my birthplace. My English is still terrible even after all this time. Why you cannot speak Greek with us, Katerína?'

'Sorry I'm so English, Mum,' Kat said, acknowledging her mother's disappointment in her.

'You must never be sorry for who you are.' Mína turned from the washing-up pile.

'But you haven't been back to your birthplace for so long, *Mána*. That's who *you* are,' said Kat. She never could understand her mother's reluctance to return to Agístri when she fervently celebrated everything else about Greece. Mína dried her hands on a dishcloth and sighed. 'No, Katerína, that is where I am from, it is not who I am. I haven't been to Agístri for many, many years – not since I took you and Nikólaos. There is no point; it is not where I belong. For me, home is wherever your father goes.'

Kat smiled, comforted by the romance in her mother's words. At least her parents had each other to battle through their grief. Kat tried to be brave, but she didn't feel it. She looked down at the wooden tabletop covered in dents and scrapes. Slashes of knives marked the countless kilos of vegetables peeled by her mother over the years. She suddenly noticed a small pebble in the centre. It was tinged a light, shiny pink, almost quartz-like. As she picked it up, the hairs on the back of her neck prickled.

'Look, Mum, what's this?'

Mína turned and took the stone from Kat's fingers with a puzzled expression.

'No idea. Maybe it's us speaking of Greece; we conjure the beach from the heavens. My own *Mána* used to say be careful what you say aloud; you bring things to you when you give them energy. She was so superstitious your *yiayiá*.'

Mína crossed herself in deference. Kat didn't remember any of her grandparents; they'd all died before she and Nik were old enough to recall. Though she couldn't imagine there was anyone on earth more superstitious than her mother.

'Maybe it's Nik sending us a sign. He always had pebbles in his pockets when we were little. I don't know where he got them from. Croydon is hardly near the seaside,' mused Kat.

'Perhaps it is a sign or perhaps not. We do not speak of such things; it is ungodly. But it doesn't mean they don't happen,' said Mína, her face becoming stern as she pointed at the edge of Kat's tattoo, which was peeking out beneath her watch strap. 'Regrets are the very, very worst, Katerína. That terrible mark is there forever!'

Kat held up her arm to look at the bow and arrow inking both she and Nik had. It represented Apollo and Artemis, the twins from Greek mythology, affiliated with the sun and the moon respectively. Kat had the moon beside her bow and arrow and Nik the sun. She caressed the faded lines.

'Well, I don't regret this at all.'

'That's as may be now, Katerína, but you will when you are eighty years old, and your skin has become folds of wrinkles and sags to the ground, it will look quite ridiculous! Why you scar your beautiful skin this way I will never understand.'

Kat's mind reached back to the moment she and Nik arrived home at seventeen, freshly inked, unsuccessfully hiding their arms throughout dinner that night. They were quickly found out by Mína who scolded them at length. Kat had felt instantly guilty but Nik persuaded their parents it was a tribute to their Greek heritage, which had impressed

Gióргios immensely, and he'd lauded their dedication to the motherland.

Mína dabbed the corner of her cloth with tea tree oil and rubbed at the stain on Kat's vest. There was no point resisting: it was likely ruined, but Mína thought she could fix it, and Kat permitted her fussing. While her mother tutted at the greasy mark, Kat remembered the pile of post she'd brought.

'There's a bunch of letters under the counter for you. One's from Greece – quite official-looking – I had to sign for it. Maybe they're calling you back, *Mána*,' Kat joked. Mína pulled a strange expression and paled, then marched out front to find it.

Kat sat at the table, removing Nik's *máti* from her pocket. She turned it and the mystery pebble in her fingers, wondering how long grief lasted and when she would finally wake up feeling half full rather than half empty. The evil eye had been retrieved from Nik's jeans before his cold body was covered with a sheet and tucked away in a clinical hospital drawer. Kat shuddered at the thought.

A cry came from the front of the restaurant, and Kat snapped to attention. She rushed to see what had happened but before she could enter the room, she stopped still in the archway at the sight of Mína brandishing a letter in her father's face, holding a large file in her other hand.

'It's his will, Gióргios, look!' Mína waved the document in the air and Kat's father gently extracted it from her hands.

Kat stepped a little further into the room unseen, her heart picking up pace.

'He cannot have received my letter about Nikólaos and now it says Katerína must go there.' She pointed out something to her father who hummed agreement.

'That island is determined to persecute me,' Mína cried as Giórgios read studiously. 'And now I will have to tell her everything.'

Kat's pulse began to pound even harder as she watched her father take her mother's hand.

'Not everything, Mína *mou*,' he said then began to read aloud. 'In association with the relevant municipality offices and the Greek Ministry for the Interior, Pétros Tzanos hereby issues his notarised last will and testament indicating his wishes to leave his literary rights, some monies and his house on Agístri to Nikólaos and Katerína Konstantópoulos.'

'What?' Kat couldn't help but shout as her parents turned sharply towards her, grim-faced. The silence stretched with no response. 'What are you talking about? And who is Pétros?'

Mína's bottom lip quivered, but she managed a response. 'Pétros was . . .' She looked to Giórgios for reassurance, who placed his hand on her shoulder.

'You must tell her, Mína,' he said as she nodded in defeat.

'He was . . .' She began to cry, her voice rising in pitch. 'Pétros was your uncle. My brother.'

Chapter 3

Kat walked uncertainly towards her parents, waiting for someone to elaborate further. Her mind whirled, trying to make sense of what she'd heard. She had an uncle, her mother's brother, who had made the twins beneficiaries of his will. But Nik – like their mystery uncle – was dead, leaving only Kat to inherit. She was bewildered and light-headed. For all the emphasis her parents put on the importance of family, they had inexplicably hidden a relative from her.

Giórgios fetched a tall decanter of Metaxa and glasses, setting them on one of the restaurant tables, beside the large file sent from Athens. He gestured for Kat to sit, and she obliged, but shook her head when he offered her a glass.

'Are you never going to drink again, Katerína? Would your brother really want this for you, because of the actions of a terrible man drunk-driving? You used to enjoy glasses of wine with your dinner, but now you punish yourself, and yet it changes nothing, not the outcome, nor our grief.'

Kat pushed the glass poured for her to the side, ignoring her father's queries about her sobriety.

'I'm so confused. You had a brother?' Kat said looking

to her mother for an explanation. Mína remained silent, her lips pursed tightly together. 'But you said you had no family. Why would you not tell me and, worse than that, lie about it? Did I meet him when you took us to Agístri?'

Mína rose from her seat and removed the last of the birthday bunting from the wall and folded it up with painstaking precision before putting it in a cardboard box. She looked agitated. Eventually, she returned to the table, having collected a new white tablecloth and her sewing box from behind the counter. Mína began to expertly attach a string of the fresh gold tassels to the linen, frowning in concentration. The quiet was unbearable.

Giórgios tenderly patted Mína's shoulder. 'Mína *mou*, you should explain to Katerína. Please. She deserves to know. It is time.'

Mína glanced up from her task with an expression of immense pain. She looked defeated even before the story began.

'Which part do you suggest I tell, Giórgios?' Mína asked as they locked eyes for a few moments. Taking a hefty glug of brandy, she continued, 'I am sorry, Katerína, that I never told you.' Mína's chin wobbled as she fought back more tears. 'Pétros, your uncle, died just before Christmas, my poor Pétros.' Mína crossed herself several times, and the length of tassels rustled between her fingers. Kat felt for her mother having lost Nik then her own brother in such close succession.

'*Mána*, start from the beginning...' Kat gently prompted, as her father handed Mína a paper napkin.

Mína shook her head then blew her nose loudly. 'You will think badly of me. You won't forgive me. Pétros never forgave me and I cannot forgive myself.' Silence again, broken only by her sobs and the wall clock beating the seconds as they passed. Mína gathered herself with another sip of her drink and continued. 'His will means I have to tell you . . . He is in your jigsaw, in the red shirt facing away. That was the only time you met him. We went to Athens, and then stayed in his home on Agístri that is now yours.' She paused and exchanged a look with Giórgios that Kat couldn't interpret.

'I can't believe he'd leave a complete stranger his house,' Kat said looking at the ceiling trying to process the little she knew thus far. 'What happened between you and your brother? I don't get why you hid him from me.' Again, Mína looked to Giórgios who took up the story on his wife's behalf.

'They had a . . . disagreement during that trip, and sadly didn't speak again. Time it seems does not heal all wounds.' It did little to enlighten Kat and her frustration rose.

'Please, *Mána*, I don't understand.' Kat's mind drifted to their earlier conversation in the kitchen about regrets. She must have been referring to Pétros. Mína went back to sewing and didn't look up, as if the matter were closed.

'Your mother and her brother were estranged. They had been for many years,' interjected Giórgios. 'Pétros was an eccentric, but also somewhat of a recluse; he became a very successful novelist – a writer like you, Katerína. In different ways you and your brother are much like your uncle. He was what you might call a confirmed bachelor.'

'And?' said Kat, still unable to grasp the gist. The only thing they shared so far was creativity.

'We were so close when we were young and nobody made me laugh like him.' Mína gazed into the distance as if she were reliving her happier past. 'But people grow apart, and Pétros refused to live a lie, never conforming to what my parents wanted for him. I suppose I admired that conviction, but my family disowned Pétros and I failed to stand up for my brother when we were younger, and as adults, he still held it against me all those years after.'

She snipped at a length of cotton and tried to rethread her needle, but her tears dropped onto the fabric and she abandoned her task.

'Why did your parents reject him?' Kat asked. 'Please tell me what happened,' she insisted. Mína burst into noisy sobs and Giórgios pulled her into his arms. Kat's frustration sparked again – why couldn't her mother talk plainly? Finally, Mína lifted her head and sighed in resignation.

'Because my brother, he . . . he never married because he preferred the company of men. He was gay.' She took a steeling breath to carry on. 'Back in those days when Pétros and I were teenagers, such a life wasn't accepted. Not like it is now. You wouldn't understand, Katerína. Our culture had very strict views on what was acceptable.' She rubbed an eye so hard with her fist, it was as if she was trying to erase the thought. 'I think he held me responsible for the shame he was made to feel. And I am so disappointed with who I once was on that island.'

Kat closed her eyes tightly, as her mother wept again. She wished more than ever that Nik was beside her. He would have loved to know one of their family was gay too, though he would have been saddened to learn that Pétros had been ostracised because of it. But it was too late. Pétros and Nik were gone, and those who remained now had to find a way to piece together what was left.

Chapter 4

When she'd returned home with her parents, Kat went straight to the jigsaw in the lounge to seek out the image of Pétros. He was the one facing away from the camera, his arms splayed like Nik in reverse. What comfort Nik could have brought him and vice versa had they been in one another's lives. Her twin had been so proud of his sexuality, but her uncle had been made to feel disgrace.

She looked up from the jigsaw and noticed her father in the lounge doorway holding the file from Athens.

'Is *Mána* OK?' she asked as he walked wearily to the sofa.

'She will be. She has gone to bed. Today was difficult for many reasons. And now this.' He handed her the documents. 'It is yours, Katerína, to make of what you will.'

She opened the binder, unsure where to begin.

'I don't want to hurt *Mána* any more than she has been. What should I do? I need your advice, *Babá*.'

'Do what you think is right, *angheloúthi mou*. Follow your heart. But if you wish for my opinion . . . life is a beautiful collision of circumstances that none of us are able to predict. Who we love, where we go, who we meet. So, if you ask me, I think you should go to Agístri. Pétros' will states you must, so why not? You get to see Greece and your new home; nobody loses.'

Kat felt torn. How could she enjoy this fortune, when it had come at the expense of her mother and Pétros' estrangement? And she was meant to share it with Nik.

'I'm not sure. What will *Mána* say? It's a big step, and then there's my job . . .'

'Work can always wait and it's all you do, work, work, work!' Giórgios gestured to her with both hands in exasperation as Kat looked back at the jigsaw. 'I will deal with your mother. And she will speak about it when she is ready. Please do not press her to. You must be patient, Katerína.' He hovered beside her, looking at the puzzle. 'All I hear is you finding excuses not to go. I am yet to hear a good reason for you to stay away from the island. A good sleep will help you arrive at a decision.' Giórgios kissed the top of her head before adding, 'Happy birthday and *kaliníchta*, Katerína.'

'Goodnight, *Babá*,' she responded.

Kat remained on the floor leafing through the paperwork from her uncle's estate until the pins and needles fizzing in her legs forced her to move. She sifted through various forms stamped by the relevant authorities until her tired eyes stung from the endless translating via an app on her phone. She gulped at the amount of money she'd been left, added to her bank account from the sale of her marital home, she was now incredibly comfortable. In the very back of the file, she found a picture of the house that was now hers along with an address and transfer of deeds she was required to sign. It wasn't a very clear image. Nothing about any of this was clear.

Since her parents had gone to bed, Kat retired to her bedroom but couldn't sleep. Instead, she searched online for more photos of the house, zooming in on satellite images. It was slightly set back from the shore though would likely have a wonderful view of the sea. Then she sought out pictures of Agístri itself. The photographs almost vibrated on the results page, drawing her in immediately: calm turquoise waters, both sandy and pebbly beaches, red-roofed traditional houses and a stunning whitewashed church with a cornflower blue dome. It was breathtaking. Dare she go there to claim her home? Though it was a place filled with people who had shunned Pétros for being his true self. But she wouldn't learn any more about her uncle here in London, and Agístri may answer what her mother wasn't prepared to. Besides, she hadn't taken any extended leave from work since her honeymoon fifteen years ago and goodness knows a holiday of sorts would be welcome. At thirty-seven, it bewildered Kat that she had been alive long enough to have had a marriage last so long and fail, when she was currently sleeping in her old room, in a single bed covered in tasselled cushions and gaudily embroidered coverlets. Yet here she was.

If she went away, took a break from life to reassess her plans, she could even find time for creative writing, maybe rework the novel she'd abandoned. The idea nudged at her, giving her a giddy feeling. The first and only book she'd written years ago while at university was still consigned to a drawer following a stream of rejections from agents. It was too crushing and disappointing, so she'd focused on interior design journalism instead, harnessing the flair for colour and décor that she'd possessed since she was a child; redesigning her dolls house every year using her mother's nail polish – much to Mína's irritation. Her current position as lifestyle editor at *Love Interiors*, a glossy monthly magazine, was hard won, but she had been there since graduating and she couldn't remember the last time she'd felt challenged.

Turning over in bed, she tucked the ugly baby pink duvet beneath her chin.

'*Night, night moonlight,*' she whispered in her mind, trying to conjure up Nik's voice and failing. In that moment, her head was too full of Agístri and her uncle to find her twin, and she became afraid of the day when she couldn't imagine his face anymore. Surely that would never happen. Dismissing the idea, her thoughts returned to the little Greek island and the house. Having a focus that was entirely her own could give her the space she needed to process Nik's death without supervision from her parents. Maybe next month she'd go – she didn't need to set a date tonight. Yes, Kat definitely needed a break, she just needed to break it to her editor-in-chief and friend, Amelia, on Monday morning.

Chapter 5

The house was empty when she padded downstairs on Monday morning. Her parents started early at Zorba's Kitchen. As Kat ate breakfast, she was lost in thought. The sense of betrayal from her mother hiding part of her family stung so much that she hardly noticed each bite of toast. But she'd been told not to mention it by her father. It was infuriating, though she acquiesced given she was living under their roof. For now. It only strengthened her decision to go to Greece. She just needed to work out when.

She was so caught up in thinking about her family that she spilled apple juice across the table, which splashed her white shirt. After changing her outfit, she was now running late. She grabbed the box of *portokalópita*, a Greek orange cake that her mother had set aside for her colleagues to enjoy, and dashed to the station.

Arriving breathlessly at work, she headed straight to Amelia's office, hoping to catch her before the Monday morning editorial meeting. She rapped on the glass door garnering the attention of her boss, who gestured for her to enter.

'Morning, belated birthday girl! How was the rest of the party after I left?' Amelia asked, before eyeing the box Kat was carrying. 'Please tell me that's your mother's orange pie cake thing!' Kat opened the lid to give Amelia a glimpse of sweet sticky glaze. A drizzle of sweetness glopped out of the box and landed on her skirt. Kat didn't notice until she caught Amelia's sympathetic grin.

'It went pretty much as expected,' began Kat, trying to brush away the evidence of her mess. 'Except . . . well, something's come up and I might need to take some leave soon. I'm not sure when, but I wanted to give you the heads-up.'

Amelia's face fell in concern. 'Of course, you're owed tons of holiday, and God knows you need to get away after what you've been through. But why now?'

'Long story, which I haven't got to the bottom of yet, but after the party, there was a bit of a revelation. It turns out I had an uncle who died last year. And he left me and Nik everything in his will.' Amelia gasped as Kat continued. 'Except obviously it's just me now, but it includes a house on a Greek island.'

Amelia's blue eyes widened as much as they could, given her face was aesthetically frozen. 'A house? In Greece? Tell me you have pics.'

Kat dipped into her handbag, pulling up the photographs on her phone.

'Here. It looks out to sea, three bedrooms, two bathrooms, huge patio with an amazing tree and garden—'

'Oh my God, it's heavenly!' Amelia interrupted. 'That stonework . . . those shutters need a lick of paint, but wow!' Amelia pressed the intercom, ordered coffee from her assistant then asked her to let everyone know she'd be late for the meeting. Leaning back into her leather swivel chair, she grinned at Kat. 'Your Greek grand design . . . I can see the masthead in the mag now. Have you thought about the amount of content we could get from this? Oh, this is brilliant! You've been working like a machine and some distance and sunshine would be so good for you. When do you leave?'

Amelia's questions came thick and fast as she handed the phone back to Kat, whose eyes glanced over the pictures on the screen. Kat still couldn't believe she was looking at somewhere she owned; it felt so unreal.

'I actually wanted to take a clean break for a bit and not work. Maybe write for myself . . . do an eat, pray, love, decorate type of thing. Actually, scrap the love.'

An intern knocked at the door, and Amelia nodded warmly. The girl almost bowed into the room with a tray of coffee, the china cups rattling against their saucers as she placed drinks in front of them, then made to leave.

'Thanks, Libby,' said Kat. She deliberately made a point of remembering everyone's name. She was once an intern too and the editors had seemed like inaccessible glamazons. Now an editor herself, Kat was reassuringly approachable for the junior staff: never very well put together and her clumsiness was often the source of office jokes. She looked at her boss's sleek blonde blunt-cut bob, shining like a sheet of golden glass. Her white shirt was pristine and unblemished, unlike the rumpled replacement Kat had chosen this morning after unceremoniously splattering her first with juice.

'I insist you take this as a new challenge, Kat. Starting now – no time like the present. Yes, of course, have some holiday, but how about you write the redecoration as you live it? Share your experience of grief within it all. The house was supposed to be yours and Nik's, so . . . it could be like peeling back layers of wallpaper and discovering what's beneath, unearthing hidden treasures – literally and metaphorically. You absolutely have to go at the soonest opportunity.' She clasped her hands in front of her. 'Do this not just for the magazine, but for yourself. Please. We've all been so worried about you. Now you can turn your hand to something even more creative and blend what you're best at – writing *and* design. It's a stroke of genius, even if I do say so myself!'

Kat shook her head, appalled at the thought. Work had been her one escape. Losing herself in the detail of colour palettes and textures stopped her reliving the crash with Nik. Writing about interiors and lifestyle trends gave her the distance she needed to survive the daily pain in her heart. But she balked at Amelia's suggestion. Why would she expose her private thoughts to anyone else, let alone pepper her lovingly curated pages with the grim inner workings of her own mind? Her misery did not want company.

She promised Amelia she'd think about it, and walked in a daze to her desk on the main floor, depositing the box of orange pie in the kitchen on the way. As she joined the meeting, Kat realised her boss wasn't on the same page as her at all. After apologising for being late, Amelia said she had an announcement.

'Well, it's already been an exciting morning because Kat has news! She is going to be working on a very special project . . . in Greece! That's all I'm saying at the moment, but I know it's going to be huge for her and for the magazine. Online content, print, giveaways . . . I can't wait for her to get started. She's off soon – we will keep you posted!' As Kat listened, her mouth dropped open and a bubble of anger formed in her stomach. Amelia was her boss, and they were friends, but this major life occurrence wasn't supposed to be page-filling fodder for public scrutiny. She hadn't even agreed to the assignment yet. She'd only just resolved to go to Greece but hadn't put that plan into action. Kat hated decisions being made for her, yet it was all anyone seemed to do.

Her colleagues offered their congratulations, and excited chatter rippled around the office. She set her jaw rigid out of fear of saying what she actually thought. Amelia was as bad as her parents, inserting herself in Kat's business. Or perhaps she enabled everyone to take charge of her life. She bit her tongue and plastered on a smile, already eager for the day to finish so she could see her parents, hoping they might reveal more about Pétros.

But when she got home that evening, there was a note with instructions for reheating a lamb stew and a request for a family meeting at 9 p.m.

She watched the kitchen clock tick-tock the minutes away, then paced between the jigsaw in the lounge, which was still intact, to the photographs on the credenza, pushing the wedding picture of her and Jamie to the back. Again. She couldn't help but chuckle, which cut through her impatience. The frame was his choice and although it wasn't one Kat would have selected, Jamie had already given it to her parents before she'd seen it. She sent him a message.

> *Hey! Wedding pic still up and I'm off to Greece soon. Not sure when. K x*

He replied immediately. She still had him saved under 'HUSBAND' in her contacts and it amused them both that she'd kept it.

Wow – Greece! Have you been married off already?! Your folks move fast!

Ha! Kat responded. *Not happening ever!! Big family news – fill you in tomorrow night xx*

She was relieved they could behave normally within their separation, but then they'd always had more of a friendship than a great sweeping love. Her thoughts were interrupted by the sound of a key in the front door.

'*Kalispéra!*' Kat shouted good evening in Greek, hoping they'd follow her voice to the lounge, and her parents entered the room. 'Can we have our family meeting now?' Giórgios lingered by the door. '*Babá?* Someone please say something!' Since Saturday, they had both been deliberately evasive, and she couldn't stand it any longer.

'*Angheloúthi mou*, there is no more to tell than you already know,' her father stated as if it were an end to the matter. 'I understand you will have questions for your mother, but I fear you will be disappointed.'

Kat slumped into an armchair, making the gold tassel trims waggle. She didn't mean to behave like a teenager, but her parents insisted on treating her in such a way that she organically morphed into a sullen younger version of herself.

Her parents took their place on the sofa opposite Kat, identical in their stance, hands clutched tightly in their laps.

'*Mána*, when did you last speak to Pétros?'

Mína's mouth remained tightly shut and Giórgios placed his hand on her knee, giving her leg a squeeze to spur her on.

'During the trip with you and Nikólaos. Your father remained here to look after the business.' She shot him a guilty look and he nodded, encouraging her onwards. 'But my brother and I were unable to repair our relationship. Even though I told him myself in person and in letters ever since that I accepted him as I did Nikólaos. That love is love, no matter who you choose.' She inspected her fingers and avoided Kat's eye for the remainder of her story. 'But on that holiday, we argued. I never heard from him again, and now I never will. I wrote to him after Nikólaos' accident, but I don't know if he received the letter . . . I only found out Pétros had died from his obituary in the Greek newspaper. I don't even know where he is buried. I never got to say goodbye.' Her voice choked at the end of her sentence, and she dabbed at her eyes with a handkerchief that had been tucked up her sleeve.

'But I don't understand why you didn't try harder. You could have gone to visit, found a way while there was still a chance to fix things. You could have done more than just write a few letters.'

Giórgios' face became stern, and he smoothed his thick salt-and-pepper hair.

'Do not criticise your mother, please, Katerína. Our generation was brought up in a way that is incomprehensible for you to grasp. Especially being raised in a very conservative family as we both were.' He leant forwards, splaying his fingers on his knees. 'Until you are an adult or married, you didn't dare to go against your parents' wishes. It was not the done thing in those days and still isn't now. Something you may like to remember. It is ingrained in us to obey family, to be loyal no matter the cost, *angheloúthi mou*.' The softening of his words with his usual term of endearment did little to comfort Kat. She simply couldn't understand why her mother wouldn't have reached out to Pétros with greater urgency, though she had some comprehension of the Orthodoxy that her parents grew up in. But Kat would never risk being estranged from a friend or family member, because you never knew when your time was up or when it would be too late to retract cross words.

'I don't know what to say other than I'm sorry for you, *Mána*,' Kat said moving to crouch in front of Mína who could hardly meet her eyes. Kat mustered the strength to announce her plans to travel to Agístri. 'I also wanted to let you both know that I plan to go to Greece soon, to the house. Do some decorating, write . . . have a bit of space. I haven't quite decided when but it's time I went to the motherland, right?'

Giórgios suddenly laughed, and Kat was startled by his gleeful response, which was in stark contrast to his scolding moments ago. Her father reached into his jacket pocket.

'This is most fortunate indeed, Katerína.' His voice boomed with the tone that signalled a forthcoming monologue. 'In life, you must bend with the wind, be shaped by the elements; it is God's way of telling us we are setting out on the right path though we, of course, believe we make our own choices without fate or destiny. Yes, the ancients speak of such things. We take what we will from their musings and do not discuss it.' The contrary nature of Orthodoxy, philosophy and superstition fused with confusion in Kat's brain, but she let her father carry on. 'However, I had a word with Amelia, and then a great discussion with Jamie at the party, and he gave his blessing to my idea that you needed time away even before we know about Pétros' house. But now it is more pressing. So, as a birthday gift, I have decided to help you towards your future. This is exactly the right thing for you.'

Mína looked at Giórgios and then to Kat. 'What are

you talking about, Giórgios?' Mína asked, panic evident in her voice.

Kat's irritation rose at the thought of a conspiracy behind her back between her father and Jamie. This was what her family and Jamie did: thrust themselves into every element of her life and made decisions on her behalf. Her father retrieved an envelope from his blazer.

'Given how much you have been through, the sadness and sorrow our family has shared, it is time for you to find joy and there is only one place that will give you this – Greece! I have spoken to Pétros' housekeeper, and it is all arranged. You are going to Agístri. It is time for change, Katerína. The will states you must go to claim the house, so go you shall!'

'No, no, Giórgios, don't make her go there.' Mína clung to his arm, but Giórgios dismissed her, shaking his head at her insistence.

'It is time, to put the past behind us.' He looked to Kat. 'We will take you to the airport, all of us together, the whole family. Mína, phone everyone at once and alert them to be free very early on Monday.'

He thrust the envelope at Kat and she uncertainly unfurled the paper nestled within. Her eyes absorbed the printed page in front of her:

BA0640 07:45 T5 LHR to ATH.

A flight to Athens along with a ferry booking from Piraeus port to Agístri.

Leaving next Monday morning and returning two months later.

Chapter 6

Kat caught Lizzie's eye as she walked into the crowded Soho bar and was relieved to see her best friend. After exchanging hugs, Kat launched into her spiel.

'Right, before Amelia and Jamie get here, I need to offload.' She babbled out the whole story of betrayal. 'I want to break something I am so bloody cross!'

Lizzie handed her a large soda water with a fresh lime.

'Look, your parents are always in your business, but I can't fucking believe Amelia and Jamie would join in too.' Lizzie was always straight to the point and, as abrasive as her language could be, it was right for the moment. 'You need to start setting some boundaries. Did you tell them how you felt?'

Kat gave her a withering look; Lizzie would know she had stayed silent for fear of upsetting anyone.

'I don't want to make a big deal of it, and a trip to Greece to write isn't the worst idea. I just wish I'd had a choice about when and what kind of writing,' said Kat.

'Or at least been consulted,' agreed Lizzie, tying her newly platinum blonde hair in a ponytail. With her overlined kohl eyes, she looked like Brigitte Bardot. 'The house is an exciting windfall, but those two . . . I'm going to say something when they get here.'

'No! Please don't. It's fine, I was planning to go anyway. And some sunshine wouldn't be too hideous . . .'

'Well, give me the nod and I'll unleash on your behalf.' She took a sip of her drink. 'Anyway, I have the best gossip for you ever . . .'

Lizzie was a showbiz editor of a tabloid newspaper and the most indiscreet woman Kat had ever met. They'd been friends since university and Lizzie was maid of honour at her wedding and, happily, they'd all remained the greatest of pals – so much so, Lizzie had asked Kat's permission before setting Jamie up on a date. Like all chosen families, it defied reason or explanation. As Lizzie finished her salacious celebrity story, she spotted Jamie and waved to attract his attention.

He looked flushed and stressed. He was a wine merchant, and his ruddy colouring was either from a lengthy lunch or a deal gone bad. He greeted Kat with a kiss on each cheek and she almost winced as a waft of booze engulfed her.

'Long day . . . ?' Kat asked. Jamie had somehow stumbled into a job that seemed like he was on a permanent gap year, gadding around the world visiting vineyards and tasting booze.

'Long day doesn't even cover it. Someone tell me something of substance, please. And I mean Kat, not you, Lizzie – none of us know who you're talking about half the time.'

'That's 'cause you're not down with the kids, babe,' she joked.

'Oh, I'm sorry,' said Jamie, his pale blue eyes twinkling,

as he looked at Lizzie's artfully ripped denim trousers. 'The Nineties called; they'd like their jeans back.'

Kat couldn't help but laugh despite being cross at Jamie. The teasing rhythm of their friendship was an instant comfort regardless of what she was stewing about. Her phone beeped and she opened the message.

'Amelia's running late,' said Kat. 'And I'm starving. Let's eat.'

They ordered a selection of small plates to arrive at random, then Kat filled Jamie in on her family drama about her uncle. He looked more shocked about her hidden dead relative than her inherited house, but Kat agreed that was the most astonishing part of her tale. He then became uncharacteristically quiet for the remainder of the conversation. She hadn't had a chance to chastise him about his covert collaboration with her father yet. Lizzie was loudly unpicking Amelia's announcement that Kat would be writing about grief and decorating just as she entered the bar. The table immediately fell silent. Amelia rolled her eyes and shrugged off her jacket.

'I know what you're all talking about,' Amelia said sitting heavily into a wing-back chair. 'Kat, I'm sorry, don't hate me, but it's a great idea for you to take a break and be more creative. Everyone thinks so – it's not just me and your father. Jamie basically spearheaded the whole thing.'

'Way to throw me under the bus! Thanks, Amelia,' said Jamie, nervously running his hand through his sandy hair.

'Sorry, darling! Look, Kat. I told everyone about the house but not your uncle. That was yours to tell,' said Amelia as she beckoned a waiter over then ordered a double vodka soda before helping herself to a truffle arancini. Kat looked at Jamie with a furious scowl then at

Lizzie and back to Amelia. Her friends became sheepish, as Jamie spoke.

'Inheriting the house is like a sign you can't ignore. I think we can all agree on that. In fact I know that we all do.'

'Oh, you *all* think so, do you? And you two already knew about the house, pretending to be surprised when I just told you?' Kat glowered at Lizzie and Jamie. 'And what's worse, you've all been sharing your thoughts behind my back. What, do you have some secret tragic group chat called "rescue Kat"?'

Their expressions collectively became even more suspicious.

'Oh my God, you do, don't you?'

Jamie placed his hand on hers and she stared down at it.

'Kat, we all love you and as irritating as it feels right now, you must agree you need to get away from everything – our break-up, Nik, and now this house has landed in your lap, giving you the chance to decorate – which you absolutely adore – but more importantly, you can do what you love more than anything: write!'

Lizzie let out a throaty giggle before saying, 'And our message group isn't called *"rescue Kat"* it's . . .'

'Don't, Lizzie!' barked Amelia in horror.

'No, go on . . .' said Kat sitting up straighter. 'Tell me.'

Jamie took a deep breath. 'It's my fault. I named it. It's called *"help Kat find herself again"*.'

Lizzie mimed vomiting and Amelia smiled at Jamie, shaking her head. Kat's outrage dissolved with a sigh: it was too tragic. Her friends only confirmed what she already knew but wasn't bold enough to say aloud. She'd fallen out of love with life and with herself; she'd lost her purpose.

'Fine, but if I plummet through a rotten floorboard,

you are all responsible. I better get the front page of the magazine for my obituary.' She fixed Amelia with a mock glare and any remaining tension evaporated, replaced by an eruption of giggles as they tucked into a new round of delicious tapas.

'Kat, just go. You can file copy from there, but please, for your sake and ours, get to that island and work out how to live again. What on earth is stopping you?'

Kat bit into a croquette stuffed with mozzarella. She chewed, seeking an answer to Amelia's question. What *was* stopping her? As she picked the string of cheese tangled in her curls, she finally landed on a response.

'Absolutely nothing.'

Chapter 7

Six days later

The queue at the airport bookshop was moving slowly. Kat grabbed a bottle of Coke from a fridge near the till, ignoring the loud tut from the man behind her as she dashed out of the queue and back to her place.

'Sorry,' she muttered not meeting his eye. She would bet money that she had more reason to be grumpy than him.

The car ride to the terminal had been tense since it followed a heated exchange with her mother at four in the morning. Mína had apparently been through her suitcase and substituted several clothes with her own choices, meaning Kat had to panic-pack until the last moment. Her mood had retreated slightly at her mother's well-intentioned gift before they left the house, which was as absurd as it was touching.

'I have this for you.' Mína had thrust a plastic pod-shaped device towards her. 'You mash up a cucumber, put it in here and keep it in the freezer. Then you run under your eyes. It takes away the puffiness.' Her mother's eyes critically roamed Kat's face. 'Such a shame I didn't prepare it for you ahead of your flight.' Kat had always wondered who bought products from pop-up adverts online. Since moving in with her parents, now she knew: her mother was one of them and the parcels of tat arrived daily – a device that claimed to save electricity yet you had to plug it in therefore defeating the purpose, a plastic container that shaped portions of rice like a duck and the crowning glory were socks to relieve fluid retention in diabetics – neither of which her mother suffered from.

Other relatives had arrived at her parents' house, waving frantically from their respective cars, and they'd all driven in a motorcade to Heathrow airport to send her off to the motherland. Kat stewed throughout the journey, disappointed by her mother's unwillingness to speak more about Pétros during the past week. She'd burst into tears whenever Kat raised the subject, which made her feel guilty, so eventually she'd stopped mentioning it.

Now, as the man behind her huffed and puffed at the glacial pace of the queue, Kat felt her blood stir in irritation. They wouldn't move any faster no matter how much he exhaled. She moved her shoulder bag further up her arm, as it kept sliding downwards, and she clasped the books, magazines and fizzy drink to her chest. But her grip slipped, and the bottle dropped to the floor. It bounced on the tiles and exploded with a pop and hiss, spraying dark brown liquid everywhere.

'Oh!' she cried, looking down at her trousers. Miraculously, not a drop had splashed her, though she noticed the remnants of her mother's home-made *bougátsa* breakfast pastry on her leg.

'You have got to be kidding!' She heard an American

accent behind her and whipped around to see a pair of once pristine cream linen trousers now streaked with dark liquid. The stains were spreading, and Kat began to panic. Usually, her clumsiness only affected her; this was mortifying.

'I'm so, so sorry, I've got a tissue here somewhere,' she said rummaging in her bag with her free hand, the motion of which sent her paperbacks and interiors magazines to join the puddle of drink on the floor. But she located a tissue and flourished it aloft, daring to meet the eyes of the grumpy man splattered with her beverage.

Kat almost stepped backwards at his glare. He was breathtaking. His piercing blue eyes bored into hers, though they were narrowed in fury.

'I think you've done enough,' he said. His voice was low and steely. 'People are looking.'

Kat pulled herself together, despite the flush creeping across her face. 'Please, let me help.' She reached forwards with her napkin to dab at his leg, trying to ignore the effect he had on her insides. She'd never seen eyes that colour before, apart from in the pictures on the wall at Zorba's Kitchen; they were the same shade as the shallow waters of the Aegean. He pushed her hand away.

'That's enough,' he snapped. Kat was aware that heads were turning in their direction, and she thought she heard someone take a photo on their phone.

'I was only trying to help. There's no need to shout,' she said, her own temper beginning to rise. 'It was just an accident.' The beginnings of a smile crept across his full lips, and she scanned his face for any other sign of warmth, but it was gone as soon as it arrived. He deposited the book and car magazine he'd intended to buy on top of a pile of travel pillows and left the shop. *Some people are so uptight,* she thought to herself, but she didn't like the feeling of having upset someone – even if it was a stranger. Determined to fix it, Kat grabbed the items he'd left behind with the intention of giving them to him as a peace offering. After paying for her soggy reading materials and the cross stranger's, she raced out of the store, wheeling her suitcase as speedily as possible, searching the rows of people at the check-in desks for 'Mr Linen'. She eventually spotted him in front of the airline she was headed for – only at the business class desk.

'Sorry,' she said to the couple waiting behind him in line. 'Would you mind if I just gave these to that gentleman over there. I'm not pushing in, I promise.' Kat wasn't sure why she'd referred to him as a gentleman when he'd behaved as anything but. The would-be holidaymakers were only too happy to acquiesce and continued mooning at each other. Another check-in desk opened and the woman called Kat forwards.

'Where are you flying today, miss?'

'Oh, Athens. But I'm not at the right desk. I only need to give these to him.'

As she spoke the blue-eyed man turned to her. She took in his features again, noting his height and broad shoulders encased in a cream linen jacket. His caramel skin boasted a suntan that indicated regular international travel. He raised an eyebrow and leant his elbow casually on the check-in countertop. *He's never panic-packed in his life,* she thought. Kat noticed the woman dealing with his paperwork send her an angry look at the interruption.

'You forgot these – for the flight.' Kat proffered his abandoned reading materials and noticed he had different cream trousers on. He must have an unlimited supply of identical linen to hand.

'Oh good, you've changed your clothes. I didn't mean to be clumsy.' She thrust her apology purchases at him, realising that she also had a splodge of vanilla custard on the sleeve of her black jumper – another casualty from her mother's *bougátsa*. His eyes caught the stain too and he smiled, affording a brief glimpse of perfect white teeth.

'Well, for someone who doesn't mean to be clumsy, you appear to do it very well. But thank you.' He continued to look at her as he received his papers and boarding pass from the woman.

'Thank you, Mr Eliópoulos,' the woman said, before blushing. 'I mean, Mr Ellis of course.' Kat briefly wondered why he had two names, but he still hadn't removed his eyes from her, which she found as disarming as it was compelling.

'Enjoy your flight,' he said. 'And try not to spill anything else, although that is your forte, it seems.'

He continued to look at her and Kat felt trapped within his stare. She couldn't pinpoint what was travelling between them, but it was powerful. It was both if he felt it too, as he took a step backwards, his brow furrowing, trying to understand. It was the work of a moment, but there was a definitive shift in energy that was both silent and beautiful like a butterfly's wing fanning the air. But as whatever it was dissolved, he turned on his heel and left. Kat couldn't work out whether he'd been funny, flirtatious, rude or all three.

'Your passport, please, miss,' said the woman at the desk.

'Of course, sorry, though I'm not flying business.'

'No problem. Miss Konstantópoulos, we can check you in here. Or you can upgrade if you like?' She relayed what it would cost. It was a luxury, but Kat felt decadent at the idea of a first foray into business class. Surely she deserved a treat after the last few months and, besides, she worked hard and rarely splurged. Making the exciting decision, she slid her credit card across the counter. She was beginning to feel the effects of only a few hours' sleep and couldn't wait to board the plane for a nap. After moving through security, she entered the executive lounge, which was swarming with people loading up at the free buffet. She hunted for somewhere to sit and found a comfy armchair to snuggle up in. As she flicked through her magazines, her eyes began to feel heavy so she closed them. *Just for a few minutes,* she told herself.

* * *

'This is the last call for British Airways flight to Athens. Would passenger Katerína Konstantópoulos please make themselves known. This is the last call . . .' Kat stirred as the voice over the loudspeaker repeated the announcement. It took precisely three seconds for her mind to digest the message and a further two before an earthquake of horror cascaded throughout her body, spurring it into urgent action. Grabbing her things, she sprinted out of the lounge and towards the gate. Her legs weren't working properly having been curled up then suddenly forced to run at full pelt. The roped-off sections in front of the gate seemed to go on for miles as she curled her way around the makeshift maze, doubling back on herself every few paces. Why did she have to always follow the rules, instead of vaulting the lot of them?

'Is it gone? Did I miss it? I'm so sorry,' she panted as she reached the desk feeling droplets of anxious sweat trickling down her back.

The gate attendant looked suitably furious.

'We need to get you on board as soon as possible,' she said, herding Kat swiftly onwards. She burst onto the aircraft apologising, a flustered wreck. One of the crew took her to her seat and she absorbed irritated glances from the other passengers. Kat wished she could be one of those effortless carefree types and pretend that she always breezed through life being tardy but fabulous.

Nearing the vacant seat on her walk of shame, her heart leapt into her throat, and she suddenly wanted to be sick. Before she could protest, she was deposited by her row and told to sit immediately. Her seat was beside the window, which was the only good news. Because for the next few hours, soaring across the distance between England and Greece, she would be sat next to the now stain-free but completely mannerless Mr Linen.

Chapter 8

After he'd made way for Kat to sit, Mr Linen stared at her, which did something peculiar to her stomach. He then smiled wryly before pulling on an eye mask. At least she didn't have to deal with his impoliteness for the duration of the flight.

She picked at the blob of custard on her sleeve absent-mindedly and settled down in her spacious chair. She was almost able to swing her legs; she was so short and the seat so roomy. She glanced to the side and found herself wondering if the two-surnamed stranger's stubble was a consequence of the early morning or if he carefully man-scaped his chin to the perfect level of fuzz. He'd removed his linen jacket, and the black T-shirt beneath afforded a glimpse of dark chest hair. His expensive-looking charcoal suede loafers were pristine. Her mother always said you can tell a lot about a man's willingness to open his heart by the way he cares for his shoes. Kat had no evidence such a thing was true, but her mother firmly believed it. He probably had enough money to buy new ones as soon as his others were scuffed, so she didn't think the theory applied to him. And if such a principle had any sway, Kat would currently be navigating the world barefoot.

Forcing herself to read the still-sticky magazines was preferable to scrutinising the grumpy perfection next to her. If she were in a movie, they'd fall in love and run off into the sunset. But the reality of Kat's world was quite different. She was headed for a probably dilapidated house to be alone on an island to grieve for her brother and, she hoped, somehow open the next chapter of her life. The thought of a Greek adventure now it was happening was thrilling because it heralded a gateway to the creativity she had neglected for too long. She could redecorate Pétros' home, breathing new life into it and making it hers. And she'd have the space to turn her hand to that old dream and write properly – not just the task Amelia had given her, but she might find her real creative voice.

Change had been thrust upon her in the cruellest and most unwelcome of ways; now it was up to her to make some alterations of her own. And Kat couldn't wait to get started.

* * *

The flight had felt like luxurious bliss. Kat slept, read each magazine cover to cover and devoured a delicious hot breakfast, though she'd refused the champagne on tap. Her brooding fellow passenger remained beneath his eye mask until it was almost time to land when the cabin crew fawned all over him upon his waking. Clearly a frequent flyer.

Now, after a speedy cab drive towards the port, she waited on the dock in Piraeus for the ferry to Agístri. The feeling of hot sunshine on her skin and the sight of a clear cobalt blue sky was heavenly. A car pulling up at the far end of the harbour was causing commotion, but she paid no mind to the crowds that swelled in the distance surrounding the vehicle. The waves sparkled and although the larger ferries spewed diesel fumes into the atmosphere, nothing could dull her delight at finally being in Greece.

Morning, sunshine, she said to her brother in her head.

She wished she hadn't waited her whole adult life to return to a place that ran through her blood. Though she and Nik went to Athens and Agístri when they were little with their mother, Kat regretted not coming more recently with her twin who had been to the country several times. Almost every summer. But then, she'd not taken a holiday abroad since she married. Jamie was always travelling for work and wanted to use his time off to relax at home, and she had been focused on climbing the ranks at the magazine. Until now. Henceforth, it needed to be all about her, her own choices and the house waiting to be claimed on Agístri.

According to her father, Pétros' housekeeper, Mrs Rálli, would meet her boat when it arrived. Just a little further across the sea and Kat would see her new house.

The island ferry neared, parping its horn as it docked. Kat stood from her seat on a stone wall, knocking over her suitcase in the process. Her handbag had been sitting on top and it emptied on the concrete. She gathered up her belongings with the help of a kind woman who'd taken pity on her frantically crawling around, chasing after a lip gloss or grabbing a paper that threatened to blow into the sea. Heading up the ramp to board, she prayed she'd collected everything. Passport, phone, credit cards, papers from Pétros' estate with the address for the house and phone number for the housekeeper on it . . . nothing was missing. Phew!

Kat found her seat at the front of the boat and through the salt-coated windows she made out the towering shapes of large cruise ships, industrial boats and other passenger ferries. As the vessel's engine roared indicating departure, excitement nudged at her with a sprinkling of nerves. She was on her solo voyage. Nobody else could make decisions about the house or how she spent her time, only her. The thought was thrilling.

'Here I come, Agístri,' she whispered to herself.

Her fingers instinctively went to Nik's red evil eye in her pocket, but it wasn't there. She rummaged in her bag, pulling out the contents; it wasn't in the side zip or any compartment. She piled everything onto her lap, then tugged at the lining, willing the *máti* to appear. But there was no sign of it. She sunk into her seat, crestfallen before she'd even arrived. It must have fallen out on the dock. Her breathing began to shallow and unshed tears stung at her eyes. Losing something Nik always had with him was like losing another part of her twin that she wasn't prepared to let go of. Though just a trinket, nothing valuable, it was his and now it was gone. Another connection severed that she hadn't been ready for.

'Don't be sad, Kitty Kat!' She heard Nik's voice in her mind, recalling the time she'd been dumped by her first boyfriend at the age of seventeen. *'Be brave. I still love you, and I'm the best judge of character because I know just how fabulous we are!'*

She grinned despite the pang his voice caused in her heart, but she was glad she could still hear Nik. He was so alive within her memories and thoughts, it still felt impossible to believe he was gone. As she gazed through the dirty windows, it felt like she was the only person in the world, no other in sight – just her, sea and sky, a thousand shades of blue and Greece, enveloping her in its embrace. She only hoped her bravery in coming alone wasn't misplaced.

* * *

Megalochóri, or Mylí as it was known locally, wasn't really a port on Agístri; it was barely a harbour. Just a shelter beside a long concrete sea wall, though it did the trick, and Kat was happy to be on dry land after the hour-long boat ride. More importantly this was the land of her mother's family – no matter how secret that history was regarding her reclusive uncle.

Her eyes scanned the length of the island opposite her vantage point on the jetty. Mylí had some new construction up on the hillside: villas and apartments set back amongst the trees ready to greet the influx of tourists in the summer months. The buildings were quintessentially Greek from what she could see. Familiar colours greeted her: whitewashed houses, stone buildings, burnished-orange-tiled roofs and clear turquoise waters – the colour of grumpy linen man's eyes. Shedding her cardigan beneath the hot afternoon sun, she tied it around her waist. She turned to walk along the pathway and as if summoned immediately from her thoughts, there he was.

'You again!' she blurted out. 'What are you doing on Agístri?'

Mr Linen looked guilty as he slung the jacket in his signature fabric over his shoulder.

'I owe you an apology. I am not good with early mornings,

or unexpected dry-cleaning errands.' His voice was low and quiet, with a hint of a Greek vowel concealed within his American accent. She'd expected more bravado given how speedily he'd hastened to rudeness earlier. But Kat bristled. One of her pet peeves was people who said, 'I owe you an apology,' then omitted the word 'sorry'. She waited to see if it would come, but the silence lengthened, punctuated only by the lapping waves from the wake of the departing ferry.

'Well, are you going to accept my apology?' he asked, frowning with what seemed like puzzled amusement. But Kat was still smarting from having lost Nik's evil eye and had no time to massage this man's ego.

'When it arrives, I'll be sure to let you know.' She surprised herself by being so assertive but enjoyed her unexpected nerve. Greece had already changed her, it seemed.

'Excuse me?' he said clearly taken aback. 'I just apologised.'

'No, actually you didn't. I'm happy to stand here all day while you work it out, but I have somewhere to be.' She pulled up her suitcase handle with a clunk and wheeled it away with considerable difficulty. It snagged on the uneven paving and clumsily tipped from side to side, twisting her wrist and aggravating her elbow joint which she'd fractured in the accident with Nik. It was yet another reminder of what happened. She then had to manoeuvre out of the way of a smart black town car. Probably to collect *him*, bound for some bougie hotel with its own jetty and bespoke fragranced lobby – if the island had such a place. Despite the pain in her arm, she wasn't going to give him satisfaction by stopping her flounce.

There was no sign of her uncle's housekeeper, Mrs Rálli, on the dock, so she decided to keep walking in the hope that someone eventually would point her in the right direction. She lifted her chin defiantly as the black car zoomed past her again, in the other direction, and sweated her way onwards, imagining with envy the air conditioning and chilled mineral water in the vehicle.

The heat was fierce as Kat rounded the side of the island from the ferry mooring. She spotted a café on the corner. An ice-cold frappé was precisely what she needed to improve her mood. Her mind flitted briefly back to the linen-clad man. Someone that attractive would be used to people caving with just one look from those electric blue eyes. She'd done it at the airport, but not anymore. The new Kat who'd unexpectedly emerged on Agístri would stand up for herself from now on. And she rather liked this incarnation of herself. She was free, without opinions or judgement. She hoped.

Kat took a seat at a table outside the café, and her stomach lurched as she caught the scent of late lunch from the nearby tavernas. Now she was on the island, it seemed bigger than she'd initially thought, and Kat had little idea exactly where her uncle's house was. It could be on the other side of Agístri for all she knew, but she would consult the map on her phone after refreshment. She ordered her iced coffee and some *micró mezze* – small savoury plates. Checking her phone, she had missed calls from Jamie and a message:

Where are you??!! Have you eloped or already been waylaid by fabric swatches and scatter cushions? Let me know you're safe J x

SO sorry, J. Yes, am in the motherland as per your grand plan! K

She left a kiss out of her reply, still punishing him for his interference, then took a snapshot of the view she hadn't had a moment to properly absorb and sent it to him.

See? Saying sorry was easy and painless.

If I didn't love you, I'd hate you! he replied.

She sat back in her chair and looked at her surroundings. Working life had always moved at such a frantic pace that when she stopped, it was disconcerting. She didn't know how to slow down.

Her gaze swept along the promenade as far as she could see to get her bearings from the images she'd found online. The blue domed church was on this side of the island but out of sight for now. The beach didn't stretch the entire length of the seafront but was shingle-like below this part of the promenade, turning to golden sand in the middle and then beyond that . . . she'd find out at some point.

As her coffee and food arrived, Kat's tastebuds sprang to attention. A few marinated anchovies, slices of crusty sourdough topped with her favourite ochre split pea dip – or *fáva* – and *keftedés* – miniature lamb meatballs coated with a smoky tomato sauce. Kat was ravenous and tucked into the assortment of tastes and flavours with enthusiasm.

'Katerina?' came a croaky voice, startling her as she took a huge bite. Sauce dribbled down her chin and she scrambled for a paper napkin to save her clothing. Kat turned and saw a lady beside her around her mother's age, maybe late sixties.

'Yes? Sorry, excuse my mess,' she said mopping at her face and chewing speedily. 'Are you Mrs Rálli?' she asked in Greek, knowing she would have to brush up on her language rudiments. Though she spoke it occasionally with her parents, living back at home with them had been a reminder of just how rusty her language skills were.

'Eat, eat!' Mrs Rálli said nodding that she was indeed the housekeeper. 'Come afterwards. My English – bad, we speak in Greek.' She reverted to her native language. 'Go past the yellow building, then a terrible modern glass house. After many trees the one after that is Pétros' house. Your uncle's former home.' She sniffed and crossed herself piously. 'I have made the house very, very nice for you. There is a washing machine.' She fixed her beady eyes on the blob of tomato sauce glistening in Kat's lap.

Mrs Rálli was dressed head to toe in black and Kat wondered if she was mourning Pétros or someone else. Everyone carried grief with them, only in Greece you wore it like an emblem from head to toe. Mrs Rálli shuffled off to speak to someone inside the café, then returned and made a great show of taking the stone steps one by one back down to the road. Kat wasn't sure how effective a housekeeper she'd be since she appeared to move with difficulty, but she was a welcome connection to Kat's mystery uncle and hopefully a helpful local to show her the sights. Although given the pace Mrs Rálli moved, Kat wasn't sure there was enough time left in the world for a guided tour.

Chapter 9

Mrs Rálli's directions were spot on, and Kat finally found herself in front of her uncle's house.

It was a beautifully simple structure and the blurred photographs she'd scrutinised back in London didn't do it justice at all. The stonework had an almost pink hue and was well pointed, and the orange roof perfectly intact. Or so it appeared from outside. The lawn was bordered by fruit trees which would yield their harvest throughout the year and a vibrant magenta bougainvillea clung to the side of the house; its blooms crept like floral tentacles to the upper level. Sun-scorched flowers sang their fragrance into the gentle breeze, and dominating the terrace was an ancient lemon tree. Its gnarly bark seemed twisted beneath the burden of its fruit-laden branches. It was as if the house had been constructed around the tree and its wooden arms reached across the terrace to join with the large pergola-like overhang affording more welcome shade.

She walked up the short flight of stone steps to the pathway for a closer look. Double French windows stood on either side of the front door and she could imagine throwing them all open to create a feel of inside-outside living. She turned around to face the water and breathed in, then exhaled. The scent of lemons tinged the air along with a comforting hint of wild herbs. The empty horizon boasted so many blues: pale, deep, rich, royal – countless vivid shades. It was hard to see where the sky ended, and the sea began with Greece uniting the two in between.

Oh Nik . . . what fun and mischief we could have had here.

'Kitty Kat, we will always have fun, in this life and the next,' he replied in her head.

A slinky cat with patches of three different colours trotted past her and started to dig in one of the flower beds.

'Ela tóra! Óchi gatoúla, stamáta!' she shouted to tell the little cat to stop. She suspected what the cat was about to do, and she was correct. It deposited something in the earth, covered it with soil, then glanced at her. Mewing, it rolled on its back in the dirt, begging with the most astonishing yellow eyes for a tummy rub.

'Argótera!' She promised later and walked through the garden. She would leave a saucer of food for it that evening. It accompanied her along the pathway leading to the patio then slumped beneath the lemon tree in the shade.

The front door was painted a forget-me-not blue. *Cheery*, she mused, though it was too much of a contrast against the simple frontage. Cream definitely. The same for the peeling, tatty shutters she thought as she glanced upwards to the first-floor windows. She was already decorating, though she didn't know how much resistance Mrs Rálli may pose.

'Yiássas, Kyría Rálli . . . ?' she asked opening the door tentatively. Cool air rushed forth as her voice echoed in the gloomy hallway and she thanked the gods that there was

functioning air conditioning. The afternoon heat outside had a heaviness to it, but that could simply be travel fatigue weighing down her bones. Wafting from within came the smell of delicious home cooking, dragging her into a soporific state. The comforting hint of buttery baking coupled with a familiar savoury something floated forwards: dill, tomatoes and onions. She repeated her greeting and eventually Mrs Rálli shuffled into view.

'*Yiássas, Katerína, Kalós írthate sto spíti sas,*' she welcomed, referring to it as Kat's house, which felt odd as she'd only just taken her first steps over the threshold. '*Pou eínai o adelfós sou?*'

She'd asked the question Kat had dreaded; nobody on Agístri knew.

Where is your brother?

Kat gathered strength to utter the words that cost half her soul, made even more difficult because she was forced to say them in another language. Every word she considered hurt more than the last as she translated in her mind.

'My brother died, a few months ago. In a car accident.' Kat briefly squeezed her eyes shut to stop the flashback that threatened to replay.

A question about her hair, Nik's sweet face, the mirror image of hers, his fingers reaching for a stray curl, tucking it behind her ear . . .

Don't remember what came next, don't remember, she told herself. *Send it away, far, far away into the darkness.*

Pushing it from her memory, she opened her eyes. To Kat's surprise, Mrs Rálli had covered her mouth in shock at the news, her cheeks glistening with tears. Then she clutched at her chest, shaking her head and muttering a prayer. She made the sign of the cross several times, before moving to a cluttered shelf to light a tiny candle. Kat was touched by the gesture and display of sympathy, realising she hadn't had to say that sentence aloud before in any language. She'd been surrounded by people who knew. Now, she was alone in her grief.

'My brother died, a few months ago . . .'

She should be talking about an elderly relative, not her twin who should have turned thirty-seven with her. But he would always be paused in time, immortalised in her heart, preserved in family memories the way he was when they last saw him. Though Kat didn't wish to think of how he looked the final time as she cradled him in her bruised, broken arms. Her eyes had locked with his as his life slipped away, his last breath leaving his body like the gentlest rush of a wind.

'Such tragic, terrible news,' said Mrs Rálli, wiping away her tears, breaking through Kat's painful recollection. They stood in silence, both women appearing to need a moment. 'So, food first, then tour, yes? Or you prefer other way around, though you eat very little at the *kafenion*, Katerína.'

Kat thought she'd escaped being force-fed at home, but she was in the land of ultimate hospitality now. 'I'd love to see the house. I can eat after . . .'

The hallway was darker than it seemed moments ago as she'd closed the front door behind her. Despite the unrelenting sunshine outside and the high ceilings, thick tapestry curtains choked the light. The furniture was an oppressive mahogany. Most of it needed to go. Kat wasn't sure how receptive Mrs Rálli would be to change. Their communication would be challenged enough with Kat's poor Greek and Mrs Rálli's strained command of English. Nevertheless, a bubbling in her bones began at the thought of the looming project. She knew she would be overcome by the amount of work before dicing it up into manageable chunks and tackling one space at a time. It had been so long since she'd had a project of her own.

She'd transformed the Victorian mid-terrace house she and Jamie had bought. Designing and decorating it had given her almost as much joy as creative writing. Both those skills had fallen by the wayside as life took over. But now, she could flex those muscles again. The entrance was a quick fix: replace the drapes with light translucent ones, change or paint the furniture and add a vase of fresh flowers. The stonework walls were stunning and Kat couldn't help but reach out to touch one. Small sparkly granite-like flecks peppered the rock, and she knew a large candle would encourage the stone to shine. She followed her tortoise-paced tour guide into the kitchen where a large saucepan was simmering – the source of the savoury smell.

Mrs Rálli had made *fasolákia* – green beans with carrots and potatoes in an oily rich tomato sauce, perfect for dunking slices from the freshly baked crusty loaf. Despite the heavenly scent, Kat's heart sank at the state of the large kitchen. Makeshift counter units had been constructed out of a series of cheap rickety pine frames with pieces of limp mismatched floral fabric drawn across to hide what she assumed to be storage underneath. It was like stepping back in time. There were no sleek clean lines, and it was devoid of the charm such a sizeable rustic kitchen should afford; in fact, it was devoid of design. The only decent aspect was the large wooden dining table. It had an upholstered corner pew, which created a casual seating nook, and tucked beneath the table were gorgeous benches made from the same oiled oak. The double doors leading to the terrace were closed but she longed to let in what light there was. In her mind's eye she saw how the space could look. There was even room for a central island, but it was a gut renovation job; she would need to start from scratch.

On they traipsed throughout the property and Kat became increasingly despondent with the sheer amount of work that would be required. Each room was more depressing than its predecessor and upstairs was an assault on her eyes. It was the opposite of everything she curated on the 'Love Interiors' pages and in the home she'd made for her and Jamie. Every room in this house had several things in common: dark furniture, crowded spaces and terribly outdated textiles. Her uncle may have shared her creative genes, but they had not shared the same taste. Kat kept any comments to herself for now, as Mrs Rálli was watching her reaction closely.

As they finally reached the lounge downstairs, Kat couldn't suppress her laughter, which bubbled up from nowhere surprising Mrs Rálli. Every cushion and armchair was adorned with gold tassels. He was her mother's brother all right, despite their estrangement. It was genetic! Her giggles were born of the unexpected sight of the familiar and, although it jarred with her own aesthetic, it made her feel at ease in the strange house she now owned. Even if Mrs Rálli did now think she was completely mad.

* * *

Mrs Rálli, it transpired, was a superb home chef and would be available for cleaning and cooking duties as per her uncle's arrangement. She was paid from the estate and Pétros had made provision to keep her on, which was a great relief, though why the woman would want to continue manual labour in her advancing years was beyond Kat. Her own talents in the kitchen were limited, and her proficiency in Grecian cuisine was lacking, much to her parents' chagrin. As a child she'd once suggested *hórta* – mountain boiled greens – was basically spinach. Her father had remonstrated with her in exasperation.

'How can you possibly suggest these things are the same? It is a great shame you do not understand these most simple of things at the heart of Greek cooking... Is like comparing cheddar with feta – is all cheese but so very, very different. I sometimes wonder why this child wishes to hurt me this way!'

Kat had been baffled at his reaction to a bunch of leaves. Until she'd tasted *hórta*. Then she understood his point.

With the cooking and cleaning taken off her hands by Mrs Rálli, she could focus on the renovation and her writing, and at least there was Wi-Fi. Mrs Rálli left for the day but would be back in the morning. Kat watched her drive away in a car that wouldn't pass inspection in the UK. It rattled noisily along the road. The woman had an intimidating energy about her. It was understandable: there was an interloper in what had been her domain, another lady of the manor. From what little Kat knew of her uncle, any house guests were unlikely to have been female.

After unpacking in the gloomy master bedroom, she found the fridge to be well stocked. She emptied some olives into a hideous floral bowl and filled another with pistachios that were harvested from the nearest island of Aegina, according to the packet. Through the double doors in the lounge, she stepped into the garden. Kat put her snacks and laptop on the patio table beside the dominant lemon tree beneath which the cat was still snoozing. She was unsure what to do next. Look online for some builders nearby, she supposed, and a hardware store. Maybe Mrs Rálli would lend her the battered car so she could buy supplies to at least make a start. Some of the furniture could be upcycled, sanded and given a lick of neutral colour. The ceilings all had a stained pine panelling between chocolate-coloured beams that needed lightening to lift the rooms away from this obsession with dark wood of varying brown hues. She was firmly in the swamped stage of the process, which she knew too well, but this was more than she'd ever taken on before. Picking up her phone she called her mother to leave a message, knowing she wouldn't answer as it would be the after-school rush in Zorba's Kitchen.

'Hi, *Mána*, I'm here in the house and it's going to be a beautiful evening. There's a lot of work to do, but I'm fine. I've eaten and I'm going to have an early night. Love you, love to *Babá* and speak tomorrow.'

Perhaps her mother would like the opportunity to help with the house if she ever came back to the island. There were a few boxes of papers piled in the study adjoining the living room though most had been dealt with by Pétros' estate office in Athens and his clothes had been donated, Mrs Rálli had informed her almost tearfully. Kat didn't understand her mother's resistance to Agístri. From here, it was beautiful. But Pétros had been mistreated by the community and his family. It must represent such an immense shame for Mína never to have returned.

Sitting back in her chair, Kat tried to digest all that had happened to lead her to this moment as the sunset's oranges and pinks danced across the sea. The world seemed to be kissed by a warm peachy light. But she felt unsettled having lost Nik's evil eye; it was so careless. When she'd unpacked her suitcase and bag, she'd turned everything out again, searching every pocket, but it wasn't there. It had probably found its way into someone else's hands by now or was lost to the sea.

As she watched the waves gently roll towards the shore, the peace on the island was almost deafening in contrast to the constant hum of London traffic. She needed to acclimatise gently and break up the silence. Music! That would lift her from her funk and maybe even inspire her to write. She'd spotted a record player in the lounge on Mrs Rálli's house tour and went in search of vinyl to help shift her gloom. It would make a change from playing digital music and she wanted to embrace all this experience had to offer her, no matter how archaic it felt.

The walnut cabinet, which housed a modern music system, opened with a sliding concertina door straight out of the 1970s. It had a vintage charm and after a coat of paint, it could stay. Inside were stacks of CDs and records. It was so strange to see such clutter when she streamed everything. She leafed through them before settling on a folk singer she knew from her parents – Dimítris Mitropános. He was much adored amongst Greeks, and she had absorbed a love for him by osmosis. A loud thump echoed through the speakers as she switched on the machine and carefully placed the needle. The crackle at the start of the record felt like something from another time, before a bouzouki strum was followed by the familiar rich voice.

Kat turned it up so she'd hear it from the garden and hoped it would drown out any thoughts of despair. Taking the remote control for the stereo, she stopped in front of the double doors and forced herself to see her surroundings as if for the first time again. The view was spectacular, a complete panorama with little between her and the vast expanse of ocean apart from the lawn and branches of the lemon tree. It felt freeing in the moment, and she resolved to cling on to that feeling. This could be her purpose and lesson to come from months of sadness: to find joy and make the most of every second, because life was too precious to be taken for granted.

As the music boomed, she stepped onto the grass but not before tripping on a loose patio tile by the tree, which sent the cat fleeing for the undergrowth. She apologised, noting to feed him before bedtime. Then, she began to spin, dancing to the voice of the singer who had been a soundtrack to her childhood and now provided the musical backdrop for this new solo adventure. She giggled as she flung her arms aloft and danced a traditional Greek dance, the *Zeibékiko*, one that Nik had been able to do with effortless expertise. Her version was awkward, but she didn't care. It was the first time she'd danced since the accident, and she was testing her limbs for aches, but the warm Greek air seemed to have soothed them for now. Even within her elation, the gap her brother had left in her life was like a physical pain, more acute than she had ever felt. Despite her celebratory movement, tears arrived as she recalled her twin dancing at family functions, their relatives making space for him to leap high and crouch low.

As she claimed the ground and the music as her own, her pace increased with each step. She didn't notice a man walking up the stone stairway at the end of the garden until she heard a voice.

'Hey! What are *you* doing in Pétros' house?'

Chapter 10

The sun had set rapidly and, in the twilight, Kat couldn't quite make out who was shouting at her. It had caused such a fright that she'd ceased dancing immediately. Panting with exertion, she scrambled back to the terrace to mute the music, which she had to admit was rather loud. Wiping her face of any residual tears, she turned towards the intruder.

'I'm so sorry,' she said tentatively nearing the silhouette who stood with both hands on his hips. The dusk revealed his features as she took a small step closer. The glint of his eyes flashed through the darkness and she recognised their unmistakable colour with a sinking heart, which began to beat even faster. Him!

'This is a crazy amount of noise! I can hear you from my house next door,' he said sternly. 'Why is it that whenever there's a problem this past day, I find you?'

Mr Linen: the man she'd covered in Coke and endured a flight with. Maybe he'd come to apologise for his ill manners, but from the tone of his voice, that seemed unlikely. And it appeared he was her neighbour who lived in the modern glass house. This was fast becoming a nightmare.

'I don't know why you're always so angry,' Kat retorted, fed up with his attitude. 'It was only music. You should learn to relax.'

They squared up to each other and Kat boldly faced him, folding her arms. Again, she admired her own tenacity in stating what she thought. She'd never done it before, always holding her tongue in case she offended someone, but here, she could be her authentic self. Even if it displeased her handsome neighbour.

'And *you* should learn it's a quiet island. It's not Mykonos. And this is Pétros' house, so again, why are you here?' he said holding his own ground.

'I'm family. I have every right to be here,' Kat responded, yet she immediately regretted her harsh tone seeing his reaction. His face fell in a cloud of sadness.

'I've been away,' he said looking up at the house and back to her, his voice strained with emotion, and Kat found herself softening towards him. 'I can't believe he is gone.' His unshed tears glistened in the beams of solar lamps that flickered on around the lawn and shadows marked his chiselled features. Kat's gaze left the lights and returned to his.

'I . . . I don't know much about him, to be honest. He left me the house in his will.'

He tilted his head to the side as if trying to comprehend how a relative could have so little information. Kat agreed, it was embarrassing, but she'd embarrassed herself constantly in front of this man since meeting at the airport. She noticed he'd abandoned his linen get-up in favour of jeans and a T-shirt, so his nickname no longer applied. His dark hair was damp, and she caught the fresh scent of his citrus cologne on the evening breeze that danced gently around them. That or it was the fruit trees offering their zest to the balmy night air.

'Then since you are my new neighbour, we should be properly introduced, though you may already know – it is a small island.' His arrogance temporarily dampened her attraction to him, though he still made her nervous. 'I am Andreas,' he said extending his hand with genuine warmth for the first time. His eyes flicked across the tattoo on her wrist, and she saw him frown. But Kat clasped his hand wishing the touch of his skin didn't send tingles everywhere.

'Katerína. And no, I didn't know who you were. Sorry, again about the noise. I'll try and keep it down. I've got to go and . . . work on something,' she blustered as she headed for the house.

'*Kalispéra*, Katerína. Maybe work on your *Zeibékiko*; you missed some steps,' he said bidding her good evening with a laugh, but his dig made Kat stop in her tracks.

'Maybe *you* should work on your manners!' She'd meant to make a joke, but it came out wrong; he seemed to bring out that side of her. Usually, she'd err towards timidity and politeness but something about him caused a need to defend herself, like he was constantly judging her.

Seeking safety through the double doors of the lounge, she stepped behind the heavy curtains to peer out at the lawn. He was still there, looking at the upper floor. What was his connection to Pétros? His sadness was beyond that of a neighbourly acquaintance. Then he walked to the lemon tree and placed his hand against the bark. She darted backwards out of sight. By the time she'd mustered the courage to peek again, he'd gone.

Chapter 11

'Good morning, sunshine,' she whispered as she opened her eyes the next day. The chasm that marked the absence of Nik's messages or calls was stark first thing and every evening.

It was early and Kat was covered in sweat. She hadn't pulled the ugly drapes before tumbling into bed, exhausted, and now the sun poured through the bedroom window. The thick sheets weren't helping her body temperature, so she kicked off the covers.

Despite the crisp morning light, the bedroom looked dreary and uninspiring. Though she was grateful to have been gifted the house, she wondered whether a simple sale would be her best bet, swallow the capital gains tax bill and move on. But Pétros' former home ignited her need to fix something, to channel her passion into an all-consuming project that was only hers. She wished her brother could have shared it, but maybe it could be a tribute to him of sorts, and also pay homage to her uncle who had been treated unkindly by his own flesh and blood. Perhaps she could right that wrong by breathing a loving energy into his home.

The thought stirred her creativity, and she reached for her notebook on the bedside table. She started to jot down some ideas, dividing the rooms into an order of priority. When her scribbles were finished, she realised she'd been sitting on the scratchy sheets for over an hour and was wringing wet from the stuffy, overheated room. The picture she had just sketched represented the final job for the house. It would have to wait until the last moment, but when she brought her drawing to life, she would know her work was done. At least she had a finishing post in mind to mark completion, and it would be a magical ritual to place the remaining part. Now it was a matter of dealing with all the bits leading up to that which would be her epic challenge.

She still didn't know what Amelia wanted from her in terms of copy for the magazine. Kat could easily compile an inspiration article that would work beautifully with the summer holidays looming:

'*A piece of Greece for your home.*'

Simple! But intertwining her grief with the virtues of a set of mezze bowls seemed flippant; she didn't want to do Nik or her family a disservice. She threw her notepad on the bed as she sprang up, needing to shower and suddenly noticed a little pink pebble beside her pillow. A prickle rippled across the back of her neck, barely noticeable, but there nonetheless.

'Nik,' she whispered, then dismissed the thought, fearing she was becoming as superstitious as her mother. Placing the pebble on the dark brown chest of drawers, she stripped off her vest and pyjama shorts, letting them fall to the floor, grabbed a towel from the dresser and went to the bathroom.

'Saints preserve me!' screamed Mrs Rálli on the landing as a naked Kat collided with her.

'Oh! Morning, I'm so sorry, I didn't know you were here yet,' Kat blundered trying to preserve her remaining modesty. Before, she was sure Mrs Rálli had seen it all, but now she most definitely had.

'It was good morning,' replied Mrs Rálli, but she had a glimmer of amusement in her eyes, which disappeared as they alighted on Kat's tattoo on her wrist. She tutted and shook her head but said nothing. Kat sheepishly retreated to the bathroom.

When she arrived fully clothed downstairs, Mrs Rálli had made a pan of *strapatsada*, scrambled eggs with feta and tomatoes. Kat thought she could get used to being waited on, but inevitably it would come at a price, as she suspected Mrs Rálli had strong ideas about how Kat should live her life. She was already exhaling heavily as she scraped the remains of last night's supper into a bowl from the saucepan and put it in the fridge. Kat hadn't had much of an appetite after being told off by her new neighbour. As he crossed her mind, she wondered what Mrs Rálli could tell her about him. She started by asking if she could borrow the car to go to Aegina island on the ferry, to which Mrs Rálli reluctantly agreed. Then Kat began to delve into the mystery grump next door. 'I met Andreas last night,' Kat said searching for a reaction.

Mrs Rálli's demeanour changed immediately, almost flushing with youthfulness.

'Ah, yes, Andreas, he is much loved. He was very good to your uncle, as Pétros was in return. He is private. Do not bother him now he is back home.' She broke off to cross herself, leading Kat to suspect there was more to the man she'd coined as Mr Linen.

'We were on the same flight yesterday and didn't hit it off,' Kat said between mouthfuls. She was suddenly ravenous, and the home-cooked breakfast was hitting the mark. 'He came over last night to tell me to keep the noise down.'

Mrs Rálli fixed Kat with a look that would have struck down the fiercest of Greek gods. Kat felt like she had swapped one set of parents for another and returned silently to her food as Mrs Rálli shuffled off armed with a broom. At least she had the day on Aegina to look forward to, though she ought to get a move on. The ferry left at eleven and she'd almost wasted the whole morning sketching and flashing her housekeeper.

* * *

On the ten-minute boat ride, Kat made a list of everything she needed to buy, having requested quotes from local contractors online. Some things she wouldn't consider tackling, but when armed with a paintbrush, she was more than capable. She only hoped the house didn't need rewiring completely, as that would eat into her savings as well as her inheritance and curtail her grand design.

Aegina was a busy place and much larger than Agístri. The harbour front was bustling; cafés swarmed with people whiling away the remaining moments of the morning over coffee. Games of backgammon or *Távli* were in full swing and shouts of elation and despair rang through the air, only to be drowned out by the zoom of a moped or a bellowing bow thrust from a mooring boat. It was positively teeming with life, though Kat could imagine during the summer months there would be little respite from tourists on both Agístri and Aegina, as was the case throughout Greece. But it felt authentic, not a sideshow town pretending to be Greek. This was real life, and Kat was determined to embrace it.

Winding through the cobbled side streets and alleys, she smiled at the number of cats lounging in plant pots. Some even sat on shelves inside window displays – though they surely weren't for sale. She was easily distracted by the local stores and bought herself a simple gold necklace with a pendant featuring the Greek geometric symbol for earth according to the philosopher Plato – so the sales assistant had informed her. Her father would be thrilled with her nod to the ancients. She'd spoken to her parents briefly as she alighted the ferry, reassuring them she was eating well and was happy. True on one count, but she was convincing enough to appease them. For now.

As she sauntered through the streets, crunching on a slice of pistachio brittle bought from one of the stalls on the front, she planned to return when her decorating mission wasn't urgently pending. The shopping was fantastic and not pricey, and she snapped shots of the artisan home goods on sale along with ceramics she'd earmarked for when the kitchen was done. She then sent them to the newly named – by her – messaging group with her friends entitled: *my new island home*. Much less tragic.

She hoped that the same good value she'd found in the shops extended to builders. She'd already had a response from a decorating and construction firm who'd promised to come to the house to cost up the job this week. In the meantime, she'd bought several sizes of paintbrush, sample pots in various shades of her chosen colour scheme, full-size neutral tins of paint, primer, countless swatches and enough sandpaper to shred and make a new beach.

After loading them in Mrs Rálli's car, she had an hour to kill before the ferry. There was a fish market and deli within a row of grocers' shops at the far end of the town beside the waterfront church and she selected various treats to fuel her endeavours on Agístri. She wondered whether a peace offering would smooth things over with Andreas. He'd annoyed her, but she hated leaving things on a sour note, having learnt the hard way how precious life was. And, she hoped she may be able to dig a little more into his relationship with her uncle.

Kat selected a bottle of organic ouzo that would appeal, no doubt, to his fancy expensive taste given his high-end get-up and smart shoes. Then, she changed her mind and bought a small platter of crispy *kataífi* – topped with pistachios. She hadn't eaten it for ages though her taste-bud memory immediately recalled the clove and cinnamon flavours wrapped within buttery shredded filo bathed in lemon-scented syrup. Traditional, simple and unfussy.

Finding respite in a *kafenío* and grateful to set down her bags of food, she ordered an *espresso freddo* and watched the bustling harbour front. A man playing bouzouki was wandering around the tables smiling in the hope of inspiring a euro or two. Her phone on the table flashed with an incoming call: 'HUSBAND'.

'*Yiássou*, husband! How are you?' she asked Jamie.

'Oh fine, dodging the rain, tasting wine, same old. Come on then, torture me with your current view.'

She looked around the busy coffee house and along the shoreline to the large cream church with its terracotta roof. The bell tower chimed noisily to mark the hour.

'Contrary to all the clanging, I haven't joined a convent. Just on another Greek island in baking sunshine watching the world go by. Same old,' she joked.

'Maybe I should stake a claim. That house is technically half mine since we're still married – I'm packing as we speak!'

She paused, wondering whether there was seriousness beneath his jest. No, she'd known Jamie for so many years; he'd never try and claim it in their divorce. Though now she thought about it, he had form for making rash decisions on her behalf, taking things out of her hands without consultation. He'd put in the offer on their house without speaking to her first, assuming she'd go along with it. Which she did because she adored it, but that wasn't the point. And, of course, he'd orchestrated this trip behind her back in cahoots with her father. Jamie continued to be involved in her life as if they were still together. But Pétros' house wasn't in the bargain.

'My uncle left it to me and Nik. It belongs to us,' she said firmly, repeating what he already knew for clarity.

'Kat, I was kidding. As if I'd do that. So, what's the place like?' She was reassured and the tension in her shoulders retreated.

'Well,' she began. 'You know how our old spare bedroom looked when I'd finished it, oak sanded floorboards with muslin drapes?'

'Oh wow!' said Jamie.

'And then remember the outhouse with mould, crammed with someone else's furniture and crap we didn't want?'

'Yes . . .'

'I'm basically living in our old outhouse minus the rot. At least I hope there isn't any . . . and the dream is to turn it into light, bright fabulousness. There's so much to do, but I'm kind of excited.' She said it with false enthusiasm as she considered the sheer amount of work the place needed.

'Kat, I've known you for nearly twenty years. I know how you sound when you're excited and this isn't it. Do you want me to come out there? I'm not sure you should be alone.'

'No!' she exclaimed, then tempered her tone. 'Sorry. I'm just thinking a lot about Nik and what it would be like doing this with him. I'm fine, honestly. I'll soon buck up. I've only been here a day. Once things get going, I'll be good as gold.' She slurped at her cold drink, which ran with drops of condensation.

'The moment you don't feel OK, I'll be on the next plane. You can talk to me, Kat, you know that. I don't want you to burn out. Take the time to relax, please.'

'I will and thanks, husband.' She smiled. Jamie always cheered her up and despite her recent irritation at him, she needed a friendly, familiar voice in her day. 'Anyway, tell me about single life – anyone special I need to know about? What about that date Lizzie set you up on . . . ?'

They chatted easily, though Kat couldn't help but replay Jamie's comment about claiming the house. Maybe she *should* seek legal advice now she solely owned something of value. Their amicable separation could become acrimonious if things went awry. Usually, Kat would merrily think the best of people. But she'd learnt that nothing turns out the way it should. And not everyone was who they seemed. Little over a week ago, Kat had thought her mother incapable of keeping anything secret from her; Mína was usually so indiscreet. Perhaps she should be on her guard from now on and think the worst; that way she would never be disappointed.

Artemis & Apollo

Artemis was gentle, unlike her tempestuous brother who roamed the world seeking out passion and amusement, often incurring the wrath of their father, Zeus, the King of the Gods. She permitted her twin to bask in his sunshine, as she came alive by moonlight, stealthily moving through the shadows, seeking a quiet life without drama or consternation. But in the realms of both gods and mortals, things rarely play out as expected.

Chapter 12

Mint green paint stripes, in varying subtle shades, adorned the walls of the master bedroom. A colour choice in homage to the pistachios grown nearby. Kat would let them dry overnight before she made her decision. Streaks of narrow tester strips decorated every room of the house, and she braced herself for the wrath of Mrs Rálli when she saw them in the morning.

Kat had insisted Mrs Rálli left for the day when she'd returned from Aegina in the clunking car and reassured her she was capable of making her own dinner. When the older woman was satisfied that Kat wouldn't starve overnight after leafing through the bags of shopping, she had nodded and bid her goodbyes.

Having sanded the dark stereo cabinet, Kat primed it ready for painting but a growl in her stomach told her it was nearing suppertime. She looked around the gloom of the lounge, massaging her aching elbow, then removed the awful thick curtains. Bracing herself, she decided to complete one more job before sustenance: to deliver the peace offering to Andreas next door.

Without a care for her appearance, aside from pulling her tangled brown curls into a makeshift bun, she took the small platter of Greek treats and headed out of the garden bound for the adjacent plot. The sea was calm and the air heavy as if a storm were brewing. Dark indigo clouds peppered the pink sky like fading bruises. As they collided with the sun's diminishing embers, parts of the vista were tinged with a vibrant scarlet. The richness of colour was almost violent, and a muted grumble of thunder sounded far out at sea as Kat made her way along the front.

Andreas' land was several thousand square feet with towering palm trees planted around the perimeter. Probably to contain his moods, thought Kat. But she pushed away the sting of his barbs about her dancing. She was only sensitive because she'd been reminiscing about Nik when he'd interrupted her. An electric entry gate on the seaward side of the house blocked the view of what lay behind. Was he trying to keep people out, or pen himself in? She pressed the buzzer and noticed surveillance cameras fixed to the walls. The fancy security system was at odds with the simplicity of what she'd seen of the island thus far. As the gates swung open, they revealed a jungle-like almost tropical garden. She moved through the foliage, and Andreas' house emerged.

In terms of architecture, it was more in keeping with something from the Beverly Hills property programmes she binge-watched. Floor-to-ceiling windows with black metal casings framed the boxy modern structure. Long rectangular fire pits illuminated a white marble patio that stretched the width of the impressive house. Black rattan L-shaped sofas and matching armchairs created a cosy outside seating area and a long dining table that could accommodate at least twelve sat beneath an ebony overhang at the far end. The pocket doors were pushed back, creating the illusion that the house was part of the garden. What on earth did this guy do for a living? Hedge fund or trust fund? Kat suddenly became aware of her scruffy painting clothes and tangled, knotted hair, and felt distinctly out of place. She couldn't simply wander in.

Andreas appeared on the terrace through the open doors just as she was working out which window to knock on. He was back in his usual linen attire but this time wearing white loose-fitting trousers and a black short-sleeved button-down shirt. Maybe his wealth came from shares in the material's manufacture, she thought. As sunset beams kissed his tanned skin, she caught her breath; he was positively glowing in the golden light. Nearing, she saw a look of delight on his face. The way his lips formed a smile ignited a spark that pinged around her body, something she hadn't felt for as long as she could remember. She reminded herself that as charming and jolly as he seemed this evening, he could also be rude and abrupt, though it did little to quell her admiration.

'*Kalispéra*,' she began finding confidence, proffering her plate of goodies. 'I come with an olive branch.'

He held out his hands to receive the gift and their fingers brushed briefly.

'Thank you,' he seemed surprised. '*Kataífi*, my favourite. You must have done your research,' he said raising an eyebrow, which caught Kat off guard.

'Um, no. I guess I struck lucky,' she stammered feeling her cheeks heat. He was so annoying; how could she possibly have had the time to ask around about his preferred delicacies?

'I guess you did strike lucky, in many ways,' he said

looking towards the imposing fence bordering his property, which hid her inherited bolthole from view.

Kat was unsure how to respond. She found him so hard to read. For someone who was able to charm with such ease, he could switch to brittle delivery in an instant. She'd seen the reaction of the flight attendants and check-in staff at the airport, blushing and preening in his presence. But he was also guarded, almost suspicious. Though maybe only with her.

'Look, I'm sorry about last night. I should have been more sympathetic. I didn't know Pétros existed until recently. It's been a lot to take in and you were obviously close,' she said looking towards her new house. 'I should know better than to be careless with grief.'

His face became serious as he stared at her. 'There is nothing to joke about when it comes to death.' His eyes flicked to the floor momentarily then back to her. 'Thank you for my gift.'

Then his fingers travelled the distance between them. The space between her cheek and his hand almost crackled in anticipation and charged the air as, in the distance, another grumble of thunder boomed. His skin made contact with hers, and Kat flinched.

'You have paint, here,' he said removing his fingers as quickly as they'd landed, which made Kat wonder whether she'd imagined it. 'Nice colour.' His eyes twinkled, but Kat feared he was laughing at her. She wanted to ask him about her uncle, but he made her so edgy and at the same time inexplicably cross that she couldn't find the words. He turned and walked into his house. Should she follow or leave? Was their conversation over? He was incredibly frustrating. Through the open doors, she saw a sleek, sunken lounge furnished in a muted cream and grey colour palette that created a peaceful environment. It was precisely her taste, though lacked colour and warmth. Andreas returned holding a damp cloth which he gave to her.

'Here.' He pointed to his cheek indicating she should wipe hers and she obliged. He grinned. 'And here.' His gaze travelled to her forehead and once again, she mirrored his movements. 'And there. But I like this shade the best.' He gestured to the tip of her nose.

'Oh, for goodness' sake! Why didn't you tell me?' she said, wiping it away, mortified that she was unknowingly covered in streaks of paint. They shared the same preference for colour, though. The daub on her nose was her favoured choice for the master bedroom.

'Any more?' she asked feeling uncomfortable, shifting from one foot to the other as he shook his head, still grinning. He was so well put together in his perfect house with his pristine crease-free outfits and she was a paint-splattered shambles.

'Do you have no mirrors in your new home, or running water, Katerína?'

Lightning streaked across the darkening sky. He had ignited her irritation again but the way he said her name sent a shiver down her spine. She thrust the damp cloth back in his hands. Whether it was him or the brewing storm, she felt disarmed and unsure what to do next. Andreas said nothing but continued to look at Kat. It was unbearable. A crack of thunder startled her.

'I have to go,' she muttered. As she turned, her flip-flop caught on a step, and she broke into a half jog to compensate, cursing her clumsiness as she went.

'*Kalispéra*, Katerína! Don't you want to stay for a drink

and *kataífi*?' he shouted after her, but she didn't respond only flinging up an arm in the air as a wave of sorts.

Neighbours could be a godsend or a giant pain in the behind. She wasn't sure which category Andreas fit into, but he was both intriguing and maddening in equal measure. It may be wise to steer clear. Life was tricky enough without Mr Linen complicating it.

* * *

'Mrs Rálli, how did you meet Pétros?' Kat asked as she tucked into a bowl of yoghurt the next morning. She'd generously drizzled it with honey and topped it with chopped walnuts. The creamy texture complemented her French-press coffee, its bitterness tempered by a teaspoon of cinnamon.

'I look for work as young girl.' Her eyes lit up when she spoke of Pétros as she attempted to speak English. 'He offers me the job as cleaner. My family was poor. We have no choice but to accept, and he helps me learn the English – though not much as you hear.' She switched into Greek and Kat had to put her spoon down to concentrate on translating. 'No matter what many on this island once thought of him, I and my family will always be grateful. We had trust and respect with each other and he gave me the greatest gift of all.'

Kat nodded. Long-term employment and security were certainly something to treasure. They were both making hard work of the other's mother tongue so compromised by switching between the two. Mrs Rálli continued as she scrubbed at the work surfaces.

'But he was a good man. The best of people. Not judgemental unlike some. It is strange when those who cast aspersions make their own mistakes and suddenly need help,' she paused, raising her eyebrows indicating that Kat should agree, though she didn't know to what and thought she had missed something important. 'He gave much to others, though many chose not to acknowledge his generosity. Where do they suppose the new roof on the church came from or the memorial benches in the pine forests? There are questions people never ask because they know they will not like the answer. He loved this island despite all that happened.'

Mrs Rálli was proving as cryptic as her parents when it came to Pétros, but Kat was determined to drill as deep as she dared.

'Is he buried in the churchyard? Nobody seems to know,' she asked, but Mrs Rálli either didn't hear or understand her question. Kat wanted to lay flowers for her uncle at least, though she'd had no inclination to ever visit Nik's grave since the funeral. She simply didn't believe in the obsession with a pilgrimage to wail over a mound of earth and headstone. Nik wasn't there; he was in her heart and all around. She tried a different tack. 'I understand how conservative this place used to be, but was Pétros alone all his life? I hope not.'

Mrs Rálli forced a sad smile. 'Not everyone, Katerína, is destined to have love; it is not a divine right to experience it. You young people expect to find your heart's desire with the click of a finger, but love is never guaranteed and if it is, it isn't always reciprocated.'

She sounded more like Giórgios now, philosophising on the trials of love. Kat wondered whether Mrs Rálli was speaking from experience.

'One love you are yet to learn, Katerína, is the love of cooking. Please, if I meet my maker tonight, you, I fear, will go hungry. You cannot survive on marinated anchovies and olives. So, I am making some dishes to keep you going on this crazy decorating marathon.' She fixed Kat with her watchful eyes then began to decant various ingredients into mixing bowls. 'Here – filo pastry. Keep between the tea towels to stop it drying out. Now light the oven please.' Kat obliged, fearing for her eyebrows and lashes as she ignited the ancient gas oven. 'You think new things are good but change for change's sake is like running from the truth. Now, one kilo of spinach after leeks and onions in the pan – a little butter and oil. I make *spanakópita* – spinach pie.' For one so slow, Mrs Rálli moved around the rickety kitchen with astonishing deftness as she continued chattering. 'A sea nymph will change his shape if you attempt to capture it, which is like trying to trap a lightning bolt. And then you have gone to such effort to chase the source of what you want that you will turn mad when it doesn't come.'

Kat expected to meet some resistance on the refurbishment plans, but she now had real concerns about Mrs Rálli's sanity. What on earth was she on about? Between Mrs Rálli barking cooking instructions and her philosophical musings, Kat's head was spinning, and her coffee had gone cold.

'But did Pétros have love? You didn't answer,' she tried again, hoping for more detail.

'He had friendship and companionship. He wrote of this – albeit fiction. Have you read his work?'

Kat shook her head, feeling ashamed as Mrs Rálli continued.

'You should. His writing is much adored in Greece, and he won prizes throughout the world. As for Pétros himself . . . he had many different loves in his life. Now melt some butter in another pan, please, Katerína, and be useful. You will brush the layers of pastry when it is ready to assemble.'

Kat felt she wasn't going to get a straightforward response. The only other person who could give her any information about her uncle was Andreas but she'd vowed to avoid him. Maybe there was a clue in one of Pétros' novels.

She became Mrs Rálli's sous chef for the rest of the morning. Though itching to get on with some painting, she realised it would be prudent to have the housekeeper onside. Already, she'd made an enemy of sorts out of her neighbour, and she needed all the friends she could find on this island.

Chapter 13

Kat was surprised to have been visited by a builder in the afternoon. She hadn't been expecting someone to turn up when they'd said they would. Mrs Rálli was lingering near the lounge doors pretending to clean the terrace table in a non-subtle attempt to eavesdrop. The surface was already spotless.

'I would say, there is much to do, but we are very experienced,' Kostas said – he was the only builder who'd responded to her email but he appeared trustworthy, reinforced by the nods and hums of agreement from Mrs Rálli out on the patio. 'There are some building supplies that must travel across here on the boat. It is good you are near one of the island harbours. Then the kitchen must be ordered from Athens, the bathroom fittings too – though my sons and I have enough to make a start if you wish. Bad weather is coming so we have cancellations and can begin almost straight away.' He nervously handed Kat his written quote but she secretly breathed a considerable sigh of relief. It was much less than she'd been expecting. Her only reference point was the contractors she'd used for her and Jamie's home. This was far cheaper, and now she could afford to include marble counters in her kitchen design.

Kostas left her with several brochures from which to select tiles and units and she'd agreed to engage him immediately, hoping he wasn't a 'bodge it and scarper' contractor. He'd said it would take four weeks to complete, maybe longer but perhaps faster. Very vague. Work would begin tomorrow according to him, which Kat knew was Greek for between now and Christmas. There was plenty for her to get on with in the meantime.

After Kat waved him off, she went to sit in the kitchen looking around her, trying to imagine it when she'd finished. She recalled Nik coming armed with a magenta orchid to see her and Jamie's house in Tooting, which she'd lovingly refurbished from top to bottom.

'And this can be your room if you ever find yourself in this part of town and need somewhere to sleep,' she'd said opening the guest room door with a flourish. It was furnished with second-hand Victorian antiques, and she had firmly leant into the period by choosing authentic colours befitting the era. There was even a battered copper bed pan dangling from the wall, which made her twin laugh. Above the vanity, she'd hung one of Nik's black and white nude photographs, and he blushed with faux modesty.

'You are so talented, Kitty Kat. But I wish you'd write, not just about design – which of course you're brilliant at – but a novel. That's what you really want to do. Promise me you'll find a way to follow your heart. It will make you happier, I swear.'

'*I wish you'd follow your heart.*' It was one of the last things he said to her before the accident too. But she hadn't had the courage to take the plunge and be an author then. She only hoped she could find the guts and inspiration she needed now, on this little island. As Mrs Rálli bustled around the outdated kitchen, Kat sighed before returning to the brochure from Kostas. She was surrounded by strangers because she couldn't deal with her family and friends' smothering. But now, she longed for a familiar face and to hear her brother's voice again even if only to call her his silly nickname, Kitty Kat, which nobody else had ever used. She looked around for a pebble as a sign of comfort, but found none. And his red evil eye was lost forever.

Mrs Rálli placed a piping-hot cup of coffee beside Kat with some freshly made baklava. That pastry lesson had been missed while the builder measured up.

'Have you got family, Mrs Rálli?' Kat asked taking a break from pictures of bathroom layouts and finishes, having folded down several page corners. The housekeeper sat at the kitchen table with her own cup.

'There is nobody left.' She took a slow sip. 'It was not in God's plan for me to have all I wished for. I never married, but your uncle insisted I should be called *Mrs* Rálli; it was more respectable and avoids questions. But you, you should have a family and a husband, not be here by yourself, Katerína. There are many bedrooms upstairs to turn into a nursery . . . It is not seemly for a beautiful, young woman to be alone and you have such wonderful skin.'

'Well, I'm about to get divorced, good skin or not. And I didn't want kids. I know that's hard for some people to understand. I love children; I just never wanted my own.'

'Ah!' beamed Mrs Rálli. 'This is because you have not yet met the right man. How old are you – what thirty-nine, forty?'

Kat balked at the increase of years at the hands of a woman who shuffled around like a geriatric.

'Thirty-seven, actually,' she responded tersely. She wasn't looking her best of late. Grief had carved time and age into her features. 'And man or no man, children aren't part of my future. However, these bathroom tiles are!' She held up a page from the builder's merchant magazine and showed Mrs Rálli the sandstone she'd selected.

'Hmmm. Very nice. Expensive. You will turn this house into a shiny box like him next door.'

'It will be a little more modern, but it doesn't mean you won't still belong, Mrs Rálli.' Kat closed the brochure. 'You'll love the new kitchen I've designed in my head, I promise. Though there will be some disruption for a bit. Maybe you could take some holiday – there's no point cleaning while there's workmen here.'

'Holiday?!' she shrieked. 'Where on this earth would I go? Why would I wish to travel somewhere else only to be alone like you?'

'You could go and hang out with your friends . . .' Kat stopped, given the look of horror on Mrs Rálli's face.

'What would I do all day? I'm used to working, being in a home to make nice. What else do I have if not this? Many of my friends and those I loved are gone.' Her eyes began to water, and Kat felt dreadful.

'It was only a suggestion,' she said quickly, though she did want to reduce the hours Mrs Rálli spent at the house. Kat liked her own space and after living back at home with her parents these past few months, she'd been feeling hemmed in. A feeling that endured in the company of this overbearing but well-meaning lady. Mrs Rálli moved to the sink to start washing up. 'Just don't feel you have to tidy up so much when the work starts. Because there will be a new mess the next day and the one after that until it's done.'

Mrs Rálli seemed satisfied and cleared the cups from the table. Kat wasn't comfortable being waited on yet, but she didn't want to offend. Happily, Mrs Rálli must have read her mind, as she lowered onto a seat again.

'Then perhaps I come just in the mornings. I will make sure you have food for the evenings, but only if that is agreeable. Pétros wanted you and your brother to be cared for when you came to the island, and he left arrangements for the house to be filled with provisions.'

At the mention of Nik, a breath lodged in Kat's throat, forming a knot.

'I am very sorry about your brother. Pétros spoke of you both with great fondness. I remember when you came here with your mother.' Mrs Rálli pulled an odd expression as she knitted her fingers together on the tabletop. Kat wished she could remember that trip. 'You were such a pretty little girl, much quieter than your brother. Though Pétros only met you that one time, he was quite taken with you. Terrible about Nikólaos – I am sorry.'

Kat managed to swallow away the lump of emotion in order to speak. 'I haven't spoken about Nik dying much. I don't want to upset my parents, so I try to keep it in.'

Mrs Rálli crossed herself out of religious piety and superstition as was the case in their culture – to prevent further misery from descending.

'It is a tragedy for someone so young to be taken away. He was so alive and so beautiful – outgoing and charming. His smile would light up the darkest room like the sunshine on a dull day; he was the same as a child,' said Mrs Rálli.

'Sorry?' said Kat, unsure she'd heard correctly given

they were currently speaking Greek and she doubted her translation. 'You mean when he was a child?'

Mrs Rálli shook her head.

Kat's skull pounded with her heartbeat, confused as to how this was possible. She hadn't been aware of Pétros' existence until the will arrived. Mrs Rálli couldn't have any idea who her brother grew up to be. Could she? 'How do you know what Nik was like as an adult?'

'Because Nikólaos and your uncle were like kindred spirits in many ways. They would often write to each other, and he came to stay several times. He was with us in August and September last year. Pétros dedicated his last novel to him – it is in the bookcase in the lounge. If only we'd known it would be his and Pétros' final summer.'

Kat stared at the table, trying to make sense of what she'd just heard.

'Nik came here? I . . . He—' She broke off as emotion strangled her voice. Why would her brother keep this from her? She couldn't comprehend the purpose of hiding it. She recalled his trips abroad to Greece, claiming he was away with friends, but he'd never said he'd visited this island or mentioned Pétros. She'd thought they'd told each other everything and had no secrets.

'Yes.' Mrs Rálli continued chattering away in her mother tongue as she rose and returned to the washing up. 'He brought such life into the house, and he made Pétros laugh – a rare sound in his later years. Although unhappiness initially brought Nikólaos here, it became his haven for joy. And his photography . . . some of the pictures, I admit, made me blush!' She giggled like a young woman, covering her mouth with her hand.

'When did he first come to Agístri?' Kat felt outraged

that someone else had shared a part of Nik that he'd kept from her.

'Six maybe seven years ago was his first trip to the island. Mína always wrote letters to Pétros on your birthdays filled with news as if nothing had transpired between them. In it, she spoke of Nikólaos and his . . . his relationships with men.' Mrs Rálli wrung her hands and Kat wondered whether she disapproved of such a lifestyle. It may be at odds with the old version of Greece and her interpretation of doctrine, but then, she'd served Pétros so faithfully and spoke of him with such affection, she must have let it pass without judgement. 'I am a simple woman, not one to say aloud what is right or wrong. But out of the blue, a letter from Nikólaos appears.' She smiled. 'And your brother and uncle became great friends. Nikólaos gave us all new life. I am glad Pétros died without knowing what happened to your brother. He stopped opening your mother's letters years ago; they couldn't find a way back to each other to repair what was broken between them.' She crossed herself again. 'He loved Nikólaos like his son. Your brother was the only blood family who never judged him,' she added bitterly.

Again, Kat was racked with confusion at the hands of her relatives, though these ones were gone and couldn't answer for themselves. She wouldn't have judged her uncle – she'd embraced her twin's sexuality – but the fact they didn't give her the opportunity and deliberately excluded her tugged at her insides. She took her leave of Mrs Rálli, longing to speak with her parents, but she wasn't sure what to say. Nik had betrayed them all and she didn't know how her mother would react. She stood in front of the bookcase housing her uncle's novels, which were all stamped with 'Bestseller' from respected international institutions. Surely her mother had been aware of Pétros' success and yet she'd kept him a secret. And now Nik had kept something from them all. Was this his last laugh? Kat wasn't smiling.

She leafed through the novels' dedication pages and found inscriptions with various names:

Mína, my sister, may you find the forgiveness you seek; Nikólaos, my sunshine . . . They'd shared the same nickname for her brother and she suddenly felt territorial. Another book had: *Katerína – may we meet in our next life*, and the last she found simply said: *Andréa mou*

My Andreas.

Chapter 14

As Kat walked along the seafront, the storm clouds huddled on the horizon and the wind increased, whipping at her curly hair, wrapping it around her features. She didn't care. The pain in her chest grew until she could no longer stem her tears. Thick and fast they streamed, soaking her cheeks. She hadn't explored the far end of the island, only having whizzed along in Mrs Rálli's car from the other ferry port, but she was in no mood for sightseeing. Her conflicted feelings whirled and stung like the harsh breeze. She needed to find shelter from the weather.

The large white church loomed ahead; its enticing blue dome looked out of place against the grey murky sky. This wasn't the Greece she'd imagined. It was beginning to feel like a terrible mistake.

Inside the holy place, she found a welcome respite from the gusts outside. It was silent save for the odd crackle from flickering candles placed around the various shrines. She sat in a pew and looked at the stained glass above. Even on such a cloudy day, the colours sang brightly in the cavernous roof, as she searched the heavens and saints for guidance and comfort. This trip was supposed to be, in a way, a pilgrimage for her brother. She wanted to renovate the house in honour of him since they should be sharing it. All it had done so far was shine a light upon all the unknowns about him and her family. And now there was a possibility Andreas had been in a relationship with her uncle. Her grand adventure felt like a misjudged plan. The whole reason she'd found herself on Agístri was due to a family secret and she hadn't planned on unearthing any more. But now that she had, she didn't want to be there at all.

In the far corner of the church, someone cleared their throat. Startled, she followed the sound with her eyes and found an ancient priest sitting on a chair with a book in his hands. She assumed it was *The* book but had no queries as to his reading matter. He nodded at Kat before resuming his studies. His straggly ponytail was tied at the nape of his neck and his long grey beard twitched as he read. He looked at peace and Kat envied his harmonious posture, when she was riddled with tension. Eventually he closed his book with a gentle thump and rose, moving towards her.

'*Yiássas*,' he said by way of greeting and took a pew across the aisle from her. Kat's eyes drifted upwards once again. The striking image of Christ was surrounded by the apostles, each with their own different-coloured window that made a rainbow as the light refracted. She'd been told that her uncle paid for the roof renovation, so perhaps the priest could enlighten her.

'*Yiássas, Páter*, I'm Kat – Katerína – you may have known my uncle, Pétros.' She waited for a signal about his attitude towards her relative. Either the priest had no feelings about Pétros, or an excellent poker face. His eyes lifted to the ceiling, and he nodded.

'I am *Papa* Serafím. We have Pétros to thank for all of this.' He waved his arm in an expansive gesture. 'A good, kind man.'

It was all anybody had said about him so far – good and kind – but it gave her little insight.

'That much I've heard, but I'd love to find out more. I obviously know bits about his life – the more controversial aspects . . .'

The priest smiled and nodded again, but said nothing, his eyes busily tracing the icons above.

He moved to the main altar and after muttering an incantation, crossed himself and went through the motions of kissing depictions of saints and the Holy Mother. Then he retrieved his tall wooden staff and turned to her.

'Come, Katerína. Before the storm arrives, let us walk.'

It all felt rather biblical as his stick clacked against the stone floor. His brown monkish robes billowed as they emerged outside into the wind, which seemed to have grown in strength since she'd sought shelter in the church. They headed up a steep incline around the far side of the island past the main harbour where larger boats and ferries docked. A pristine beach with sun loungers stacked atop one another sat in front of a closed-up taverna. The path was hard going, but the priest forged on with Kat following.

'There are several parishes on the island and many churches. I try to visit them all each day, though it is many miles to walk. I do not wish for anyone to be neglected, whomever they are,' said Father Serafím raising his voice to be heard against the elements. As they crested the brow of a hill, passing a row of shops and a hotel, the scent of pine permeated the air. The dense forest that dominated the centre of the island seemed to grow from the roofs of houses.

'This may be a difficult question, Father, but how was my uncle viewed here and by you?' she panted, observing how fit the priest seemed to be despite his advanced years.

He paused, leaning against his staff and took a deep breath. Kat turned to look across the island and out to sea as another ferry defiantly crossed the choppy waters from the mainland in the distance. She was grateful for the priest's command of English for such a conversation.

'Ah, Katerína, I sense your question is about the community but more so about our religion. Am I correct?'

Kat hesitated. Her own Orthodoxy was questionable, especially having been brought up in liberal London. Though her family was affiliated with their local church, she only attended out of duty at Easter or on celebration days.

'I guess. I'm just struggling to get a sense of who he was. I haven't read his work yet, but I've heard stories of his amazing philanthropy and kindness. He even left his house to me, but he's like a stranger with barely a wisp of a memory from when I was five to back it up. I'm working with nothing here . . . I don't even know where he is buried.'

The priest chuckled. 'Nobody knows where he is laid to rest. Perhaps it is his final act beyond the grave to wield his own judgement on our religion. But his writing is wonderful; it is abstract and lyrical. I would suggest his spirit is expressed between the pages, so you may find part of him there. Yes, his altruism knew no bounds, but as for what I or the church considered his choices – they are different things,' he started walking again and Kat joined him in step. 'My role as father to this island is that of upholding our doctrine. Now, if God made man in the image of himself, who am I to judge how right or wrong He may have got it? I speak as I find and over time, what I've discovered is that human kindness remains most important of all – a generosity of spirit along with deeds to match. If a person does not hurt or harm, destroy or kill and strives to be the best version of themselves, then they are welcome. Suggesting otherwise is an implication that God made a mistake.'

Kat had never heard such measure from a holy man.

'I think you've cut through an ancient debate, Father, with a lot of sense. And assessing people in terms of their kindness is a pretty great benchmark. I should take note too.' She was thinking how quick she'd been to judge her neighbour and make assumptions about his relationship with Pétros. Perhaps it would be better to broach the subject directly. 'Pétros was close with Andreas too, I understand, and of course Mrs Rálli.'

He smiled and looked down at his feet as the terrain roughened.

'Some stories are not mine to tell. There is only one story I am prepared to pass on and that is the holy story. You see, there are always three versions of every tale – other than the story of Christ: the opposing versions, and then the truth. Truth is what you should seek.'

She laughed. He had such a simplistic but beautiful view of the world. Oh, to have such faith!

'And that's my struggle. I've found out some things about my family – secrets – and I'm trying to digest it all, which is hard when nobody is here to answer my questions, and I suppose—' She broke off unable to complete her sentence, which she finished in her mind: *I feel so alone.*

That was what she wanted to say, but somehow the words wouldn't come. She felt as if she were naked, being battered and bruised by the elements before the summit of the island, yet still, she couldn't bare her feelings out of fear of what would tumble from her lips. 'Anyway, thank you, Father. I'd better get back before the rain starts,' she said as black clouds loomed ominously.

'And I should get up this hill before I am washed back down again,' he joked continuing on his relentless hike. As they parted, Kat looked upwards to the little church further up the mountainside that Father Serafím was headed for. His life was true service. Kat wished she had such purpose, to feel like she'd contributed something significant to a community as her uncle had also done. He'd left the world a better place. What would she leave behind? Recommendations about curtains and tablescapes . . . hardly a significant legacy. But perhaps she could change that by writing in the way she'd always wanted.

Father Serafím stopped ahead and turned. 'Are you certain you are strong enough for your journey onwards?'

Kat nodded, touched by his ability to instantly reach the heart of what she was wrestling with. 'I'll be fine, Father. Thank you.'

He nodded and dug his staff into the ground to move on, shouting as he went, 'Good luck to you, Katerína! Remember, the answers you seek may be right in front of you.'

He spoke into the wind, but she heard his words just as her toe caught on a shiny pink pebble under her foot.

Chapter 15

~~Grief~~
~~Greece~~
~~Grief in Greece~~
~~My Greek Grief~~
Oh good grief!!

Kat had deleted every word and phrase she'd attempted to write that afternoon following her hike with the priest. Eventually she admitted defeat and abandoned it. What was her editor thinking when she commissioned her to combine decorating and bereavement? It simply didn't work – that, or Kat wasn't in the right mindset. She'd have to speak to Amelia and beg her to change her mind. Kat was beginning to doubt her ability to write about anything other than décor and design.

She'd received a message from Kostas who said he'd arrive as planned tomorrow to begin the upstairs bathroom demolition and to take up the floorboards in the primary bedroom. Beautiful as they were, the wood needed some intensive love and care.

Kat moved her belongings into one of the guest rooms and started to strip the floral wallpaper back in the master. She worked into the evening, uncovering beautiful brickwork beneath the strips of paper, which she then scrubbed clean. But a single wall was made of the same granite-like stone as the downstairs hallway and exterior. She planned to put a simple coat of whitewash over it, and her chosen shade of minty green over the other three brick ones, which would allow their pleasing wonky shapes to shine through the paint.

The lights suddenly flickered on and off and, concerned about the resilience of the power supply, she went in search of candles to have on standby, which she happily found downstairs in a kitchen drawer.

She was about to head back to the bedroom, when an almighty howl came from the garden. Was it the tri-coloured cat she'd seen on her first day? He was probably wild, so opening the doors and giving him access was pointless, and she wasn't sure whether she could cope with the stream of cadavers that ensue when inviting a cat in. But his tuneless wailing persisted, penetrating the windows.

'All right! I can hear you,' she said, decanting some tinned fish onto a saucer. Venturing outside with the offering, she looked around. The cat was nowhere to be seen, though his screeching song travelled on the air. She placed the plate beside the lemon tree, hoping if the cat was hungry, he would find it. She decided to call him Patch if he returned. It would be good to have a friend.

Kat usually enjoyed time to herself; loneliness was a very different problem, though. The omnipresence of her family could be stifling, but now the deafening silence was too quiet. She couldn't phone her parents, because she hadn't worked out what to say about Nik's relationship with Pétros and his trips to Agístri.

As she walked back inside, she sent a message in her '*new island home*' group:

> *No concrete news about the uncle. But he dedicated a bestseller to me! I'm immortalised in literature if I achieve nothing else. House demolition/renovation starts tomorrow. Paint and colour schemes chosen, storm out at sea, grumpy but very handsome neighbour and randy cat in the garden. K x*

Cracks of thunder boomed around the island like a cannon being fired as she sat shrouded in lamplight in the lounge to rest her aching limbs. She opened the novel Pétros had penned for Andreas. She wasn't quite ready to delve into the one devoted to Nik and although vanity had tempted her to read the one written for her, at the moment, she was more intrigued about the man living next door and his connection to her family.

She sipped at sparkling water infused with lime, mint and cucumber, trying not to flinch at the rumbles echoing over the sea, and opened the first page of Pétros' book, entitled *Versions of Love*.

> Geometric shadow shapes merged to form a layer of pristine skin as I sat and observed. The candlelight wavered, forming a blanket over bare muscle and sinew, curves and sharp edges. It would be impossible to reduce this form to lines and angles, such was his beauty. I longed to plummet into the depths and draw his soul towards my blank page. My pencil hovering,

uselessly pointing, awaiting impulse and momentum. It was not love, nor would it ever be such, but I knew I had to fall in love with him, break him apart to make him whole on the paper before me.

I searched his eyes for discomfort, but none was forthcoming; sought out the pain I knew of his past, but found no trace. He was feigning life, as we all do in one guise or another, purporting to live. He'd made it his work to fool admirers, a convincing portrayal for a fleeting moment, a professional pretender. To fall for his deception was to tumble into the chasm, the darkest of abysses where the murkiest moments of human existence thrived. Those deeds would guide me downwards to meet my fate with no siren call to yield salvation, no nymph to spirit a journey to the promised land in search of nirvana. Only the basest of thoughts and desires remain when skin and bone, love and loss are stripped away. Blood is all that could hold any worth; for it is within its cells and structures that the heart seeks and finds its true purpose.

Kat squirmed in her chair and placed the book in her lap. Outside, the dark sky ignited orange with a flash of sheet lightning. Was this novel of Pétros' a love letter to Andreas? The intimacy of the writing transported her into the scene, but she had been confronted with the mental image of her neighbour naked. Was he the subject of the passage she'd read? Her mind travelled unwittingly to what might lie beneath his linen. As she flicked through the pages, a handwritten note slipped from the back of the book and onto the floor. Holding it to the light, she saw it was written in English:

> *Dearest Pétros, I can never thank you enough, I owe you everything and would be nothing without you, A x*

She frowned. Could 'A' be Andreas? And if it was, the nature of the relationship he had with her uncle seemed pretty clear.

Lost in jumbled musings, she went into the kitchen to make supper. She'd convinced Mrs Rálli that she didn't need a full gourmet performance each day, reassuring her that she was capable of fixing something herself. Nevertheless, in the fridge there was an individual moussaka for her to reheat along with a 'gardener's salad' made of shredded white cabbage, carrots, sun-dried tomatoes and celery with a home-made olive oil, vinegar and honey dressing.

While she waited for her dinner to warm up, she glanced around the kitchen, comparing her vision for the space with the tattered reality. The platters she'd spied on Aegina would be a wonderful centrepiece on the new central island, piled high with lemons from the tree in the garden. She had no idea what the end goal for the house was. There were no plans in her immediate future to up sticks, move to Greece and embrace island life. A holiday home, perhaps for her family if her mother ever agreed to return to Agístri, or she could rent it out. But that may be too much work for Mrs Rálli. It all suddenly seemed like a half-baked plan, not fully realised and slightly mad. What was the point of this renovation expedition? What was she doing with her life? She had no answers for either. Grief seemed to be clouding her judgement, and she felt stuck in the fog. She had an urge to speak to Jamie.

'Hey,' she said as their call connected. 'I have a question.

You know you always used to tell me I work too hard, giving my all to the magazine, but did you ever feel like I pushed you away? I know my family are a lot . . .'

He laughed in surprise at the other end of the phone. 'Hey, yourself. That's a random one. Could you give me some context?'

Kat took a deep breath. 'I've got a lot of time to think, which isn't always a good thing, but I wanted to know if it was me who caused the end of us.' She suddenly felt silly embarking upon such a discussion. 'Ignore me, I'm just second-guessing myself.'

'Wow. You do have time on your hands. I mean . . . maybe . . . Hang on let me step outside. Just at a wine-tasting thing. Do we really want to rake over old ground?'

'Probably not, but . . . I'm not sure what I'm doing here, or if I'm making the right choices.' She nibbled at the skin beside her thumbnail. 'Did we waste time, Jamie? Or make a mistake . . .'

'What do you mean? Have you changed your mind about our divorce?'

Kat hadn't expected her initial question to invite this one.

'Oh . . . no. Sorry. I don't think so.' Why was she trying to let him down gently when they'd already let each other down in the kindest way possible? She ought not to give him hope – if he harboured any, which, until now, she had been certain he didn't. She accidentally nudged her glass of water, which promptly smashed to the floor. 'Oh, for goodness' sake!'

'You don't sound very sure, and you don't sound very OK,' he said.

'I am OK, I promise. Just having a small crisis. I found

out Nik came here and knew my uncle but he never told me. I don't know how to broach it with my parents, so I'm saying nothing. Not really a solid plan.'

'I can't believe Nik didn't say anything about your uncle.' Jamie sounded as surprised as Kat was. 'What else did you find out?'

Kat explained the little she knew as she cradled the phone to her ear and swept up the shards from the tiled floor with a dustpan and brush.

'We will never understand why Nik didn't want you to know he came to Agístri, Kat, but it's pointless to dwell. Everyone has their secrets, don't they?'

'I don't,' she said indignantly. 'Maybe I'm too much of an open book.'

'Goodness, listen to you, all feisty in Greece!' Jamie said laughing. 'As for open book . . . I'm not so sure.'

'What's that supposed to mean?' Kat bristled slightly.

'Only that I didn't always know what you were thinking. You confided in Nik and sometimes I felt left out. That's the problem with twins, someone always gets stuck in the middle and they're the ones who lose out. And your whole sunshine and moonlight thing . . . you said good morning to him before me.'

'Excuse me?' she snapped. 'You adored Nik.'

'Kat, calm down. That's not what I'm saying.'

'Well, it certainly sounds like it. I've got to go, I'm about to burn a moussaka.'

She hung up abruptly, but his words left behind an uncomfortable sting. Their amicable break-up didn't feel much like it anymore.

Her phone pinged with replies to her earlier message to the group.

Hoping for a hot builder to replace the grumpy neighbour for you! Lizzie x

Love you, Kat, and miss you. Just relax and write from your heart. Amelia x

Worried about K – should one of us go to Greece? J

Kat recoiled. Did Jamie mean to send that to the group chat she'd created? It was probably meant for the other secret one where they discussed her life behind her back. For the first time in as long as she could remember, she felt angry with Jamie – no, it was more than that. It was resentment. He couldn't choregraph a rescue for her and she wouldn't let him. She was the only person who could rescue herself.

As she took the moussaka from the oven, her mind drifted back to the note in her uncle's book signed '*A*'. Was it from Andreas? And what had Pétros done for him? There was someone who could enlighten her, but she had no idea how receptive they'd be to sharing their story. *Only one way to find out,* she thought. Tomorrow, she'd pop next door and ask him. It was time to get some concrete answers to her growing list of questions.

Chapter 16

Kat was intrigued by the slip of expensive-looking stationery she found on the doormat early the next morning:

Come to my home to celebrate the terrible weather! 7 p.m. bring nothing, just yourself!
Andreas x

She ran her finger over the embossed initials – AE – in the top corner. It was a more friendly offering than of late, but Kat hadn't brought anything to wear to a sophisticated soiree in a glass house. There was no dress code, nor indication of what kind of event it would be. She compared the handwriting to the note she'd found in the novel last night; it was identical. One mystery solved, but it prompted more queries. Though she could ask a few leading questions later on now she'd been presented with an opportunity to see her neighbour. She only hoped she liked what she heard.

Her tense exchange with Jamie on the phone last night still stung, and the fact he continued to drive a discussion about her welfare amongst their friends was more than irritating. But she needed to get on with another island day, plus Kostas was due, and she should ensure they had snacks and drinks to sustain them. This was her chance to demonstrate her version of Greek hospitality.

It was too early for Mrs Rálli to appear, so Kat decided to walk up the hill behind the house where she'd been told by the housekeeper there was a convenience store and bakery. She was setting a precedent for the builders if they showed, but she wanted them to love refurbishing the house; it was her chance to change her life and it felt significant. The colour strips she'd splashed on the walls had looked different in the morning light, but her preferred shade for the main bedroom, endorsed by Andreas, had developed into a more complex pistachio hue than she could ever have imagined. It was ideal. She walked past a dormant taverna with blue tables and chairs and a striking pink bougainvillea overhead, then rounding a bend saw a church made of the same stone as her house. Inspired by her surroundings, she began to write in her mind.

The difficulty with grief is you never know which version will show up. Rather like an undercoat of the perfect colour, after the overnight test, nothing is the same in the cold light of day – everything is different. Again.

Maybe Amelia wasn't wide of the mark with her suggestion to write about loss in tandem with renovation. It was a rebuild in every way. Her assignment was gradually making sense.

Dark charcoal clouds hung threateningly above the horizon like they were gathering to decide on their next move. The claggy air prophesied the impending storm, which, when it broke, would be welcome to clear the atmosphere. The sea was strangely glassy now the wind had dropped away, but the grey shapes reflected in the water seemed as foreboding as the sky.

As Kat reached the bakery, several people were milling about taking coffee outside or standing and conversing, munching on the contents of paper bags, allowing the morning to unfurl. The scents of pastry and freshly baked bread connected with her appetite and she had a sudden hankering for *tirópita* – cheese pie. She received several nods and good mornings as she entered the furnace-like temperature of the shop. It was hard to breathe. The ovens were blazing, churning out baked goods as she looked through the display cabinets at the vast array of delicacies, cookies, glazed cakes and pastries.

She selected several savoury slices and a few tubs of cinnamon biscuits to sustain the builders should they arrive. If not, she could always take the leftovers to Andreas' later on. Though scraps from a bakery may not be his vibe. Kat wasn't sure what his vibe was at all, and his moods were subject to as much change as the sea-state.

Returning to the house, she found Mrs Rálli at the kitchen table.

'The power is gone,' she began the moment Kat entered, omitting a greeting. 'There are no lights, no hot water, we are without air conditioning. We are waiting for a delivery of gas for the cooker. What on earth will we do?'

Though it may seem like a disaster to Mrs Rálli who was frantically mopping her brow, Kat didn't mind. She'd half expected this to happen and although being without air conditioning would be a challenge given the humidity, Kat had plenty of food that would keep. She encouraged Mrs Rálli to return home, arming her with a salty cheese slice sprinkled with sesame seeds, insisting there was nothing to be done.

By lunchtime, Kat had given the master bedroom its first coat and even in the muted light, the pale shade of green opened up the space with a tranquil energy. It seemed to have doubled in size now the stone was exposed and painted white, and the pine-planked ceiling covered in the same shade. A knock on the front door drew her downstairs, grateful for the interruption as she'd worked up a thirst from her labours. She saw Kostas' large outline through the frosted glass panel and her heart leapt. Work could finally begin and now she was acclimatised, Kat could focus on writing.

'*Yiássas*, Katerína. We are here! There is no power on the island, but there is still much we can do. These are my sons – Àngelos and Chrístos. They work with me whether they wish to or not.' His brown eyes twinkled as he towered over her and his handsome sons mumbled hello.

'Welcome! I can't offer coffee as we're running low on gas, but please help yourself to drinks while they're still cold and there are snacks on the side in the kitchen.'

Kostas' troupe trudged in. The two young men glistened with sweat she assumed from the weight of their tool bags slung over their shoulders coupled with the mugginess. After they'd hungrily tucked into the food, she showed them upstairs to the master bedroom and talked them through her plans for the floorboards. Kostas stood and nodded at her ideas as his offspring sprang into action, moving furniture and dismantling the bed. They also planned to pull apart the upstairs bathroom and a skip was due any moment.

With all the mess and dust, Mrs Rálli was sure to have a fit. Kat knew the banging and crashing would be distracting, so she planned to take her laptop to the beach and use what remaining battery there was to write. If it ran out of charge, she could continue reading Pétros' book, *Versions of Love*, though it was in Greek, which made it extra hard going. It was also a bit too literary and highbrow, though that had clearly served him well over many years judging by the value of his estate.

There were very few people frequenting the stretch of road in front of her house save for the odd moped whizzing along or handfuls of tourists on hired bikes taking in the sights. Further down, she saw a row of sunbeds and, although there was no sun, she jumped down from the pavement onto the sand, took a seat and unpacked her laptop. The little bar was shut, and the peace was welcome on the deserted beach. She momentarily stared at the horizon, assessing the threat of rain, and her eyes traced the crystal-clear waters, which were inviting despite the day's dullness. If she felt inclined, she had her bathing suit on beneath her sundress. Inspiration began to bubble, and her fingers flew across the keyboard. It was more of a mind-dump than a structured, planned piece of writing, but she allowed her feelings to connect with her hands and the words flowed.

> *At the start of any design project, regardless of scale, it's hard to keep the end vision in mind when the minutiae of the moment feels all-consuming. That's how I felt when I first came to Greece, to tackle the renovation of my late uncle's house. I was also reeling from the death of my twin brother. You may ask, what's the connection between death and decorating? There isn't one unless you're incredibly clumsy! But an aesthetic revamp, whether a room or an entire home, is like giving the*

space another life, almost a rebirth. Stripping away what was there before, what was lost, broken or decayed then breathing fresh energy into it. Taking something that seemed useless and orchestrating a renewed purpose is immensely satisfying.

If you've ever pulled something apart, be it a piece of furniture, your own thoughts, or a relationship, you traverse a similar process: devastation, despair, a glimmer of hope and then, eventually, bright light emerging from the darkness. The heaviness that troubled you, the regret at having set upon a course of destruction slowly shifts. There is no shame in admitting failure, but there is strength to be found in taking that hopelessness and allowing it to fuel change. Whether a brand-new colour palette, a daring fabric, or leaning into your grief and hoping that one day, just as a discarded dressing table can be stripped back, then repainted, somehow your heart will also be repaired; be valued by someone who may find it, allowing you to remember what it's like to feel joy again.

Kat's eyes swam as she reread what she'd written. It was a relief to set some of her thoughts free. After adding the lines she'd thought up as she walked to the bakery that morning, she connected her computer to her phone and attached the copy in an email for Amelia along with some photographs of the sea she'd taken on Aegina:

Hi Amelia,
    Not sure if this is anything like what you had in mind but am playing with the idea and you were right – there

is a lot to be said for writing renovation while exploring loss. My 'Grief in Greece' or 'Death and Decorating' is in motion! (Do NOT use either for the masthead!) Anyway, let me know what you think. Will keep sending pics in the group chat if you need them. I have no Wi-Fi as there's a power cut, so message me. K x

She pulled out a bottle of water from her bag after closing her laptop and took a thirsty gulp. Reflecting on the words she'd written, her throat narrowed as she imagined her brother beside her on the beach, or watching him dive beneath the surface of the sea. He'd already been here, likely had swum in this water. Why didn't he tell her? She pushed her things into her bag, and as her fingers brushed a pebble nestled at the bottom, her nerves began to jangle. It was pink and shiny, like the one she'd found in the bedroom and on her hike with the priest. Identical to the one in the back kitchen of her parents' restaurant on her birthday; a time before she'd entertained the idea of travelling to Greece, let alone learnt of her inheritance. She must have picked one of them up and put it in there. Their appearance seemed to coincide with her thinking of Nik or doubting herself, but then isn't that what bereaved people do – cling on to what brings them comfort – things and knickknacks, imagined or real? Her phone trilled, pulling her from imminent malaise. It was Lizzie.

'Hey – you've saved me!'

'What? Are you OK?' Lizzie sounded concerned.

'I'm joking. I'm just thinking about Nik, about to fling myself in the water . . .'

Lizzie laughed. 'Well, you won't be alone for long, my friend.'

Kat frowned. 'How's that?' she said looking around her, but there was nobody in sight.

'Because, I've just fucking been made redundant, can you even believe it? You'd think years of compromising my morals as a professional gossip would count for something, but they'd rather employ some inexperienced bloody teenager to save money. I'm too expensive apparently. All those years of loyalty mean nothing.'

'Oh, Lizzie, that's terrible. You've worked so hard for that paper.' Kat felt awful for her friend who'd lived for showbiz gossip so much, she'd made it her career. And she was brilliant at it. Everyone loved Lizzie, and Kat couldn't imagine her being let go from her job, nor how she'd respond to dismissal: she was incredibly headstrong and determined. From the moment they'd met at university on the same journalism course, Kat was in awe of Lizzie's cut-throat approach to every module of their degree. She was always destined for the ruthless world of tabloids. Whereas Kat's more lyrical approach leant towards feature writing or gentler, less controversial subject matter. And, she hoped, one day, novels.

'So, to lick my wounds, I'm inviting myself to Greece. For a couple of weeks, maybe longer. I have nothing to do apart from count my severance money and cry into a bottle of gin and plot the downfall of my former employer. So, while my useless hands have no purpose, I beg of you, arm me with a tin of paint and put me to work before I go bloody mad.'

Kat closed her eyes in silent thanks to the heavens: her friend was just the tonic she needed, and she would have help with the house. A friendly face might even make her feel more at home.

'Lizzie, that would be amazing! But you need to know,

it's a conservative place so you can't swear so much in public. And there's no power, the builders have started demolishing one of the bathrooms though there's another one downstairs, and there's only the box bedroom free and it's filled with some of my dead uncle's papers.'

'God, sounds wonderful!' Lizzie said, sarcasm travelling the distance. 'Honestly, I don't give a shit – sorry! Anyway, Jamie's worried about you, so I'm being efficient – helping you and reassuring the gang that you aren't really going to drown yourself in the sea.'

Kat ignored the stab of irritation at Jamie's continued clandestine discussions about her. She still hadn't spoken to him since their call.

'I'll message you with my dates when I've finished making voodoo dolls of my ex-boss who of course kept his job with his inflated salary. Wanker! If I get myself together it might even be at the weekend. Yay!' Lizzie enthused.

'Just tell me when and I'll meet you off the ferry on the next island, Aegina. I need to go there again anyway and you can see two islands in one day! Can't wait!'

As they hung up, Kat's heart soared at the thought of having a friend to share all of this with. Maybe Lizzie could put her journalist's instinct to good work and do some sleuthing into Pétros and Andreas' pasts. It was about time Kat unearthed all her family secrets, which seemed to be increasing in number with each day she spent on Agístri.

Chapter 17

Kat woke with a start; she'd fallen asleep on the sunbed and was roused by a clap of thunder. She felt sticky, as if her skin had been coated in a syrupy glaze like the pastries adorning the bakery counters. The sky was a collision of murky purples and greys, yet it was still beautiful. Even a dull overcast sky in Greece was preferable to the equivalent in London.

Stripping off her olive-green dress, she looked down at her swimsuit-clad body. She knew she'd lost weight since Nik died as her mother often reminded her. Grieving was a rapid diet. She burned thousands of calories with the effort of getting through another day without her twin. But another week of Mrs Rálli's cooking would help regain any lost pounds.

She dived beneath the sea's flat surface, and the cool water was a welcome respite. Lengths of seagrass tickled her limbs as she swam beyond the shallows and out of her depth. Swimming had been part of her physiotherapy routine after the plaster casts were removed from her arm and leg following the car crash and she felt her muscles respond.

Her bones had healed and, aside from the odd ache, it was as if the accident had never happened. If only there was a similar rehabilitation for her heart. Floating on her back, Kat watched the undulating clouds, which resembled cake batter churning in a mixer on a slow-motion setting.

An almighty splash came from beside her as something surfaced, and she whipped her head up, yelping in fright as she did so. She accidentally gulped a mouthful of the sea, which made her cough as she took in the source of the sound. It was unmistakably a male figure given the breadth of his wetsuit-clad shoulders and he was wearing a snorkel and mask, but more worryingly he was brandishing a spear gun aloft. Kat continued to splutter, alarmed that the person was armed, and her eyes stung painfully from the saltwater. The masked merman pulled their goggles back, revealing their identity. Andreas.

'I am so sorry to scare you. I thought you heard me call your name.'

Kat finally ceased choking and was able to respond, though her chest still pounded with fright. At least, that's what she put it down to.

'Sorry, I didn't hear you.' She wasn't clear why she was apologising, but couldn't help but notice how droplets of water clung to his dark lashes like miniature icicles.

'Did you think I was a shark, Katerína?'

'Ha!' she declared out of relief more than anything. 'Is that what you've been hunting? How very alpha.' She nodded at the large metal spear that looked more like an assault weapon. She'd never trust herself to operate one; her own toes and fingers and those of anyone nearby would be at risk of amputation.

'No, I've caught *lavrakiá* – seabass – and octopus for this evening,' Andreas replied, shifting a strap across his body to proudly show her the bag, which was moving like an alien trying to escape an embryonic sac.

Kat began to swim to a place where she could touch the sand with her feet.

'I fear your hunting and gathering may be in vain unless you have a generator.' Her foot brushed a rock and she flinched. Andreas made her jumpy with or without having surfaced like a sea monster beside her.

'The electric's out at mine too. I saw you swimming and wanted to tell you the power was down in case you didn't know, as I don't have your number. Tonight is still on.'

Kat felt self-conscious and chilly as the breeze increased, making waves that splashed at her face. Was he asking for her number? Maybe he wasn't in a relationship with Pétros in the way she'd first thought. His eyes were piercing even in the dull light and became the most colourful thing she'd seen on the island that day aside from the blue dome of the church.

'Then how do you propose to make use of your catch? I mean, you can't let it go to waste or you may as well set them free, assuming they've not already suffocated.'

'I was going to serve them for us tonight.'

She couldn't work him out. Since they'd met, he had been rude, flirtatious, apologetic – without having said the word sorry – and incredibly grumpy. He was a puzzle.

'I'm not a huge fan of sushi . . . I have a gas stove if it helps unless you have a barbecue.'

They both waded towards the shore and Kat did her best to focus on the beach. Out of the corner of her eye, she noticed him turn his head to her and she couldn't resist meeting his gaze. His wet dark hair was swept back from his face, exposing his pronounced cheekbones and a jawline that looked like it had been made from marble. He was so attractive, it was captivating; he was almost too beautiful. No wonder her uncle had been inspired by him.

'Come at seven as planned and let me surprise you. There will be no sushi, I promise.'

'OK . . .' She was unsure about dinner alone with him, but she needed to unpick Pétros' past. Plus, the alternative was spending the evening solo, nibbling at olives by candlelight with a paintbrush in hand. 'I should go; the builders have started at the house.'

'Could I come with you? I'd love to see your plans.'

Again, she was thrown off guard by him. 'Of course, but I fear it may be carnage in there. It's day one and all about demolition. The plans are all in my head, not written down anywhere.'

'Another time then.'

Although Kat smiled, she was disappointed not to share her vision with him yet and couldn't pinpoint why she felt so crestfallen.

When they reached the shore, she quickly threw on her sundress, feeling vulnerable beside him while her mind flashed back to the paragraph she'd read in Pétros' book: *'. . . bare muscle and sinew, curves and sharp edges. It would be impossible to reduce this form to lines and angles, such was his beauty.'*

She glanced fleetingly at Andreas as he rolled down his wetsuit to his waist. Her uncle's words came to life, personified on the sand next to her – muscle, sinew, brown smooth skin. Kat tore her gaze away. He waited for her to finish dressing, and she felt the heat of his stare as she gathered her things, stuffing the book into her bag, hoping he hadn't seen. She felt like a voyeur having delved into precious private text, yet the novel had been published and consumed by thousands, so why did she feel like she was trespassing on something she shouldn't be privy to?

'I'll walk you to the house,' he said. She stepped forward and stubbed her toe on a corner of the sunbed, but gritted her teeth to keep from yelling out. His expression, when she managed to meet his eyes, was one of amusement. They walked in silence up the stone steps from the beach to the road. The short journey seemed to take forever. A heavy atmosphere hung between them, in addition to the weight of the stormy air that still hadn't been released. The tension all around was unbearable and Kat felt like she was on the brink of bursting. She had to know about him and her uncle but didn't know how to broach it without prying about his sexuality, so remained silent instead.

At the house, the skip that Kostas ordered was now in situ, filled with shards of an avocado-coloured cistern, a broken-up pedestal sink, fractured tiles, chunks of carpet and lumps of rotten wood. Kat reminded herself that things had to get worse before they got better – that sentiment applied to both life and renovating. She ought to write that.

Kostas strode down the steps from the front lawn and ignored Kat, heading straight for Andreas and heartily shook his hand as he said in English, 'Andreas, you are back! I heard you were. You have been gone for so long, almost a whole year, yes? But we keep up with your news. Welcome home again. We are all so proud.'

Kat was taken aback. What had Andreas been up to that summoned such pride from Kostas? Perhaps he was a medical genius and had cured the incurable or led a humanitarian quest to liberate someone from political persecution.

Maybe she'd judged him solely on his appearance and made assumptions by virtue of his good shoes. She watched him become bashful upon receipt of Kostas' compliments before he responded in Greek, 'It's been a while, I know. How is Nicolétta and . . . your sons?'

They fell into conversation. She hadn't heard Andreas speak Greek before and it was excruciatingly alluring. But he looked uncomfortable enquiring after Kostas' family, though that may have been the switch in language.

'Forgive me, Katerína,' said Kostas suddenly noticing her. 'We have made a good start. The boys are gone for the day, but the floorboards need treating. And there were boxes of papers beneath the bed when we take it apart. I would not dream of prying, so I have left them for you in the small bedroom. We will see you tomorrow, very early.' He almost did a small bow to her and then turned to Andreas. 'Chrístos and Àngelos would like to see you before you leave Agístri again. Never forget where you are from, Andreas.'

After Kostas had jumped onto his motorbike and roared off along the road, Kat turned to Andreas who was looking up at her house.

'I think we just met your number-one fan,' she joked, but he didn't reply and she regretted her jest. The silence grew, interrupted only by thunder rolls.

'Hadn't you better go and murder your fish?' He directed his intense gaze at Kat who felt like it had pierced her skin. She couldn't read what he was thinking. His hair was still damp, and a kiss curl had formed on his forehead. It was shaped like a perfect question mark – ironic, given that she had so many questions about him. Her fingers itched to reach out and touch it, but instead she made a fist and kept her hand by her side.

'Seven o'clock, let us meet on the road between my house and yours . . .' He looked to the upper floor again before returning his attention to her. 'And I promise – if you can trust me and I hope that you can – there will be no raw seafood for dinner.'

As Kat watched him walk away, transfixed by his shoulder blades, she was intrigued and – against her better judgement – excited. How would the food be cooked? Why was he flirting with her when he had been in some kind of relationship with her uncle? And why did he ask her to trust him? Anyone who made that request usually had something to hide; it was a preface to untruths. She knew all about that from her family. Her mother and now her brother had both deceived her and she couldn't help the disappointment she felt. No, it was more than that, it was betrayal. Despite her cynicism, words from her uncle's novel drifted through her mind

'He'd made it his work to fool admirers . . . a professional pretender.'

Kat was now more resolute than ever to unearth who Andreas really was.

Artemis & Apollo

Apollo was a fervent lover, but his passion was matched by his capacity for destruction, whether wreaked upon himself or others. His humours ran high. In contrast, Artemis felt love with the greatest purity, remaining a maiden without children. But she could equally fall victim to trickery, such was the belief she had in true affection. On occasion Artemis was disappointed by those closest to her and left with an empty heart longing for the love she dearly desired.

Chapter 18

Hosing herself down with freezing water made Kat breathless despite the air being thicker than ever. The downstairs shower was as cramped and dated as the rest of the house.

The box of tattered papers that Kostas unearthed beneath the bed had revealed little about Pétros – at least those she'd read before getting ready for her evening. Letters from various charities or institutions based all over the world profusely thanked her uncle for his support. He was a benefactor for many arts organisations and had funded bursaries for creatives in both Greece and abroad. What a wonderful thing to have done, Kat had thought. Pétros was more than generous when he was alive and remained so in death. She was a beneficiary of his endless philanthropy, and only wished she could have shown him her gratitude in person, or knew where his resting place was to pay her respects. It would make it more palatable to be the recipient of his money and his home.

There were also handwritten notes of thanks to Pétros from various individuals. One was signed from 'A' – like the note that fell from the novel and seeing the handwriting matched, she'd started to read the first line of several pages:

> *My love for you knows no bounds, Pétros, and will always exist wherever I am in the world, no matter how great the sea that parts us . . .*

She'd immediately refolded the papers, having felt embarrassed to be holding it let alone consider reading on. On the reverse of the envelope was the sender: *Andreas Elìopoulos*. It must be from her neighbour. Kat tried to recall the two surnames he'd used at the airport, and she was certain that was one of them, but she'd been somewhat distracted by him at the time to pay attention. She'd decided to take it with her that evening and hand it over. He might like to have the keepsake, and the gesture could prompt more information. She didn't dare read it. At times, she already felt like she was walking over her uncle's bones simply by being in the house.

Out of the shower, she towelled off and combed mascara through her lashes. She allowed her hair to air dry in the humid evening air and it formed into ringlets and fluffy waves. As she walked upstairs, the house was dim and it felt like in each corner lurked a secret and the shadow of a stranger.

The main bedroom and family bathroom were the bombsites she'd predicted. Dust coated every surface like nobody had set foot in the home for decades.

It will all come good, Kat told herself.

After choosing a navy cotton maxi dress from the spare-room wardrobe, she slipped on simple tan leather sandals. She accessorised with chunky gold bangles, the new necklace she'd bought on Aegina and hooped earrings, then surveyed her reflection. Being an identical twin in different genders was a fascinating puzzle: Kat and Nik had truly been carbon copies of one another in male and female form. When they were younger, each had found it annoying when strangers or family members declared how much they looked alike. They veered between casting aspersions on the intelligence of the remarker or resenting the fact that they resembled their sibling, especially during the slightly awkward teenage years.

Now, Kat found enormous comfort in the fact that Nik would always be with her as she stared back at herself in the mirror with his reflection living on inside her own eyes. It also meant there was no escape from what was missing, no respite from her grief. She needed to learn to make peace, which would require her remembering how it had all ended after the accident. But she couldn't; she wasn't strong enough. Not yet.

* * *

Before she left for her dinner assignation, she refilled the saucer with fish for Patch the cat, who she hoped was enjoying her hospitality. From the empty dish, she was certain he was. The storm clouds occasionally illuminated with lightning, and Kat wondered whether it would ever get properly bright again, in terms of weather and in her heart. She fired off a message to the friend group chat:

> *Hot date – it's very hot tonight and I have dinner with my neighbour – unclear whether the two are linked. He is much less grumpy than before. More soon! K x*

She also sent a message to her parents, omitting her evening's plans. Best to stick to safer subjects that wouldn't prompt a thousand queries: her wellbeing and the weather.

Power out on the island, storm brewing but am absolutely fine. Lizzie coming to stay soon and am saving my phone battery! All fine and have made friends with a neighbour. Love you, Kat x

Her phone battery had seventy per cent left. She scanned the sent message to her parents, which had mentioned she was 'fine' twice. People who insisted they were fine tended not to be fine at all. She only hoped her parents hadn't picked up on it. They would certainly try to call, but she couldn't risk draining her power so turned it off. She didn't know when she could next recharge.

And as to whether she had made friends with him next door, she remained unsure. She was certain there was something between them but could have read it wrong, especially given what she'd seen at the start of his letter to her uncle and the way Pétros had written about him. But from the moment they'd met at the airport there was an unmistakable crackle, despite his rudeness. Although, she'd been rude the next time they met, and on it went. Her neighbour was increasingly perplexing, but until she knew about his relationship with Pétros, she would try to temper any flirtation. She patted her shoulder bag, which contained the letter from 'A' then stepped onto the road.

Andreas was waiting for her on the tarmac dressed in his favourite fabric. His grey trousers almost appeared lilac in the light and his navy shirt showed off his skin tone as much as her dress in the same shade complemented hers.

'I swear you must own a linen factory. It's all I see you wear!' she exclaimed. '*Kalispéra!*'

He stepped closer, laughing at her jest. '*Kalispéra*, Katerína.' He kissed her on each cheek, and she caught his freshly showered scent tinged with citrus. 'This is not true. I believe you saw me in a very tight wetsuit earlier.' He pulled away from their intimate greeting, his eyes sparkling. He was playing with her, and she felt her cheeks heat but held his gaze defiantly.

'Sorry to disappoint you but I didn't notice,' she fibbed.

He chuckled and put a hand on her shoulder, which sent a shiver down her arm.

'You don't care what you say, do you? I like your honesty; it's fearless.'

She continued to look up at him, wishing she could work out if she'd fabricated their attraction and he was just incredibly friendly instead.

'I guess not.' She tried to step out of herself to see the Kat he saw. She didn't think herself fearless. 'I'm intrigued. Where is this mysterious dinner you promised . . . I see no oven and no fish. There is still no power . . .'

'Patience, Katerína. All good things . . .' He placed his hand in the small of her back and guided her along the seafront and down the steps to the beach. Kat stopped in her tracks, astonished by what she saw. A fire glowed on the sand with a metal grill on top ready for cooking. It was surrounded by large rocks to contain the flames along with oversized cushions, beanbags and blankets creating a seating area. Votive tealights flickered in glass holders around the edges of the picnic rugs with crockery laid out for a fireside supper.

'Oh wow!' she exclaimed. 'How did you do all this?'

'My secret.' He smiled down at her and her eyes couldn't help but travel to his mouth and then up to his mesmerising stare.

'I didn't have you down as a caveman – hunting for your supper and now outdoor grilling. Your shoes misled me.' She glanced down at his suede loafers. They were a different shade to the ones he wore at the airport, but still pristine and untarnished.

'Come on.' He took her hand to lead her down to their encampment for the evening. 'I have no idea what my feet have to do with this. But given the circumstances, we must cook our own food that I wrestled from the sea with my bare hands.' He broke their connection and showed his palms to her, and she suddenly felt light-headed.

'Bare hands? I recall that you had a very large gun,' she said playfully.

'I thought you said you didn't notice what I was wearing,' he retorted.

Part of her wanted to cringe at his joke, but the other half – no, more than half – couldn't help but think about what he was referring to. There was something about him that encouraged her to feel bold, less apologetic, a more honest version of herself. She'd noticed the shift ever since she arrived on Agístri but the fact he'd remarked upon it made her wonder if that was who she really was: the person she'd hidden beneath years of acquiescence, doing the right thing by everyone except her. He raised an eyebrow. She was none the wiser as to his intentions. She couldn't pinpoint the energy between them: it was impossible to analyse. A silence stretched for an age as they stared at one other, as if time had paused. Finally, he spoke.

'This isn't me spinning you a line, believe me, but do you

ever get the feeling that you've met someone before? Like in another life yet you can't quite explain it?' He took her hand again then turned it over, his fingers gliding over the curve of the moon in her Artemis tattoo. The intimacy of his touch on her wrist was surprising but Kat knew precisely what he meant. Her stomach grumbled loudly with hunger, making a peculiar sound that almost drowned out the waves. They giggled, instantly breaking the tension. He moved to tend to the fire before looking back to her.

'What are you waiting for? I want to get to know my neighbour and I think I better feed you from the sounds you're making!'

Kat sunk inelegantly into a beanbag beside him and shuffled around trying to get comfortable. 'Not sure there's much to tell but ask away.'

'Well, what do you do? Where are you from?' he asked as he fished a bottle of rosé from a cool box.

'Wow, this is an inquisition. By the way, I don't drink. I can grab some water from my place.' She made to get up, but it was tricky to stand from a beanbag embedded in the sand.

'I think I have some. I do – sparkling or still?'

'Sparkling, please. Someone came prepared!'

He poured her drink into a crystal glass and Kat became afraid for its safety in her clumsy hands. Who took glassware to a beach?

'I confess, my housekeepers packed everything, so the stuff in here is as much a surprise to me as it is to you – apart from the fish.'

He had multiple staff, then. His house was massive. Clearly, he was fancier than his shoes first indicated; he oozed wealth and success. She added his profession to the long list of questions she had for him.

'And did your Michelin-starred chef clean and gut the seafood too?'

'Sorry to disappoint *you* now—' he was mimicking what she'd said to him earlier and she enjoyed the banter '—but no, I did it all on my own. And I got covered in fish guts – it went all over me. I did a bit of a Kat.'

Kat wished she could be outraged that he had coined a phrase to describe her tendency to be splattered with something, but she was flattered. Andreas had noticed her.

He held his hand above the grill, though Kat could have told him it was more than ready to start cooking. Years of watching her father preside over the coals in Zorba's Kitchen had taught her something. She watched the octopus, almost translucent in hue, constrict and shrivel in shape, darkening to a deep burgundy over the flames. Andreas' eyes gleamed in the firelight as he spoke. 'You don't mind if I have a glass of wine, do you?'

'Not at all. I've only been sober six months and I'm not one of those militant anti-drinkers.'

'Can I ask why? You didn't answer any of my earlier questions, so I'm asking another.'

Kat was hardly ready to admit what had happened to herself let alone a stranger, so she glossed over the real reason without being untruthful.

'Just going through a bit of a change. Not that I had a problem with it – let's call it a major life admin phase and it may or may not be forever.'

'A lot of people are trying sobriety. I think it's great,' he responded. 'I've been in America recently and most people freak out if you order a glass of wine at lunch.'

Kat watched him cook and wondered if it was the moment to mention Pétros. Now was as good a time as any, so she bravely began as gentle an interrogation as she could.

'Tell me about my uncle. I don't know much. I found this letter you sent him amongst his things.' Kat reached into her bag and handed him the envelope. He took it but placed it to the side. 'I didn't read it, well maybe a little bit, but I started the book he dedicated to you and assumed—' She broke off, embarrassed to have made assumptions about him but he saved her blushes.

'You assumed we were lovers,' he finished the sentence for her and shook his head but didn't seem surprised. Kat wondered whether others had thought the same thing. 'No, we weren't. I'm straight. Yes, he wrote about me. He used to say I inspired him, but we weren't romantically involved. I loved him. In a very different way.'

Kat's stomach flipped at the sudden clarity of their relationship.

'There was also a note from you in one of his novels thanking him for everything . . . How did he help you?'

Andreas looked beyond the smoking grill before returning his stare to her.

'I wouldn't be here today if it weren't for Pétros. Every single thing I've achieved is because he cared when nobody else did. Now it is too late.'

Their dance between sadness, flirtation and reflection ebbed and flowed like the tide that was making noisy work of the shore. Andreas seemed unwilling to elaborate, but Kat pressed on, keen to uncover more.

'Did you get to say goodbye to my uncle before you left? Kostas said earlier you'd been away for a year,' Kat asked, hoping he'd reveal something tangible.

Andreas shook his head sadly and flipped the fish on the

grill. The smoke from the barbecue rose into the night sky and wafted away, sending charred smells up towards the heavens.

'I wrote or emailed and when I didn't hear back, I assumed he was busy writing.' He seemed to delve into his memories then laughed. 'You never interrupted Pétros when he was in the grip of a novel. I knew he'd been sick and had cancer, but I thought he was in remission; I never thought he would die. Not yet. It's hard to imagine him being gone. Mrs Rálli called me with the news just before Christmas. I missed his memorial in Athens because of work, and nobody knows where he is buried. He is as elusive in death as he was in life.' There was a genuine sadness in the way he spoke about her uncle.

She put her glass carefully beside her, pushing it into the sand for safety.

'I wish I'd known him. My twin brother, Nik, did. He often visited Pétros, which I only found out about recently.'

Andreas handed Kat a plate of octopus, squeezing a generous amount of lemon juice over the top. He held her gaze for longer than was comfortable; he seemed to be scrutinising her face.

'I thought I recognised you. You're Nik's sister! I didn't connect the dots as he always called you Kitty Kat when he mentioned you.' Andreas slapped his forehead. 'How is he?'

Kat inhaled deeply, wondering why she was forced to repeat her most painful experiences over and over since reaching this island. And now to learn that her brother had also met Andreas. It was like being submerged by a wave, barely managing to surface before another came crashing down.

'He died last October. Car accident.' It was all she

could manage and didn't want to go any deeper than was necessary.

Andreas clasped her arm and held it firmly as she gripped on to her plate.

'What? I . . . Kat, I am so sorry. That's terrible. He was . . . God, I can't believe it.' His eyes glistened in sympathy; the flames from the fire danced light across his face. 'I'm just so, so sorry. I can't imagine how devastated you must be, losing your twin. You were incredibly close from what he said.'

Kat appreciated his compassion, but it seemed like Andreas was better acquainted with her family than she was, along with all their secrets.

'Please, I beg of you, no more talk of death. It's everywhere I turn at the moment. Tell me something interesting, like about your job or at least something hilarious,' Kat said, locating her appetite and digging in. She moaned in appreciation at the tender octopus, impressed he'd timed the cooking to perfection; it was so easy to ruin. Flakes of white seabass fell off the bone as he served her a piece, like a shining sliver of mother of pearl.

'Work is just work. Given what we've spoken about tonight it seems even less important and as for funny . . . I can tell you about this intriguing woman I've met, and she does make me laugh, but has no idea how I feel,' Andreas said, spooning beetroot salad onto her plate. She suddenly felt cold despite the warmth from the fire and the humidity in the air.

'Oh . . .' she said not wishing to hear about his love life.

He continued, 'She's pretty hard to unpick. You know those kinds of people that you want to be near, but they don't reveal much. She has this incredible courage, an infectious strength. And she's beautiful.'

Kat understood: she felt all of those things about him, but

now couldn't say anything. His face lit up when he spoke of this woman, so she obviously meant something to him.

'And what do you want to do about it?' Kat was trying to be nonchalant.

He shrugged and took a forkful of salad. 'Not sure there's anything I *can* do about it. My life is complicated and I think hers is too, so I probably won't act on it. I also may have got it wrong; I don't know if she feels the same. We only met recently.'

Pushing away her disappointment at offering romantic counsel to someone she was incredibly attracted to, she placed her plate onto the white rug, taking care not to spill beetroot on the cashmere.

'Well, if you want my advice, given what we've been talking about, all the tragedy and death, life seems far too short not to take a risk. And what's the worst that could happen – she says no or rejects you? I'm sure even your considerable ego would eventually recover.'

Andreas burst out laughing and Kat admired his profile as he threw his head backwards, wondering what the skin above his Adam's apple would taste like. She shook herself back to reality as he spoke.

'I'm inclined to agree especially when you say exactly what you think. It's refreshing, and so . . . so unapologetic,' he said putting his food down too.

'I think you'll find *you're* the unapologetic one. I'm still waiting for you to say sorry after all the airport rudeness,' she was teasing, though meant what she said.

He angled his head to look at her, then his eyes slowly travelled around her face. He'd been talking about someone he couldn't read but he was just as tricky to understand. It sounded like he and this woman were a good match.

'Then, even though I believe I've already apologised, I'll sacrifice what you consider my giant ego to say . . . Katerína, I am sorry for being ill-mannered and giving you such a poor first impression of me. How's that?'

Kat couldn't conceal her amusement. 'Not bad. It's a start at least.'

Andreas leant back on one arm and the beanbag moulded around his form. He reached for her hand and again marked out the mythical arrow on the inside of her wrist. 'Nik had a similar tattoo, didn't he?' She nodded at his words, unable to speak; his fingers felt so soft. 'What can I do to convince you that I'm truly sorry for being such an ass?'

Kiss me! Kat shouted to herself, but she found self-control despite the electric shocks his touch was sending throughout her body and changed tack.

'My *Mána* always says life is too short for regrets and since the wind is howling, maybe you should throw caution to it and grasp whatever it is you want. To hell with the consequences and complications. I'm trying to live like that from now on.'

Andreas suddenly leant over to her and his hand reached for her face, snaking around to the back of her neck.

'That's the problem – I'm not sure I can be like that.' He was so close that Kat could hardly breathe. Their faces were merely inches apart as his eyes continued to bore into hers. Up close they were bluer than she'd ever seen before, in nature, or in life. 'The woman I was speaking of earlier is you, Katerína.'

How had they suddenly arrived at this point?

He rubbed his thumb over her cheek and his eyes followed the movement as if he was absorbing every millimetre of her skin. Andreas opened his mouth to speak again, then thought better of it and pulled away to pick up the letter he'd written to Pétros. He began to read. She saw a tear escape, tracking down his cheek like an orange crystal, illuminated by the firelight. Eventually, he screwed up the paper into a ball and threw it onto the hot coals below the grill and it caught immediately. He moved to face her again, his beautiful eyes streaked with emotion, as part of his past was eaten by the flames. She felt as if he was asking a question of her soul: one she could neither interpret nor answer. As the wind circled in the silence surrounding them, Kat was confused. Finally, he broke the quiet.

'I know you didn't read the letter, because if you did, you wouldn't be here having dinner with me.'

Her mind became so cloudy, she couldn't form a thought nor string a sentence together, but tried nonetheless. 'You can't have done anything that bad. Pétros clearly loved you.'

His eyes flashed, and he shook his head. 'Katerína, you have no idea. And if I told you, it wouldn't only ruin tonight, not just me and you or whatever is beginning here, but it would wreck everything.'

Chapter 19

As Kat made coffee for herself and the builders on the gas hob the next morning, she reflected on her dinner with Andreas. They had left the beach picnic shortly after he refused to elaborate on his past. The ideal setting for a romantic sojourn had instead become a maelstrom of conflicting emotions. Whatever Andreas was hiding, she simply didn't have the appetite to press him to reveal it – he seemed unable to answer a question with simplicity. She also knew he felt something for her but wouldn't act upon it. It was drama she could do without, but reluctantly admitted she was as drawn to him as he claimed to be to her, and she couldn't stop thinking about him.

Mrs Rálli was tutting at the dust and noise from the builders as she chopped vegetables, so Kat absconded to the terrace with the stormy sea for a soundtrack, interspersed with the odd bang and crash from Kostas and his sons. She began to write, hoping her laptop battery would last until she'd finished.

Uncovering something unexpected rarely leaves you

feeling better than before you began. Like unearthing a secret, if something is meant to be kept from you, there's a good reason, and you're seldom better off for finding out. Removing a sheet of wallpaper more often than not makes way for cheap, rotten plywood or a pattern worse than the original you were trying to replace. It is unusual to find a gem, a beautifully preserved brick or glinting granite stone or to remove the lacquer from old furniture and find a flawless frame without the telltale signs of a woodworm in residence. The urge to replace and renew consumes us all, but can leave you unsure, with further questions and more frustratingly without any answers. Curiosity killed the cat, but I won't let curiosity kill this Kitty Kat.

The wind wafted the scent of citrus across her face as she sat back in her chair. The smell reminded her of Andreas. Though he wasn't the source, he crowded her thoughts, interrupting her writing flow.

She turned on her phone and sent the piece to Amelia. Then her eyes travelled up the contorted trunk of the ancient lemon tree, along its branches before finally resting upon the fruit. The lemons weren't quite yellow, though they must be ripe for their tangy flavours to be tinging the early morning air. She stood and reached up to pick one, holding it to her nostrils and inhaling deeply. Looking down, beside the now empty saucer she'd left for Patch, she saw there were three pink pebbles. Her blood cooled as she scooped them up. The ping of messages from her phone drew her back to the terrace table. The first she opened was from Amelia and it simply read: *We need to talk about your writing ASAP!*

Putting the little stones on the table, Kat called Amelia who answered immediately.

'Kat! What the hell did you send me?'

Taken aback, Kat tried to respond.

'I thought . . . I mean, I was having a bit of trouble . . .'

'I didn't like it. I *loved* it! This is *exactly* what I'd hoped you'd come up with. Tell me there's more. I'm putting the first one you did online this afternoon. You've given me your second, so we'll release them on the website every couple of days to keep momentum up. Then I'll do a compilation for print next month,' Amelia interrupted with great enthusiasm.

Kat's blood was practically frozen now. Online this afternoon? She hadn't edited any of what she'd written yet let alone done a proper proofread. She was simply trying on the idea to see if it had legs. 'But . . . I was just playing around. None of them are finished,' Kat protested.

'What you've sent is perfect. The whole team love it. Send over everything you've got so far.'

Kat felt the clutch of panic grip at her as she paced the patio. The renovation and Andreas were dominating her thoughts before she got to Nik having known Pétros. And she'd only been on the island a few days.

'I've got some other pieces, but I'm not ready for anything to go out yet. And Lizzie's coming here soon. I need another week. There's no hurry, Amelia, let me get ahead of this as much as I can.'

Kat heard Amelia sigh and crossed her fingers that the deadline could be extended. It was unfair to be thrown into work when this was supposed to be a break. But Kat knew she was onto something and had enjoyed the freedom of the writing process without the constraints of her day job.

'Fine. You have until early next week. But let me say that

you are a brilliant writer; I wish you'd believe you have something important to share. I have a feeling about this and I'm never wrong. Got to go, need to brief the team. Love you and speak soon. But next week, right?'

Flames of creative excitement began to spark deep within Kat as she walked around the garden. The flowers and foliage attracted her with their patterns and textures. As she traced variegated leaves with her fingers, she was certain that circumstances had conspired to afford her the space to explore her dream of writing. This could be a chance for her to finally branch out, emulate her uncle and become a novelist, or at least attempt to write something that felt more significant than only decorating advice. Like Pétros, she could leave something behind that was authentic and born of her personal experience. She simply needed to be given the time to find her own voice. This was too important to rush.

She sent a message to Lizzie asking for an update on her travel plans and hoped that she wasn't too bruised after the redundancy news. Poor Lizzie. She'd worked relentlessly for that newspaper and went above and beyond the call of duty, securing exclusives nobody else could get. They'll rue the day they let her go, thought Kat. Lizzie responded straight away.

Coming Saturday! Ferry gets to Aegina at 11.30. Can't wait! Have told Jamie and he approves!

Kat was thrilled beyond measure at the thought of seeing her oldest friend: it was the boost she needed to keep her energy going with both the house and her writing. She then sent Jamie a message to repeat the news that Lizzie was coming and tell him he could stop worrying and discussing her behind her back! He responded too.

> *I feel odd about our conversation on the phone the other evening. Let's not fall out – you're too special to me. Glad Lizzie's heading out there. J x*

She couldn't be cross at the motivation behind his meddling but at least he understood she was fine. More than fine; in fact, she was feeling inspired.

Finally, she dialled the number for Zorba's Kitchen.

'*Kaliméra*, Zorba's Kitchen, Mína speaking,' trilled her mother's voice with faux politeness.

'*Mána*, it's me. Just wanted to say hello.'

'Oh, thanks goodness, Katerína. IT'S KATERÍNA,' she bellowed, presumably to Giórgios. Kat moved the receiver away from her ear. When her mother raised her voice, it could make the hairs on Kat's neck stand to attention. 'So, Katerína, the power goes out on Agístri and then *poof*! Nothing from you. We think the house is being struck by lightning and *poof*! You burn in the flames. But how would I know? There is no way to reach you, and I try but there was no connection. *Poof* my daughter is gone, disappearing into the thin air!'

'*Mána*, calm down. I'd turned everything off to save battery after I sent you messages. No need to be so frantic.'

'But if there is an intruder in the night, what will you have to dial a number if everything is off? Is like cooking in a saucepan made from chocolates: useless!'

'*Mána*, please. Try not to worry,' Kat attempted to appease her.

'Try not to worry, she says. TRY NOT TO WORRY,

SHE SAYS!' she repeated louder again, Kat assumed for her father's benefit. 'Because you insist on not having children you will never experience the anxiety and worry you feel as a mother. I have not slept; I hardly eat a single thing since you leave and . . .'

There was a muffled scratching as her mother stopped speaking mid-sentence and then her father's low tones began.

'Pay no mind to your mother, Katerína. She is eating and sleeping very well. I am glad you are safe. Tell me, what is it like being back in the country that flows through your blood like the Haliácmon River?'

Kat didn't know which stretch of water he was referring to, but could safely assume it was somewhere in Greece.

'I love it, *Babá*. It does feel like coming home in a lot of ways. I just wish Nik was here with me.' She risked mentioning her brother to Giórgios as he seemed the calmer of her parents at the moment.

'I know, *angheloúthi mou*, but he is with you in your heart and spirit and how he loved Greece. He is all around. His soul is with the saints but he will always guide you on the island.'

Kat widened her eyes and was grateful it wasn't a video call, because Nik had certainly been there already, but she chose not to mention that.

'It's so peaceful, well not so much today as it's quite windy, but I'm writing as well as redesigning the house. I'd love you and *Mána* to see it. I wish she'd come here.'

He replied so softly that Kat could barely hear.

'Do not mention it to her, but I agree. I will work on your mother. It is a very nice idea for her to return to Agístri and make peace with the past. It is time we all find closure.

Otherwise, we will carry yet further sadness into our futures and become beasts of burden and I do not speak of donkeys.'

'OK, *Babá*.' Kat smiled, enjoying her father's wisdom. In fact she'd missed it. She'd love to have her parents with her and there were conversations she needed to have with them in person about Nik having known Pétros. They ended the call with a promise to speak soon and Kat returned to her laptop, but not before tripping over the loose tile on the terrace beside the tree. She tutted and pressed on it with her foot. It would all need replacing. Sitting back down, she began to type, her fingers flying over the keyboard as an idea took charge and she yielded to her thoughts, trying to block out her own imposter who wondered whether it was good enough.

'Katerína!' she heard and saw Father Serafím on the road. She jumped up to greet him.

'*Yiássas, Pater*,' she said formally. 'Are you on your rounds?'

'Of course. There is no rest for me, despite this weather. And please, call me *Papa Serafím*.' There was something comforting about his demeanour, a tranquil certainty in his purpose. It reminded Kat of her own father with bountiful wisdom on tap.

'I have a question for you, if you have time,' she began, and the priest gestured for her to continue. 'How do you cope with doubt? I'm writing and it's very personal. I've never done anything like this before. But it feels right like it's what I was meant to do.'

Father Serafím smiled. 'You answer yourself, Katerína. You have the strength within already and what greater way to express your feelings than in creativity. Saint Joseph, The Betrothed, was also a carpenter. Now, this is a practical craft, but it is also creative – an ancient art.' He paused and stroked his wiry beard as he looked up at the house. 'You renovate Pétros' home with the same love. If artistry is done correctly, it is seamless and meaningful. But when a joint doesn't quite fit, no matter how much you sand away, it will never be right. You need to learn when to begin all over again rather than persist. Sometimes you must decide to walk along a different road. And only you will know when that moment is.'

Kat looked out to the roughening sea, which foamed like the jaws of a rabid animal. The island waters seemed to change so rapidly when the weather was this unpredictable. She wondered whether she was on the right path. As she opened her mouth to ask for clarity, she noticed he had walked away, covering considerable ground while she was lost in thought. In the distance his cloak billowed around him, shifting in shape like a droplet of ink in water. He seemed to float along the seafront.

As Kat returned to her writing, she thought about the priest. He made such perfect, elegant sense that it almost brought tears to her eyes. She'd never met anyone like Father Serafím before. He was an exceptional man and his words not only inspired her, they also spurred her onwards to follow her heart.

Chapter 20

Time passed with astonishing speed as Kat worked fuelled by regular cups of coffee from Mrs Rálli since the stove's gas supply had been replenished. Her neck protested from being hunched over her laptop in the garden, but she sent all her pieces to Amelia. There was little battery left, so she'd have to stop. But at least she'd made headway and edited everything she'd written. She was happy with what she'd achieved. It was thrilling to be writing something so different for a change.

After checking on Kostas, who was making excellent progress with the bathroom upstairs, she went for a swim to restore her body. Now the wind had dropped, it was as if it had never been there, as the calm sea cradled her in its watery embrace. She floated almost in an embryonic state in the salty ocean, watching the rippling storm clouds above darken to a deep charcoal grey. Heavy raindrops intermittently began to plop on her face, so she quickly headed back to the house. Finally, the storm showed signs of breaking and the island could return to peace and sunshine. With power, she hoped.

Wrapping a pale pink sarong loosely around her, she reached the garden to find Andreas and Mrs Rálli at the terrace table, their heads bowed almost in conspiracy. In front of them was a huge bunch of flowers. As he spotted Kat, a huge smile broke across his face. She could feel the heat of his stare from the lawn and Kat suddenly felt shy.

'*Yiássou*, Katerína,' he began as he stood and moved to greet her using the informal version of hello. He kissed her on both cheeks, and she received his salutation on her salty skin. They remained on the grass as the rain increased, but neither seemed to notice.

'*Yiássou*, yourself,' she said, mirroring his hello, unable to decipher his mood. He was so contrary. Her eyes met Mrs Rálli's, who smugly shuffled away.

'I wanted to apologise for last night. You must think me rude. Again. Come, let's get out of the rain.'

Kat tightened the covering around her body and knotted it at her chest as she felt his warm hand on her waist through her damp swimming costume. As they watched from the shelter beneath the overhang, the rain became positively monsoon-like. She searched his face for a clue to enlighten her as to his intention, but there was none. He was both breathtaking and confounding.

'The great news is I already thought you were rude before last night, so it made no difference at all,' she teased, hoping it would read as mild flirtation meets nonchalance and not blatant offence. Kat realised she'd forgotten how to flirt, if indeed she'd ever learnt how. 'The flowers are beautiful, thank you. You didn't need to.' She squeezed the sea from her long brown hair, trying to casually mask her delight at the bouquet of white orchids and roses on the table.

'Things ended abruptly last night, I know, but I'd like to explain myself properly. If you want to see me again that is.' He suddenly looked unsure of himself and put his hands in his pockets, which was in such contrast to his usual confidence.

'I'm seeing you now, aren't I?' Kat was unsure if she had the appetite for this push-pull between them. It only increased the number of things she needed to sort out.

'*Mesimerianó*,' Mrs Rálli announced as she emerged from the kitchen patio doors holding two bowls that she plonked inelegantly on the table followed by cutlery.

Kat turned to Andreas. 'Apparently, it's time for lunch. Are you hungry?' she asked.

He looked embarrassed as he responded, 'Um . . . Mrs Rálli already invited me. I hope that's OK?'

Kat shot a glance at the old woman who moved away as fast as she could holding the flowers that dwarfed her slight frame. Why did everyone feel compelled to meddle in her affairs? Not that she and Andreas were having an affair as such – Kat didn't know what to call it. She plastered on the most hospitable expression she could.

'Of course, you're very welcome. And you're lucky Mrs Rálli is here otherwise it would be a paltry feast if I was in charge.'

As they took their seats beside one another, Mrs Rálli deposited a basket of crusty sourdough and wished them a good meal: '*Kalí órexi!* Thank goodness for the gas stove!' she declared, then disappeared again.

The heady scent of cinnamon from the *mosharáki kokinistó* travelled straight to Kat's appetite. The tomato beef stew was also spiced with cloves and she almost felt drunk from the aromas swirling around. Or perhaps that was just the effect Andreas had on her. It felt too intimate to be sitting in her bathing suit with only sheer material preserving her modesty, when Andreas was fully clothed and, as usual, incredibly well put together. They both moaned in approval at Mrs Rálli's efforts: it was utterly delicious. Kat tore a hunk of bread from the loaf, scattering shards of crust across the table, and offered a piece to Andreas.

'Probably a bit more rustic than you're accustomed to,' she said as he accepted and dunked it into the thick sauce as if to make a point. He raised his eyebrows.

'I think you have the wrong idea of me, Katerína. From the start I've given you the wrong sense of who I am.'

Kat followed suit, except a dollop of tomato fell in her lap. She rolled her eyes at herself and reached for a napkin from the bread basket, only to make an unsightly smear on her pale sarong.

'You don't give much away, Andreas. I have no idea who you are.'

He raised just one eyebrow this time as he looked at her.

'You don't need to pretend for my sake.'

'Seriously, I have no clue what you're on about. Which goes for most of our conversations. You say a bit then back away so fast I feel like I imagined it. Being guarded or private is fine, but what you need to know about me is I'm incredibly straightforward.' She discarded her serviette onto a side plate. 'If you want to really get to know me, then great. But you also need to give a little back. Friendship or any ship for that matter is a two-way street but with you, it's mostly one-way traffic and I feel like I'm heading towards a dead end having mistakenly passed a no-entry sign that I didn't see.'

Kat put her hands on either side of her bowl, pleased

with her analogy. It perfectly described whatever was going on between them.

'Are we in a car, Katerína? Now you're the one not making sense.' He was evidently amused, but she didn't want to be mocked.

'You know exactly what I mean, Andreas. I don't have the time nor inclination to mess around.'

He put a hand on hers.

'And I don't either. I've never met anyone like you. I'm surrounded by people who say yes to me all of the time; nobody challenges me. Until now. And I like it. I like you.' He traced the back of her hand with his fingers as he spoke. 'There is something here, so I don't understand why you're talking about road signs or trying to resist this.'

Kat's heart began to thump inside her chest; he could surely feel her pulse through her hand. She felt the same about him, but he was the one resisting. He almost kissed her last night, but then stopped. She didn't know what to say or how to break through this apparent stand-off, but he saved her the trouble.

'How about we start all over again?' he said, his eyes sparkling. 'Let me invite you to dinner, like a blind date. Come to my house this evening and we can ignore everything that's happened so far.'

'OK.' Kat hesitated. He'd used the word 'date'. She hadn't been on a date for years, not since before Jamie. She'd forgotten how it was all supposed to work. 'So, we pretend we're strangers and begin again?'

He nodded and returned to his almost finished lunch. 'Exactly. It'll be fun.'

'Fine. But I'm a terrible actress; I fear you'll be disappointed.'

Andreas sent her a strange look. He was at it again – approaching intimacy and then retreating as fast as he made any progress. Wiping his lips with his serviette, he folded it neatly then said, 'Half past seven come to my home and I want you to be yourself, Katerína. Never pretend with me, please.' As he slowly leant forward, the sound of the raindrops seemed to grow in volume, clattering against the wooden structure overhead, making the leaves on the lemon tree vibrate. His fingertips found her face and he pushed her wet hair away before tenderly brushing his lips to hers with the lightest kiss, gentle and softer than a feather pillow. It tasted like autumn as a cinnamon sweetness lingered between them.

Time stood still and Kat couldn't tell if seconds or minutes passed as they remained pressed together, until he moved back an inch and opened his eyes. The scent of the earthy herbs on the wind married with citrus hints wrapped around them. Kat didn't dare move in case he performed another of his hasty retreats. He leant in again, but with a certainty that took her breath away. Kat's hands reached for his neck as his found her waist and their pent-up passion finally unleashed. His hands moved up her ribcage, which made her squeak into his mouth, breaking the moment.

'What happened? Are you hurt?' he asked pulling away and frowning.

'No,' giggled Kat. 'Ticklish. Sorry.'

'Clumsy, ticklish and beautiful. And you have no idea just how beautiful you are.' He lifted her wrist to his mouth and whispered onto her skin. 'Will I see you later?' He looked vulnerable. He was such a contradiction of strength and gentleness when he revealed glimpses of the real him.

'Later,' was all Kat could manage before watching him

walk across the lawn. Patch the cat returned and made a beeline for her, headbutting her calves as he rubbed his head against her skin with enthusiasm.

'You're back!' she said, scratching Patch behind his ears, pleased to see him again. 'Did you see what just happened?' she asked, reliving the kiss in her mind. Patch mewed at her as if in answer then found his favourite spot beneath the tree.

Kat was startled by the clearing of a throat and saw Mrs Rálli who met her with a knowing smile, though said nothing, which Kat was grateful for. Then the housekeeper, began to sing quietly as she piled the empty bowls atop one another. Kat followed her to the kitchen with the rest of the tableware. She recognised Mrs Rálli's song from her parents' music collection: '*Apópse tha'thela . . .*' which translated as 'Tonight I'd like to.'

Kat couldn't help but agree; tonight she would like to indeed. Very, very much.

Chapter 21

The upstairs bathroom had been stripped to rivets and posts and the floor was gone. Kostas and his boys had achieved so much; Kat was overjoyed at their work rate. And they'd heard the power would be fixed tomorrow according to the jungle drums on the island.

The floorboards in the master had been re-laid and coated with oil to treat them. They looked exquisite against the light green walls. It was gently feminine and transformed the bedroom. Though every room looked huge without anything in it. Kat had plans for the dark bedframe when the builders reassembled it: she'd use white paint to match the exposed stone wall and fix four wooden posts at each corner from which she'd drape sheer fabric to create a canopy. That would look incredible. Kostas could find the wood and cut them to size when the electricity returned. She needed to look online for some curtains; pale muslin would do for every room. Easy and simple. If only the same could be said about her growing feelings for Andreas.

She folded her arms and leant against the sanded doorframe, admiring the beautiful new colour palette. Kat needed to move back in here to make the guest room ready for Lizzie when she arrived. It would be a push to get it done, but she knew she could if she focused. And therein lay the problem. The diversion that lived next door.

She had taken considerable care over her appearance ahead of dinner before the light faded from the house. A fluttering in her stomach tickled at her insides. She sent a message to Jamie asking how he'd felt about diving back into dating again after they'd separated. He hadn't wasted any time. 'HUSBAND' flashed on her phone alerting her to his reply.

Dating?! Are you seeing the same guy again – the neighbour?

Maybe! she responded, not wanting to get his hopes up, let alone her own.

It's nerve-racking but not so bad once you take the plunge. Good luck! Will phone later to check he's not a mad stalker – they're out there walking among us – I've done the legwork! Text me to let me know you're safe mid date, otherwise I'll summon the coastguard!

Kat laughed. It would be prudent to keep him updated so he didn't worry and send any more messages to his private chat group. She'd keep her phone on since she had plenty of battery and if the power returned tomorrow, she could refuel all her devices and go back to her new normal on Agístri.

Her reflection in the full-length bedroom mirror showed a twinkle of anticipation in her eyes. She was wearing a simple black dress that tied at the neck, exposing her shoulders and back. Unsure if it was nerves or the drop in temperature following the rain, she shivered as her fingers brushed her lips where Andreas' had been earlier. After adding a stack of bangles to her wrist followed by some drop earrings with a lapis stone, Kat was ready for whatever the night held.

* * *

Andreas opened the heavy front door that seemed to fold back on itself. Its hinge mechanism defied engineering, but Kat hardly noticed the design, something she would normally get excited about, because she was drowning in topaz pools as she looked up at him. Even though all the patio doors were folded back, it felt too casual to wander in, hence why she had formally rung the bell. He leant forward and they kissed, picking up where they left off after lunch.

'You look beautiful,' he almost whispered as his fingertips traced her naked spine, sending delicious ripples along each vertebra.

'Thank you,' she replied casually as his eyes flicked up and down her body. His crisp white shirt gleamed against his skin, which looked the colour of butterscotch in the evening light.

'Welcome to my home, though at least this time you're not covered in paint!' he said, taking her hand and leading her into the hallway that glowed with warmth from the countless candles placed on every available surface. Larger versions sat in hurricane lamps on the floor lined up at intervals along the skirting board. The effect was beautiful and incredibly romantic, which made her nerves increase.

Andreas' house was finished to monochrome perfection with splashes of colour from oversized artworks on the walls. The marble floor was seamlessly laid, the natural charcoal streaks resembling brushstrokes lined up perfectly on the white background.

'This is stunning, Andreas,' exclaimed Kat. She had never seen such a home in real life, only in luxury property magazines.

'Thanks. It's kind of my sanctuary away from the noise of the world. I designed it to feel peaceful, but I wonder whether it's a bit stark. What do you think?'

They stopped before the sunken lounge, which looked out onto the terrace and the sea beyond. The sun had almost set, and Andreas' house was aglow with candle flickers. The smell of wax hung heavily in the air like a church.

'If I were you, I'd find a way to add more colour. The artwork does it, but then you need to follow through to the furnishings. So, the oranges in that painting,' she pointed at an abstract piece on the far wall. 'I would pull out that colour and find a way to add it, maybe with a throw. And metallic bronzes somewhere on the table.'

Her eyes traced the carefully placed trinkets, but they were all in the same muted palette. What she wouldn't do to get hold of the lounge and show him how cosy it could feel even in such a cavernous building. It had been done by a professional interior designer, she had no doubt, but it was missing something. As her gaze eventually returned to him, she found him looking at her as if he was trying to work something out.

'Tell me, what is it that you do? You clearly have great taste in design . . . and men, of course.'

She appreciated his flirtation but chose not to respond. She needed to make him work for her affection. A little.

'I'm a writer for an interior design magazine, so it's my

area of expertise, I suppose. I admit, it's also a hobby that somehow became my job. It's been a passion of mine since I was a little girl. But writing is what I really love.'

Andreas seemed to approve.

'Then Pétros' house is in great hands, and you share a love of writing with him. He'd like that. I'll ask my designer to find something . . . unless you would like to do it? I'd pay – you're a professional, of course.'

The idea of mixing an element of her work with pleasure was tempting, but she didn't want to complicate life any further.

'Tell you what, when I next go to Aegina, I'll have a look for a throw and if you like it, your designer can take it from there. And no payment necessary, just feed me!' She returned his smile and felt her colour rise at the thought of finding the perfect something for his lounge.

'That sounds like a great deal to me,' he said then his face became unexpectedly serious and she wondered what he was about to say. It was too early in the evening for him to pull back. 'I'd like to show you something, but I'm worried it will upset you, Katerína.'

She couldn't imagine what it could be.

'Why would it upset me?'

'It's a photograph. A portrait of me from two summers ago. Nik took it.'

Her breath caught in her throat. Another reminder of the secret her brother had kept. But knowing it was near, she needed to see the picture.

'Please, I'd really like to look,' she said tentatively. She followed Andreas through the lounge, spotting several staff in black uniforms busying themselves in the open-plan kitchen. Lines of giant pillar candles lit the sparkling black granite countertop, making it seem as if the work surface was illuminated by fireflies. She itched to touch the industrial-style design and swoon over the luxury appliances, but there was something more pressing to see.

Andreas opened a glossy black door with a large chrome handle to reveal an office space, which was also littered with candles. A huge picture window would reveal the spectacular sea view if it were light outside, but only a slice of crescent moon stood out in the darkness. Andreas gestured to a wall, which had shadows like fingers across it, cast from the blazing wicks. Beneath the streaks of darkness, was the most beautiful black and white portrait. The muted, soft light almost heightened the image.

Andreas looked beautiful in extreme close-up, every angle and feature in the sharpest possible focus. The glimpse of his naked shoulders was tantalising; she could see his skin in exquisite detail. It was as if the passage she'd read in her uncle's book had come to life under Nik's lens. Andreas was looking directly at the camera and almost beyond it, like he had immediate access to her most private thoughts. It was unsettling, captivating and deeply erotic; she could hardly tear her eyes away. The power of his stare reached every part of her. She'd never experienced such a physical reaction to a piece of art before. There was something in his expression that conveyed so much, yet it was a glance that could have been lost in the second that followed. A lump lodged itself in her throat; it was an effort to speak.

'I've never seen Nik take a picture like this. So . . .' She couldn't find the right word.

'Moody?' said Andreas. She could hear the smile in his voice without turning to him.

'No, much more.' She stepped even closer. Her fingers

longed to touch the photograph, to trace the lines of his mouth, his cheekbones. She need only take a step backwards and she could practise on the subject in real life. Andreas' fingers caressed the nape of her neck, brushing her hair to the side as he lightly kissed her shoulders. The sensation grew as she gazed into his eyes on the wall, intense darts of desire rushed throughout her body. 'He captured something in you. It's stunning,' she managed breathlessly.

Kat finally turned away from her brother's picture, because Nik had caught on film the way Andreas had looked at her last night on the beach. And he was giving her the same look right now.

'I won't tell you what he said to get that expression out of me,' Andreas said, making Kat laugh, though it was fleeting.

'I wish he'd told me he'd been to Agístri before. I had no idea Nik knew our uncle or you. And I don't know why he kept it from me.' She was unashamed of the tears pooling in her eyes. Kat refused to hide her grief or put it on pause any longer, having masked her pain for her parents' sake. But here, there was nobody to check or scold the magnitude of feelings she'd bottled up for so long. It was like she'd been freed from shackles she didn't know had bound her. Andreas placed his hands on her shoulders; the contact on her skin almost made her jolt. Warmth and kindness radiated from him as he brushed a tear that slowly snaked its way down her cheek.

'I am truly sorry about Nik. I usually hate my photograph being taken, but he was so easy to be around. Funny and incredibly rude.' He smiled with sympathy as Kat blinked, sending more tears down her face.

'He was,' she agreed. 'We're so different and yet so alike. Were. I can't get used to speaking about him in the past tense.' Andreas folded his arms around her, and she released the remaining tears in silence, absorbing the heat from his body, his scent, not just cologne but him.

'He is always with you. Nobody ever leaves their loved ones, even when they die.' His words brought some comfort. Kat was beginning to believe Nik was leaving her signs in the little pink pebbles, but what he meant by them, she had no way to decode. She spoke into the warmth of Andreas' chest.

'I'd never keep a secret from Nik and I didn't.'

'I'm the same. I hate secrets too.' He unwrapped his arms, then kissed her cheeks in the furrows where her tears had been and finally her lips as their need for each other rose. As his mouth moved to her throat, her body was almost quivering with desire. He pulled away and looked at her. The shadows from the dim light created a grey wash across his face like in the photograph and he was replicating the expression Nik had immortalised. 'I guess you're not hungry right now,' he said.

At the idea of food, her stomach protested at its emptiness, thankfully without sound.

'Andreas, you will come to learn that I can always eat, no matter what's going on,' she replied and let him lead her back to the terrace where the outside dining table had now been set for a candlelit supper.

Chapter 22

Andreas' chef had conjured up a feast in the outdoor kitchen, grilling meat and fish over charcoal. His housekeepers had a knack for making dishes appear and disappear unnoticed – unlike Mrs Rálli, who laboured, huffed and puffed with each step. But Kat had grown fond of the woman, and she didn't know what she'd have done without her during the first week on Agístri.

'You have served every single thing I adore,' Kat said to Andreas, placing her knife and fork neatly on her dinner plate. She didn't think she could eat another thing.

'I confess, Mrs Rálli gave me a few suggestions. She likes you, and believe me, she is a hard lady to impress.'

'Well, I'm the one who's impressed. That *souvláki* was as good as my father's. My parents have a restaurant back in London and absolutely nobody is allowed to go near his grill. I should get one for the garden when the house is done,' she said. It was strange to be without the gaggle of relatives ready to offer advice or suggest alternatives to her choices. On Agístri she could make her own decisions, and she enjoyed being without such constraints.

'Tell me about your folks,' he said, his American accent more pronounced.

'Not much to tell. My mother, Mína, was born on Agístri and *Babá*, Giórgios, is from Thessaloniki, and they are hopelessly in love. My mum would follow him anywhere and so, when my dad wanted to move to England, they ended up in London with most of their extended family. Apart from Pétros . . .' She hoped he would speak about her uncle a little more. She watched him carefully as he took a slow sip of his wine.

'Pétros said she came to stay here, and Nik spoke about it too, saying you were both too young to remember. They talked a lot about your mother.'

'What do you mean? The family disapproval about Pétros being gay?' Kat asked.

'I got the sense that Nik and your mom had been fighting. I wasn't party to those conversations.'

Kat was bewildered. Her brother and mother didn't really argue. But her memory was muddled since Nik died and though she could recall the odd disagreement, which was natural, nothing stuck out in her mind. But then, she had been living with Jamie, work had consumed her, and she may have been kept out of their quarrels. Kat admitted she felt a creeping guilt about how much time she had devoted to her job, occasionally going weeks without seeing her brother, though they'd spoken or messaged every day.

'Did my uncle not talk to you about it?'

'He didn't speak of Mína much, only that they couldn't find a way to make amends,' Andreas said sadly. 'When life is so precious, it seems like a terrible waste of time holding on to the past or to conflict. Refusing to forgive. Easy to say, harder to do.' Andreas seemed to be speaking to himself and the warm air rather than her.

'I don't seem to know much about anyone I love,' she managed, confusion racing through her mind as she tried to make sense of her family.

'Do any of us?' He reached for her hand as he spoke. 'But I reckon you're a true romantic; you see the best in everything. Like the renovation, taking something and making it beautiful; you see potential wherever you go.'

A wave of affection rushed through her as their fingers entwined.

'The fact you've said that means you're also a romantic. Though the beach picnic kind of gave that away, and the flowers, and now this . . .' She couldn't stop looking at him; he was so striking, like a magnet drawing her in. But she couldn't help steering the conversation back to her uncle – she knew there was more, otherwise Nik wouldn't have hidden it.

'I wonder why Pétros couldn't forgive my mother even after so much time had passed. She said she wrote to him and told him when she came here that she accepted his sexuality. My brother was gay as well and though it was a shock for her at first, she supported him. We all did.'

Andreas shrugged. 'I wouldn't know. For Pétros, sadly, your mom represented the cruellest time of his life, though I know he loved her. He would talk about her needing to forgive herself for what she'd done, but that's all he said.' Andreas sipped at his wine. 'Regrets are the worst, Katerína, especially for those who don't find that forgiveness.'

Her mother's words echoed in her mind's eye as Andreas repeated them: *'regrets are the worst'*. A large fruit platter had been placed in front of them. Kat didn't know when, but she bit into a slice of peach, licking the sweet juice from her fingers even though she was full up from supper.

'What about you? Do you have regrets?' she asked tentatively, wondering if the gateway to who he kept hidden could be prised open.

'Many. Too, too many to mention . . .' he began, then seemed to check himself. 'And I'm guilty of not taking my own advice about forgiveness either, but you don't want to hear about my demons.' He reached for her hand again, not knowing that she really did wish to delve into his past. She allowed the silence to stretch, hoping he would fill it with nuggets of information. As the chorus of cicadas filled the air, he seemed lost in his own thoughts, almost wincing at his memories. At last, he spoke. 'When my father died, I'd just turned sixteen. He was my idol, my hero and then he was gone. I didn't know who I was without him, and I was lost. He died out of the blue; it was such a shock.'

'I'm sorry, I didn't know.' Kat squeezed his hand tightly, not wishing their connection to break as he slowly peeled away his first layer. She understood the time it took to process someone dying unexpectedly; she was still wrestling with that.

'My mother remarried, quite soon afterwards, and I rebelled. Badly. I refused to move to California with her and her new husband. That's where she's from originally. There's so much about that time I regret, but Pétros saved me and took me in.' Kat longed to know more. She nodded, encouraging him onwards. 'He was very special. I'm sure you've already heard the stories of what he did for the community that treated him so poorly. In a way, he became like a father to me. He was my guardian when my mom left for America.'

'He sounds like an incredible man,' Kat said. 'If Nik

loved him then that's good enough for me. My brother was such a good judge of character. He had an ability to see to the core of a person instantly. Whereas I trust far too easily and then end up disappointed.'

Andreas lifted his hand away from hers and cupped her cheek.

'It's not a fault, Katerína. Your uncle was the same; in that way you're quite similar and he also often ended up hurt by those he trusted. But wouldn't you rather be that person than cynical and jaded?'

'For sure,' she agreed. 'Though like I said before, I hate secrets – that's my current source of disappointment. Or people bossing me around like I'm a child, especially since my brother died. Everyone's forgotten I am a grown-up.'

'What happened to Nik? I don't want to upset you but you didn't say much about it on the beach,' he said carefully, searching her face for the answer. Grief was certainly etched into her skin, but the terrible story was not. She outlined the bare minimum of information, trying to separate the facts from her broken heart.

'He was killed in a car accident . . . by a drunk driver. I was with him . . . he died in my arms.' She felt the surge of emotion travel up her throat threatening to strangle her, but pushed it away. 'I don't remember all of it, or my brain won't let me, but I do know that anyone who gets behind the wheel of a car drunk has no place in my life. I know we've talked about regrets and what a waste of time it is to live without forgiveness, but the man who drove into us deserves all the guilt I hope he feels. I will never forgive him for what he did to Nik and to my family.'

Andreas withdrew his hand. Again, the silence lengthened like a shadow in a summer sunset.

'Not great conversation for such a beautiful dinner,' she said as her phone beeped in her bag. 'Sorry.' She pulled it out and saw that Jamie had messaged to ask if she was all right on the date. She'd call him later.

'Listen, I have an early start tomorrow. I have to go to Athens for a few days for work,' Andreas said, apparently drawing the evening to a close.

'Sure,' she said putting her phone on the table as she stood pretending not to be disappointed. Never mind; he was busy and she definitely was.

'Can I use your bathroom before I go? And I promise I will think of something fun to say when I come back to end the evening on a happier note.'

In the downstairs restroom Kat caught sight of herself in the mirror. Lit by candles, the effect on her reflection was not warm and soft, as if speaking about her twin's death had added another decade to her features. Knowing the portrait Nik had taken of Andreas was nearby proved too much to resist. She tiptoed along the corridor for a quick peek before returning to the dinner table. Andreas' eyes pulled her towards them like a siren call. Although the photograph was black and white, the real-life colour she'd grown to know so well almost glowed from the picture as if his spirit had slipped behind the frame.

Her eyes travelled around the shadowy room that she hadn't taken in before. Several ornaments stood on a shelf, like a line of trophies. Stepping closer, she selected one. A tall gold column topped with three prongs that resembled a mishappen trident. Trying to squint at the inscription in the dim light, she fumbled and it landed with a thud on a thick rug. She exhaled with relief it wasn't damaged. Touching precious or expensive things was always a risk, but her curiosity had won. As she turned it over, gripping tightly, she almost gasped in shock. She reread the words on a small plaque that said:

Best Actor, Hellenic Film Awards

She'd heard of the awards, they were the equivalent of the Greek Oscars. Looking at the others on the shelf, she saw they were all for best actor, best newcomer, rising star . . . She bristled that he'd withheld his profession because he may not trust her. He'd evaded any queries about being in America for a year, saying he was visiting family and working. She heard her phone trilling from outside and took the statuette with her. As she exited the terrace doors, Andreas' back was to her. He whipped around as she spoke.

'And the award for biggest drama queen goes to . . .' she exclaimed, grinning and brandishing the accolade in the air. 'Why didn't you tell me you were an actor?'

But Andreas' face was stony, and the smile fell from her mouth as he held her phone aloft. It flashed with an incoming call. On the screen was the word 'HUSBAND'.

'And why didn't you tell me you were married?'

Chapter 23

They stared at one another for what seemed like an age. Kat felt her privacy had been unjustly invaded and the wrong conclusion teased from her history.

'I don't owe you an explanation, Andreas, any more than you should have told me about this.'

'Hiding an award is hardly the same as hiding a husband!' He moved to her and took the statuette from her hand. 'Why were you snooping in my things anyway?'

'I-I wasn't. I went to look at Nik's photograph again and saw all your trophies, that's all.'

'Well, at least you didn't take pictures to send to the papers since your phone was here, keeping all your secrets.' His voice was as ice cold as his eyes and his stance rigid. The unsaid accusation travelled the distance between them, hitting her firmly in the ribs.

Kat's anger swelled.

'Sorry to burst your bubble, but I still have absolutely no idea who you are. And up until I had the misfortune to bump into you at the airport, I'd never heard of you either. You're just my rude neighbour with lovely shoes, who occasionally kisses me, but ends every dinner prematurely and has absolutely no clue how to behave in polite company.'

'Polite company?!' he exclaimed. 'I'm not sure you're being so polite right now, and you're in my home.'

'Well, let me rectify that immediately.' She grabbed the phone from his hand, snatched up her bag and stalked towards the pathway to the sea, before turning to him once again. 'For your information and for what it's worth, I don't have secrets. I'm separated, about to be divorced. I hope you and your loafers will be very happy together. Good evening!'

* * *

That night, Kat was plagued with strange dreams. Snippets of scenes from the car accident were her usual visions, but instead of Nik, her mother was in her arms begging for forgiveness. Then as she tried to escape the wreckage of the car it started to rain pink pebbles, penning her in until she could no longer see the sky nor breathe. She woke several times panting, her mouth open in a silent scream, but when she dozed off, she returned to the same dream, reliving it in multicoloured horror.

In the morning, she groggily forced herself from bed and could barely utter 'good morning, sunshine'. Between nightmares, she'd replayed her altercation with Andreas and her heart had pounded with fury before confusion descended. To be accused of concealing something when she'd been nothing but open from the get-go was desperately unfair. *He* was the one who had evaded straightforward answers. But now she knew the truth, she did understand a little. Still, it didn't give him the green light to jump to incorrect conclusions about Jamie. She was better off without Andreas anyway; show business was not a world in which she belonged.

Kat was ashamed to admit that she'd googled him in the early hours and was astonished by his popularity, especially in Greece. There was gossip that he was set to be the new leading man in Hollywood. She stopped herself from obsessively delving any further and felt sick and embarrassed. If anything happened between them now, he would always suspect her motives. At least she had Lizzie's visit to look forward to tomorrow and Kat couldn't wait to catch up with her friend. She had an awful lot to tell her.

Suddenly, the lights in the house flickered and dimmed before shining brightly even in the morning sunshine. Power and weather had been restored. Kat rushed to charge her laptop and phone before almost skipping downstairs to use the bathroom since the upstairs one was out of action. The sense of optimism was welcome, and she pushed last night along with Andreas firmly to the back of her mind.

'*Kaliméra*,' she almost sang to Mrs Rálli in the kitchen who responded with one of her knowing looks.

'Ah, last night went well it seems. I am happy for Andreas; he is a good man.'

'I'm afraid you'll be disappointed, Mrs Rálli. I don't think things will go any further. Thanks for trying to matchmake, but you've wasted your time.'

The old woman looked crestfallen, but Kat explained about their imminent guest and her housekeeper rállied quickly. The thought of having Lizzie to fuss over seemed to cheer her up.

Kat spent the rest of the morning readying the bedrooms, then borrowed Mrs Rálli's car to visit the mini market at the other end of the island. She needed to stock up and fill the now-functioning fridge with booze as Lizzie loved a drink. Kat knew her friend was disappointed in her choice to be sober as they'd always partied hard together at uni, but her friend also understood the underlying reasons. Would it last forever? Perhaps not. But for now, Kat needed as much clarity as possible to navigate life without her twin and to write.

After toiling in what would be Lizzie's bedroom past lunchtime, much to her housekeeper's chagrin who was desperate to see her eat, Kat finished. Adding a final flourish with an earthenware jug filled with some of the white roses from Andreas' now-bittersweet bouquet on the dresser, it was ready, and Kat had moved back into the newly decorated primary bedroom. In there, she'd already painted the bedframe with the newly attached corner posts and needed to let it dry before adding the new mattress topper and linen. One room done, so many more to go. Maybe Lizzie could help her decorate the second and third bedroom during her stay.

Kostas was banging around with his boys in the bathroom upstairs, laying tiles, and the screech of the stone cutter was deafening. Mrs Rálli had gone home after complaining about the noise for what felt like an hour but not before she'd force-fed Kat a large late lunch. Taking a milky coffee to sort through Pétros' papers in the third bedroom, Kat filed them into neatly labelled boxes: personal correspondence, charity work, book things and household affairs, all annotated on her laptop to send to his estate office. She found a letter addressed to her mother's maiden name – Mína Tzanos –

from someone called Yiánnis Papandréou. Strange that mail would ever come for her mother here, especially since the postmark was dated seven years ago. She put it to one side for now.

As she sat amongst the boxes, she felt sad that a lifetime of work and existence could be piled into a few containers to be distributed, donated or recycled. Though Mrs Rálli had said most of Pétros' papers were at his solicitor's in Athens, life seemed so disposable and far too temporary. Taking that thought further, she began to write.

> *When a home changes hands, often the new owner cannot wait to put their stamp on it, marking their turf like a feral cat. Eroding evidence of another's existence eventually removes any sign that someone dared to live where we dwell. But what is the rush to erase the past? We don't do it with one another – unless we are deeply wronged, hurt or broken-hearted. What has gone before shapes us into who we will become; it is unavoidable. We carry our memories into the future, such is the privilege of existence. The bereaved cling to recollections like plaster to a wall; it is embroiled in the process of letting go and learning to live with a heart that will always feel different, an empty space never to be filled.*
>
> *Whether it is a design or a dream, redecorating can be a resurrection of sorts, allowing history to peek through the cracks, enhancing the present. Like paint on a stone frontage, you can improve it without diminishing its original state, merely amplifying it for a new age. Be it body or building, all things have a past that beats a unique rhythm like a heart. Fashions*

come and go, but they always return, often bolder and evolved beyond their beginnings. Muscle memory applies to people, cabinets or rocks. Sometimes I wonder, what is the point of attempting to hide it?

As she finished writing, her eyes travelled back to the letter meant for her mother. It had already been opened, so there was little harm in looking, surely. Kat couldn't work out why it would be sent to Agístri, when her mum hadn't been back to the island since the trip she'd taken with her and Nik over thirty years ago. Though Kat was beginning to mistrust all she'd been told, or not told, by everyone around her. Regardless, she ought to mention it to her mother first.

Mína answered after two rings.

'I had the most awful dreams last night about you, Katerína. I am so glad to hear your voice,' she babbled, not that Kat had even had a chance to say hello yet.

'The power is back on, but listen, I'm sorting some things out in the house before Lizzie comes tomorrow, and—'

'I am so happy she is coming,' interrupted Mína. 'You shouldn't be alone while you are so fragile. Is important to have people around you that you trust, especially on that island.'

Kat didn't feel fragile; her writing was giving her a new strength. But in the spirit of sorting out life, she needed to ask her mother about what she'd found.

'There's a letter for you here, *Mána*. Shall I post it?' Kat managed, finally completing a sentence.

'What letter? There is no letter,' Mína said, and Kat thought her dismissal odd, but her mother was prone to heightened emotions.

'It looks like it's been opened. It's addressed to you here at Pétros' house from Yiánnis somebody. I could read it to you now if you like?'

'No!' Mína shrieked. 'Please, Katerína, whatever you do, please, please, *angheloúthi mou,* do not read it.' Her mother started to cry, and Kat knew she'd be frantically crossing herself.

'Mum,' Kat began sternly. 'Why can't I read it?' Her mother was now sobbing at the other end of the phone.

'Because you mustn't – you have to promise me. It is from the past and has nothing to do with us now. Ancient history, please destroy it,' she said between gulps.

'So, you know what it is?' Kat had deliberately avoided promising anything to her mother.

Mína exhaled heavily. 'Yes, I know,' she said quietly. 'Please, Katerína, it will hurt us all. I beg of you, do not read it. For mine and your father's sake. Please.'

Kat heard the service bell at the restaurant ding in the background, but neither of them spoke. It repeated its tinny ring several times.

'*Érchoumai!*' shouted Mína, saying she was on her way. 'Can we speak later? I have to go. Katerína, I ask you for very little in my time as your mother, but you must throw away that letter. It does not belong in our lives. Please, there has been enough sadness. You would not wish to make more for us all, would you?'

She hung up, reeling from Mína's attempted guilt-trip as she felt the blood run colder in her veins, prompting goose bumps to rise on her skin. Kat had never heard her mother sound so desperate, not since Nik died. But this was different. What on earth was in the letter that could hurt them any more than they'd already been? She picked up the envelope and faltered, suddenly afraid. What excuse could there be for such a reaction? Despite being fed up with lies and secrets, Kat wasn't one to break the rules and preferred to keep the peace. She put the letter in one of the boxes and only hoped she'd be able to forget about it.

Artemis & Apollo

For all his perceived immorality, and penchant for careless endeavours, Apollo held his values dear and opposed those who slighted him and his family. Artemis shared his moral compass. When it came to their parents, the twins defended them at all costs. But when they were wronged by their mother or father, it would be nigh impossible for them, or any of those embroiled in their drama, to recover.

Chapter 24

Waiting on the harbour for Lizzie's boat, Kat enjoyed the bustling hum of Aegina at the weekend. It was in complete contrast to her sleepier island. The morning sun beat down fiercely on her skin and despite the heat, it was preferable to the stormy weather of the last few days. It felt like the beams were coaxing her back to life.

As the ferry docked, Lizzie was first to rush down the ramp, dragging a large suitcase and an oversized holdall hooked over her shoulder. Kat hardly recognised her. Lizzie's hair was no longer platinum blonde but bright titian, like one of the buoys providing a buffer between the sea wall and the boat.

'Kat!' Lizzie shrieked as she flung herself forwards, folding Kat in such a tight embrace the force almost knocked her flying.

'I am so glad you're here. Lizzie, your hair is so . . . so red!' Kat stood back and surveyed her friend. The effect was striking, making her bright green eyes shine.

'Part of my renaissance. Right now, I need a drink! That

boat was bloody bumpy.' She preened her newly blunt-cut fringe then apologised for swearing.

'How are you bearing up? I still can't believe they made you redundant,' Kat said taking Lizzie's giant shoulder bag which pulled at her elbow, so she switched hands then headed for the strip of eateries on the front.

'I'm completely over it. Almost. Nearly. Oh, who am I kidding?' she replied throwing her spare arm around Kat's shoulder. 'I'm just hurt and feel horribly betrayed. But when I get the biggest scoop and sell it to all their competitors, they'll be sorry. Not that I'm being vindictive, simply serving my fabulous version of justice. And speaking of a story . . .'

They took a seat at a busy bar, managing to snag a table overlooking the harbour.

'Don't tell me you've got one already. You've only been in Greece a couple of hours.'

'I do and it's good, but it's not quite a story yet. I need to do some digging. More in a moment. Waiter!'

Lizzie beckoned to the boy taking orders and requested an ouzo, olives, fried potatoes and bread. Kat ordered a soft drink, though she felt tempted by an ouzo. Lizzie had an infectious energy, the ultimate party girl, but Kat was set on sobriety for now. Though she did feel like she was missing out to an extent and often her friends encouraged her to have a drink, which almost made her more determined to abstain. If she drank again, it would be her choice entirely. And she intended to pursue her dream of writing, so access to every thought and feeling was necessary. She wanted and needed to be authentic in this new venture.

'You look thin, Kat, and tired, beneath that stunning suntan,' Lizzie said grabbing her friend's hand.

'I don't know how I've managed that; it's been cloudy

for days. I've done nothing but eat. I did have some crazy weird dreams last night but I've been working so hard on the house. And writing . . .'

'That sounds like a great holiday, said no one ever! Kat, you were supposed to take time off and reset after everything that's happened. Why are you doing so much?' Their drinks arrived and they clinked glasses.

'Amelia's idea has taken hold, so I've done a few pieces, only as an experiment. But she loves them and wants more.'

'Tell her to sod off! She coordinated this plan with Jamie and your parents to make you take a break and now she's set you to work. I'll tell her if you won't.'

'It's fine, Lizzie, honestly. It's become a kind of therapy anyway. I'll get it all done, somehow; I always do.'

'Well, I'm here to help.' She smiled grabbing Kat in a hug again. 'Just don't push yourself so hard. This is the only time you'll ever get away from life. I don't want you to fall apart. And you won't because . . . enter Lizzie!' She gestured to herself and then hugged Kat once more. 'It's so good to see you.'

'You too, but we've tons of time to catch up apparently, given the size of your suitcase.' Kat eyed her luggage, which would contain enough clothes for a month. Lizzie was welcome to stay as long as she wanted. Their food arrived and Lizzie took a handful of *patátes tiganités* that were sprinkled with oregano and flecks of feta. Speaking through her mouthful she said, 'Gossip first, then I need to hear about your love life and the hot neighbour. You will never ever guess who I saw on the dock at Piraeus.'

Kat shook her head not wishing to play the guessing game, which could go on for some time from past experience. Happily, Lizzie launched straight into it. 'Andreas Ellis!'

Kat balked, grabbing the table edges with both hands. 'Who?'

'Yeh, his original name is Andreas Elio . . . popo . . . hang on.' She consulted her phone. 'El-io-pou-los, that's it. No wonder he changed it. Hollywood's hottest new thing. He's already a big star in Greece apparently.' Lizzie proffered her phone with the search engine results for Andreas that Kat had already seen from her own brief hunt online.

Kat's mouth went dry and she took a swig of her Coke. 'How do you know who he is? I'd never heard of him . . .' Kat chose her words carefully, not wishing Lizzie to press her for details.

'He's been shooting this movie that already has Oscar buzz. And he is seriously fucking hot. Sorry. No girlfriend with him, so not a story yet, but he is absolute heaven in person. Tragic backstory – teenage grief, father dies, mother elopes back to America and he stays in Greece.' She clasped her hands at the tragic romance of his past before continuing. 'He was born on Agístri, is forty years old . . . Quiz me and I will tell you everything I know until I find out more. It's like fate sent me here all sad and redundant to get a huge scoop!'

Kat wondered whether to mention that he lived next door, but since he was away in Athens, there seemed little point bringing him into their day. Plus, she and Andreas weren't really speaking. Though she also didn't like keeping things from her friend.

'Oh, I know who you mean,' Kat said, attempting to be nonchalant. 'I've seen him around.' She helped herself to an olive.

'You're kidding! What's he like? God, imagine waking up and being that beautiful every day. Does he live near you?' Lizzie asked squirming in her seat with excitement, but she changed tack when Kat shrugged in response to her countless queries. 'Speaking of, I cannot wait to see what you've done with the house and you must tell me all about your date with the boy next door.'

Although she smiled, Kat already regretted her words and the fact a potential story and Kat's questionable love life were both interlinked. The last thing Andreas needed was to be alerted to a former tabloid journalist scouring the island for gossip. He was private and guarded; that much he had made clear.

Kat filled Lizzie in on her renovation progress instead, dismissing her date as a one-off or two, unlikely to progress, before paying the bill and heading for a thrift store to pick up some glass containers for the almost finished bathroom. Then she would introduce Lizzie to Agístri.

* * *

Mrs Rálli had formed a solo welcome party with a cold mezze on the terrace table. After showing Lizzie to her room and depositing her luggage, they returned outside to eat. Mrs Rálli fussed around Lizzie, who couldn't understand a word she said, and the older woman looked at Lizzie's hair colour quizzically with each exchange. As Mrs Rálli's car clattered along the seafront, Lizzie and Kat feasted on the patio as the sun began its slow descent over the sea.

'Mrs Danvers is scary.' Kat thought Lizzie's comparison to the housekeeper from the novel *Rebecca* a little unfair, but she'd also felt intimidated by her initially. 'This is paradise, Kat. It's absolutely incredible. And it's all yours!' It was supposed to be hers and Nik's.

'Not if Jamie has his way.' Where had that come from? Kat thought she'd shaken off his strange comment. But she decided to elaborate, wondering if he'd repeated his 'jest' to Lizzie. 'He said since we're still married technically half is his, though I think it was a joke.'

'He wouldn't! No, that's Jamie's rubbish banter. He thinks the world of you, Kat, and would never hurt you.'

'That's just it, I don't know. Thankfully my uncle sorted all the paperwork in advance – the Greek inheritance laws can be pretty complex, though it was all sewn up before he died and all I had to do was sign a form. But Jamie also asked if I'd had second thoughts about breaking up – not in so many words, but basically he did.'

'What?!' exclaimed Lizzie refilling her glass with rosé. 'What did you say?'

'No, of course! But things have felt a bit weird, him organising this trip for me with my dad. He's behaving like we're still together, always interfering and overstepping. I was probably kidding myself thinking we could stay friends after the divorce goes through. *If* it does. And he called when I was on a date and made things awkward and kind of ruined the night.'

'What could he have done all the way from England to wreck your hot neighbour dinner?' asked Lizzie.

'I still have him saved as "HUSBAND" on my phone and Andr . . .' Kat almost said Andreas but speedily checked herself. 'And the guy I was with saw my phone. It kind of put the brakes on things. Jamie called to see how the date was going and managed to sabotage it instead.'

'Oh, Kat, the universe is piling it on.'

'And now my mother is being strange. I found this letter addressed to her from some bloke called Yiánnis and she completely freaked out when I mentioned it. Then she cried and said I had to throw it away. It's already been opened though.'

'Where is it?' Lizzie sprang from her seat so abruptly that it made Kat jump up too.

'I said I wouldn't read it.'

'Kat, you are a grown-assed woman. For fuck's sake, stop letting your parents boss you around. Aren't you dying to know what it says? *I* can read it if you want to be such a goody-goody.'

Lizzie's summary was correct. Kat was fed up being ordered around and smothered by her family. Her time on Agístri had shone a light on the freedom she didn't know she'd been missing. She also couldn't deny her own curiosity about the contents of the letter. Kat hesitated, scrolling through the various outcomes in her mind before eventually walking back into the house. Lizzie followed her upstairs into the box room, trying to hurry her along before Kat handed over the envelope. Her mother forbade Kat from looking at it, but said nothing about anyone else, so technically she wasn't going against orders. Her pulse began to thump in the silence as Lizzie's eyes scanned the pages. She held the papers to her chest looking disappointed.

'It's all in bloody Greek,' said Lizzie shaking her head and handing it back. 'Your turn.'

Kat hesitantly accepted the pages with a slight tremor in her hands. Her mother had been vehement she mustn't read it and Kat already felt guilty about disobeying. She looked up at Lizzie who nodded encouragement, gesturing impatiently. Kat needed to translate as she went along. Speaking her supposed native language was one thing, but reading it was much harder. She was out of practice and as her eyes traced the neat calligraphy, letters of the alphabet swam in front of her eyes. Her heart pounded so loudly, it felt like her chest might split open. The paper blurred as tears clouded her vision. She couldn't believe what it said, though as she turned the envelope over in her fingers again, there was no mistaking who it was meant for.

'The suspense is killing me. What does it say?' pressed Lizzie.

Kat tried to speak but her voice stuck. She cleared her throat then tried again. 'My mother was right. I shouldn't have read it,' she said quietly.

'Why? Bloody hell, Kat, tell me what it says!'

As she was jarred back to reality by Lizzie's coarse language, the revelation within the lines prompted a thousand questions to thunder through her brain. It explained why there had been so much talk about forgiveness from Mrs Rálli, and within the conversations between Pétros and Andreas.

When Mína brought Nik and Kat to Agístri over thirty years ago, her mother did something that she still couldn't forgive herself for. And now nor could Kat. She'd heard as much from everyone who'd known of her mother back then, but Kat could never have imagined she'd be confronted with this. Scrunching up the pages, her tears gathered, poised to disperse as Lizzie touched her arm, eager to know more.

'It's a letter from a man called Yiánnis . . .' Kat began but couldn't continue.

'Even I worked that out. And . . . ?' Lizzie was like a frenzied terrier in front of a burrow full of rabbits.

'A letter . . . from Yiánnis saying goodbye. That he will always think about her . . . how much he loved her . . . and he would always remember their time together on Agístri. My . . . my mother had an affair with him thirty-two years ago. Here on this island. In this house.'

Chapter 25

After reading the letter, rest was firmly out of reach for Kat. She was up before sunrise the following morning, attempting to distract her mind from her mother's indiscretion. She'd been writing at the patio table, filled with décor inspiration after her trip to Aegina yesterday and had finished her usual column in record time before turning her attention back to her newer writing project. It was helping her make sense of her emotions, like a cognitive therapy of sorts.

'How did you sleep?' asked Kat when Lizzie finally emerged into the garden yawning loudly.

'Like the dead!' said Lizzie stretching her arms high above her head. 'Shit, sorry, terrible, terrible choice of words.'

'It's fine, I knew what you mean,' said Kat. 'It's odd, you know? Just being here, I feel closer to Nik somehow. I can't explain it.'

'Are you going to speak to your mum about the letter?' Lizzie said accepting a cup of coffee from Mrs Rálli who shuffled away to make a fresh pot for the builders due at any moment.

'Don't know. She tried to call me last night. Several times

at three-minute intervals, but I didn't know what to say so ignored her. How could she, Lizzie? And my poor dad. He'd be heartbroken if he knew.'

'Kat, try not to leap to any conclusions until you know the details. But I get it, I can't imagine your mum doing that. Your parents seem so in love.'

Kat laughed sarcastically. 'Yeah, that's what I thought too. Anyway, this is your holiday – enough about my endless woes. What do *you* want to do today?'

'Him, please!' said Lizzie, grinning as she nodded at Kostas' eldest son who beamed a winning smile their way as he carried a large box across the lawn. 'Why didn't you tell me you had delicious builders working here? I would have come sooner.'

They watched him walk into the house, admiring the retreating view.

'Can't say I'd noticed, though now you mention it . . .'

'Hands off. You snooze, you lose!' joked Lizzie sipping her coffee.

'Be my guest,' replied Kat then grabbed Lizzie's arm. 'And I am so glad you are my guest, despite the letter drama. I'd be in such a state if I was here on my own. Now, Chrístos aside, what else?'

'Let's walk and swim, eat – all the good holiday things. Your vacation starts now, Kat. Give me ten minutes to get ready.'

When Lizzie finally reappeared much later than promised, Kat had written several more pages for Amelia.

'Good morning again, Greece!' declared Lizzie dancing onto the patio. Kat shot her a suspicious look, taking in the flush on her pale skin and smudged eyeliner.

'Don't tell me,' said Kat closing her laptop and taking it

inside. 'I don't want to stop you having fun, but please don't distract my builders. They're on such a tight schedule.'

'And in such tight jeans . . .' Lizzie giggled making Kat roll her eyes with laughter.

'Come on, the beach calls,' said Kat then she shouted to Mrs Rálli to let her know they wouldn't need lunch.

As they left, Chrístos walked outside, shirtless, which Kat thought somewhat unnecessary. Although the day was already warm, the air conditioning was blasting inside. There was little need to remove his clothes unless Lizzie had already done it for him, which seemed likely. It was going to be a struggle to keep things on track. He winked at Lizzie who coyly flicked her fringe from her eyes.

Kat and Lizzie set up on some loungers at the far end of the village on the golden sands of Skála beach and Kat began to relax. Having Lizzie nearby made her feel so much better.

'This is heaven, Kat. Look how beautiful and healthy-looking everyone is. I feel pale and so English.' She stripped off to her bikini and lay like a starfish, willing the sun to tan her. 'Any ideas what you'll do with the house when it's finished?'

'Nope,' Kat replied rubbing sunscreen onto her arms. 'I could let it out long term, but the more it goes on, the more I'm falling in love with it. And the island.'

'I don't blame you. Greece does rather suit you. Maybe it's where you belong.'

Kat contemplated her friend's words. 'My life is in London though, work, you guys . . . I admit that being here makes a kind of sense. I can't explain it. You know Nik used to come here.'

'Did he? Wow!' Lizzie said loudly. Kat frowned as her

friend picked up her book and frantically leafed through the pages.

'Yes,' Kat said with a suspicious tone. She knew Lizzie too well and could spot when she was being deliberately evasive. Kat continued, scrutinising her reaction. 'Nik used to come to Agístri to see my uncle.'

Lizzie didn't reply or pretended not to hear, so Kat repeated her statement. Lizzie put her book down and eventually turned her head to Kat.

'I know,' she said quietly.

'What?' Kat almost shouted.

'Don't get angry. I didn't know about your uncle, only that Nik used to come here. He told Jamie years ago, but they didn't want to mention it to you.'

'*Jamie* knew?!' Kat exclaimed. 'But *you* didn't mention it to me either. I can't believe this. Why is everyone around me complicit in secrets and trying to protect me all the time? From what? Myself?'

Lizzie sat up on the lounger to face her.

'I don't know all of the info.' Kat shot her a look of disbelief. 'I didn't want to get involved between you and Nik and then you, Jamie and Nik – that would be a recipe for ruined friendship. Honestly, that's all I know. It wasn't my place to go digging – I do have some scruples.'

'I can't believe Jamie,' said Kat. 'He should have told me, and I don't understand why he kept it quiet. How can I ever trust him again?' Kat suddenly jumped up. 'What if he knew about my mum's affair?' She reached into her beach bag for her phone. 'I've had enough of this; I'm going to ask him.'

'Kat, wait. Don't do anything rash, just think about it. How could Jamie possibly know about your mum? He didn't even know about Pétros.'

Kat rested the phone in her lap then pulled on her cover-up.

'Because the letter had been opened. What if Nik found it? Or maybe Pétros read it, but I have no way of asking either of those people.' Tears pricked at her eyes; she was so sick of crying. 'I'm trying to make sense of my life, but every time I feel just a tiny sliver of hope, another secret springs up to bite me. Lizzie, I don't know how much more I can take.'

'Kat, please, try and get some perspective.'

'But I had this grand romantic idea about my parents' relationship, which is a lie. I don't want anything else unpicked.'

Lizzie perched on the edge of her sunbed facing Kat.

'I know you miss Nik. We all do, but you must keep living, Kat.' She gestured to the calm sea gently lapping on the sand and the clear sheet of blue that stretched above. 'Be present and don't drag up the past to look for something that might only hurt you more. Some things are secrets for a reason. Trust me I know from my job. Nine times out of ten, they only cause pain and damage.'

Kat lay back down on the comfy bed. 'I'm so furious with Jamie and my mother. And I just don't understand why Nik didn't tell me about coming here and meeting my uncle, and he met Andreas as well.' As soon as she said his name she wished she could take it back.

'What did you say? Andreas as in film-star Andreas?' Lizzie moved with such speed over to Kat's sunbed that she nearly toppled them both over.

'It's a very common Greek name.' Kat shifted to the edge of the lounger, trying to dismiss it.

'I've known you for twenty years, Kat, and you're a terrible liar. Why didn't you tell me you knew him? Does he live near you?'

Kat didn't know what to say but Lizzie could see her squirming.

'Hang on, you said you'd been on a date with your neighbour and the house next door has huge gates and security cameras that stick out like a sore thumb. Oh my God. Andreas lives next door, doesn't he? And you've been seeing him – why didn't you say anything?'

'I didn't want to . . . He's so—'

'You didn't trust me, did you?' Lizzie interrupted. 'You'd thought I'd sell the story.'

Kat felt ashamed because that was precisely what she'd thought. Lizzie's face fell and Kat thought she saw tears in her eyes. Her friend began to pack up her things, flinging suncream, her paperback and towel into her bag.

'You can't be angry with people for keeping things from you, Kat, when in principle you have done exactly the same to me.'

'Oh, come on, not telling you who my famous neighbour is, is hardly the same. You and Jamie chose not to tell me that my dead brother came to an island where my uncle lived – a relative I didn't know about until recently You're supposed to be my best friend.'

'And you're supposed to be mine. I didn't realise you thought so poorly of me,' Lizzie said as she stood up and flounced away, her bright red hair like a warning of her anger as it shone in the sunshine.

* * *

Kostas was grouting the tiles when Kat returned from the beach. She'd waited on the sunbed for half an hour, but Lizzie hadn't come back. There had been no response from her friend to the several messages she'd sent either. The argument had depleted Kat's excitement about the almost finished upstairs bathroom, though the effect of the sandstone tile and cream stone basin had transformed it. Removing the bathtub and creating a walk-in shower rejuvenated the old-fashioned room. Now it wouldn't look out of place in a high-end hotel.

'We make a beginning on the downstairs bathroom tomorrow and then there will be a few days before the kitchen arrives. If you need us to decorate any of the other rooms while we wait for the delivery, my sons would be very happy to help.'

Kat asked them to start on the lounge and small bedroom if they had time and tidy up the garden, which she would be happy to pay extra for. She was certain one of his sons would be delighted to spend as much time here as possible – if Lizzie ever came back to the house.

A cloud of despair settled over Kat's heart as her mind reached back to her brother and Jamie's friendship. They were always close; they'd had to be since Kat and Nik came as a pair, such was the nature of twins. But she'd never imagined her then husband and brother were keeping secrets from her. It made her more suspicious of those she was supposed to trust and she didn't like that feeling at all.

As her plans to have lunch with Lizzie were clearly cancelled, Kat grilled some sourdough and drizzled the toast with olive oil, adding a generous sprinkling of oregano. After decanting some tzatziki into a bowl, she went into the garden. She set up her laptop again, seeking a diversion instead of angrily calling Jamie or her mother or weeping about the quarrel with Lizzie. She decided to channel her feelings into writing instead.

When it comes to a house, discovering a secret can be thrilling, whether it be a wooden floor beneath a carpet or stumbling across a box of treasures in the attic. But in life, unearthing a secret can be devastating and unwelcome. Pain can be caused by the smallest of things when you're in the depths of coming to terms with loss. The wrong thing said can jar and grief can rise up.

Like sandpaper will stealthily erode a surface, stripping away the layers of time, so a secret can eat away at those trying to contain it. Renaissance and rejuvenation aren't always for the better if we cannot learn from the past – the trace of which will always remain. But in the fullness of time, it becomes possible to find the strength to forge onwards and see clearly again without being blinded by the blinkers of loss. And though you may not like what you see, it is the view you have and only you can change your perspective.

Kat looked up at her own view, which was stunning. Greece had certainly changed her own perspective on life. The sea sparkled in the sunlight as if a million white lights were flashing within the waves, like a daytime phosphorescence. It was hypnotic, though the feeling of true joy was missing. But it was up to her and her alone to alter what she saw and how she felt about it. She needed to heed her own advice.

Her phone rang as she was rereading the last lines she'd written, filled with a renewed strength and determination from her own words. There was no sense putting off the inevitable. She answered and took charge of the call immediately.

'I think you owe me an explanation.'

Chapter 26

The silence at the end of the phone seemed louder than the waves on the shore. Wind crackled into the receiver.

'*Mána*, did you hear me?'

She heard her mother breathing and eventually, she responded, 'I assume you decided to read a letter that was not meant for you, Katerína, against my request.' Her voice was devoid of emotion. Kat wasn't used to this stony version of her mother and it was disarming.

'Don't make *me* feel guilty. I wasn't going to, but Lizzie insisted. Unfortunately, she doesn't read Greek and though I hardly can, I know enough to pin together your escapades on Agístri. I can't believe you'd do that to *Babá*.' A knot lodged in Kat's throat. She still wished she'd never read the letter and had done as she'd been told. Though that hadn't got her very far in life, behaving in the opposite manner had resulted in just as much heartache and misery.

'*Angheloúthi mou*, this is a conversation we must have in person. I'm disappointed you have also shared this with Lizzie and were so easily led by her. I need to explain so much to you and . . .'

'Well, that's not going to happen since I'm here in the house where you decided to be unfaithful to my father. No wonder you never wanted to come back to Agístri. Is he still here on the island? Yiánnis, the man you chose over *Babá*?'

'It was a very long time ago, many years. As I tried to say, it is old history and has nothing to do with life now.' She was being so matter-of-fact about something so devastating, that Kat almost preferred her mother overwrought and weeping.

Kat scoffed. 'And yet here it is in *my* life.'

'Please, Katerína, I know you will never understand, and I do not ask for your forgiveness as I do not deserve it, but your father has mentioned about coming to the island. With me.'

'Well you can't stay here! It's a mess and even if you could, I don't think that's appropriate.'

'Of course not, but Jamie was suggesting he may like to see you as well.'

'Jamie? What the hell has he got to do with it?' Kat couldn't keep track of the tumult of emotions racing through her, though anger was now dominant at Jamie's over-involvement.

'He is only concerned about you.'

'More like he's concerned about getting half of the house that was supposed to be for Nik and me . . .' At the mention of her brother's name, Kat dissolved. She'd foolishly thought things might get easier at some point, that by being in Greece she'd somehow find a way forwards. But all she'd done was blindly trek along a new path with nothing but drama and sadness at every turn. 'I have to go. I can't talk about this right now.'

She ended the call and sat at the table, sobbing into her hands for such a length of time that the sun moved across the terrace unnoticed, the overhang no longer providing shelter. Eventually she dried her tears and plunged a slice of cold toast into the tzatziki, dropping a large dollop on her keyboard.

'Great. That's just about right,' she said to herself knowing her laptop would smell of garlic for weeks.

She went to grab a cloth from the kitchen. Inside, she saw that the lounge had been covered in dust sheets and painting had begun in the hallway too. The builders were nowhere to be seen, and she assumed they'd either left for the day or were taking a break. She had no idea what time it was. Upstairs they'd also made a start in the little bedroom and the walls had their first coat of the palest yellow, which gave a warm hint of sunshine to the space. Everything was moving so quickly, that Kat wondered if it was all a bit too fast. Plans for her own future weren't travelling at the same speed. She was drifting aimlessly around the house, just like she was pointlessly wandering around her life, longing for something to make sense.

As she tackled the blob of creamy dip on her laptop, she saw Lizzie walking across the lawn. Kat felt terrible about their disagreement and wished for no further drama. They owed each other an apology.

'Lizzie!' she said moving to meet her friend halfway on the grass. 'I know I should have told you about Andreas. It's not a big deal but now it's become one. I don't want to fight. I do trust you, though it doesn't seem like it, and I'm sorry.'

Lizzie took Kat's hand and squeezed it warmly. 'You're not as sorry as I am. I should have apologised first just like I should have told you about Nik coming here, but I swear I knew nothing about your uncle. Having half a story is worse than knowing nothing. As we've found out with your mum's letter. I know you trust me; I'm just feeling insecure about being made redundant. It's knocked my confidence a bit.'

'You are brilliant and talented, and I love you,' Kat said bringing her friend in for a hug.

'Tell that to the bastards who fired me.' She sighed. 'But you know me, I'll recover and be better than ever.' Lizzie pulled back and scrutinised Kat. 'You know what I've forgotten, though?'

'What?' asked Kat frowning.

'I'd forgotten just how bloody tiny you are. You're the size of a hobbit!'

'Thanks a lot!' joked Kat, grateful to be back on track.

'Honesty is always best, mostly. So come on, my miniature friend, let's put the world to rights and decide what to do about your mother.'

They went into the kitchen and Kat poured Lizzie an Alfa beer in a glass chilled from the freezer. It frosted as she decanted the liquid, then she grabbed herself a non-alcoholic version.

'Mum called,' Kat began as they took a seat at the kitchen table. She nestled in the corner nook and hugged her knees. 'It was not good. And apparently Jamie's been speaking to them as well. I don't get why he's interfering. I can't work out what to be the angriest about, but I think my mum's affair wins.'

Lizzie took a thirsty gulp of her beer and hummed appreciation at the cold liquid.

'Jamie we can deal with. He only cares, we all do, but maybe you guys never set proper rules when you split up. You're so used to being in each other's lives; you should talk to him.' Kat raised her eyebrows, suggesting that wasn't an easy conversation to have. 'As for your mum, that's the tricky one.'

'She said it was a chat we needed to have face to face, which is the last thing I need.' Kat sighed and pulled her long hair into a topknot. 'I hate things left hanging. There's been too much of that since Nik.' Lizzie moved to sit beside her in the corner pew.

'Don't hate me, but . . .'

'Nothing I ever want to hear begins with that, Lizzie.'

She smirked. 'Hear me out. Since Nik was killed . . .' Kat winced at the words. Hearing someone else say it made it real. It was too painful to think about, yet she hardly possessed the strength to keep the image of him dying in the wreckage of the car from her mind as Lizzie continued. 'You've become used to not making your own decisions but then get angry when things are taken out of your hands. You're reacting to something terrible that was senseless and incomprehensible. Nik's death was a tragedy, but an accident – you know that, Kat.'

Kat digested her friend's words and lifted her drink to her lips but said nothing, allowing Lizzie to share her thoughts.

'There was nothing you could have done about what happened. You're my best friend and it hurts me to see you so weighed down, not just by Nik but by everything. I wish you'd find a way to free yourself.'

'Whilst I appreciate the psychoanalysis, I can't shift . . . this massive sense of loss and I feel so lost, Lizzie.' Tears began to fall down her face though they hardly registered. 'And I'm tired of this.' Her fist pressed against her heart. 'It hurts. Every day I wake up and know I can't call my brother or hear his voice ever again. He wasn't just my brother, he was my twin. We were two parts of the same thing and now

I'm without him, I'll never be complete again. I miss him so much. And I'm sick of my family and friends keeping things from me and constantly interfering.' She needed to release her frustration. Every single person she loved tried to control her and she knew she had been compliant in enabling them. But she had to put a stop to it, for her own sanity. 'And before you say it, Lizzie, you might have all been trying to protect me, not telling me about Nik coming here, but I am a grown-up. Every time I find something else out, I get even more hurt. My mum betrayed my father and I'm horrified. And Jamie betrayed me by keeping something about Nik secret, and Nik did the same thing. I can't forgive any of them for it. I don't know how much more I can take.'

She wiped her face and Lizzie went to get a tissue for Kat, who blew her nose noisily then sighed just as loudly.

'Tell me how I can make it better, Kat,' said Lizzie taking a seat again.

Kat sadly looked at her oldest friend.

'You can't; nobody can. Only me.'

* * *

That evening, Kat cobbled together supper for them both, making a delicious *briam* – roasted vegetables sprinkled with capers, lemons and fresh herbs from the garden. Chrístos had returned before they'd started eating under the guise that he'd 'forgotten something'. Kat watched from the corner of her eye as he flirted with Lizzie and made a date to go out for a drink the next evening before exchanging numbers. Lizzie had asked Kat's permission with her eyes. They knew each other well enough to communicate with a glance and Kat smiled her encouragement. She was glad her friend could let loose after losing her job; she deserved some fun. And Chrístos was gorgeous. But he wasn't Kat's type: he wasn't Andreas.

After dinner, Kat and Lizzie spent their time in the little bedroom giving the walls a second coat of yellow paint along with the fitted wardrobes to keep the lines uninterrupted. They listened to music from their university days, singing and giggling until their stomach muscles ached. It was precisely the tonic Kat needed: a trip down memory lane with only tears of laughter for company and she felt lighter for it.

The little room wouldn't take long to complete. She'd already ordered a new bed and side tables online. Jamie could stay in this bedroom, if he came to the island with her parents and if she ever decided to forgive him – that was still up for discussion. The existing terracotta-tiled floor was perfect for the Mediterranean vibe she wanted to create. One less job for Kostas to tackle.

'How is it I am absolutely covered in paint, and you have only one splodge on your arm?' Kat asked as they sat on the tiles admiring their work.

'Because you're the clumsiest person I've ever met and don't apologise for it, whereas I'm pretending to be anything but me.'

'So not true, Lizzie. You're incredible and have the most magnetic charisma of anyone I've met.'

Lizzie slung her arm around Kat's shoulders.

'More than Andreas?' She giggled, slurring slightly as she'd started on a bottle of a Greek spirit – tsípouro – after she'd finished a couple more beers.

'I don't want anything from Andreas, thank you very much.'

'Bullshit,' she said waving her hand. 'He is one of the hottest guys on the planet who lives next door and clearly wants to date you from the teeny bits you've told me. For what it's worth, let me say this . . .'

'No more amateur psychology, Lizzie, I beg of you.'

'When was the last time you had any excitement with a guy? Your eyes light up when you mention Andreas. You must remember what it was like with Jamie at the beginning.'

Kat's mind reached backwards through the years: a chance encounter in the student union bar and she'd settled for him immediately, almost stopping life before it had begun.

'I don't think we ever had that. Not a single thunderbolt or earthquake; nothing ever really tingled. That's not being in love, that's friendship. I didn't know the difference at the time. Loving someone and being in love aren't the same thing.' Kat felt her colour rise as she recalled the physical reactions she'd had to Andreas, which could be dismissed as lust initially, but that had always been missing with Jamie. She'd married him because it seemed like the right thing to do. For everyone else but not for her.

'Then what *is* it you want? Manifest it from the Greek gods,' shouted Lizzie to the ceiling, her eyes glinting in the low light.

'I . . . I want passion,' Kat began tentatively. Out of the window, she saw the almost-half-moon rising and she directed her words to the lunar light. 'Someone who makes me want to throw them on a bed because I need to be with them, who makes me sad to go to sleep because I'll miss them, whose touch is the first thing I think about in the morning. Someone who looks at me and it's like the rest of the world doesn't exist and all that matters is being near one another, can't keep your hands off, can hardly breathe at the thought of being without them.' Kat turned to Lizzie, panting with the excitement of her imagination. '*That's* what I want.'

'Wow, that is a very specific list,' said Lizzie grinning. 'Anything else?'

'Yes, I also want a new lamp for that table.' Kat pointed at the console in the corner.

'Jesus Christ, you really need to get laid.'

Chapter 27

Early the following morning, Kat woke up happy, sing-songing 'good morning, sunshine' to the windows and jumping out of bed. Having Lizzie to stay was the ultimate balm for her wounds. Inspiration was coursing through her and after making a pot of coffee, she started writing in the kitchen immediately.

> *Unless you mend a table with a wonky leg, it will always be off balance. But how do you tackle it without a manual or the right tools? If you're resourceful and practical you may work it out, but rushing a quick fix will inevitably require further repairs in the future. Such is the journey of navigating a grieving heart. There is no textbook to show you how to move on. Because every version of grief is unique and related to the irreplaceable relationship you had with the person who is no longer alive. The Japanese repair method of kintsugi enhances the flaws of a once broken vessel with gold. Maybe we are better for our*

imperfections and more beautiful for having loved and lost. Nothing can teach us how to journey through bereavement. Nobody can do it for us, nor can we do it on another's behalf. We are given instruction on how to live, but there is no guide about how to journey onwards without each other.

Her writing was now flowing with ease, and Amelia said they would be posting the first piece in the next few days. Kat felt nervous, almost nauseous as she contemplated something so personal being shared. It was quite a departure from the usual advice she imparted, which was strictly limited to fixtures and furnishings; there had been no mention of her own life before. But she was filled with an energy that had been lacking for months and was determined to mend every aspect of life she could find, including the house.

Kostas and sons arrived at eight on the dot, and she made more coffee, letting them know about the delivery of furniture bound for the lounge. The unwanted pieces would be removed by a house clearance scrap merchant at some point today too. Then it would start to feel more like hers. There was still so much to be done but for now, she could add the final touches in the upstairs bathroom.

Kat filled three mismatched vintage glass canisters with water, then added a drop of food colouring into each to create three different tones of blue. Such a simple idea, but incredibly effective. She clustered them together on the tiled shelf above the sink, then added a cream stone dish, placing some locally made olive oil soap in it. She was yet to pick the succulent cuttings for the windowsill display, but as she looked around the bathroom, the varying neutral tones were warm and comforting. She sent pictures to Amelia to use for her forthcoming pieces online, delighted that the accessories photographed so beautifully.

Passing Lizzie's room, she heard the telltale signs indicating she was not alone in bed. They'd shared a dorm at university and Kat knew every noise in Lizzie's repertoire. She couldn't help but giggle as she tiptoed downstairs. She went to tell Kostas which furniture was destined for scrap while he was painting the lounge.

'This colour is very, very nice – it is white but yet not white as there is green. Quite wonderful. You have a very good eye for design, Miss Katerína. We will soon be able to begin on the kitchen, which will be the biggest of the jobs yet – and ahead of schedule!'

'I can't wait for it all to be finished and you've done so well. I'm really grateful to you and your sons.'

As she spoke, Kostas looked around. 'I don't know where Chrístos is. That boy! Always up to no good.'

'Oh, don't worry. He's just finishing something off in another room, I think. No rush.' Kat's cheeks warmed and she stifled a snicker as she excused herself to find Mrs Rálli.

She located her at the stove boiling split yellow peas.

'Mrs Rálli, you're making *fáva*, my favourite!'

The old woman turned and nodded as Kat took a seat at the table.

'There is much change in this house, so I try to keep some things the same. And what is the most consistent thing in our lives – food. And family of course.'

Kat wasn't sure what point she was trying to make and wondered if Mrs Rálli was aware of her mother's shenanigans decades ago.

'Is there a man called Yiánnis who lives on Agístri?' Kat asked tentatively.

Mrs Rálli whipped her head around. 'There are many, many called Yiánnis on the island. You could be speaking about anyone.' She turned back to her saucepan as if that was an end to the matter.

'What about Yiánnis Papandréou?' Kat saw the woman's shoulders tense at the name.

'My memory is not what it once was. I cannot be certain.'

'Mrs Rálli, please. I know about him and my mother,' said Kat, unable to believe she was saying those words aloud.

Setting her spoon beside the stove, Mrs Rálli lifted the pan and drained the water in the sink, huffing with exertion. Kat watched her closely and waited.

'The trouble with delving into the past, Katerína, is what you may find. And this is what you experience. I see in your face it has made you unhappy, yes?'

Kat nodded as Mrs Rálli shuffled over to join her.

'So, you can ask me as many questions as you wish, but you should be prepared not to like the answers. I also would suggest that you speak to your mother instead; it is a family matter and not one I wish to be involved in.'

There was a finality to her words. The tears swimming across Kat's vision betrayed the bravery she was attempting.

'My father has mentioned bringing my mother to the island. It'll be hard to talk plainly with him nearby.'

Mrs Rálli patted the top of Kat's hand.

'You will find a time when it is right. And it might be nice for me to see your mother again after so many years. She loves my food.' She burst into laughter, which was such a rare sound it made Kat doubt that were true. Yet another family connection. Kat sighed. They were all so interlinked, but she couldn't quite untangle the web. 'Your friend should be careful.' Mrs Rálli indicated the ceiling with her eyes.

'Chrístos? Why do you say that?'

'Let's just say he can lead people astray. He was at school with Andreas and things could have turned out very differently if your uncle hadn't stepped in. Bad influence.'

Kat was starting to realise that Mrs Rálli was the keeper of all secrets on Agístri and, in particular, those under this roof.

'In what way?'

Mrs Rálli stood with great effort. 'I need to make the *fáva* and then I make *lemonópita* – it is my specialty.' Kat's mouth watered. Another of her favourites, like her mother's orange pie; this was lemon-soaked citrus heaven.

'Let me go and pick some lemons for you, oh, and I need a trowel for the garden. Do you have one I could borrow?' asked Kat picking a basket from the hook on the wall.

'Garden equipment is in the shed around the side of the house, and I need eight lemons.'

There was a shed? Kat had been so consumed with the interior that she'd only got as far as the front lawn and hadn't even considered there could be more hiding around corners behind the shrubs. She stepped over brambles and through tall rustling bamboos to find a lean-to that barely qualified as a shed. But within the little hut, aside from several lizards, was everything required to make the garden neat again. She took what she needed to clip some succulents for the bathroom, then returned to the patio to pick the fruit.

The tree almost vibrated as she picked the beautiful lemons, and she rested her hand against it in thanks for the harvest. Patch the cat was lounging in the shade of the branches, watching her gather the fruit. Along the seafront, she saw Father Serafím walking with his tall wooden staff, marking each pace. She raised her hand, dropping one of the lemons, and he waved his stick aloft in greeting. She bent to pick the lemon up. On the ground beside it was another small pink pebble. Goose bumps rose on her skin. They seemed to appear when the priest was around, but then they'd also shown up when she'd thought about Nik. Patch fixed her with his yellow eyes and mewed.

'Sorry for disturbing you!'

He watched her put the pebble in her pocket before mewing again. Kat once again rested her hand against the trunk of the lemon tree.

'Hugging trees now, are we?' said Lizzie walking through the patio doors. Her striking red hair resembled a bird's nest. 'Who were you waving to?'

'Just the local priest. Maybe I should call him back so you can repent,' joked Kat.

'I have nothing to confess. A lady doesn't tell.'

'There was nothing lady-like about what I heard.'

Lizzie laughed. 'I wish I'd taken a greater interest in your culture years ago. God, I love the Greeks!'

'And on behalf of the motherland, we thank you for your sudden enthusiasm. Coffee?'

Lizzie nodded and Kat went to fetch her a cup, meeting Chrístos – who gave her a wide grin – in the hallway. As he swaggered away, Mrs Rálli's words echoed in her mind. He had an arrogance about him and Kat hoped Chrístos didn't get her friend into trouble, not that Lizzie wasn't capable of fending for herself.

Stepping back outside, she saw Lizzie with her hands

pressed against the lemon tree looking upwards. She turned her head to Kat.

'Are these limes or lemons?' she asked.

'Lemons. I know I sound like my dad, but they were known as golden apples in Greek mythology, I think – something to do with immortality.'

'Lemons, limes . . . the same but different,' Lizzie almost whispered. 'Like you and Nik. It's weird, but I get what you mean about him feeling near. It's almost like he's here.'

Kat raised an eyebrow at her friend. Her unexpected spiritual musings resonated with all she'd felt too since coming to Agístri. Finding the pink pebbles whenever she thought about her twin made her wonder if Nik was telling her to stay on the island, or urging her to flee? She needed to work that out for herself.

'I've decided that I'm going to speak to my father and get him to arrange coming with my mum to the island. And he can bring Jamie. Their trip is going to be on my terms,' said Kat determined to confront those who had wronged her or betrayed her in person.

'I like you in Greece; you're ballsy. I think that's a great idea,' Lizzie said. 'Oh, and I'm out with the sexy builder tonight. You don't mind do you?'

'You enjoy. There's tons to do.'

Lizzie exhaled dramatically for effect. 'And I've got Chrístos to do.'

Kat swiped her arm playfully, glad that their friendship was restored.

'Mrs Rálli warned me about Chrístos being a bad influence. Be careful, Lizzie,' Kat said.

'I can spot a bad boy a million miles away. Don't you worry about me, just worry about your next lot of visitors,' she replied as her eyes travelled in the direction of the sea. Then, a large grin spread over her face. 'Speaking of. I think there's someone here to see you.' She nodded towards the end of the garden and Kat turned around. Her eyes locked with her favourite shade of blue. Standing on the lawn and dressed in linen was Andreas.

Chapter 28

Lizzie's elbow poked Kat's side, nudging her forwards, but her legs felt like lead.

Andreas smiled, again so contrary to their last encounter and how it had ended. So far, spending time with him was like riding a roller coaster of emotions.

As Lizzie escorted Kat over to him, she whispered, 'Does he always wander around your garden?'

Though it was too late to reply as Andreas was now in earshot, yes, was the answer.

'Katerína, *yiássou*! I should have called, but I still don't have your number . . .' He was like a magnet, drawing her in as she neared. He then turned to Lizzie who thrust out her hand.

'Hi, I'm Lizzie Parish, Kat's best friend. *I* will send you her number.' She shook his hand, staring at him with unabashed scrutiny. She gave him her phone and Andreas surprisingly inputted his number. He was unknowingly giving his private line to a journalist, which he may not be too happy about.

'Good trip?' Kat had found her voice and discovered it

to be more clipped than she'd intended. 'I mean, how was your Athens thing?'

He dug into his pockets for nothing. He seemed nervous, which was so unlike him or at least what she knew of him so far. As he shrugged, the open neck of his white shirt revealed a tantalising glimpse of caramel skin. She heard Lizzie sigh beside her as he replied, 'Just work stuff. It's fine.'

They fell silent. Kat and Andreas stared at each other, waiting to see who would make the first move.

Lizzie rescued the quiet. 'I'm out tonight, so maybe you could keep Kat company. Otherwise, she'll be all alone covered in paint.' She smoothed her red hair from her face and Kat wondered if she was flirting a little. Turning to Lizzie, she shot her a furious look. Not at the preening but at her suggestion. Yet again her life was being orchestrated by a loved one. She was not a puppet for them or anybody. Lizzie got the message from Kat's glower.

'I'll leave you to it then. I'm off in a bit, so you have the place to yourselves.' She turned her back on Andreas and mouthed to Kat with a glint in her eye. '*Wow!*'

Skipping through the patio doors, Lizzie disappeared behind the new white muslin curtains Kostas had hung.

Kat met Andreas' eyes and could hardly take a breath. He was more beautiful than she recalled. The air felt like it was closing in around her, almost too thick to inhale as the sun illuminated the lawn. There was nowhere to hide from its glare nor was there shelter from Andreas.

'Your friend's funny,' Andreas said clearly amused by Lizzie's meddling, as his features shone in the light.

Kat laughed, breaking the tension. Gesturing for him to follow, she walked back to the terrace to seek out shade beneath the tree.

'Friend? Not sure after that performance. I honestly don't need company; I'm quite happy on my own. I've got loads of decorating to do and writing, in fact boring things that wouldn't interest you and . . .'

He suddenly stepped forwards and placed his hands on her shoulders.

'Shhhh, Katerína. I came to offer another apology. I'm sorry. You see how much I've grown? You've taught me the joy of saying sorry.'

It was all she could do not to shiver at his touch, though she was grateful he'd stopped her babbling.

Here they were once more. One apologising to the other, and repeat. A fascinating if not tedious circle they were stuck in.

'Maybe we should both stop doing things to be sorry for. It's all we've done since we met,' she said.

His lips parted as he considered her words. 'Then let's make a pact to do just that.'

Kat held out her hand to him and out of the corner of her eye, she saw the upstairs curtains twitch. Lizzie was watching and Kat wanted to tell her to mind her own business. 'Friends?'

He frowned, looking at her outstretched hand. 'Friends? Really, is that all?'

Kat felt her cheeks blush but stood firm. 'I think it's a start.' Kat dropped her hand. Her legs now felt like they were made of sherbet, fizzing and tingly.

'Ah, so you said, "a start",' he said. 'That means there is more to come – maybe not just friends in the end.'

'Look,' Kat began. 'It strikes me from what little I've learnt so far that your life is very complicated. As are you. I have enough going on without adding you and all your trophies into the mix.'

Andreas stepped even closer and towered above her. She caught the scent of lemons on the wind. From him or the tree, she didn't know and didn't care as her mind flooded with flashbacks from the passionate moments of their previous meetings, particularly their kisses on this terrace and at his house.

'I know you trust your heart, Katerína, but you fight it. What's the worst that could happen?'

My heart getting shattered! But she didn't explicitly say that aloud.

'The trouble is, you look like my next mistake and that scares me,' she said bravely.

'Making mistakes is sometimes the only way to learn. Maybe we are both afraid, Katerína, but you're the only one of us who admits it,' he replied with a wry smile.

'Why don't you come over later and help me finish painting the lounge?' She thought it unlikely he'd agree, but he surprised her.

'Deal!' He took her hand to seal their agreement, and the feel of his skin sent darts of desire through her. She wanted him to step even closer and . . . the list she'd spilled to Lizzie last night floated through her mind, increasing her heart rate further. He lifted the hand he was still holding and lowered his lips to her wrist. His long eyelashes almost touched his cheekbones as he kissed the bow and arrow tattoo. Kat sucked in a breath at his touch. He opened his eyes to reveal his dazzling stare as his mouth lingered above the moon.

* * *

Lizzie came bounding down the stairs ready for her date as Kat pushed the modern light grey sofa into position in the lounge.

'Amelia's just put your piece online and everyone is going nuts for it! It's been shared over twenty thousand times. Kat, it's just incredible. Holy shit! So is this lounge.' Lizzie twirled in a circle, speedily taking in the new room before whipping around to face Kat. 'Have you seen the editor's note about Nik?'

Kat had been so engrossed in rearranging her new furniture now the old had been removed, that she hadn't checked her phone. She didn't know where it was in fact. Her mouth dried and she suddenly felt nauseous at the thought of her private musings being read by strangers, open to dismissal or unkind scrutiny. Lizzie thrust her iPad towards her and Kat digested the words on the screen, her mouth drying in anticipation as she read Amelia's introduction.

Our immensely talented lifestyle editor, Katerina Konstantópoulos has turned her attention to renovation and rejuvenation. In a new exclusive online feature, we will follow Katerina's journey in her motherland of Greece as she decorates a house from top to bottom. But this isn't just any grand redesign; this is so much more. Allow me to be personal for a moment. Katerina's twin brother, Nikólaos, was tragically killed in a car accident last October and for those of us who knew and loved him, our lives haven't been the same since. He could walk into a room and make it gleam, as though sunshine lived in his heart, lighting everyone with his energy. It's impossible to think we will never hear his laughter again. But for Katerina, the world is half empty. As twins, they shared everything, and should have shared a house on an idyllic Greek island, left to them by their uncle, the notable Greek literary fiction writer, Pétros Tzanos, who died last December. Katerína is taking on a mammoth solo project and is sharing her journey with us all. This isn't simply about tips and tricks to make a house a home, this is about rebirth through renovation – literally and spiritually. I want to thank her for her candid writing, and I know you will all take so much more from her than just the usual exceptional taste she brings to this magazine. Together we will share her Grecian odyssey and I can't wait to hear what you think.

   With love, Amelia

   Editor-in-Chief, *Love Interiors*

Tears pricked like needles at the backs of Kat's eyes as Amelia's description of Nik rang through her mind. He had been Kat's sunshine, yet he'd also been everybody's. She was flattered by the introduction, but began to worry about how it would be received. Lizzie's hand rested on her shoulder.

'Don't get in your head, Kat. I promise you it's brilliant. I want to read more.' She pulled the tablet back from Kat and scrolled through the article again. 'And the comments are amazing, thousands already. It's your dream and you're living it; show the world who you really are.'

'I don't think I want to show anyone that,' she replied, reluctantly taking the compliment. But Lizzie was right. This was her opportunity to experiment and write something totally different within the safety of what she knew and loved. A hybrid of new and old; precisely what she was doing with Pétros' house. She felt a bubble of excitement at the thought of her long-held ambition to write take shape. Then she noticed Lizzie's eyes were red and Kat realised she must have been crying when she'd read the article upstairs. Amelia, Lizzie and Jamie were all part of Nik and Kat's world, and it was time she acknowledged their pain as much as her own. There was comfort to be found within shared sorrow. Though she didn't feel quite so generous towards Jamie at present, but that may be remedied soon when she gave her father the green light to bring him along with her mother to Agístri.

She only hoped she was prepared for their trip. There was no escaping any of them on a tiny Greek island.

Chapter 29

While Lizzie was out to meet Chrístos for an early drink, then onwards to sample what nightlife there was on Agístri, Kat was digging in one of the sea walls. She planned to gently extract three bulging succulent heads.

'*Kalispéra*, Katerína,' came a voice wishing her a good evening. She looked up to see Father Serafím peeping over the wall at her.

'*Yiássas, Papa* Serafím, how are you?'

'As always, on my rounds. I see you have discovered an island treasure, Katerína.'

She felt like she'd been caught robbing apples from a neighbour's orchard.

'I hope it's all right. I'm just taking a few cuttings for the house.'

Father Serafím waved his hand. 'The plants do not belong to me or indeed to any of us. They are there to be loved and nurtured, tended by those who have the foresight to notice them. Even the weeds are not to be dismissed, though I don't suppose you wish for those in your garden.' He laughed and the sound resembled the wind. It was almost a whistle, and the strangest laugh she'd ever heard.

'I might let the side passages of the house stay wild for the bees and butterflies,' she said and the priest clapped his hands.

'Bees are the true industry of nature, generously giving us their bountiful gifts in the form of honey and as for the butterfly . . . we admire them for their beauty and then we forget them as they flit away. Yet butterflies have a life destined to be cut short, so beautiful, fragile and precious, not with us for long. It is why we should appreciate them while they are here.' His cloudy eyes sparkled as he beamed at Katerína. 'I see you picking fruit from the lemon tree in your garden. It is very special, one of the oldest trees on our island.'

Kat smiled. Busted again.

'Mrs Rálli wanted to make *lemonópita* and who am I to resist that?'

Again, the priest chuckled to himself. A breeze lifted the sleeves of his robes.

'Temptation is spoken of much in scripture, but can sometimes be impossible to resist, especially when it seems like the right course to take. Yet then comes consequence, and one cannot help but wonder if it would have been better to relent.'

For one so lyrical, his sense was clear. It was almost as if he'd spoken Kat's thoughts about her mother aloud, yet they'd been talking about lemon cake. Hadn't they? As she contemplated his words, she looked to her hands, which were coated in earth. A trickle of blood interrupted the layer of dirt. She had somehow cut her wrist beside the moon in her tattoo.

'Oh.' She winced as it stung in the salty air. Looking up to ask if Father Serafím might have a tissue, she discovered the top of the wall was empty. Clambering up the slope armed with her succulent cuttings, she scanned the seafront, but he was out of sight. He must have popped into someone's house to check on his flock. For his age, he was lithe, able to appear and disappear with ease like an apparition. Cupping her scratched wrist that was still beading with blood, she deposited the plants on the patio table back at the house. A blue butterfly had landed on a thick branch of the lemon tree that reached under the awning like a woody finger. She stopped to watch the insect open and close its wings, recalling Father Serafím's words, which prompted a new thought in her mind.

The fragility and beauty of life is all around, but why does it take a tragedy to make us stop and notice our surroundings, the people in our lives, or what is special to us? Never have truer words been spoken than 'you don't know what you've got until it's gone'.

Kat wrote in her head, then rushed indoors to commit the passage to paper before she forgot. As she sought something to make a note with in the hallway, she overheard voices coming from the kitchen and stopped still. It was Mrs Rálli and Andreas.

'No, Andreas. She has had enough in her life with her brother, her uncle and now what she has discovered about her mother. It is not for me to say what. Her burden is enough.'

'I need to be honest,' he said firmly.

'You should be careful about what you are prepared to reveal. Which version will you tell? The truth or what some others believe? It is too dangerous.'

Kat crept closer to the kitchen, not wanting to miss a word yet fearful of being discovered. As she pressed herself against the wall, the stone was a cold shock to her exposed skin, and she had to stifle a yelp.

'I plan to tell her everything tonight. I care about Katerina and don't want any secrets in my life. Or in hers.' His voice was so tender that Kat had to call on all her resolve not to run to him.

Kat heard Mrs Rálli tut several times.

'It could ruin so much for you, Andreas, if the wrong story gets out. Then what was Pétros' sacrifice for? Nothing! If it weren't for him, who knows where you would have ended up, but it would certainly not be on the pedestal our people have put you upon.'

Kat had never heard Mrs Rálli say so much nor with such venom. Instead of anger, she felt ashamed for eavesdropping, so tiptoed backwards, taking care not to knock into anything until she was outside again. She looked to the lemon tree, but the butterfly had gone and she wished she could retrace her paces to the moments before she'd heard anything. More secrets awaited; Andreas said he was going to tell her. She rushed around the side of the house and sought solace in the shed. Settling on a lumpy bag of compost, she examined her wrist, which had now stopped bleeding. She ought to clean the cut but didn't want to face anyone. She shifted awkwardly on the plastic beneath her, stifled in the musty confines of the hut. Yet again, everything had changed, shifting further into deception. How many more secrets could one island hide?

Chapter 30

She waited until she heard Mrs Rálli's car drive away. Levering herself upright in the shed, Kat managed to pull down a shelf laden with pots in the process. With muted thuds, they bounced off the floor, which was covered in old tarpaulin and hessian sacks.

Dusk was falling and the outside temperature, although still balmy, was a welcome respite compared to the suffocating atmosphere of the garden lean-to. There was no sign of Andreas either. It seemed that he'd been withholding more than just his profession. But they weren't even together; she had no right to delve into his secret history any more than he did hers. Though she had nothing to tell. But he said he cared about her, and the idea that his feelings were growing in line with hers gave her a warm but uneasy glow in the pit of her stomach.

Whilst in the little hut, she'd become even more determined to untangle the web of lies and deceit. Secrets were too exhausting. She walked back over to the lemon tree to see if the butterfly had returned. It had not. Looking at the branches, she wanted to ask her father about the origin of the golden apple mythology, but more importantly she wanted to tell him to come to the island. She dialled his mobile, hoping he would pick up rather than her mother intercepting the call, and she was in luck.

'Katerína *mou*, how is it on Agístri? Are you feeling that you are home again?'

Kat couldn't answer his first question with complete honesty so opted to respond to the second.

'It does feel like home, *Babá*, and I can't wait for you to see the house.' She took a steeling breath. 'I want you to come with *Mána* to the island. And I hear that Jamie wants to visit so you may as well bring him too. As soon as you can. I think it's time *Mána* came back, don't you?'

'Your mother is very worried about you. But yes, it is a most wonderful plan. I will organise it immediately. I have already looked at the flights and had a quiet word with Cousin Eléni to see if she could look after the restaurant – just in case the moment arose. And I may have said something in passing to Jamie too. So, our great minds are thinking alike!' Kat rolled her eyes but laughed. She should have known her father would take it upon himself to start a plan before it was a fully formed thought in her own head. 'Katerína, I hope you and your mother can make things right. Did you have a disagreement? She will not say, but it is obvious to me.'

Kat hesitated, but it was pointless to deny. 'Sort of. I think she's feeling a bit churned up about the island and Pétros. It will be good for her to finally put the past behind her when she gets here.'

She waited for him to respond and noted his pause.

'There are burdens for us all to bear, Katerína. We all have our histories. Is like a crack in a slab of marble, what put it there could be an earthquake, a defiant act of God or simply carelessness at the hands of man. Behind everything there is a tale that leaves a scar forever. It is our duty to learn to live with the marks of time.'

He sounded like he was writing a piece for Kat's column, and she found herself moved by his wisdom.

'You should have been a writer, *Babá*. You have such a way with words.' For all the jokes she and Nik had made behind his back or the secret snorts they'd shared when their father would launch into one of his stories about Greece, she found that when she listened properly, he had a beautiful rhetoric. And Father Serafím's lesson about appreciating those in our lives had worked its way into Kat's psyche. She was surrounded by wise men, aside from Jamie. And possibly Andreas. She didn't know what she could learn from either of them.

'I leave the writing to you, *anghelouthi mou*. Your article was quite something. I take credit of course for your philosophical musings, but you have a style that is all yours.' His voice wavered as he continued. 'And I am very proud of you. We all are. Your strength teaches us all so much. That you get from your mother.'

But Kat hadn't inherited her mother's appetite for deception, though she couldn't say that aloud. Instead, she led her father back to the Greek myth.

'I wanted to ask you about golden apples. There's this amazing lemon tree in the garden. It's like the whole house has been built around it.' She knew her father would relish the opportunity to share the tale.

'Ah, I remember that tree, is almost sacred on Agístri. The mythology is not so straightforward, yet I am pleased you ask . . .' He wove the myth as if he were inventing it himself, adding that the garden of Hesperides where the apples grew was akin to Eden, riddled with temptation. When eaten, the apples could bestow innate wisdom but were the property of the gods and fiercely guarded by a serpent.

'There is always a price to pay for vanity and yielding to temptation,' her father concluded. An unkind thought formed in her brain that he'd best tell her mother that, but Kat bit her tongue.

'Thanks for the story, *Babá*, but I better go. I need to feed the cat – you'd love him. He has three colours – brown, white and black. I called him Patch.'

'A tri-colour cat means success; is very lucky.'

'I could certainly do with some of that.'

'I am sad you only have a cat for company. You shouldn't be alone at this time, Katerína.'

'Lizzie's here and my neighbour said he might pop over.'

'He? You said he, Katerína. Is he Greek?'

Kat sighed wishing she hadn't mentioned him.

'Greek American and he's just a friend.'

'Greek American is better than no Greek at all.'

She couldn't help but laugh. 'Bye *Babá*.' They ended the call, and nervous butterflies began to flit around her stomach, even though there were none to be seen in real life. She felt the beat of their silken wings deep inside at the thought of Andreas and what she may find beneath his carefully crafted façade.

* * *

The crackle of vinyl interspersed with Greek folk music blasted from the stereo as Kat dipped the paintbrush into the pot. Her new furniture was in place but covered with protective dust sheets while she applied the final coat of white paint with a hint of mint to the lounge walls. The old record cabinet was painted a shade of light grey similar to that of the sofa fabric. She loved the retro feel juxtaposed against her modern makeover.

Kat was having fun, losing herself in the work rather than contemplating the conversation she'd overheard between Mrs Rálli and Andreas. Again, she had nobody to press for answers apart from Andreas and things were only just back on an even keel. Though he'd said he planned to tell her, as yet, he hadn't turned up. Maybe it was for the best, but as soon as she thought it, she knew she was lying to herself.

Her phone beeped with a message from her father.

We all arrive in two days! Greece beckons us home. I will email you all the details. We stay for a little over two weeks!

Her phone immediately pinged again with the confirmation from Jamie too. The smoke signals between him and her family seemed to be instantaneous.

Can't wait to see you and catch up properly! J x

You can stay with me and Lizzie – we need to talk! replied Kat hoping he took the hint that despite her invitation via her father, all was not well between them.

But she'd made it happen and taken charge of her family for the first time in forever, and felt a deep satisfaction at her decisiveness. Despite the confrontations she would need to have with her mother and Jamie, it was high time they all faced each other along with their past.

She heard a sharp rap on the open terrace doors, which made her jump despite the music filling the room. Kat burst out laughing at what she saw.

'What?' Andreas asked grinning, knowing full well what she'd found funny. He was dressed in pristine navy overalls with a white vest beneath and an empty tool belt around his waist as if he were playing a role.

'This isn't a costume party!' Kat giggled. 'It's a far cry from the linen but it's too much.' She couldn't help her persistent laughter as she stood to greet him, clutching the paintbrush to her chest. He'd moved so close that she could count his eyelashes. He kissed her on one cheek, then the other, pulling back to look at her. It was painfully slow, teasing and tantalising. Then he leant forward and brushed her lips with his. It was a forward movement given their tumultuous history, yet somehow it seemed right. She pushed away her concerns about what she'd heard, trusting he would reveal the truth to her as he'd assured Mrs Rálli he would. But for now, she couldn't refuse the delicious moment. As he smoothed her hair from her forehead, she felt like he was looking inside her.

'I thought about you every moment when I was away, Katerína. There's something about you that I can't shake. What is it with you?' He ran his thumb across her cheekbone as he cupped her face, and she shivered, wanting to forget about decorating.

'I . . . I thought about you too.'

He leant his head down to meet her mouth and pulled her to him, their kiss deepening with every second. Kat longed to run her hands through his hair, feel his shoulders, caress his tanned muscular arms, but she couldn't and realised why. She was still holding a paintbrush, which was crushed between them depositing splodges on their clothing. She burst into laughter once more, stepping backwards.

'So, kissing me is funny is it?' he said puzzled before following her eyes to look at his chest. There he found a huge splat of paint.

'Sorry about your brand-new dungarees. At least they're more authentic now,' Kat joked as he moved towards her again, removing the paintbrush from her hands. As he kissed her again, she felt the tickle of bristles beneath her chin and he trailed the brush slowly along her neck, downwards across her chest, over the top of her singlet to her middle.

'Andreas!' she exclaimed pulling the paintbrush away and flicking speckles of paint at him.

'This will not end well for you, Kat,' he promised mischievously and plunged his hand into the paint pot, re-emerging with a fistful of white that he held out to her. It trickled along his wrist and droplets plopped onto the dust covers spread over the floor. Kat submerged her hand to match his. They laughed as they circled one another, feinting, then dodging and darting around the covered furniture. Kat shrieked as he managed to catch her around the waist with one arm and gave her a coloured sleeve with his paint-coated hand.

She whipped around slipping in his grip and with a wicked glint in her eye she reached up to kiss him. He was unable to resist and grabbed at her waist to pull her against his body. She didn't want to stop but the competitive part of her couldn't let him have it all his way. As they kissed, she deposited her handful of paint on his head, deliberately smearing the side of his face, covering his ear and eventually giving him a matching painted arm. Their lips didn't part for a moment, and she pushed her fingers into his dark hair then gripped the back of his neck as he lifted her off the floor and carried her to the sofa. They moved seamlessly as if they were one person. Landing, Kat felt cocooned in plastic dust sheets. They stuck to every part of their bodies as she clung to Andreas above her. He suddenly pushed up to his knees.

'OK, you win. I can't hear anything.' He tilted his head to one side and tapped at the other ear to dislodge the paint that must have trickled inside.

'I got a bit carried away,' said Kat.

He looked at her, his blue eyes twinkling. 'You bet you'll be carried away.'

Kat was unsure what he meant, whether the game was over or if he was being serious. Before she could unpick his words, he jumped up and scooped her into his arms. He ran out of the doors into the garden, across the lawn and down the steps to the beach. She barely noticed her surroundings as she begged for him to put her down. But she didn't mean a word of it, wishing she could stay in his embrace for the rest of the evening. He splashed into the water still holding her and waded out waist deep.

'One, two . . .' He swung her back and forth, threatening to fling her into the depths. At the last moment, as her muscles tensed, preparing to be dunked, he gently sunk to his knees, allowing the warm sea to swirl around them. She held on to his paint-covered neck and looked at him, breathless from their ridiculous game. His face became serious as he kissed her again, loosening his hold, and Kat wrapped her legs around his waist. Their shoulders submerged as the water tinged pink from the sun's dying light. She had never felt anything like this before. Andreas was different. His touch sent darts of electricity into her body, waking up every corner that had been shrouded in grief and unacquainted with true passion. He cupped a hand of seawater and washed her neck clean, kissing the skin beneath as he loosened her hair from its clip. Her curls cascaded down her back, pooling on the ocean surface. He repeated the action across her chest, his lips replacing the paint then tracing her tan lines until her desire rose to the highest point tolerable.

'What did you do here?' he asked finding the plaster beside her tattoo.

'Just a scratch, it's nothing,' she said huskily; her scrape was the last thing on her mind. He raised her wrist to his lips and kissed around the small circular Band-Aid. She mirrored his action from moments before and trickled the crystal-clear water over his face, his neck and shoulders in a kind of unholy baptism until neither could stand the teasing.

As they faced each other, the intensity of their connection consumed them both. The air was charged with an energy that made it almost impossible to breathe. But the thoughts Kat had tried to suppress sprung forward, bringing a dose of reality alongside.

'I care about Katerína and don't want any secrets in my life. Or in hers.'

The conversation she'd overheard couldn't go unmentioned. She didn't want things to progress until she knew who she was letting into her life. Passion had overruled her rational mind but she wouldn't allow herself to be hurt. Although she feared it was almost too late; the dam she'd sworn to build around her heart was weakened. She began to tremble as the sun finally disappeared behind the headland and a wind whistled across the water.

'Come on, let's get you warm,' he said and scooped her up once more.

'You don't have to carry me everywhere. I am capable of walking, you know,' Kat said squirming in his arms.

'But there's always a risk of you tripping over.' She relented and allowed him to carry her back to the house.

'I'll get some towels,' she said when they reached the patio, still in his arms. 'You need to let me go or we'll freeze.'

'I don't want to let you go, Katerína.'

His words almost winded her. He said all the right things, though they could be lines from a film for all she knew. He kissed her as he placed her down then stared for a moment.

'Katerína, I really need to talk to you.'

Chapter 31

Andreas was beside the lemon tree when Kat returned having stripped off and flung a kaftan over dry underwear. Without any men's clothes in the house, she'd grabbed a hammam towel for him.

She handed it to Andreas. 'Do you want a beer?'

He shook his head. 'I have to drop a few kilos for my next film, so I'm off the booze like you.'

'I have *Fix horís*,' she said offering him a Greek brand without alcohol. 'I'll get you one.' In the kitchen as she poured drinks, their looming discussion hovered like a spectre. He had worked his way into her heart, and she hated to admit she'd developed feelings for him.

She walked outside, watching as he took a seat at the terrace table wrapped in just the towel she'd given him. He looked pensive but it was better off he told her what she needed to know, before things became more complicated.

She placed both glasses down and sat opposite Andreas, gesturing for him to take one. 'What did you want to talk about?' she asked, deciding to start the conversation.

'Your writing is beautiful.' He rested his hands on the

table before taking a small sip of beer. 'I read your piece online and it really touched my heart. The way you write about grief is so . . . universal. I felt it. I think you've found what you're meant to do. And the comments from readers, it's been shared everywhere online; you've really connected with people.'

'Have you been researching me . . . ?' she said, flattered he'd read her work.

'Maybe a little,' he said. His slowly spreading smile was deeply seductive; it sent the butterflies in her stomach into a frenzy.

'You didn't want to chat about my writing, Andreas . . .'

He sighed. 'I wanted to be honest with you about my past, how I came to be in Pétros' care,' he then paused as the music in the lounge finished and the sound of cicadas filled the quiet like relentless percussive heartbeats. 'If this is going to go somewhere, you and me that is, you need to know who I am. The real me, or who I was once, at least, and the moments that brought me to this place, here, with you now.'

Kat gave him the time to develop and order his thoughts, knowing any interruption could cause him to retreat into his shell. She picked up her glass with both hands, hoping not to break it or the moment.

'I've told you some, but there's more. After my father died, I started to act out; hanging with the wrong crowd . . .' He looked down at his drink, clasping it hard. 'I was a teenager and I needed to grieve for my father, but my mother was set on playing happy families with this new guy of hers. I wanted no part of it. So I hardly went home; I was out all the time with friends. Or people I thought were my friends. The only thing that gave me joy was studying acting, but I couldn't see a way to make a living from it, so I tried to hide it from everyone. On a small island like Agístri you have few choices for work. I wanted to get away from here: it represented all I'd lost. I grew to hate my mother and blamed her for everything. The only person who let me be myself was Pétros, and I believe he saved my life. I owe him.'

Kat digested his words, but there seemed to be a gaping hole in his story. Bad behaviour, fast-forward to Pétros. She had to know what happened in between; that was where the truth lay.

'What did my uncle do to help you?' she asked.

Andreas hung his head. 'The gang I hung out with used to graffiti his home, this house, or throw litter on the lawn. We knew he was gay, and I guess we carried on the persecution because we thought he was different. It was cruel and I'm ashamed to have played my part in that.' He broke off and took a drink. 'One day, I was so low, the lowest I'd ever felt. My friends dared me to steal his car; the one Mrs Rálli drives now. It was brand new in those days and hardly anyone had a new car on the island.' His eyes watered as he met her stare. He looked tortured, in physical pain from his recollections. 'It's all a bit hazy and happened so fast. But the car crashed into that wall down there and your uncle came out of the house. My friends all ran away, leaving me to face the consequences alone and take the blame for it all, which I was happy to do. I felt responsible and guilty for everything we'd done to him, and I didn't want to betray my friends or get them in trouble. I just didn't care what happened to me anymore. I told Pétros it was me; I was the culprit and had acted alone. Instead of calling the police, which he had every right to do, your uncle talked to me instead; I mean really talked to me. He asked me what I was so angry about. Nobody had ever bothered to ask me that.'

He paused to look at the lemon tree before picking up the story again. 'Pétros said he was sorry to hear about my father and it all poured out. I sat on the sofa in there.' He pointed to the lounge, which no longer resembled the room it once was. 'I cried for my dead father, for the family I'd lost and the new one I didn't want. But most of all, I told him how I wanted to be something better. That's when I confessed my dream that I'd never spoken aloud: to be an actor.'

Andreas rubbed his eyes and Kat reached for his hand.

'Your uncle promised me that after my national service, he would send me to drama college in London if I got in. But my mom was set on going to America. Pétros insisted he would become my guardian if I stayed, as I was still only sixteen, and he promised to ensure I completed my education. I think Mom was glad to have me off her hands to focus on her new family so she agreed. Pétros paid for me to fly to England and audition for drama schools and I won a place that I deferred until after the army. He gave me somewhere to stay, a place to call home. That's all I've ever wanted – somewhere or someone to belong to.' Andreas sat back in his chair and his shoulders dropped a little. 'The rest, I guess, is history.'

Kat was moved. Andreas targeting her poor uncle for his sexuality was awful, but Pétros' generosity shone through along with his capacity for forgiveness; it was nothing short of inspiring and it made her wish again that she'd known her uncle. To crash Pétros' car was dangerous and stupid and Kat shivered as her mind briefly showed her Nik's body in the wreckage of the accident. But the circumstances were different; it wasn't the same at all. Andreas was lucky nobody got hurt. She took his other hand and held both.

'My uncle clearly adored you. He saw what I can see

now: someone who needed to be loved and cared for,' she said realising how quickly she was falling for him.

'You are so like him in a lot of ways,' Andreas said tenderly. 'Kind, caring, talented . . .'

The solar lights around the garden flickered into life, and branches cast shadows across the terrace.

'Why acting?' she asked.

'Simple psychology, I guess. Acting meant I could choose to be anyone. Anyone but me. I could escape, not think about my father's death or my mother's new marriage and the kids she went on to have. I could conjure up a new world for myself within each script. It was my release from this island prison.'

'But you still live here,' she said, and he laughed.

'It's funny, no matter how far I ran towards work, overseas or anywhere in the world this was the only place that felt like home. And that's because of your uncle. I didn't deserve his kindness, but he opened up his life to me. You can imagine that there were rumours of course about us; you thought it too when we first met. Those lies were mainly spread by my so-called friends, who'd stopped speaking to me by then, but I didn't care. I realised it didn't matter who he loved or preferred; his soul was good. I'm living testimony to his generosity. If it weren't for him, I hate to think what could have happened. He saved me, Katerína. I just wish I'd got to say goodbye.' His voice choked, and she moved to fold him into her arms.

It struck Kat as sad that he'd been lacking not only guidance but love at a time when he needed it most. No child should lose their parent so young. She couldn't imagine being without hers despite the current frostiness she felt towards her own mother.

Andreas' fragility and honesty meant he was imperfect, which made him even more attractive. His looks were only the surface; locked inside there was still a sensitive little boy who craved acceptance. Pétros had paved the way for Andreas to find himself and unearth his own joy, and in a way her uncle had done the same for her. If he hadn't left her the house, her life wouldn't have been given this new purpose, which wasn't just about decorating or design, but about writing, rediscovering herself and letting go of the past to lead her towards her future.

* * *

'We have to eat at some point, so I'm taking over your kitchen,' Andreas said after Kat had given him a tour of the downstairs. 'I can't believe what you've done; it looks nothing like it used to.'

After grabbing what he needed from the fridge, he cracked some eggs into a bowl and indicated Kat should whisk them. She enjoyed being bossed around the kitchen by him – it was preferable to Mrs Rálli. As he sliced onions, peppers, tomatoes, olives and cut a block of feta, the aromas wafted around the room. It was incredibly distracting to watch him cook bare-chested. She wondered how tightly fastened the towel was at his waist.

'I shouldn't ask, but I'm intrigued. Exactly how famous are you?' said Kat as she finished her task.

'I don't think they've invented a measurement for it yet,' he laughed. 'In Greece . . . pretty well known. Outside of that, unclear. The movie I shot in America is about to be released and if it's well received, things might change. Or not. I try not to think about it. At first it was novel being recognised; it felt good, but sometimes it can be overwhelming.'

As he lit the stove and drizzled olive oil into the pan, Kat set the kitchen table and took a seat. 'Fame is weird, isn't it? It's such a temporary idea, and there's so many celebrities these days, it's impossible to keep track, so I don't.'

Andreas fried the onions, tinging the air with sweet tempting smells. 'It's better that way I think. It's why I stay pretty low-key when I'm here. And you know, I liked that you had no idea who I was. You gave me a reality check before my head got too big.'

'I bet you haven't been spoken to like that in a long time – the way I did at the airport . . . or on the harbour . . . or on the front lawn . . . we've been pretty unpleasant to each other, haven't we?'

He turned from the stove to look at her after adding peppers and tomatoes to the pan. 'I think our moods kind of collided in great ways and some not so great ways. I like the good bits. A lot.' He pointed at her with the spatula. 'Why are you so far away? Get over here.'

She jumped up to sit on the work surface beside the cooker to be closer to him. He poured the egg mixture into the frying pan, adding a dusting of dried oregano.

'Mrs Rálli would have a fit if she saw me up here and you with hardly any clothes on,' Kat said with a laugh. 'She's a funny one. I can't quite get the measure of her . . . and I don't get why she wears black since she isn't widowed.'

'She's had a lot of sadness, and was super close with Pétros,' Andreas said carefully. 'She means well underneath her stern exterior.'

Andreas then sprinkled black olives and some feta into the omelette before expertly folding it in half. He pushed it under the grill and moved to stand in front of Kat. She slid her hands around his neck and trailed her fingers across his broad shoulders and down his arms. He stepped between her legs. They were at eye level and as she kissed him, being at the same height felt deliciously strange. Though she was hungry, the last thing she wanted was an omelette and salad. His effect on her was immediate as her hands wandered over each curve and muscle of his exposed body, before resting on his taut waist. As he pulled back to retrieve their food, she took a seat in the dining nook.

'By the way, you might want to make yourself scarce for a few days. My parents are coming to visit on Wednesday.'

He dressed the salad then sat opposite her at the table, setting the plates down. The glistening heap of oiled peppery rocket was mouthwatering along with the enticing aroma of the herb-scented eggs. He signalled she should eat as he replied, 'Then I'd love to meet your folks if you'd like me to.'

Kat took a mouthful of food, trying to conceal her delight. This was moving fast, and she wasn't sure what it was but it felt right. She chewed slowly, savouring the taste and working up to telling him who else was inbound. 'And you should know that my almost ex-husband, Jamie, is coming too.'

Andreas' head shot up from his plate. 'That is less exciting. But he is welcome to the island, I'm sure.'

Kat didn't quite believe him and wondered whether he was the jealous type.

'I know it's hard to understand but he's been part of my family since I was at university. Nobody did anything bad, no big dramas. We weren't meant to be together, that's all. I promise you, there's no feelings left for me other than friendship,' Kat explained hoping this didn't set her and Andreas back again.

'And how does he feel?' he asked.

'The same. Maybe you should ask him,' she teased but he shook his head.

'I need to trust you, so I believe you. I can't imagine you looking at anyone else the way you look at me,' he said resting his fork on the table. Kat couldn't remove her eyes from his.

'What do you expect? You're basically naked; it's hard to concentrate on anything else,' she replied as her gaze travelled to his mouth and back again. 'I kind of like the way you look at me too.'

'Kind of? We need to make that definite. You didn't finish your food.' He stood to gather the plates and put them in the sink. Kat slid her arms around him from behind, allowing her fingers to travel up to his chest, exploring his body as she burrowed her face in his back. She could taste the sea on his skin, the scent of ozone and citrus and another note that was uniquely him. He turned around and took her face in his hands. As she looked up at him, she felt emboldened by their honest exchange about his teenage years. She trusted him too, and believed he felt something significant for her.

'I didn't finish the grand tour. We haven't been upstairs yet,' she said.

His eyes sparkled with mischief. 'It would be a terrible shame not to finish what you started, Katerína.'

She took his hand and led him straight to her bedroom with no intention of showing him any of the other rooms. They could wait. She could not.

Artemis and Apollo

Falling in love at first sight was commonplace amongst the gods, and for Artemis, a mortal named Orion became the target of her affections. Like her, he was a hunter who embraced the moonlight as opposed to the day.
On one occasion, the ever-competitive Apollo convinced his sister to try and shoot a black shape in the water for fun, suggesting she'd never hit it. Artemis gladly took the challenge and found her mark first time. But the moving target in the sea was Orion. She had been tricked, such was her innocent nature; she would have believed anything she was told by those she loved.
Artemis learnt the hardest of ways that being too hasty, too trusting and not weighing up the consequences could have a heartbreaking outcome.

Chapter 32

'*Kaliméra*, you,' said Andreas as the sunlight crept across the bed. Kat squinted in the morning sunshine. She hadn't closed the curtains last night; she'd been too preoccupied with Andreas.

'*Kaliméra* to you too,' Kat said as she stretched her hands high above her head then rubbed her eyes. He looked so perfect, and she hated to think what her hair resembled. She'd slept entwined in his arms and there hadn't been a single nightmare to break her bliss.

'I like waking up with you,' he said propping himself up on his elbow, then running his fingers along the inside of her arm. It was too ticklish, almost painful yet utterly heavenly to feel his touch. She giggled. If this was a dream, she didn't want it to end.

He leant down and kissed her, rolling over to cover her with his body. Their passions rose as he retook the space within her that he had left merely a couple of hours prior. As Andreas moved gently and slowly, in contrast to their frantic fervour the previous evening, the world seemed to work in slow motion, with only him in it.

Kat abandoned herself to every sensation pulling at her insides, teasing and goading, daring to build with delicious intensity. She held Andreas as close as she could, clutching his back as he moved above her, their skin connected as if they'd become one person. He lifted his face from her neck to watch as she arched her back, inviting every second of pleasure into her body. She looked into his clear blue eyes as she crested over the peak of the wave, before matching his rhythm once again as they ascended together. Something between them shifted while she basked within the purity of the sensation, so exquisite it was almost agony; words were unspoken by their lips, but their bodies said all they were too afraid to give voice to.

After dozing, the sheen of sweat drying from their skin, Kat stirred.

'I need a shower then coffee. You?' she asked lifting her head from his chest.

'Yes to both,' he said pushing the bed sheet from his tanned waist. The sight of his body against the crisp white linen almost made her jaw drop; he couldn't be real. She felt her desire flicker into life again.

The new walk-in shower met with both their approval and though they may have used every last drop of hot water, Kat thought it was the best bathroom she'd ever created. Showering would never be the same.

'Let me get you that coffee,' he said after, wrapping a thick fluffy towel around him.

'No!' she almost shouted. 'Mrs Rálli might be here, and I can't face the inquisition. And I don't know if Lizzie had an overnight guest either.'

She threw on her kimono-style dressing gown and combed her wet hair, watching him behind her in the mirror as he kissed along her shoulder. They looked good together, but Kat checked herself, trying not to jump ahead. Her situation was about to become even more complicated with Jamie arriving tomorrow and her parents staying at the hotel along the seafront. Nothing in her life, it seemed, was destined to be straightforward. And now Andreas was in the mix. Her muscles ached but without the hint of pain she'd become accustomed to after the accident. She noticed a glimmer in her eyes that had been missing for far too long. Extracting herself from further temptation, she left him in her bedroom promising to return with caffeine. Lizzie's bedroom door was closed with no sounds of life. She'd either stayed out or was still unconscious.

Downstairs, Mrs Rálli was bustling around tutting at the abandoned omelette pan and plates in the sink.

'Sorry, I didn't have time to wash up last night. I'm just grabbing some coffee then heading back upstairs for a lazy morning.' Kat smiled as Mrs Rálli fixed her with a beady stare, noticing the two cups Kat set on the side.

'Kostas will be here soon. I will tell him you've taken unexpectedly to your bed, with two coffees,' she said raising an eyebrow, then turned back to the sink.

'Could you ask him to assemble the bed for the third bedroom when it arrives? And also I need to chat with him about the patio. There's a loose tile I keep tripping on, and we'll need to fix it or start the garden early. I haven't chosen the stone yet. God there's so much to do.'

Mrs Rálli whirled around; Kat had never seen her move so quickly.

'No . . . I . . . Pétros' home.' Her breathing suddenly became laboured and she grabbed the kitchen counter for support. Kat rushed over and took Mrs Rálli's elbow, guiding her to a seat. She'd turned terribly pale and was gasping for air, muttering something about the garden in Greek, but Kat couldn't catch her words.

'Andreas!' Kat shouted, hoping he could help. She fetched a glass of water and encouraged Mrs Rálli to take a sip. Andreas appeared wrapped in a bed sheet that made him look like he was imitating a god at a fancy-dress party. The sight of him could have tipped Mrs Rálli over the edge. 'I think she needs to see someone.' Kat wanted to get her checked over.

'I will call my doctor,' he said, racing to find his phone.

Mrs Rálli raised her head to look at Kat. Even between rasping snatches of air she managed to say, 'Andreas . . . is your . . . lazy morning . . .' She found a smile. At least her funny turn hadn't affected all her faculties.

'Try not to speak and be calm. This renovation is too much. It's my fault.' She felt utterly selfish disrupting Mrs Rálli's workplace. It was as much her home as it was Kat's. She was eroding memories of Pétros with every strip of wallpaper she removed and could kick herself for being so careless with Mrs Rálli's grief by being so wrapped up in her own. She felt her hand being gripped and their eyes met.

'None . . . is your fault . . .' Mrs Rálli broke off and pressed her hand to her chest as Andreas reappeared.

'The doctor is coming straight away.' He crouched down in front of the housekeeper and took her hands. 'I think you should lie down. Can I get you anything?' He lifted the water to her lips. Kat couldn't help but notice how caring he was, but after all, Mrs Rálli had seen him grow into a man. The colour gradually returned to her cheeks and her breathing steadied after another sip.

'Please, there is one thing you could do for me.'

'Anything,' Andreas replied.
'Find some clothes to put on before the doctor arrives.'

* * *

Mrs Rálli had been taken to the hospital by Andreas' driver at the doctor's recommendation. Andreas had gone along to keep her company after dashing next door in his damp, splattered painting overalls to seek more appropriate attire. Kat didn't know he had a chauffeur or doctor on standby. There appeared to be so much she didn't know about those around her; there were still too many missing pieces of information. But at least she now knew about Andreas' past.

Stepping out onto the patio, she looked around at the terrace. What had Mrs Rálli been so upset about? Probably Kat's pulling apart all she'd known. And with her parents and Jamie coming tomorrow, it was too much for her housekeeper and it was beginning to feel too much for her.

Her eyes followed two butterflies flitting above the lawn, tangling together and dancing apart as the scent of lemon filled the warm air. They flew upwards until they landed in the bougainvillea on the side of the house. Kat's gaze then fell upon the loose tile in the floor – the scene of several stumbles. She wondered whether she could find a way to fix it into place temporarily so it didn't protrude as much. As she dug her fingers down, trying to get purchase, her mind meandered through her recent history. Her feelings for Andreas were undeniable and, in the heat of the moment, it felt like his attachment to her was growing too. But he had form for stepping forwards and backwards with as much regularity as the tide and she acknowledged she should have guarded her heart more carefully.

Sitting down, she tried again to pull the tile from its place. She'd noticed a new optimism building within her, in contrast to the heavy burden of grief she'd been carrying. Tracking back six months ago, she was married, and her twin was alive. It was almost incomprehensible how life had changed. She found herself wishing she'd been more aware of how precious time was rather than going through the motions of a half-lived existence with Jamie. It was nothing compared to the feelings she already had for Andreas, and she'd only known him for ten days. As she reached beneath the stone with her hands, she felt one of her nails chip. Examining the damage, she urged her mind to stay in the present and give her tears the day off. But she couldn't help her thought. Had she appreciated Nik enough when he was alive? If only she'd seen him more often, despite their daily exchanges, and hadn't been as consumed by work. Yet she had to take the comfort from his last words:

'*I love you . . .*'

How many bereaved people in the world can say hand on heart that they knew just how much they'd been loved? There were blessings to be found, and Kat made a resolution to be more thankful and only hoped Mrs Rálli would make a speedy recovery.

Patch the cat appeared from the undergrowth and howled loudly at her.

'In a minute, Patch. Let me just . . .' He repeated his mew, circling between her arms, his fluffy tail brushing her face. He then sat staring at the tile as she continued to wrestle with it. Finally, she managed to lift the stone, showering the patio with creepy-crawlies who scurried off to find new hiding places. Patch watched them disperse, pouncing on a centipede, before quickly losing interest. He turned his yellow eyes to Kat. Buried in the hole was a small wooden box with a gold plaque and plastic sleeves. Kat tried to dislodge it from its tight nook with difficulty, collecting more dirt on her skin. Eventually she won the fight, and loosened it from the ground. Goose bumps rose immediately as she found a cluster of shiny pink pebbles beneath where the box had sat. Brushing the layers of stubborn earth from the inscription, she slowly revealed the words beneath. She gulped in shock at the discovery, covering her mouth with her dirty hand.

Pétros Tzanos, may you finally find peace.

Wind wrapped around her as she recalled her uncle's burial place was a mystery; nobody appeared to know where it was. This looked very much like a container for ashes, but it was incredibly unorthodox to be cremated. Then again, Pétros seemed to have been anything but conventional.

Her suspicions were confirmed as she gently extracted the papers from the plastic: Pétros' death certificate.

Poor Mrs Rálli. Now it was clear why she wore black all the time and shuffled around like an old lady. Grief had aged her; she'd lost Pétros, and now Kat had threatened to dig up the sacred place she must have been gatekeeping. Mrs Rálli kept the secret of Pétros' burial place and in the midst of the merriment of renovation, Kat had threatened to exhume his ashes. Her skin now prickled with the shame of what she'd literally unearthed. Mentioning the tile must have caused Mrs Rálli's funny turn. Kat hurriedly replaced the pebbles, box and papers in their original resting place and wedged the stone tile back on top, pressing it down as firmly as she could. She frantically swept away the earth with her hands then rose to her feet.

As she stood over her uncle's secret grave, Patch padded over to the tile and settled down. He also had a covert task it seemed: to stand sentry over what lay beneath. There would be disruption for the creature, but even more so for Mrs Rálli if Kat dug up the patio. How on earth could Kat broach the subject without causing further upset?

Chapter 33

Nothing compares to grief; it erupts into your world and blows it apart like a giant wrecking ball in the ultimate demolition. Then, you have to decide whether to live amongst the rubble, reminded at every turn of the cruel twist of fate. Or rebuild.

After my brother died, I thought I would never feel joy again, yet, gradually, almost unnoticed, moments began to creep in. I wondered if I'd ever laugh again. But eventually I did. You can only see the stars if the world goes dark. Recently, I laughed like I haven't for months, covered in paint and being as free and playful as a child. Within the constraints of adulting and responsibility, it's hard to seek out the sheer bliss of unadulterated fun. Though glimpses appear with greater frequency, it's a challenge to embrace them without feeling guilty. How can I have existed for months without Nik? Yes, life does go on, but it will always be different. Just like we were; twins, though unique in our own way. But with life comes death, with love comes pain. All I can do is to remodel this house in Nik's name, claim it as my own and rebuild what life looks like without him. I'm doing my best and that's all I can ask of myself today.

From her chair outside, Kat stared up at the clear blue afternoon sky with only the odd whisp of a cloud interrupting the expanse of blue. She noticed that with each piece she wrote, she was being more honest about the reality of her grief and mentioning Nik. Fewer analogies about renovating, now: she was sharing her true experience. With every word, there was catharsis, which would thrill her father, being a Greek word.

She hoped Andreas would return soon with news about Mrs Rálli. He'd been gone all morning and she was starting to worry. They still hadn't exchanged numbers despite him giving his to Lizzie, and Kat didn't understand why they hadn't. Perhaps it symbolised another step closer to making their 'something' real. But they'd already taken a significant leap. Not just by Kat inviting Andreas into bed but by him sharing his past with her. And she was grateful at how candid and honest he'd been.

A shout roused her from her thoughts. Andreas strode over the lawn.

'Hey! I was calling you, from the road for ages. Where did you disappear to in your head, *moró mou*?' he asked bending to kiss her hello and calling her his baby, which was thrilling, but her concern for Mrs Rálli overrode her happiness.

'What did the doctors say?' she asked urgently bracing for bad news.

'Mrs Rálli will be fine. They're keeping her in for observation, which she was furious about – low blood pressure and stress.'

Kat dropped her head allowing the pang of guilt to wash over her. 'I feel so responsible. If I wasn't breaking up the house, she wouldn't have been ill.'

Andreas took a seat next to her at the patio table. 'Don't blame yourself, Katerína. It's not your doing, believe me.' He lifted her chin with his finger. The power of his stare penetrated the middle of her body and beyond. Their connection was special, except she still had questions about how on earth this could work. She leant forward to kiss him again, reaching around his neck with her hands, suddenly needing him closer, if only to reassure her she wasn't making a huge mistake with the house or with him.

The overly dramatic clearing of a throat broke them apart as, through the terrace doors, Lizzie appeared in a dressing gown with Chrístos who had his arm draped around her. Something about him got Kat's back up immediately, especially after what Mrs Rálli had said about him being trouble, and she stiffened within Andreas' arms.

'Hi again.' Lizzie beamed, and Kat couldn't tell if her glow was from her day spent upstairs or the fact she'd caught her kissing Andreas.

'I thought you'd moved out,' said Kat trying to mask her embarrassment. 'I haven't heard a peep from you, which makes a welcome change.'

'*Yiássou*, Andreas, I hear from my father you came back,' said Chrístos in a gruff voice, offering out a hand with what looked like an unkind sneer on his face. Kat hadn't heard him say as many words before. She doubted his linguistic skills were the attraction for Lizzie. She felt Andreas tense as he returned the handshake silently with a nod. She looked at him and frowned. He caught her eye but said nothing. Kat wondered if Chrístos was one of the friends who used to terrorise her uncle with Andreas.

'See you later,' Lizzie said to Chrístos and Kat averted her gaze as they began an overt display of lust that they apparently still hadn't exorcised.

After he left, Lizzie sunk into a chair. 'He's adorable isn't he?'

'Do you know anything about him?' Kat said noting Andreas' stony face.

'I know all I need to.' Lizzie grinned.

'Mrs Rálli said you and Chrístos were at school together,' Kat said to Andreas, hoping he could shed some light on Lizzie's bedfellow. Andreas didn't respond, gazing out to sea instead so Kat couldn't see his face.

'Come on, spill the gossip,' encouraged Lizzie.

He turned his head back to them. 'Let's just say although we aren't close anymore, I owe him a great debt. He protected me when I had nobody else,' he eventually said carefully.

It was a tantalising glimpse of the young man he used to be and Kat needed more.

'In what way?' she asked and Andreas appeared reluctant to elaborate but his captive audience cajoled him into a response.

'I was being bullied badly by this one kid at school after I lost my father. It was pretty relentless, and I was even more miserable because of it.'

'That's awful,' said Kat. 'Chrístos wasn't the one bullying you, was he?'

Andreas shook his head. 'It was Chrístos who gave me his protection and, I guess, somewhere to belong with him and his gang. For a while he was like my family as my own one fell apart. I will always be grateful. Like I said, I owe him.'

It struck Kat as ironic that Chrístos had saved Andreas from a bully yet together they became perpetrators of such behaviour by targeting her uncle. Although Andreas had paid his penance with how much he cared for Pétros over the years. Those formative teenage friendships endure even if that bond is broken later on in life. Such social currency in the schoolyard clearly allowed Andreas to begin to navigate his grief. And Kat related to that. She respected his loyalty, though Andreas' kinship with Chrístos appeared to have fractured with time.

Both Kat and Lizzie were moved by Andreas' story, though they had quite different reactions. Kat took his hand whereas Lizzie stared at Andreas as if she were trying to process his words. She then began typing on her phone before exclaiming, 'Well, that just makes Chrístos even hotter.' Though she then frowned at Andreas before changing the subject. 'Jamie's been messaging, Kat. He said he's excited to come with your parents tomorrow, so you better work out what to say. I think we should plan a welcome dinner for everyone.'

The last thing Kat wanted to do was make supper for them all, especially here in the house.

'We'd better finish the room upstairs for Jamie. But Mrs Rálli isn't very well, and if I cook, it will open the food floodgates for a major critique from my mother.'

'Use my chef if you like. It's too much to get the house ready and make dinner. I'd be happy to host at mine,' said Andreas.

'Are you sure? My parents are a lot and you'll be bombarded with questions,' Kat said then Lizzie interrupted.

'I have some questions too.' Kat shot her a look, which Lizzie correctly interpreted. 'But they can wait. Let's get this place sorted. I just need to freshen up. Have you both finished with the shower?' she asked winking at Kat as she left.

'You don't have to stay. It's weird you helping me fix a room for my estranged husband,' she said turning to Andreas.

'No stranger than you doing it alone. We'll get it done faster and then I get my girl to myself before I have to share you with everyone tomorrow.' His hand travelled to the back of her neck, pulling her forwards. Kat couldn't help the tremor of elation at the fact he considered her 'his girl'.

* * *

Between the three of them, they completed the small bedroom in no time since the painting had already been done and the new bed assembled by Kostas. The pale-yellow walls and the terracotta floor tiles gleamed in the golden light streaming through the windows. Pétros' few boxes of papers were now all in the study adjoining the lounge downstairs.

Andreas moved the white painted chest of drawers into place beneath the picture window that boasted a wonderful view of the sea. Kat then placed a vase of wildflowers from the garden on top along with a bowl containing some of the pink pebbles she'd found.

'Who's hungry?' asked Andreas.

'Starving!' said Kat and Lizzie in unison.

'How does steak and fried potatoes sound?'

Both women groaned in anticipation.

'Never make a promise you can't keep,' Kat said as Andreas reached for her waist. He gave her a lingering kiss before leaving and said, 'I would never do that.'

As Lizzie and Kat made the bed with fresh white linen featuring delicate embroidered buttercups at the edges, they had a chance to catch up.

'I'd say someone is smitten,' said Lizzie in a sing-song voice.

'It's early days . . .' replied Kat trying to be nonchalant.

'Not you! Him!' said Lizzie as they plumped the pillows, and Kat added an ochre scatter cushion. 'Have you seen the way he looks at you? He can't tear his eyes away and God, those eyes! I'm so happy for you, Kat.' She grabbed Kat's hands and spun her in a silly dance before pushing her onto the newly made bed.

'Lizzie! Look, I don't know where it's going but . . .'

'Please no buts, Kat. Just abandon yourself to his complete and utter heavenly loveliness and enjoy. Don't overthink it. Be more me!'

Kat couldn't help but laugh. 'What, dye my hair red and bang a builder?'

'Very funny,' she said sitting beside Kat. 'You know exactly what I mean. Stop overanalysing and follow your passion. Believe me, you'll have a way better time.'

After dissecting her burgeoning relationship with Andreas for a little while longer, they were eventually lured downstairs by his voice summoning them to dinner. Through the patio doors, they discovered the table had been set and large silver domes covered three plates from a dinner service Kat had never seen before. Thick church candles flickered beside a large platter of doughnut peaches and Andreas stood beside the table with a chair pulled out for Kat.

'Dinner is served!'

The air smelled like he had delivered on his promise. Kat and Lizzie looked at each other open-mouthed.

'How did you . . . ?' Kat began, unable to believe how stunning the terrace looked. There were even fairy lights in the lemon tree. It was like a whole team had created the dining area, yet there was nobody else in sight.

'My secret.' Andreas grinned as Kat took the seat he was holding for her.

'I thought we weren't doing secrets,' Kat said. He looked staggering as the candlelight illuminated his face. To Kat, he became more beautiful as evening descended, because that was the time they'd found each other; their affection came alive beneath the moonlight, the unavoidable silver orb in the sky. As his eyes gleamed, she lost herself in his gaze before the clatter of cutlery returned them to the moment.

'Holy fuck, this is amazing,' said Lizzie hungrily tucking in.

'Lizzie,' hissed Kat wishing her friend could curb her swearing but Andreas waved his hand.

'Don't stand on ceremony for me.' He lifted off the dome for Kat followed by his to reveal glistening pieces of steak oozing with thyme-flecked butter. The meaty smell was enticing and the fragrant herbs tempted her taste buds. Discs of crisp fried potatoes sprinkled with oregano nestled alongside the ribeye. For a few moments as everyone ate, the island provided the music: the timpani of the sea along with the hi-hat clinking of knives and forks.

'This is amazing, Andreas. Thank you,' said Lizzie politely. Kat was delighted her friend hadn't launched an inquisition earlier, but her thoughts were premature. 'So, tell me about this movie. I hear it's going to be huge.'

He shrugged. 'Nobody knows that yet. Of course I'm proud of it, but I hope it lives up to the hype. Most things rarely do and if it doesn't work out . . . I'm trying not to think about it. What comes next is out of my hands.'

'Gosh, how cheerful,' said Lizzie and Kat hoped that the British sarcasm translated to the American in him. 'Who's doing your PR? What you need is something to intrigue the public. For example . . . a love interest.' She raised her eyebrows at Kat who squirmed with embarrassment. If this was a precursor for what was to come with her parents descending, Kat regretted the next two weeks of their stay in advance.

Andreas answered good-naturedly. 'I have someone taking care of PR, but some things feel too precious to share.' He put a hand on Kat's who suddenly found it hard to swallow her steak. Her mouth had gone dry as she tried to chew, feeling terribly unattractive with a hamster cheek of meat as they looked at each other. She realised that at some point soon, the whole world would know who he was, not just in Greece but everywhere. She couldn't see how she'd fit in and something akin to panic began to rise in her chest at the thought of being apart when they'd only just found each other.

'Will you have to go away to promote the film?' she asked, her voice sounding squeaky as she tried to digest her emotions and her supper. Andreas nodded with an apologetic look.

'To New York for the premiere next Tuesday, then two days later do the whole thing again in London. All that stuff that looks like fun, but jetlag and living out of a suitcase is hell. Then I start filming another movie in a couple of months. In Italy.'

'Oh,' said Kat becoming aware that their liaison may have a speedier expiry. A silence stretched that was considerably less comfortable than before. Kat had suddenly lost her appetite and pushed her plate away, realising that her white cotton slip dress was splattered with droplets of oil. She would never suit Andreas' life that was filled with flawless, blemish-free perfection. Kat needed to focus on mending her family and herself, not entertaining absurd thoughts like belonging anywhere near a film star. She dabbed her mouth with a linen napkin in an effort at elegance and plastered on a smile.

'It's all going to get rather exciting for you . . .' But she barely convinced herself let alone Andreas. Lizzie was looking down at her plate, chasing potatoes around with a fork when Kat felt a squeeze on her hand from Andreas.

'Nothing has to change,' he said. She felt her heart swell longing to reach for him, when this was the precise moment it should retreat. Instead, she absorbed his sentiment and closed her eyes briefly, willing her feelings to subside. But as she allowed his blue eyes to connect with hers again, she felt the inevitability of what she couldn't resist, like an unstoppable tsunami cresting towards the shore. She was falling in love with him.

Chapter 34

In the morning, Mrs Rálli returned to the house in anticipation of Kat's family arriving.

'It is deeply inconvenient to stay in the hospital when we have guests coming. I must see the house is ready. It is my job.' Mrs Rálli gave her a stern look. Clearly, Kat was in the way, and so she allowed the older woman to inspect the house. Happily, Mrs Rálli appeared fully restored, ensuring all was ready for Jamie to her satisfaction. There was no criticism, an absence of tutting, and she even approved of the *spanakópita* Kat had made using her recipe. That impromptu cooking class already seemed like a year ago.

'I see all is in order, Katerína. It would be a great shame to begin work on the garden when it is so beautiful. The flowers are in bloom and the trees full of fruit. Your family will not be able to enjoy it if it is dug up,' Mrs Rálli said, though now Kat knew what lay behind her suggestion.

'You're absolutely right,' Kat agreed not wishing to cause another dizzy spell. 'Why don't you take the rest of the day. We have plenty of food and everything we need. I'll see you tomorrow.' Mrs Rálli nodded and with one last look around the patio, she went to her car and drove away.

Kat walked to the harbour alone. Lizzie said she'd join her after she'd finished a call about a possible story and Andreas had interview commitments online for most of the day. They'd see each other at his house for the big family dinner although the thought terrified her. As the passenger ferry made its progress, Kat felt her nerves rise. She was still cross with Jamie for his endless interfering and for not telling her about Nik coming to Agístri, but the idea of welcoming her mother back to the island where she'd been unfaithful left an ever-present sour taste in her mouth.

'I see you wringing your hands, Katerína. What worries does this boat bring you?' She turned to see Father Serafím. He was resting on his staff, holding his already weathered face to the sun.

'It's my parents and my nearly-ex-husband arriving. Our dynamic has become somewhat complicated of late,' she replied as the priest nodded. The engine grumble grew in volume as the vessel neared.

'Well, there is no time like the present to confront what troubles you,' the priest said. 'Think of it this way: instead of running from what haunts you, if you stand firm in the face of consternation, you may find something much brighter. Like being in the shadows and stepping into sunlight.' Her affection was growing towards the wise old man, and she'd love her *babá* to meet him. They could philosophise the day away. Kat spotted her mother's face anxiously looking out of the ferry window, scanning the crowd gathered on the dock. As she saw Kat, she smiled, then visibly gulped.

Jamie was first off, wheeling his suitcase behind him. He'd gained a little weight which was noticeable given he wasn't very tall. Kat had no doubt her mother had mentioned it to him without discretion.

'Kat, darling, you look amazing!' he declared then laughed nervously, running his hand through his blond hair. 'I've already been researching local wines and looking forward to getting stuck in! I've ordered a case for delivery to yours. Hope you don't mind; Lizzie sent me the address. God, it's hot. I'll look like a tomato by lunch!'

'Hello, Jamie,' Kat said formally as the sweat patches expanded on his light pink polo shirt. 'Good to see you.' His blue eyes crinkled guiltily knowing he was still in her bad books; they weren't the shade of blue that she'd recently grown to love.

'Jamie!' Kat heard Lizzie shout across the harbour then saw her fling her arms around him. 'You're going to love it here. Kat's done the most incredible job with *her* home,' she added pointedly. Giórgios was disembarking, holding on to the side rail as he carefully walked the ramp, and Kat rushed to help.

'*Babá*, let me take that for you.' She pulled the old leather suitcase from his hand. When they reached flat ground, she hugged him warmly.

'*Angheloúthi mou*, finally I am in my Greece. Now, let me look at you.' He untangled from her embrace and planted his hands on her shoulders. 'Yes, I see our country suits you. You look healthy and happy. Greece is where you belong. It flows in your blood; it is *your* motherland. And this—' his hand swept along the length of the vista '—this is your *mother*'s land. Tell me, has your Greek improved?'

Kat laughed. Her father's presence was like a tonic and she had missed him but hadn't realised quite how much until now.

'I fear you'll be disappointed, *Babá*,' she replied as she saw her mother nearing. Kat could introduce her father to the priest another time.

Giórgios leant forwards and lowered his voice. 'Your mother is very emotional to be on this island again after so many years. It is a long time since I was on Agístri too. The place where I won your mother's heart and asked for her hand in marriage.'

Kat couldn't find the enthusiasm for his words. What she'd discovered had tainted her view of their relationship. Her poor father had no clue what had played out on Agístri behind his back while he was at home slaving over his beloved grill. But Kat couldn't bring herself to be completely icy towards her mother and despite feeling betrayal on her father's behalf found the warmest greeting she could muster.

'*Mána, kalós írthes sto spíti*,' Kat said, welcoming her mother 'home'.

'*Brávo,* Katerína!' her father said in response to her Greek then Lizzie gave him a big kiss hello. Mína opened her arms to her daughter. Kat noticed she had dark circles under her eyes that a thick layer of concealer hadn't hidden. She felt guilty at her contribution to her sleeplessness, but such was the consequence of secrets. Kat preferred it when she knew none of them at all. Their embrace was brief, then Mína said, 'Katerína, you are still thin. Is this housekeeper not feeding you at all? I must have words. Mrs Rálli was never a talented cook, and I see nothing changes,' her mother nervously babbled.

'Mum, I've done nothing but eat since I got here!' Kat responded and Lizzie stepped in.

'Mína, she looks way better than when I first arrived. She is positively glowing inside and out, with good reason too.'

Her father agreed with Lizzie, but Kat was keen to move things along before Andreas was mentioned just yet.

'Let's get you settled. Jamie, you're staying with me and Lizzie. *Mána, Babá*, your hotel isn't far from . . .' Kat broke off not knowing what to call her home. Because it was hers and Nik's but used to be her uncle's and was the scene of her mother's dark deeds. Then, Father Serafím's words about confronting troubles nudged at her, and she summoned the bravery she needed. There was still dinner at Andreas' to endure.

* * *

Having deposited her parents in the hotel to rest, Lizzie, Jamie and Kat returned to the house. After a grand tour with Jamie complimenting every completed room, they sat to eat Kat's home-made *spanakópita* on the terrace. The afternoon was warm, but a gentle breeze sent notes of wild basil on the wind to heighten their appetites.

'How come you never made this for me?' asked Jamie as shards of filo littered the table. It was a messy thing to eat, so nobody would notice that Kat's flaky pile was larger than everyone else's.

'I didn't know how; I've only just learnt it from Mrs Rálli, the housekeeper. You'll meet her tomorrow. She's quite a character. I'm reconnecting with my heritage,' Kat replied.

'In more ways than one,' added Lizzie beaming at Kat as Jamie leant forward.

'Do tell,' he said. Kat had forgotten what terrible gossips Lizzie and Jamie were when they got together. Kat wasn't in the mood.

'I think you need to answer a few things first, Jamie,'

she said. Lizzie took her cue and cleared the plates. Jamie clasped his hands in front of him.

'Go on then, do your worst, wifey,' he said trying to be charming, but it had no effect on Kat.

'First, you can stop calling me that. And second, but more importantly, I don't understand why you didn't tell me about Nik coming here. You knew and you kept it from me.' He opened his mouth to interrupt, but Kat held up her hand indicating she wasn't finished. 'And thirdly, there's the house. You've made the odd joke about "your half" but it belongs to me and my family. And I don't know why you keep inserting yourself into my business because I'm not really your business anymore, not in the way I used to be.' She sat upright, propped up by tension. Jamie tried to reach for her hand, but Kat moved it away, folding her arms.

'Come on, Kat. I'm sorry, OK? Nik didn't want me to tell you because he didn't want to upset you. That's all.'

'But he confided in you and not me.' Kat wished her tears weren't so available when it came to conversations about her brother, but they started to sting.

'Look, he'd fallen out with your mum and was hell-bent on coming here. For what reasons I don't know. I'm certain there was more to it, but I couldn't get it out of him. I asked him again over the years, but he said I should forget about it and never tell you. I absolutely knew nothing about your uncle. He didn't tell me that. Nik always wanted to protect you, Kat; you can't blame him for caring.' He brushed up some of the *spanakópita* crumbs on the table, pushing them into a small pile. 'Yes, I mentioned it to Lizzie, which is how I'm guessing you found out that I knew. I only wondered if she had any more intel, but she didn't, so I thought it best not to say anything.'

'Why wouldn't he share it with me?' Kat bit her lip to stem her emotion.

'I don't want you driving yourself mad about it, Kat. I understand you're cross, but I was only trying to protect you too like Nik,' he said standing from the table and moving into the shade beneath the lemon tree. It irked her that Jamie and her family continuously shielded her. She knew when he was being genuine: he had such an open face and carefree demeanour. It was so easy to be with him, too easy. They'd stayed together for longer than they should. But she didn't need his protection then and definitely didn't now. She'd moved on.

'And the house?' she asked wanting an end to any conflict with Jamie. She needed as many of them in a good mood ahead of Andreas' dinner and as much as possible solved before she confronted her mother. When that opportunity would present itself she had no clue.

'Jokes, I promise. Poor taste,' he reassured her with a smile. 'You've done amazing things, as you always do. Everyone is talking about your writing back home. That second piece was even better than the first and that was superb, Kat. Coming to this island has done you the world of good.' He leant a hand against the tree trunk, putting his other on his hip as he stared out to sea. 'It's like a bit of heaven. I wouldn't blame you if you never wanted to leave.'

Kat followed his eyeline to the horizon. His reaction and Lizzie's were the same as hers when she'd first arrived. It was spectacular and he was right: she didn't want to leave. But that wasn't about the island; it was Andreas. Their relationship was too new to have such a conversation. She knew he felt something for her, but her time on Agístri had an ending. She'd done what she swore she wouldn't do, which was to cause herself any more hurt. Her heart was already broken by her brother's death and now it seemed inevitable that the remaining pieces would be shattered once and for all at the hands of the man she loved. Their paths were unavoidably headed in very different directions. It was yet another twist of fate she had no choice but to accept and Kat didn't know if she possessed the strength to endure any more pain.

Chapter 35

Giórgios and Mína were waiting on the road above the beach to walk en masse to dinner. Kat thought it best not to inflict Pétros' house upon her parents and all that it contained literally and metaphorically. There would be time for that.

Her heart was thudding a persistent rhythm as they neared Andreas' gate.

'What's with the fancy security get-up?' asked Jamie sending a waft of wine on his breath towards Kat as she pressed the buzzer. 'Is this guy in tech or something?'

'Yes, Katerína, what does your neighbour do for work?' asked her father. As the gate clicked open, she became concerned about the number of aperitifs Jamie had consumed. She answered vaguely, knowing she ought to explain who he was but didn't quite know how to describe their relationship.

'Look, before we go in, this is just someone I've been sort of seeing. It's very casual, so please don't read anything into it. Any of you!' Kat felt like she was lying to herself as much as her family with her outline but continued. 'Andreas is in . . . the arts, *Babá*.'

'Ah, this is the Greek American man you mentioned. You know that our people invented theatres. He is connected with his true heritage.'

Kat caught Lizzie's arm and whispered, 'This is going to be the longest night of my life. You better help me!'

'Don't explain anything else about Andreas. I want to see their reaction!' Lizzie said mischievously. But this wasn't a game to Kat, it was her life, not some celebrity spectacle for Lizzie to gawk over. She only hoped Andreas and her friends would keep their promise not to mention her brother at all tonight. She couldn't face her parents discovering that Nik came to Agístri and had stayed with Pétros. That was a chat she needed to have with them privately.

Mína gasped as Andreas' house was revealed from behind the foliage when they neared. Kat was suddenly worried her parents would feel out of place in such a modern version of Greece. Her fears were allayed as their host appeared on the terrace to greet them. Dressed in his favourite fabric, he looked like he had been lit by the gods as the golden light kissed his skin. He strode over to Giórgios and shook his hand warmly saying, '*Kalós írthes kai hárika, Giórgio.*' Andreas had extended his welcome, saying it was his pleasure to meet him. Her father beamed. It was a smart move to speak Greek. He moved to Mína and kissed her on each cheek and Kat saw a blush creep across her olive skin.

'Andreas Ellis! I know who you are! Why did you not say, Katerína?' she gushed before turning to look Andreas up and down. 'You are much smaller in real life; the camera really does add the ten pounds.' Kat had never paid mind to the Greek newspapers that arrived sporadically at home but could only assume her mother had read about him and seen his work somewhere.

'I'm very sorry about Pétros, Mína. He was a good man, the greatest.' Andreas spoke quietly, and Mína accepted his condolences, though Kat noticed her shoulders stiffen. Andreas then said hello to Lizzie and kissed Kat lightly on the lips, remaining the right side of appropriate, although her physical response inside was anything but. She heard Jamie clearing his throat.

'Sorry to interrupt . . . Hi, mate, great house, though I have no idea who you are. Celebs aren't my bag,' Jamie said with a smirk that almost became a grimace. Kat thought there was an insult within his slightly slurred words, though if Andreas noticed, he didn't take the bait.

'Well, I've heard a lot about you, Jamie,' Andreas said shaking his hand. Kat looked at their grip and saw Jamie's knuckles whitening. He'd never been the kind of guy to posture and puff out his chest, but that's the part he appeared to be playing tonight in this strange soap opera.

'All good things, I hope. She is still my wife.' Kat winced at Jamie and found herself wishing she had come with only her parents.

'Not for much longer,' trilled Lizzie saving Kat's embarrassment.

'What can I get everyone to drink?' asked Andreas as one of the housekeepers stepped forwards and took the various orders. Then Andreas indicated to the seating area at the far end of the patio where trays of canapés sat on the coffee table.

'Bit much isn't it?' Jamie said to Kat quietly and she caught another whiff of alcohol. 'Staff and a mansion . . .

somewhat out of your league.' She ignored him but as she sat next to Andreas on a rattan sofa, she shot Jamie a filthy look.

'This was once two houses if I recall, yes?' Giórgios said, his eyes tracing the boundaries of the plot. 'Do you remember, Mína? Many years have passed since I was last on the island, but mostly very little changes.'

'It took a lot of construction, and I was lucky to get the permits, but I wanted to stay on Agístri, so built my dream home. I can be myself here.'

'And you have family on the island?' asked Giórgios. Andreas briefly explained about his father's death and his mother who now lived overseas.

'But you travel for your job as a famous actor, yes?' Mína chimed in. 'How long do you spend on Agístri?'

'As much as possible. And now I have another reason to stay.' He looked at Kat and took her hand. She wished they were alone so she could ask him how on earth he planned to make this work. Glancing to her parents, she saw their faces beaming in the sunset light as they nudged one another with their elbows. They'd have her married off by nightfall, she thought.

'You're going away to America and Europe for your new movie next week though,' said Lizzie as the inquisition continued. Kat wished they would all behave normally – whatever that was.

'I already read about this, Andreas. You will be a star in Hollywood! *A po po po po po*,' Mína was in awe uttering a Greek exclamation that defied translation.

'I don't know about that, but the premiere is in New York on Tuesday.' He turned to Kat. 'I was hoping you'd come with me, Katerína.' Her mouth dried as she contemplated the thought. Maybe Jamie was right: she was out of her depth. She also had nothing to wear to such an event. A sundress and flip-flops weren't going to cut it. As her mind raced to process a response to his invitation, her mother reacted.

'Oh, Katerína, how wonderful! America! A film premiere!' Kat could see Mína's excitement, but Jamie snorted in amusement.

'Kat on a red carpet, ha! What if you fall over in front of the world's press? I can see the headlines now, Lizzie, can't you?' His face was flushed. Every sentence he uttered seemed to be designed to put her down or dig at Andreas. Lizzie shook her head at Jamie, then picked up her phone and began to frantically type.

'How's the wine, Jamie?' Andreas asked and Kat was grateful for his loaded question.

'Pretty decent, actually, mate,' Jamie replied taking another sip before holding up the glass to the light and swirling it around. 'Not bad.'

'Katerína tells me you are in the wine business, so I chose this especially for you. It's from the Peloponnese region, organic with no sulphites. Less chance of a hangover, although it depends how much you plan to drink.'

Jamie's face flashed with irritation. 'I don't get hangovers, mate. Occupational hazard you'd think, but I've got pretty high tolerance for most things . . .'

It was like watching a fencing match, both men sparring. Kat found it irritating, though Lizzie appeared to find it humorous when she deigned to look up from her phone.

'I'm glad the expert approves.' Andreas' arm snaked along the back of the sofa and found Kat's shoulder. They were both being territorial; she wasn't anyone's property nor trophy to claim. This dynamic was worse than she could have imagined, and they hadn't even reached the dining room inside yet.

'The Greek wines are some of the finest in the world, as they should be. We've been making it for thousands of years,' said Giórgios.

'*Yiámas* to that,' said Andreas as they clinked glasses. But Kat's heart wasn't in the toast at all.

* * *

Andreas had curated the most wonderful feasting menu with unpretentious small plates that befitted a traditional taverna. Classic Greek salads, platters of perfectly crispy calamari rings with clusters of deep-fried tentacles, *fáva* dip, fried – or *saganáki* – local cheese, a whole roasted seabream on a bed of herbs with lemon slices along with skewers of lamb and charred vegetables. The informality of passing dishes around the large indoor dining table made the earlier tension almost disappear. But there was a sinister undercurrent to their gathering that Kat hadn't banked upon, and she was regretting her decision to create a happy family meal when they were anything but.

Her father had given partial approval to the chef but insisted on speaking with him in person. The poor man was forced to leave the outdoor barbecue to be quizzed on his marinades. Giórgios had sent him away with tips to improve his grilling skills. Kat had cringed, but Andreas seemed entertained and asked her father to give him a *souvláki* lesson. Unfortunately, Jamie had spent dinner trying to get a rise out of Andreas. Happily, his efforts thus far had been unsuccessful.

As most of the plates were cleared away, Kat noticed her mother gazing wistfully out to sea through the open doors and couldn't help but wonder if she was thinking about her former lover, Yiánnis, or her brother, Pétros. Or perhaps Nik. She caught Kat's eye and smiled, then looked to Andreas who was receiving a lengthy monologue about the battle for Greek independence from Giórgios, then her gaze returned to Kat. She nodded and smiled again. They were dancing politely around each other, knowing a conversation would soon come, but were also happy to avoid it for as long as possible.

'You have a beautiful home, Andreas. You know Katerína is very talented at design,' Mína said bringing Giórgios' history lesson to a premature close.

'I know. What she's done next door is astonishing. And such a gifted writer. There is no end to her talents.' He reached for her hand beneath the table as he continued. 'She gave me some great advice about my lounge and has promised to find me something more colourful to go in it.' Kat tried to accept the compliments with grace, but it was hard. She wanted to say something self-deprecating but instead was struck dumb by the way he looked at her.

'Why the hell should she buy you stuff? You're loaded, mate! Maybe it's all for show and you're actually skint,' slurred Jamie as he sniggered to himself. Nobody else was laughing. Andreas took a slow sip of red wine, his jaw set rigid.

'Will Katerína meet your mother in America when you are both there?' Mína asked desperately, trying to cover up for her erstwhile son-in-law and simultaneously accepting the invitation to go to New York on Kat's behalf.

'Mum, please . . . I only just heard about it tonight. We

haven't discussed the details.' It was a question she'd never ask or had considered, but now desperately wanted to know the answer to.

'Sadly not. My mother and I have a difficult relationship,' Andreas replied diplomatically.

'Of course, not all of us are lucky to be in a close family.' Kat could have laughed out loud at the irony in her mother's words but remained silent.

'Families, eh?' said Jamie rolling his eyes then took a huge bite of watermelon. It was the first thing he'd said that Kat agreed with. She looked around the table at her mother, who was hiding a terrible secret from her father, to her almost-ex-husband who was determined to wreck what was developing between her and Andreas and then her best friend who had been uncharacteristically quiet, preoccupied with her phone all evening. They had all, aside from her father, been terribly rude, although Kat feared he'd insulted Andreas' chef. The atmosphere grew in weight until Giórgios eventually spoke.

'I think it is time for bed. We are not acclimatised yet. I hope Greece will forgive me for staying away so long.' He wiped his mouth with his napkin.

'Hang on, I haven't finished my wine,' said Jamie, struggling to stand. He gave up and remained seated.

'Take the bottle, or I have a case. What's mine is yours,' said Andreas but Kat could see he was furious at Jamie's poor manners and slew of passive-aggressive insults.

'Well, you've already got something of mine, so it's only fair to share,' Jamie said indicating to Kat then draining his glass.

Andreas stood abruptly, his chair scraping on the marble, which seemed to echo through the room. Jamie in turn managed to jump to his feet.

'Come on, then, outside,' said Jamie, scowling across the table at Andreas who returned the look with equal intensity.

'Enough!' cried Kat loudly, making everyone turn their heads in surprise.

'This is most unlike her,' Mína explained to Andreas. 'She is usually mild-mannered and keeps a very nice house. Katerína makes a good wife . . .' Kat had stared open-mouthed at her mother until she could no longer endure another word.

'Stop it right now!' said Kat. Her voice rose as she released what she'd kept inside for too long. 'All of you, stop it! You've embarrassed me but most of all you've embarrassed yourselves. And as for you, Jamie, I do not need a show of male brutality thank you very much, so you can put your fists away and sit back down. I don't know why you're in my business but I'm absolutely sick of it. I'm thirty-seven years old and it's about time you all let me make my own choices and my own mistakes. You can't keep trying to control or protect me. And I won't stand for it anymore. It's too much! All of you, every single one of you, it's what you do and I've kept quiet because woe betide I upset anyone. But it ends now. Tonight! Do you understand me? Well, do you?' Kat looked around the table, which had fallen silent. Jamie looked crestfallen and rightly hung his head in shame. Even the staff in the back kitchen had stopped clearing up after supper. Lizzie returned to her phone, which further infuriated Kat who was breathless from the strength of her outburst. 'Why does everyone in my life have to be so bloody alpha?'

'You know that *alpha* is actually the first letter of the Greek alphabet . . .'

'*Babá*, please! Not the right time.'
Giórgios took the hint.
Kat sunk back into her chair, regretting inviting any of them to Agístri. In fact, it was fast becoming one of the worst ideas she'd ever had.

Chapter 36

'I don't know where to begin,' Kat said as she sipped at a peppermint tea. Her stomach was churning, and she didn't know who to be the most astonished by, but Jamie challenging Andreas to a fistfight was shameful dinner party etiquette.

She placed her cup on the lounge coffee table and Andreas pulled her into the safety of his arms.

'Your dad is quite something,' he said, and she felt his laugh throughout her body as he held her tightly.

'He certainly is – very proud to be Greek – you might have noticed.' Kat extracted herself from his embrace and sat forward on the sofa. 'I'm just so sorry about Jamie. It's not like him.'

'I'm sorry for my part in it too, he got to me. But maybe he isn't ready to let you go.'

Kat pondered his suggestion. There seemed to be little other reason, but she'd been sure of how he'd felt when they'd split months ago. Turning up tonight drunk was a poor show. And then there was Lizzie's failure to intervene or back her up, which was hugely disappointing. She felt let down by them all in one way or another, but at least Andreas had apologised, though he had done little wrong. Jamie had goaded him to such an extent throughout the evening, it would have even tested the patience of Father Serafím. Turning to face Andreas, she crossed her legs beneath her.

'Well, *I* let Jamie go, a long time ago.' She hesitated for a moment, but needed to ask him about America. 'Did you mean what you said earlier, about me coming with you to New York next week?'

'Of course. It's up to you. I know it feels like a big step, but I want you by my side. I said before I wanted to keep us private, but the idea of such a big moment in my life without you doesn't feel right. I'm serious about us; I want to show you how much.'

She beamed, reassured that his feelings mirrored her own, but there was a nagging sense of doubt. While they were living her island fantasy, she felt invincible, Jamie aside, but there would be a time when she would leave Agístri. Long-distance relationships rarely survived, plus if this film succeeded the way it was tipped to, she'd be left stranded in the wake of his success. Being exposed to public scrutiny on his arm didn't thrill her either, though the sentiment that put her there, did.

'Tell me what you're thinking, Katerína,' he said and she shivered, enjoying the sound of her name in his mouth.

'I'm thinking about us, what happens when I finish the house. My life and job are in London and you're at such an important moment in your career, I don't want to distract you or hold you back. I'm scared to need you too much,' she added softly.

'Kateⲅína, I understand. In the past, I've never really done relationships because I didn't believe in them. Until I met you. You're all I can think about, and I don't only need you, I want you,' he said reaching for her. 'I've never met anyone like you. I see you creating a home, writing with your heart, welcoming your family and friends. I have no measure for how a family should be, but beneath what you think is your parents' interfering, there is love. And so much given by you to those you care for. I want to be one of those lucky enough to receive your love, if you'll have me. All you have to do is choose me. Choose us.'

It sounded so simple, but it wasn't. She leant forward to kiss him, her mind racing to override her desire, but her body won the sprint as she pushed other thoughts aside. She didn't want to need or to love Andreas, because if it ended, which seemed unavoidable, she knew she'd never repair her heart, which was only just starting to mend.

* * *

In the morning, Kat reluctantly returned to her house to confront Jamie and Lizzie. She felt like a bad hostess staying out, but after last night, she hadn't wanted to speak to either of them.

Her body tingled with the surety of her feelings for Andreas and she knew they were reciprocated. Though neither had uttered *I love you* aloud, their bodies had said as much over and over again during the night. Today she was rejuvenated and determined to sort out the mess of her loved ones once and for all, to tie up loose ends before they became knots.

Andreas had arranged for a stylist to come to his house later for dress fittings to give her options for the premiere. She'd insisted it was unnecessary, but he was immovable in his generosity. It was like living in a make-believe world, but she thought it would present an opportunity to have some alone time with her mother by inviting her along.

Before stepping up to her lawn, she took in the sea then lifted her head to the sun, a solitary sphere of gold in a cornflower sky. Kat felt less alone and found a brief moment of peace beneath its beams.

'Good morning, sunshine,' she whispered to her brother. Her heart felt full. Almost undetectably, some of the cracks had begun to heal. That wasn't Andreas' doing, it was entirely hers. Patch gave her a fright as he darted past her, and she followed him towards the house.

'Well look what the cat literally dragged in!' called Jamie as Kat strode across the lawn, preceded by Patch who slumped in the shade beneath the lemon tree. She took a fortifying breath.

'Is there anything you'd like to say before I start?' she demanded with her hands on her hips.

'I haven't had enough coffee for this.' As if on cue, Mrs Rálli appeared with a cafetiere, and Kat wished her a good morning. She seemed recovered from her ailments but walked with the weight of a hidden burden. Kat still didn't know how to broach the subject of her uncle's ashes beneath the patio; it was on the long list of issues to fix. Her mother ought to know where Pétros' resting place was too, but Kat had more pressing things to discuss with her. Jamie took a sip from his cup, which made him wince.

'Damn that's hot,' he said rubbing his scalded lip. 'Kat, look, I'm sorry about last night, it's just that—'

'It's just nothing,' Kat interrupted. 'Your behaviour was unforgivable. It's not only me you owe an apology to.'

'What, pretty boy next door? You must be joking.' Jamie

leant back in his chair rocking it onto its hind legs. Kat hoped he'd topple backwards to knock out his uncharacteristic superiority. She folded her arms, silently encouraging him to elaborate.

'The chef and the fancy house, it's like he was trying to impress everyone. And I don't like how he is with you.'

'What – kind, attentive and loving? As for his house, it's where and how he lives. You're being pathetic.' Kat was seething.

'I don't buy it. It's like he's putting on an act. It's what he does for a living after all. I've done some digging online and there isn't an unkind word written about him. Anywhere! Nobody's that perfect, not even a saint.'

'Sounds like someone's been bitten by a green-eyed monster, or maybe it's blue eyes that are the problem,' said Lizzie who wafted onto the terrace in a kaftan.

'Quite!' agreed Kat, appalled at how Jamie could deign to behave this way.

'Rubbish!' insisted Jamie. 'You're trying to live some absurd fantasy. And now he wants to parade you on a red carpet like some show pony. Maybe it's time for a reality check.'

'From you?' Kat scoffed. 'If you can't accept my relationship, then I can't have you around me. I think you better stay at my parents' hotel. I'd like you to leave.'

'Relationship?! Is that what you think it is?' He laughed unkindly. 'I thought you were smarter than that.'

'Jamie, that's enough,' Lizzie said stepping between them. 'You came out here to see if she's OK and you've got your answer. Kat is more than OK. I'm sorry for you to hear this, but I've never seen her this happy.'

While Kat was grateful for Lizzie's sudden, if tardy

support, she wished her friends could take her at her own word. She wasn't sure how Jamie could continue to be in her life after this. It felt like the end of a chapter with a new one beginning in tandem. And it was incredibly sad.

She went into the house wondering if there was a way to leave her life in London behind. She'd been working from Agístri, easily meeting deadlines and filing copy. As a ray of sunlight illuminated the hallway, it suddenly didn't feel quite so impossible anymore.

* * *

Kat spent as long as she could in her room while Jamie packed his belongings. She had no inclination for goodbyes. Did she regret the way things had turned out given how close they'd been over so many years? Of course. But he clearly couldn't find joy within her choices. Perhaps because he didn't have a defined role anymore. He'd been so used to being relied upon especially after Nik died, that now, when she didn't need him in the same way, he didn't know how to be around her. She watched him from her bedroom window struggling with his suitcase across the lawn. He had interfered too often for too long. All her loved ones had, and she was determined to stop their behaviour that she'd permitted over the years.

Later in the afternoon, as Andreas led her up his sweeping marble staircase, she realised she hadn't paid attention to her surroundings last night in the midst of their passion. Upstairs resembled the lower floor with beautiful white marble and stunning artwork. From every room and along the length of the landing there was the most astonishing uninterrupted view of the sea, across to Aegina and beyond.

It was as if the house had been built solely for the ocean as hers seemed to have been constructed around the lemon tree.

'Sappho, my stylist, is very excited to dress a woman for a change,' Andreas explained as they entered a dressing room adjacent to his master suite. A large cream suede couch dominated one wall, and a vanity sat below one of the windows. The rest of the space was storage aside from a series of freestanding mirrors and clothing rails. Kat wondered just how much linen was encased behind the walnut-fronted wardrobes, but didn't wish to offend Sappho who greeted Kat warmly with two kisses. Her bleached hair was styled into a Fifties quiff and several piercings sparkled from her face, but she was dressed in a conservative satin wrap dress in a rich burnished orange. The contrast was stunning. Kat immediately trusted her taste; she wasn't quite as confident in her own style compared to the certainty of her interior designs.

'Andreas, this is where you leave. Shoo!' Sappho ushered him out of the door.

He blew Kat a kiss and she called after him, 'My mother is coming soon; can you show her up?'

'I'll send coffee when she gets here,' he replied his voice echoing along the corridor.

'This will be so easy, though I have little notice to pull this together,' Sappho said, her voice thick with a Greek accent. 'These are on loan and many designers jump at the chance to dress Andreas' girl.' She turned to one of the racks holding evening gowns in every colour hanging in branded clothing bags. There must be thousands of euros in designer clothes. Kat wondered whether she should warn Sappho about her tendency to spill everything she touched. It would surely eat into her designated kitchen funds if she ruined a frock and had to buy it. Warmed by the fact that Sappho referred to her as 'Andreas' girl', Kat suddenly felt like Cinderella being fitted for the ball and in a way she was. But not how Jamie had referred to her, living some kind of deluded fairy tale; this was real.

'He seems very happy,' Sappho said selecting a beautifully simple white gown with delicate draping. 'I've worked with him for years and it is very new to see him like this.' Kat dared to touch the material, which was the softest silk she'd ever felt.

'Perfect with your skin tone. We do gold jewellery, oversized cuffs, no necklace. Very Greek goddess and, look! Your tattoo is Artemis, yes?' Kat nodded at her recognition of the tribute inked on her wrist. 'Important to celebrate our heritage, no? Especially in Hollywood where everyone has identical noses or takes the same weight loss drugs – is all so dull. Now, try it on.'

Kat looked uncertainly to the plate-glass windows. Anyone on the road or on a boat could look up and see her naked. Sappho walked to the window and flicked a switch.

'Privacy glass. We see out – nobody sees in!'

As Kat undressed then slipped the gown over her head, she was stunned by her reflection. Her olive skin kissed by Greek sunshine positively glowed. The one-shouldered design exposed her slender collarbone, and the simplicity of the effect was striking. Fabric clung to the curves of her body like a sculptor had modelled her from white clay; she felt like a statue. She noticed that the sharp angles within her shape from months of grief had softened, thanks to Mrs Rálli's cooking. It was as if she'd been lit from within, an invisible flame illuminating the shadows of heartache that had lingered for so long. Sappho stood behind her and gathered Kat's hair up then, at her ear, dangled a gold drop earring with a large green stone in the centre.

'Perfect. My work here is done. Though dress is too long. Try these shoes.' Sappho offered a pair of vertiginous gold strappy heels, but Kat was terrified they would heighten the risk of a trip.

'What about some simple Greek sandals instead?' she suggested hopefully.

'Love!' said Sappho clapping her hands together. 'Flats on the red carpet, such a statement! I must take up the hem many inches.' She bent down and expertly scooped up the spare fabric pooled on the floor and started to pin.

Her mother's voice cut through the tranquillity from down the hall. 'There is so little furniture, Andreas. What you need is a woman's touch. *That* is what's missing.' Kat rolled her eyes. As the door opened, Kat turned her head. 'Oh, Katerina!' Mina covered her mouth with her hand. 'You look so beautiful, just like Aphrodite! Don't you agree?' her mother asked Andreas, her voice oozing delight. 'It is almost like she is dressed for her wedding day.'

Kat took the deepest breath she could find and steadily exhaled. *Here we go again,* she thought.

Chapter 37

After much cooing and ahh-ing from Mína, the dress was zipped away by Sappho ready to be altered. Then, Kat was finally alone with her mother in the dressing room.

She pulled up the stool from the vanity to sit opposite Mína who was perched so close to the edge of the sofa, her knees brushed the coffee table.

'Are you serious about this man, Katerína? Your father and I approve. He is so handsome and charming – oh those eyes – and he is Greek!'

Kat knotted her hands together, willing her courage to stay if not strengthen. 'I don't want to talk about Andreas, *Mána*, I want to talk about you and Nik and Yiánnis,' Kat said seriously as her mother recoiled at the name of her former lover and looked down.

'What is it you wish to know, *angheloúthi mou*?' she said not raising her eyes.

'Everything,' Kat cried unable to contain herself. 'I don't understand what's happened. To you and *Babá*, to our family with all these secrets. Did Nik know about your affair? I found out he used to come here; another thing you hid from me. But is that why he came, because he knew what you'd done?'

Mína nodded slowly, still inspecting her lap. Kat had deduced from the tiny threads of information she'd managed to gather that they'd argued, and it had somehow led Nik to this island. But hearing she was correct made her brother's betrayal even sharper.

'*Mána*, look at me!' Kat said, almost shouting. She took a beat to find a note of calm. 'Start from the beginning. Please, tell me how Nik knew.' Emotion saturated her voice so much so that Mína finally lifted her head to look at her daughter.

'Nikólaos found . . .' She faltered and looked to the heavens before returning to Kat. 'Nikólaos found a letter from him. From Yiánnis that came to our home just after your thirtieth birthday. It was so unlike your brother to just open it, but I suppose his instinct told him to. Nikólaos had come for lunch that day, but I wasn't home from the grocer's yet. Your father had gone to do something, I don't remember what. And I found Nikólaos standing, like a stranger clutching it in his hand. I thought someone had died from the look he gave me . . .' She winced and crumpled before covering her eyes. Kat sat in stony-faced silence.

A knock on the dressing room door broke the moment and Kat let in one of the kitchen staff with a tray of coffee and little rectangles of glistening baklava. The girl placed it on the table looking as uncomfortable as the pair of them. Her mother didn't take her face from her hands and the girl scurried away, probably relieved to escape. Eventually Mína reached for the coffee with a shaking hand, tears falling from her eyes, but Kat said nothing.

'Nikólaos and I had our only big fight that day. He said

he would come to Agístri to uncover all my secrets,' she continued. 'I will regret our cross words for the rest of my life. I don't know if he ever forgave me. He said that he did, but he never looked at me the same afterwards, I am sure of it.' Her voice was swallowed up for a moment before she continued softly. 'I had to tell him about my brother when he found that letter. But at least Nikólaos found a friendship with Pétros that I was never able to have. It is the one blessing amongst this horror.'

Kat dug her fingernails into her palm, trying to remain steady. Their secrets had not only denied her a relationship with Pétros, but prevented her from sharing this island with Nik and she resented them all for it. Kat measured her tone as much as she could before continuing. 'Your affair with Yiánnis was when you brought me and Nik to Agístri, wasn't it? We were only five. How could you when we were here, with *Babá* at home, running the business? And poor Pétros, under his roof, after what your family did to him.'

Mína shrugged the smallest amount, a careless gesture for such an important conversation, forcing Kat to grind her teeth to maintain composure.

'You are right, it was a terrible thing to do. But I'd forgotten what it was like to be desired. Or so I thought. You always say to me I am obsessed with size and shape, well you are right. My body was never the same after having you two.'

'Oh, so your adultery was mine and Nik's fault?' Kat couldn't help but say.

'*Ochi*, no, please Katerína. This is impossible to relive this piece of the past. I understand why you insist upon it, but I don't wish to lose you like I did your brother . . . I cannot survive any more loss . . .' She broke apart and sobbed like a child. She became so small on the settee that Kat couldn't help but reach for her hands, taking a seat beside her.

'You won't lose me, I promise, just tell the truth. You can't continue to keep things from me. Stop protecting me, *Mána*. You all have to stop it.'

'You are so fragile, *angheloúthi mou*, your body has only just healed. You cannot even recall after the accident properly. I'm afraid this will make you remember something so terrible.'

'I'm not as fragile as you all think. I've realised that not knowing is worse than knowing. I found that out the hard way.'

Mína slowly gathered herself with a tissue that Kat pulled from a mother-of-pearl box on the table.

'Not always. I think about the day before the accident so much, before the world changed, when my heart was intact.'

'I know. I know, *Mána*,' Kat said tenderly. She wished she could remember the world before they lost Nik with clarity, but it seemed shrouded in fog, unreachable like vapours of a ghost. Kat nodded to her mother to continue.

'Yiánnis was my childhood sweetheart. We were in love as teenagers – all very silly; we were only children. But our parents decided we would marry. And I loved him and that love grew as I became a woman. Or what I thought was love at that time. Our families were both from the island and it was an unspoken arrangement. But then your father came along and swept me off my feet.' She smiled at the memory, but Kat found it hard to share the joy of her story. 'After my parents' difficulties with Pétros, I think they wanted any solution to one of their children's happiness. I was besotted with your father; he made me feel things I had never thought possible. And his ambition, to move to

England and start a life and a business, I was caught up in the excitement.' She grabbed Kat's shoulders. 'And believe me, I still am, I feel the same for Giórgios that I always have. I made a stupid, stupid mistake. I met up with Yiánnis again unexpectedly when I brought you and Nikólaos here to try and reconcile with my brother. It was like I was suddenly a young girl again with no responsibilities. I could be free and remember what being desired was, to be more than just a mother, a wife, a cook and cleaner. It was shallow and believe me, it was nothing. I never expected him to write to me in England all those years later or mail another here. I wish he hadn't because each of my children found his letters in both the places he sent them to. I regretted ever coming back to Agístri.'

'But why did he contact you after so long, out of the blue?' said Kat, reluctantly finding empathy for her mother's feelings at the time.

The letter she'd found in Pétros' house gave no clue as to the writer's intentions; it only contained regrets and goodbyes, sweeping statements about an old great love and having lost it.

'He sent me a letter because he was dying, receiving palliative care and his time was near. I don't know if that's what he wrote in the letter you read. Yiánnis wanted to make amends and say his last words to me, to say goodbye. I never imagined what catastrophe it would wreak with your brother. And *my* brother.' She paused to gather her thoughts. 'I had hoped to tell you and Nikólaos about Pétros before your brother discovered that letter. But I just couldn't. I felt that if I told you how my family had treated him and that I was party to such terrible persecution and homophobia, you would both think so poorly of me. And

I couldn't find a way without revealing the one thing I also wanted to avoid: Yiánnis. Because of what I did here on the island, my brother and I quarrelled over my . . . my affair and although I wrote to Pétros, that argument more than three decades ago was the last time we spoke. The time just disappeared but the pain in my heart did not. And it was my fault.'

She sniffed and wiped her nose before continuing. 'What your generation will never be able to comprehend is how Greece was in those days. We upheld our Orthodoxy to the highest moral degree. Katerína, it wasn't accepted to be gay but almost worse in a way was to break your marriage vows which, I admit with the heaviest of hearts, is what I did. Adultery was such a taboo and of course remains so. And Pétros judged my affair more harshly than my parents had him for preferring men. His last words to me were, "I love you, but those in glass houses should not throw stones when they have rocks . . ." Now, I am not as clever as you or your uncle and I wondered for so long as to why I would throw a stone when there is a rock. And then I work it out: he was punishing my hypocrisy, and he was right to.'

She blew her nose loudly and Kat allowed her to finish her confession. 'I was afraid, don't you understand, afraid that my brother would tell you all the things I was ashamed of? So I had to keep him from you both. And yet my secrets emerged anyway – for Nikólaos and now for you. I have failed and my past is sent to haunt me. You, my last remaining child, must be disgusted with me.'

Kat took a moment to absorb her mother's version of events. Her mouth was bone-dry so she sipped her now-tepid coffee.

'When did Yiánnis die?' Kat asked gently.

'I do not know, nor do I wish to. I tried to make amends with my conscience and put the past behind us; there it should stay. But I take my responsibility in hurting my family.' Her voice cracked. 'And I have tried, Katerína, I have tried to make it better ever since. All I wanted was to protect you both. But losing Nikólaos is my penance for deceiving those I love the most. I know it! I have brought bad luck on us all.'

She crossed herself three times before shattering into her final pieces and Kat wrapped her arms around her mother, holding her while embracing her own tumult of feelings: sadness, anger, resentment but most bewilderingly a sense of understanding. She felt sorry for her mother, for who she'd been thirty-two years ago. She'd forgotten who she was. Wasn't everyone guilty of losing touch with who they are whilst navigating years of change in body, mind and heart? She allowed her mother to wail for all she had lost, but Mína would not lose her daughter's love, of that Kat was certain. She was also convinced that Nik had loved her mother just as fiercely, Mína had simply shattered the illusion for him. The twins were both as culpable of idolising their parents; nobody considered their mother or father fallible unless proven otherwise.

When Mína had cried her last, Kat dabbed at her face with another tissue as a mother would her child, their roles were temporarily reversed.

'I'm glad Nik used to come to Agístri to see Pétros.'

Mína agreed. 'And I also am glad. I'm only sorry that I kept your uncle and this island from you. I will regret that too along with so many other things.'

Kat couldn't help the hurt ricocheting through her body

at how many people knew about Nik coming here. Nobody had seen fit to include her, instead pointlessly protecting her as usual.

'When Nikólaos uncovered my mistake, and I told him about my brother, I had to explain about him being gay and he connected with that. Though we never spoke of it again, it seemed like Nikólaos wanted to keep this island part of his life separate from us all. Even though it was born of my treachery initially, he grew, I think, to love it. Again, I will never know just how so. I only wish I could have been part of it.'

Me too! screamed Kat in her head, but allowed her mother to work her way towards a conclusion. She needed to hear the truth in all its gruesome purity.

'I took it as more punishment for what I did, though at least my brother had some reconciliation with one of his blood before he died.' Her voice choked again, and Kat felt another swell of pain at the exclusion from her brother's secret Greek world. Perhaps Nik occasionally resented being a twin but hadn't ever said as much. It could, she admitted, be overwhelming at times, being forced to share everything from the moment you were born. Having something that was only yours felt like a rare jewel. It was how she was beginning to feel about the house. For the first time in forever she had something that was just hers. But the bittersweetness remained; it was only such because her twin was dead.

'Come, I want to show you something,' said Kat pulling Mína to her feet. She gave her mother another hug, burying her face into the scent of hairspray as her own tears fell unseen. In time she would find forgiveness, because even the most perfect people made mistakes and fell foul to errors of judgement. She took Mína's hand and led her downstairs to see Nik's photograph of Andreas. It was something she could reveal that none of her family knew about, just her. And she was incredibly proud to do so.

* * *

Mína tentatively walked over the grass towards the lemon tree. Her pace was slow and steady as she stared up at the house.

'Are you OK, *Mána*?' asked Kat, unable to imagine the complexity of her mother's current feelings. She managed a nod, but no words. She had cried again at the portrait of Andreas in his study that Nik had taken. Seeing it in daylight was more breathtaking than Kat recalled from her first viewing in the candlelit gloom. It was a collision in art of two men she loved, albeit in very different ways.

'Do you want to come inside? It's pretty different from when you last were here.' Kat took her mother by the arm and gently led her through the lounge doors away from the loose tile in the patio where Pétros was buried. Kat couldn't tell her mother in the moment. It might break her apart irreparably.

'But it is almost empty, Katerí150na!' exclaimed her mother as she looked around aghast at the new sitting room. 'There are no things or photographs, no keepsakes, icons . . . is like Andreas' house next door. You two are a very good match!' She changed tack turning to Kat. 'You like him, don't you? And he feels it for you, I see it. Your father and I would be happy for you to marry.'

'*Mána*, please, don't interfere. It's very new. Yes, I like him but, I beg of you, don't mention it at the taverna tonight.'

Kat had planned round two of the family dinner, having decided that being in public may make them all behave better. She hoped.

Mína turned away grinning, though her smile began to dissolve as she stepped towards the old bookcase. It had been sanded and painted but still held Pétros' novels along with a series of Greek classics he had owned. Her mother ran her fingers along the spines.

'Your father says living in a home without books is like living in a darkness. I am not a great reader or writer like my brother or you.' She dropped her hand away but continued to stare at the shelves. 'I am sorry I never told you about him, Katerína. I have failed. There is little I am good for.' She sniffed.

'What about being a wonderful mother and wife?' Kat forced herself to say the last word. Before knowing about what had transpired, she'd almost canonised her parents and their love. It went to prove that nothing, no matter how it seems from the outside, is perfect. Mína turned to face her daughter.

'Know how sorry I am, Katerína. For you and Nikólaos. I have let you all down. Everyone I love – my brother, my children and my husband. God, it is so warm in here!' She dabbed at her brow with her palm. 'When you become my age and everything is dried up and heads for the ground you cannot regulate your temperature. I forget how hot Greece is.' She stroked Kat's cheek with the back of her hand. 'Nikólaos made me promise never to let you know about Yiánnis because it would hurt you too much. He didn't want you to think badly of me and I was grateful, I suppose, that you could never discover what I had done. I couldn't have imagined my brother would make you a beneficiary of his will and I'd be forced to tell you everything. But know this: your father and I are proud of you. The way you write is wonderful; everyone at home says so. The whole family is so proud. And, Katerína, you are all we have left.'

How her mother could switch from the lamenting the weather to immense tenderness with such ease was astonishing. Kat put an arm around her shoulder.

'Come on, let's eat. I've also got a cushion for you to put tassels on. Only one, mind, but it's yours to keep in the house and help me make it a home.'

Kat felt a sense of relief having had such a tricky conversation and knew that with a little time, these wounds could heal. They had to. Kat was all that remained, and they in turn were her blood. As they entered the cool kitchen, Mrs Rálli turned from the stove and Mína paused in the entrance. The two women stared at each other like caged animals about to be released, poised to pounce, faces pinched in tension. The day had already felt like a roller coaster from her confrontation with Jamie, to an emotional exchange with her mother and now this. Kat was exhausted and the moon was still below the horizon.

Artemis & Apollo

Blood is what bonds us all; blood gives us life and runs faster when we are angry or feel the rush of love. Even though gods do not bleed when cut, their emotional scars cost them as much. Like mortals they only hurt because what wounded them mattered.
Though Artemis was heartbroken by Apollo's deception, she forgave her brother. No matter what the fates hold, you can loosen, but you can never undo the ties of blood; they are eternally inescapable.

Chapter 38

'Mína.' Mrs Rálli nodded, her lips pursed.

'Hello. Again,' her mother stiffly replied from the doorway.

Kat looked from one to the other, knowing if she extolled the skills of Mrs Rálli and how she'd cared for Kat when she'd arrived her mother would be jealous. And there was nothing she could say about her mother because the housekeeper apparently knew everyone's secrets. Though she was currently unaware of Kat's discovery beneath the patio.

'I'd like you to sit down and eat together,' Kat said, taking matters into her own hands.

Both women turned to her in horror, but she wasn't going to mediate their conversation that was years overdue. It was down to them and would be easier if she wasn't party to it.

She ushered Mrs Rálli to a chair and poured them both a large glass of rosé from the fridge. Thankfully, all the cooking was done save for dishing up the black-eyed beans cooked in a spinach and tomato sauce. She crumbled a little feta over the top, and filled the table with platters of salad.

'Right, this is the last supper, though it's a very late lunch snack thing,' she said as they both looked at her. 'Because the kitchen is being smashed up tomorrow. I'll be outside writing if you need me. *Kalí órexi!*'

Kat grinned her way into the garden. It felt good to take charge and boss her mother around for once.

The heavier the weight of grief, the stronger you eventually become, though it doesn't feel like it at the time. Nor do you notice your muscles strengthening, holding you up as you take weary steps onwards, but they learn as you do to face each day. Time isn't a healer, but it will march onwards regardless of whether you wish to keep up or not. And that's the trick: to set your own pace, continue breathing and seek out slices of joy through the cloak of darkness. A wise man once told me that you can find the unexpected when you stop searching for it. And occasionally what you were looking for was not only right in front of you but hidden inside yourself.

As I navigate my new normal, I have needed to dig deep for a resilience I didn't know I had nor ever wished to need. Yes, there is comfort to be found in beautiful things, but the greatest comfort of all is with loved ones: friends and family if you're lucky enough to have them. Looking outwards is natural, looking inwards is painful though necessary if a true renovation of the self is to occur. Metamorphosis literally means to change from the immature to the adult – which can happen at any stage of life for us mortals. It also comes from the ancient Greek meaning to transform. And as I've transformed this house, I've also undergone some major repairs myself. There is no fast fix, but as with any work in progress, a new and improved version slowly begins to emerge into the sunshine. It doesn't hide what lies beneath, foundations can't be altered, but fresh ones can be laid leading you to eventually face the world better and stronger than before.

Kat pressed send, having been working for well over an hour. Then, she scrolled through the thousands of emails containing messages from readers that Amelia had forwarded to her over the last few days. It seemed that everyone was indeed talking about her writing and though she rarely scrolled through social media, she'd had to turn her notifications off as her followers increased tenfold across all platforms. Excerpts had been published in tabloids and used as talking points on national radio stations too, apparently. Amelia and the magazine team were overjoyed at how it had been received. It seemed that grief and loss were universal, though everyone had their own unique version. Kat had validated strangers' feelings. They felt heard, and she was honoured that so many precious memories had been shared with her in the messages she read. As she filtered her emails, there was one Amelia had sent earlier that morning saying: *Call me – need to chat!*

Kat dialled her number and she picked up immediately.

'Kat! Where have you been? I've been desperate to speak to you,' she said urgently.

'Sorry,' Kat responded unsure if she could digest any more big news. 'My folks are here with Jamie and there's a lot going on. Is everything OK?'

'Well . . .' Amelia began. 'You've seen the response. We've

never had so many messages and emails – even letters in the post! You've touched a nerve, tapped into the zeitgeist and people want more. And it's not only our lovely readers who've noticed you.'

'What do you mean?' Kat asked. Her heartbeat increased.

'Today I had an email from a literary agency wanting to work with you. I'm forwarding it to you now. They'd like to discuss you writing a book!' She squeaked before adding, 'I knew you could do this, but it's better than I could have imagined. You're amazing, Kat, just amazing.'

Kat felt every thump of her pulse as she read the message that dropped into her inbox. She then scanned it again to ensure she'd understood. They wanted to broker a book deal. Apparently, there was 'buzz' around her writing, and they'd offered to represent her, confident of securing a publisher.

'Oh my God!' Kat whispered standing from the outdoor table. 'Oh my God!' she repeated into the phone. 'Amelia . . . I can't believe it! This wouldn't be happening without you. I can't thank you enough,' she said.

'Nonsense, you just needed a push. Now go and tell your parents! Got to dash, need to put more of your brilliant, brilliant work online,' she said before hanging up.

Rushing inside, Kat interrupted her mother and Mrs Rálli. They weren't weeping or screeching, unlike Kat. In fact, they had been holding hands across the table when she darted in.

'Kateriná, what has happened?' her mother asked in alarm.

'I've . . . I've got a literary agent who wants to work with me, and they think they can get me a book deal!'

Her mother sprang up and threw her arms around Kat.

'This is wonderful news! It is what you always wanted. To be a writer, like Pétros. Tonight, we all celebrate at the taverna – you must join us too.' She turned to Mrs Rálli who seemed overwhelmed at the invitation, clasping her hands to her chest. 'Here eat some of this bread. Mrs Rálli's baking is much better than it used to be,' Mína said with a wicked grin, thrusting a side plate at her daughter. But Kat's hands were trembling with excitement and she dropped it on the floor.

'*Opa!*' shouted Mína and grabbed another and threw it on the flagstones.

'*Opa!*' joined in Mrs Rálli who did the same.

Lizzie ran through the door. 'What the fuck is going on?' Kat didn't chide her for swearing.

'An agent emailed Amelia, and they want me to write a book!'

'No way!' She jumped up and down as she elatedly hugged Kat. 'And are we breaking shit to celebrate?'

'So it seems,' Kat said handing her another dish.

Together they smashed the outdated plates on the floor, knowing that the old must make way for the new, just as the tide is coaxed by moonlight to bring fresh sand to the shore in time for the sunrise.

* * *

'A toast, if you will all charge your glasses.' Giórgios stood at the long table in the corner of the taverna. 'As the great philosopher, Plato, once said, "*We can easily forgive a child who is afraid of the dark; the real tragedy of life is when men are afraid of the light.*" You, my sweet daughter, have found light from all of our darkness; you also found your truth. But above all, I see you rediscovering yourself and your purpose.' His voice quivered as his eyes shone brightly.

Andreas and Kat reached for one another at the table, and his touch steadied her emotions as her father continued.

'And of course, none of this would be possible if it weren't for Greece! A sad circumstance brought you to Agístri following Pétros' death.' He nodded to Mrs Rálli to acknowledge her sorrow, and Kat loved her father even more for it. 'We are proud of you and excited for what and who is in your future. To our Katerína. *Yiámas!*' His eyes twinkled as he looked from Kat to Andreas and back again, and she was glad he hadn't explicitly referred to their fledgling liaison. Jamie, at the other end of the table, was behaving well. So far. She caught his eye, and he winked warmly. Kat was relieved that they could all dine together in whatever semblance of normality her family had found.

'It seems life is going to get exciting for you too, Katerína,' Andreas said and kissed the side of her head. 'Maybe our trip to America comes at a good time before you're chained to your desk writing a bestseller.'

Kat laughed. 'It's not a done deal yet, though it's what I've dreamed of since forever.'

'You've found a way to make your dream come true. For what it's worth, I am so proud too.' He looked at her with such affection, she felt like her heart might burst out of her chest and bounce around the ceiling of the taverna. He lowered his voice, and it felt like all the other diners had disappeared. 'This isn't the place to say this, it should be when we are alone, but I can't keep it in. Katerína, since we met, my feelings have been growing and I want you to know with all of my heart that I . . .'

'My turn to say a few words,' Jamie interrupted raising his glass. Kat could have thrown the bread basket at him. She was desperate for Andreas to finish his sentence, but the moment was lost. 'Kat, I know we've had a bumpy road of late, but I wanted to say huge congrats. Though you haven't signed on the dotted line yet, good things are coming, and I'll be watching from the sidelines with awe and pride. We all will. And Andreas, mate, although we rather got off on the wrong foot, you seem a decent chap, so please, just take care of our girl. To our Kat!'

It was a kind-spirited toast though his timing was hideous having cut across what Andreas was about to say, but Kat mouthed a thank you to Jamie as glasses clinked again.

'*Signómi*, sorry to interrupt your dinner, but can I have a picture?' a blushing young girl said who'd suddenly appeared beside their table.

'Of course,' said Andreas, excusing himself from their party.

It was like the first in a long line of dominos. Once one fan had made the move, every other diner followed suit. Andreas was surrounded.

'Get used to sharing him,' Lizzie said. 'But he really does only have eyes for you.'

'I'm not sure I'm ready for New York or any of this,' she said watching Andreas encircled by admirers. 'I think he was going to say the "L" word just now, but Jamie did his speech instead.'

Lizzie's green eyes widened. 'You're kidding! Well, that's what you get for having your husband and lover for dinner. Jamie was your starter, and Andreas is the main event, that's for sure. And for my dessert, I'm heading off to meet Chrístos.'

'Of course you are. I'll leave the key for you in the usual place. Not sure where I'll be tonight.'

'In heaven I should think if Andreas says what you thought he was going to. I'm so happy for you, Kat. You deserve this more than anyone I can think of. Not just him, but success. And happiness, it's been a long time coming.' She squeezed Kat's hands. 'Just think, you could be a writer on your island paradise living the dream!'

Kat surveyed her loved ones amicably breaking bread at the same table in stark contrast to their last attempt, which had ended with Jamie almost challenging Andreas to a duel. Then, she looked towards the sea as the moon cast its light like a silver cloak across the water. She wished Nik was there to share it all and heard his voice as if he'd whispered it in her ear: *'Night, night, moonlight.'*

Chapter 39

'I'll see you at yours. I'm going to walk my parents back,' Kat said to Andreas, leaving a lingering kiss on his lips. 'Are you all right getting home? There might be a superfan hidden in a bush.'

He laughed. 'I'll be fine. Don't be long, I want to finish what I was saying earlier.' He leant down to kiss her again and she wished he'd tell her now. But it made the anticipation sweeter. Because if it's what she thought it was, she felt the same way and was dying to say it out loud.

When she reached the hotel with her parents, she gave her mother a warm hug and spoke quietly into her ear, 'Thank you for today, *Mána*, it meant a lot for us to be so honest.'

Mína replied in a whisper within their embrace, 'And to me, *anghelouthi mou*, and to me. And I'm so sorry again.'

'Katerína, let us walk. It is a beautiful night, and I would like to spend some time with my little girl,' said her father before kissing Mína on the cheek. 'I will only be a few moments, *agápi mou*.' Kat watched their look of innate understanding, a result of many years of partnership, traversing joy and pain hand in hand – so much love was visible. But it wasn't everything Kat had once thought it was.

Her father gave her his arm and they meandered along the promenade as the soft evening breeze circled around them. Waves lapped with barely any sound, gently caressing the tideline with watery fingers, all cast in metallic light by the waxing gibbous moon. They found a bench overlooking the inky sea.

'I recall when I first came to Agístri, it was very different. This is not that many years ago, Katerína.' He inhaled deeply, drinking in the night. 'But Greece at its heart is very straightforward and little changes. We revel in our culture, are fiercely proud of our history and flag, but ask any Greek what really makes him happy, he will answer: my family, love and perfectly grilled meat!'

They both chuckled at this because it was so true for them. Kat wondered where her father's monologue was heading but she was enjoying their time together.

'I have told you that I won your mother's heart with my big ideas, and I impressed your grandparents. I was so sure of myself as young people tend to be. But, Katerína, do you know what I was most certain of?' She shook her head as he turned to meet her eyes. His were the same ones she had shared with Nik and she felt her brother's presence as if he were sitting beside her. 'My love for Mína. I would have bet my life savings on us and, in a way, I did by moving to England for a new life together.'

Kat's heart began to crack again at her poor father speaking of their courting with such tenderness, not knowing what the woman he adored would be capable of only a few years after. She suddenly felt a chill on the wind and pulled her wrap tighter around her. Now, she really didn't know what to say, but it seemed her father needed no response.

'Your mother always did the best for you and for your brother. None of us are perfect, Katerína, all we can do is be the greatest version of ourselves today, then try to do better tomorrow.' He looked upwards to the stars as a lone cloud briefly masked the moon. 'What I have come to realise, is that although many things will never make sense, we must find a way to accept them. The way we lost Nikólaos, having to live without him . . . there is no silver lining in that. And yet, here we are tonight celebrating you on the cusp of becoming an author. Yes, you may always have become that one day, but it is interesting that after we say goodbye to Nikólaos, you receive this offer. Perhaps it is the reason for him leaving us.' Her father continued to look to the heavens as he took her hand. 'You must fly with the winged heels of an ancient messenger to share your experience with the world but most importantly to use your voice. Would you have written a book someday? Yes. Would you be asked to write *this* book, whatever it will be? No. I knew there had to be purpose within the tragedy. There is meaning in everything; there are reasons for all pain and suffering. It doesn't lessen the agony, but what use are we to each other or to Nikólaos if we stop our lives because his was cruelly taken away?'

Kat leant her head on his shoulder, absorbing his words.

'*Babá*, you are right – you always are. I'm glad you and *Mána* are here. I've missed you both so much.' Kat allowed her tears to come, and her father comforted her. She cried for her twin but agreed she had to seek out the positive in her heartbreak, as impossible as that felt. It's what Nik would want her to do. Giórgios let her tears flow, then finally dry. He slowly stood and offered his hand.

'Come. I have my love waiting, as do you.' The mischievous glint in his eye said he wasn't finished with her yet. 'So, tell me, Katerína, do you love him?'

Kat couldn't help the grin that spread over her face, replacing her residual tears.

'I do, *Babá*.'

He nodded then smiled too. 'And does he love you?'

'We haven't quite got there yet, but I think so.'

'Good. I like him. He is polite, successful and he speaks Greek. And you are off to America soon . . .'

They retraced their steps towards the hotel.

'How do you know it's real, *Babá*? Love. I mean really, really real.' Jamie's words about her living in a deluded fantasy darted through the night like a sprinting shadow. She resented his appearance in her thoughts and physically shook it away with a shudder.

'It is very simple: there is attraction or lust as you would call it, then comes something more than friendship, like an ancient wisdom. And once you realise this, love arrives.' Kat listened to him intently, linking her arm back through his as they ambled onwards. 'You go through these stages until it dawns upon you that you cannot imagine a life without them; it is impossible to even consider sharing a pillow with another. Then you know you have found the other half of you. All of this can happen in a few days or weeks, occasionally it takes years, but you, *angheloúthi mou*, have located it on this beautiful island where I found your mother. For me, it took just one second to know that I loved her, and I refused to be apart. And she felt exactly the same. I am a very lucky man.'

Kat's legs stopped working and she came to a halt. She willed the air into her lungs as if her last breath depended upon it. The Kat she was a few weeks ago would have swooned at her father's words. Now, they'd been sullied by what she'd learnt.

'Katerína?'

She didn't know what to say as she slowly exhaled, unable to meet his eyes.

'Katerína, know this: disappointment and heartbreak are fleeting, but love outlives the ages,' he said, his tone becoming serious. She raised her head. 'I know about your mother, what happened here with Yiánnis. It is not for you to carry. She told me when your brother discovered it. Yes, of course it hurt me, but it hardly matters now so long after the fact. It was some thirty years ago. No mother is perfect. There is only one, the *Panagía*.' He was referring to the Virgin Mary, held in the highest esteem in Greek Orthodoxy. 'All any mother or father for that matter can do is learn after we fall.'

'Why didn't any of you tell me?'

Her eyes filled as another wave of sadness swept through her.

'Because of this sweet face looking like that.' He took her cheeks in his hands. 'We were only trying . . .'

'To protect me, yes I know – it's what everyone always does,' she interrupted. 'But look what you've all done.'

He tipped his head to one side. 'And what have we done? Tried to stop you from being hurt, helped you continue to believe in true love, shielded you from disappointment in the people who are meant to lead you through life. You will never find peace, Katerína, if you hold on to things others have let go of. Find a way to forgive at some point. Not just for our sake, but most importantly for yours. The past is gone and while parts can live on, we must learn to leave the worst behind us.'

* * *

Kat wanted to wash her face before going to Andreas', needing to decompress after the chat with her father. In the upstairs bathroom of her house, patting cold water under her eyes, she realised she too was guilty of the accusations she'd levied of late. She'd shielded her father by not saying anything to him about her mother and yet he already knew and didn't need her protection. But it wouldn't have been her place to tell him just as it wasn't Jamie's or Lizzie's to inform her about Nik coming to Agístri. And who was she protecting by not sharing the location of Pétros' mystery burial place? She didn't want to be party to any more secrets. She needed to unburden herself.

'Kat, are you here?'

She heard Lizzie calling her from downstairs and, after drying her face, went to find her.

'Hey, what happened to your date with Chrístos?' Kat asked as she found her friend in the garden.

'I think you'd better sit down,' said Lizzie. She looked anxious and fidgety.

'You're scaring me,' Kat replied, taking a seat on the patio.

'I don't know how to say this, but I know you've noticed how preoccupied I've been on my phone. I've been doing research, trying to get my facts in order. And then I got waylaid by Chrístos, but he's been telling me a few things that I'd never be able to find online.' Kat didn't know where she was going with this, and although she was still concerned, she tried to lighten the mood.

'You mean you two actually have conversations?'

'Kat, listen. He told me about when he was younger with Andreas and some of the things they did with their friends.'

Kat breathed a sigh of relief. 'You're so sweet to tell me, but I already know everything. Andreas filled me in on the terrible stuff they got up to. Especially in relation to my uncle.'

Lizzie pushed her hand against her heart. 'Phew! I feel much better. I had to tell you because I didn't want to risk us falling out again if you discovered I knew.'

'You're a very good friend, but he's told me. Yes, he made awful mistakes, but they aren't mine to forgive. I'm fine with it – I don't like it, but he was going through a lot at the time.'

'I have to say, you're not reacting how I thought you would. When did he tell you all this?'

'Last week, I think. I can't remember; I've lost track of the days.' She tried to count how long she'd been on the island but couldn't order her thoughts as Lizzie's words sank in. 'What do you mean my reaction? Like I said, I don't like it, homophobia is disgusting, but Andreas made amends with Pétros.'

'No, I mean about your uncle's car,' Lizzie said leaning forwards on the table and clasping her hands.

'I know that Pétros caught him when the car crashed into the wall and Andreas took the blame for them all. It's a stupid thing to have done but no one got hurt . . . a silly dare gone wrong, that's all.'

Lizzie dropped her head.

'Lizzie, what's going on?'

Her friend slowly lifted her face, holding her hands as

if in prayer under her chin. 'Andreas knows how Nik died, doesn't he?'

Kat nodded, frowning in confusion.

'Oh God,' said Lizzie as Kat grabbed at her hands urgently.

'Tell me what I don't know, Lizzie. Now.' Her voice trembled. She was suddenly afraid of what she was about to hear.

Lizzie took a steeling breath. 'It was all a dare as you said and yes, your uncle's car was stolen,' Lizzie began and Kat nodded, hating how cold her blood had become as her heart hammered against her ribcage. 'His friends tried to stop him, worried the joke had gone too far, but apparently he was determined, showing off to them. So, he drove Pétros' car all the way along the seafront and back before colliding with the wall outside this house. There was only one individual to blame, and it was who was driving your uncle's car at the time it crashed. Hardly anybody knows the whole story. The true story. The worst of it Andreas obviously didn't tell you because . . . Kat, I'm sorry, he was . . . when he got behind the wheel of the car, he was drunk.'

Chapter 40

Kat couldn't quite believe what she'd heard and asked Lizzie to repeat everything that Chrístos had told her. Andreas had shared part of it but conveniently left out the one detail that would have sent Kat running for the first ferry off the island. The crash was a direct result of drunk-driving. He'd admitted responsibility, taking the blame, but had only told her half the story. The blanks she hadn't questioned at the time were now being filled in by Lizzie via Chrístos. No wonder the men were so frosty with each other, given the secret they'd concealed between them since they were teenagers, and it had found its way to Kat. Andreas had been calculated by omission, knowing what she'd think given her twin had been killed by a drunk driver. It was worse than a lie: it was unforgivable.

She'd insisted she wanted to be alone, so sent a reluctant Lizzie back to Chrístos – the source, it seemed, of Andreas' secrets. She simply couldn't get her head around it. She interrogated her memory to find the words Andreas had used when he'd opened up: *'It's all a bit hazy and happened so fast. But the car crashed into that wall down there and your uncle came out of the house.'*

He'd known how she would react. It wasn't simply a prank; it could have been deadly as her family knew only too well, ruined scores of loved ones' lives and though it was lucky he hadn't, that wasn't the point. There was absolutely no way past this for her. It was over between them. Looking at the moon above the sea, it was so bright, she felt like it was taunting her and needed to escape its beams.

She went inside to the kitchen and found a pile of Kostas' tools stacked in the corner. Looking around at the home she was building, she wanted to hurt it, hurt something, anything. Picking up a large sledgehammer, she swung it over her shoulder and brought it down hard on the battered wooden countertop. She repeated the action over and over until she heard the crack of splintering wood, but she didn't stop. Her furious tears fell as she gritted her teeth and decimated one of the freestanding shelves. The floral fabric that had once concealed crockery behind it, now lay under a pile of wood along with smashed china and glass. She sobbed as she continued to break the kitchen apart, crying for her brother, needing him more than ever. This was not how she thought her evening would pan out.

'Kateriína! What the hell are you doing?' She turned and saw Andreas in the doorway, taking in the scene before him. He moved towards her.

'Don't you dare come near me, Andreas. I mean it, not one more step.' Her angry tears persisted but there was nothing he could say that would make it better. He stopped where he was. The look of horrified confusion on his face nudged at her resistance. She loved him; she'd thought he was a safe haven for her heart. But she would never forgive him. Not about this. He wasn't who she'd thought he was.

'What's happened? Tell me, please, I don't understand,' he said looking at the devastation around her.

'You've lied to me! I want you to leave, now,' she said staring him down, willing her feelings for him to vanish. He'd tricked her heart into loving him and she couldn't simply wish that away. If only it was so easy.

'Katerína, please, I haven't lied to you. I don't get what this is about,' he pleaded with his eyes, which only an hour earlier had looked at her with the purity of what she'd thought was love.

'I know the truth about Pétros' car. Chrístos told Lizzie what actually happened, the version you didn't want me to know,' she said and watched him close his eyes and sigh.

'Look, I need to . . .' he started.

'I don't want to hear another word. I won't believe a single thing you say.'

'Katerína, please. What did Chrístos say?' he asked firmly, anger creeping into his voice, the muscle in his cheek tensing.

'Why? So you can change your story with another lie or conveniently leave something out again? Just go, Andreas.'

'Come to my house where we can talk.' He took another step forwards, but she backed away crunching broken glass beneath her shoes. He held out his hand to her. 'Katerína, be careful, you'll hurt yourself.'

'There is nothing that would hurt me like you have.

No, Andreas. I'm not coming with you. Not next door, not to America. I'm going nowhere with you.' She turned her back on him, wishing to hide the tears that poured out her broken heart. The sound of his footsteps retreated along the hallway and she was crushed further. He'd given up on her so easily. She crumpled onto the floor amongst the remnants of the kitchen, surrounded by her shattered faith in love.

Chapter 41

When Kat had exhausted her tears, she surveyed her makeshift demolition. She needed to erase the evidence of her heartache Andreas had caused.

Picking up piles of debris, she tidied and cleared the kitchen through the remainder of the night. Countless trips to the skip outside replaced her crying and anger with devastation. She couldn't delete her feelings for Andreas; they were too strong. But she wasn't prepared to build a relationship with someone who couldn't be honest. There had been too many lies, too many secrets and she didn't want any more.

Night gave way to morning. She was covered in dust and coated in sweat. The dress that she'd worn to the celebratory dinner in the taverna was ruined. In the garden, Patch was sleeping in his usual spot and didn't stir as she passed. Kat was determined to wash away any trace of last night and walked down to the beach and straight into the water. As she sat in the shallows, the cold made her recoil in shock. But she didn't care. Pulling her knees towards her, she rocked back and forth as the sun rose above Aegina, the light slowly creeping towards Agístri, cloaking it in a golden embrace. There was no warmth for her beneath the sunbeams. Shivering, she rested her head on her knees. The only heat came from tears she thought she'd used up as they trickled down her face, plopping into the calm water.

'Morning, sunshine,' she said aloud and squeezed her eyes tightly shut. What she wouldn't give to hear Nik's voice again, to receive his counsel about Andreas. That beautiful white dress would remain in its clothing bag, never to be worn on a red carpet, at least not by her. She longed to run away, to float out to sea and be cast away on another island, away from everyone who had let her down.

'Nik! Why did you leave me?' she shouted.

'*I wish you'd follow your heart, Kitty Kat. I love you . . .*' Nik's last words before the accident floated through her, the moment before her world changed forever. She was older by two minutes, but he'd always felt like her protective big brother, trying to wage her battles. Now he was gone and she'd never felt more alone, betrayed by everyone she loved. Squeezing her eyes even tighter, she saw Nik in her mind's eye in the wreckage of the car. She'd had the vision before but willed it from her thoughts each time: she didn't want to remember his last moments. Now it pressed forwards and she hadn't the energy to resist.

Nik's brown hair was stuck to his forehead, peppered with shattered glass and matted with blood; a stream of red emerged from his nose drawing a harsh line to his lips and another trickled from his ear. His face was turned to her and Kat was his mirror image, as if they were back in the womb, side by side, fighting for survival. Except this time, Nik couldn't fight. There was no victory to be found; this was the ultimate defeat. His lashes flickered as he struggled to keep his eyes open. And he was pale, so pale, like someone had painted his olive skin white. The odd sheen shone through the bloodstains and cuts and Kat recalled her peculiar thought at just how beautiful her twin had looked. Hissing noises from the engine, steam rising all around, a crumpled blue car blocked Nik's window. Deflated airbags hung like slack pieces of skin. The atmosphere was cloudy with a smoky powder. A tangy metallic taste coated her tongue like a penny was in her mouth. But she had no care for anyone or anything else. She couldn't take enough breath to curb her panic and terror. Nik's breathing was shallow, barely a rise in his ribcage. Her chest ached from the impact. There was a pressing weight inside her, a heaviness she couldn't describe or shift.

'Nik, stay with me, don't you dare leave me,' she heard herself say as she reached for his hand, ignoring the shooting pains around her broken limbs. 'Nik, don't you do this.' She felt the tears she was crying back then join with those she was shedding in the present as her mind played out the end. Nik opened his eyes, looking at her with warmth and love.

'Night, night, moonshine,' he whispered with a half-smile. As the last breath left his body, the sunlight faded from his eyes and her twin, her beloved brother and best friend, left her forever with words she hadn't remembered until now.

She couldn't tell if her feral cries were living within the terrible memories that had resurfaced or if she was actually making those sounds now, but it was a wailing unlike any noise she'd heard. She put a hand down to steady her body, which convulsed with cold and shock, letting her palm sink into the sand. A butterfly fluttered above the sea surface and she willed it upwards away from danger as it found the strength to fly away over her head for land. Waves started to lap around her body. What the hell was she doing sitting in the water? Scrunching her fingers, they closed around something buried in the sand. As she snatched it up, water trickled through her fingers to reveal a gold disc with a small fan engraved on it. She dunked it back in the sea to relieve it of any remaining grains and turned it over, hoping, *knowing* what she'd find. She'd seen it before. Somehow, it had found its way back to her after she'd lost it.

In her hand was Nik's red evil eye.

Chapter 42

The following week was dominated by the kitchen renovation, so Kat, Lizzie, her parents and Jamie spent most of their time together in tavernas or on the beaches around the island. Anything to divert Kat from her break-up with Andreas. Kat had made Jamie and Lizzie swear upon pain of death or worse that they wouldn't mention any details about the demise of her relationship to her parents or speak about it when Mrs Rálli was near. Her forceful insistence had summoned their instant agreement, and she trusted them to take her seriously. Though Kat was devastated, she did her best to hide it and instead devoted any spare time to writing, channelling her feelings to make sense of a different kind of heartache.

The problem was, every time she read the news online or caught sight of newspapers in a kiosk or shop, there was Andreas gracing the front pages. He looked devastatingly handsome in a tuxedo on the red carpet, lauded and adored by everyone except her. She couldn't escape him no matter how hard she tried. At least he'd convinced the world with his smile; hers was much less assured. She couldn't pretend with such ease like he apparently could.

Jamie had been surprisingly kind and he'd asked her parents not to mention anything about Andreas in front of Kat – the first welcome piece of meddling. But she appreciated his support along with Lizzie's honesty about what she'd unearthed from Chrístos. It was obvious to them both just how miserable Kat was without Andreas.

On Saturday as the kitchen neared completion and the appliances were due, Kat loaded her parents into Mrs Rálli's car and took the ferry to Aegina. It was time to purchase all that was required to fill the new navy kitchen units; the finishing flourishes were always her favourite part of the process. Jamie and Lizzie said they had plans together so remained on Agístri. Kat wondered how she would feel if a romance struck up between the two of them. It would be weird and almost incestuous, but it was something she was sure she didn't need to think about.

'The best thing to do is divide and conquer,' declared Giórgios as they entered a large store that sold just about everything from food to furnishings. 'I will take charge of the pots and pans, all things needed for grilling. Mína, you deal with baking trays, mixing bowls and everything for the oven. Katerína, you do the rest. Here.' He pushed a shopping cart towards each of them. Kat had already ordered the dinnerware, since she'd smashed up most of it, along with new mezze bowls, napkins and tablecloths from the artisan shop she'd discovered on her first trip to Aegina. But she needed glasses, cutlery and utensils. She was glad her parents were part of finishing the house – gold tassels aside – it may help dispel any darkness the island and Pétros' home had once held for them.

As she rounded a corner, Kat almost collided with her mother's trolley. It was piled high with plastic containers all stacked within one another. An unnecessary amount; not even Andreas' oversized chef's kitchen needed this much Tupperware. She jolted herself back to the present, wishing she hadn't thought about him.

'*Mána*, what on earth am I going to do with all of those?'

'What are you talking about? It is a sign of great wealth and prosperity the more containers you have. You see, you may write, but you don't know. Look, Giórgios!'

Her father appeared from another aisle and nodded his approval. If what her mother said was true, it seemed counterproductive: buying so many would surely deplete anyone's fortune. She was picking her battles, so changed the subject.

'We are digging up the patio soon and then it's all finished,' she said. Her parents exchanged a look as Giórgios parked his shopping cart alongside a wall of tins mainly consisting of chopped tomatoes. He took Kat's hand.

'A superstore is not the place, but your mother and I need to talk to you. We both agree there should be no more secrets.' He looked to Mína for confirmation before continuing. 'It is about your uncle and the instructions he left. We did not know where he was laid to rest, nobody did. However . . .'

'*Babá*, let me save you the speech. I know where his ashes are. I just don't know how to broach it with Mrs Rálli. I was afraid to cause her any more grief.' Her parents breathed simultaneous sighs of relief that she knew. 'Mrs Rálli clearly loved Pétros very much and must have put him under the patio herself, the poor woman. It's an awful burden to be left with. But . . . how do you both know? *Mána*, you said you had no idea where he was buried.'

Her mother stepped forwards. 'I promise, I didn't know

until you forced Mrs Rálli and I to have lunch in the kitchen, and I am very glad you did. She told me she couldn't hold it in any longer. Cremation is not in our culture. Pétros was determined to reject what judged him his whole life, but still he wished to remain on the island . . .' A Tannoy announcement interrupted her mother and they waited as a special deal about Greek coffee was broadcast to shoppers. Her father was right: this was not the setting for such a conversation. Her mother continued when the advert finished.

'We were busy celebrating your writing achievements, then everything happened with . . . your relationship, but I did plan to tell you. I swear. Pétros made the arrangements to be cremated with instructions for Mrs Rálli to bring him back to the house so they would always be close to each other. And never to tell a soul.'

Kat nodded, understanding Mrs Rálli's need to cling on to whatever remained, even if it was only dust. But the housekeeper was simply following instructions, though that didn't lessen her grief. And Kat believed that her mother would have told her: they'd all learnt the danger of withholding life-changing information from one another.

'So, what do we do?' asked Kat. 'She had a funny turn when I mentioned the patio before. But I have an idea . . .'

Kat outlined her plan, and her parents agreed it was the best and most respectful way for them all to be able to say goodbye properly.

'I will speak with her,' said Mína. 'We weren't the best of friends before, but as time passes, forgiveness comes easier, and we have found a closeness bonded from our loss. It's a shame we didn't have it all those years ago – such a waste.

And the same goes for my dear brother – it is time I will never get back.' Mína's eyes watered and she busied herself inspecting passata as Giórgios put his arm around her.

Kat looked at her parents. If her father had forgiven her mother, then so could she. It wasn't her fight; it had only dampened her romantic notions of their love, which appeared as strong as it had ever been. Her father was right: disappointment passes, but love lasts forever. She only hoped her feelings for Andreas could disappear. Again, she wished he wouldn't interrupt her days – though the nights were even worse without him.

'And speaking of forgiveness, can you not forgive Andreas, *angheloúthi mou*?' her father asked but Kat looked away knowing she'd disappointed them with her relationship choices again. Most of all, she'd disappointed herself by trusting the wrong person.

Kat took in the colours and sizes of the tins on the shelves, the scent from the deli counter and the electronic beeping from the checkout.

'No, *Babá*, I can't forgive him,' she said with conviction.

'But you both seemed so happy . . .'

'Please. Not today. Let's just finish my house. For Nik and for Pétros.'

'You know, something is only yours if you build it; if you didn't build it, it is not yours.'

Kat rolled her eyes, entertained as always by her father, glad that at least for now, things were on an even keel with her parents and friends. As for Andreas, her wound was too raw and there was nothing on the shelves or anywhere in the world that could help her to heal it.

* * *

That evening, with all the kitchen paraphernalia in boxes and bags in the lounge, Jamie, Lizzie and Kat enjoyed the final moments of sunshine in the garden with the last of the cold drinks from the old refrigerator, which now sat upended in the skip. The smart freestanding replacement would be installed tomorrow along with the other appliances then the patio work would begin. But at least they could toast with the new glasses she'd bought.

'Tell me what you two have been up to today?' asked Kat. They looked uneasily at each other. Perhaps there *was* something going on between them after all.

'Mainly drinking wine, exploring the island, not much.' Jamie was being shifty, and Lizzie was still preoccupied with her phone.

'This should be you,' she said thrusting the screen towards Kat. A picture of Andreas next to his beautiful co-star from the London premiere of his film two days ago. New York had passed in a blaze of glory, and the weekend press worldwide had been filled with photographs of him. Andreas was on a trajectory to stardom, like a rocket ascending, leaving Kat behind. She looked at the image, wishing her heart didn't yearn for him.

'Maybe it's for the best. I can't compete with that. That's the fairy-tale ending, them together, not me.' She returned the phone to Lizzie who snorted in disgust.

'Please!' she said. 'As if he'd be interested in that blonde plastic energy. He loves you.' She shot Jamie a look of sympathy. 'Sorry.'

'Don't mind me. Kat's happiness is all I've ever wanted. I did think he was too good to be true, and he should have been honest about his past. But perhaps he deserves to explain when he comes back. It might give you some closure.'

'You've changed your tune,' Kat said. 'I thought you weren't a fan.'

'I think he's got enough of those, but no, I wasn't. However, I do believe in second chances. Maybe there's still hope for that fairy tale. It just might not be what you were expecting. As I said, your happiness means everything. It always has and always will.'

Kat frowned at him as he and Lizzie smirked at each other knowingly. Surely, he wasn't talking about rekindling their marriage and stopping the divorce. Is that what he was insinuating when he mentioned second chances? Lizzie typed furiously on her phone again before looking up.

'All I will say is nothing is ever what it seems. Never say never, Kat. Don't write anyone off completely.'

Kat began to worry that she needed to have yet another difficult conversation but this time with Jamie, making clear once and for all there was no chance of them being together. He and Lizzie had no idea the strength of her feelings not only for Andreas, but about what he'd done in the past. Yes, she was being judgemental, but no amount of trouble or grief could excuse the recklessness of getting behind the wheel drunk. The man who killed Nik had ruined her family and changed them all forever. There wasn't enough forgiveness in her for him or for Andreas.

Lizzie excused herself, saying she was off to make a work call leaving Kat with Jamie. She felt uncomfortable being alone with him, given she was now unsure about his intentions. He cleared his throat and fiddled with the stem of his glass before taking another sip of wine.

'How are you, Kat? I mean really, how are you?'

She considered his question. 'Well, things are much better with Mum and Dad and look at this! I completely forgot to show you.' She reached into her shorts pocket to show him the evil eye. 'I lost Nik's *máti* at Piraeus port and then last Friday morning I found it here in the water.'

He took it from her hand and turned it over. 'It can't be the same one, though.'

'I don't know, it isn't likely, but I was sitting in the sea after I smashed up the kitchen thinking about Nik and suddenly there it was.'

'You were sitting in the sea . . . you smashed up the kitchen,' Jamie said slowly. 'You didn't mention any of this and yet you want me to believe you're fine? Come on, Kat, I know you too well, probably better than anyone. Apart from Nik.'

'But I'm different now, Jamie.' She shook her head in protest. Kat *had* changed since being on Agístri and he needed to understand just how much. 'You can't lay claim to me forever. You know that and so do I. It's time for what comes next. For both of us.'

He finished his wine and toyed again with the glass. 'Listen, I'm going home in a few days, but I want to do something with you, just the two of us. There's this wonderful forest in the middle of the island with a beach at the bottom of the hill. What do you say to a picnic, for old times' sake?'

'Jamie, I . . .' Kat began, wanting to let him down gently. 'I don't think it's a good idea. I've got so much to do here; I need to keep writing and speak to this book agent again.'

He leant forwards and took her hand. 'The builders will be fitting the kitchen and it'll be a while until I see you again. Just give me tomorrow, a few hours, that's all I ask. Please, Kat.'

He looked so desperate, though she didn't want to lead him on. Jamie had been such a tower of strength after

Nik died. Even though he'd caused drama with his persistent interference, she knew he meant well beneath it and she could forgive him for that. Though she wouldn't allow it to happen again. When Kat considered his unswerving friendship, she felt like she owed him one day.

'Fine. You have two hours tomorrow, though nothing heavy, please! Only giggles and fun from now on,' she said hopefully.

It was only a picnic. What's the worst that could happen?

Chapter 43

Electric bikes were a godsend. The hills leading to the centre of the island were almost vertical. Kat felt much stronger in her body, the warm climate had dispelled any residual aches and pains in her joints; if only her heart would catch up and mend. As she cycled onwards, she felt free. The resolution with her parents and having Nik's evil eye with her again had given her considerable comfort. Whether it was the same one or not mattered little – if she believed he'd found ways to send her signs and it helped her through, so what?

As she biked along the forest roads lined with fresh-smelling pines, she recalled her earlier conversation with Mrs Rálli. Kat had instructed her mother to have a quiet word with the housekeeper alerting her to the fact that the ashes had been discovered. When she'd received the green light from Mína, Kat had taken Mrs Rálli's hand and carefully led her onto the terrace first thing this morning.

'I want to firstly say to you that I can't imagine the pain you've held in for so long having to conceal Pétros' resting place. But I'd like you to know that his home will always be here. And you, Mrs Rálli, are part of our family – you always have been, and there is a place for you forever at our table.'

Mrs Rálli's eyes had overflowed instantly at Kat's words. She'd wiped away countless tears as she looked at the tile beneath the lemon tree guarded by Patch who was curled up so tightly, he'd resembled a multicoloured bagel.

'Thank you, Katerína,' she'd said placing her hand on Kat's arm. 'You know, life rarely looks like we expect it to; love isn't always the way it ought to be. I admired Pétros for staying on the island when he'd been made so unwelcome in his birthplace and perhaps that's what made me love him. I'm no fool, I knew it would never be reciprocated.' She'd broken off as her eyes travelled up the trunk of the tree before continuing. 'It was not my choice, but I am grateful because I knew what love was supposed to feel like. I felt it here, and it was true.' Mrs Rálli had pressed her heart like it might fall out from her chest. Kat admired her devotion in accepting an unrequited life. 'I also see that you had a great love with Andreas, but you allowed him to leave. I don't want you to waste your time: none of us know how much is left. As for a seat at your table, I accept, but, please, you must let *me* cook!' Kat had laughed in relief, though Mrs Rálli's words about love gripped her.

'We will honour my uncle properly when the patio is re-laid. And I'm sorry I didn't speak to you sooner about his ashes. I didn't know how.'

Mrs Rálli, who was even smaller than Kat, had gazed up squinting in the sunlight with eyes that had swum with emotion.

'You have had much pain, Katerína. To lose a brother in such tragedy, and your uncle too – is a great deal to process. And then Andreas, though that love is not yet lost; I feel it in here.' She'd ferociously clutched her fist again to her chest. Kat had realised there was no escape from opinions about her life. But from now on she would choose her own path, no longer to be steamrolled by the forceful folks around her. There was a beauty in realising she had the freedom to make her own choices and her own mistakes. She finally felt like a grown-up, which was as terrifying as it was liberating.

As her mind returned to the present, cycling through the cool forest, she still felt uneasy about the picnic. Although Jamie was in jovial spirits, she had a creeping dread that at some stage she'd have to disappoint him. Yet more unrequited feelings.

Jamie paused ahead putting a foot on the ground to steady himself and opened his phone as Kat pulled up alongside him.

'How much further?' she asked.

'Just checking the location. Not far. Off we go!'

'Hang on, I'm thirsty,' Kat said opening the picnic hamper strapped to the back of Jamie's bike and finding only two small bottles of water. She wasn't a culinary expert, but this was a poor excuse for a lunch.

'Where's all the food?' she asked with increasing suspicion that he'd lured her under false pretences.

He tapped the side of his nose before cycling on. 'That's for me to know and you to find out. Come on, Kat!'

* * *

They arrived at a clearing on the edge of a hill, beyond which the sparkling sea stretched like a length of blue satin. Kat was surprised to see Lizzie standing beside a blanket, her bike propped against a tree trunk. Maybe she had the picnic, Kat thought dismounting. She looked from one to the other.

'What's going on?' she asked apprehensively.

Lizzie gestured to the throw on the ground. 'You better sit down, Kat.'

'I'm fine where I am, thank you.'

Lizzie went to stand beside Jamie and Kat's mind started to race. *They're going to announce they're a couple,* she thought, and surprised herself as she felt something akin to excitement.

'Right,' Lizzie began looking at Jamie. 'We need to tell you something.'

Here it comes . . .

Jamie took up the mantle. 'Lizzie told me all about Chrístos and his account of Andreas and your uncle's car. There was something that didn't quite sit right with us, well, Lizzie actually.' He yielded the floor to Lizzie who brandished her phone and consulted her notes.

'It made no sense that if Andreas nicked his car and had been drunk, Pétros would take him in instead of calling the police. Especially if they'd all been terrorising him for so long. So, I did some sleuthing and found two of the other boys from their gang here on the island. They're men now obviously, and one of them is actually rather gorgeous.' Jamie tutted at her, but she pressed on. 'It's all here, I've been documenting this for ages. I was planning to write about Andreas at first, but the story took a rather interesting turn.'

Kat was astonished at the level of intrusion her friends were capable of, but she allowed them to continue, beginning to feel like she was in some kind of juvenile detective cartoon.

'We met with them both separately yesterday,' said Jamie who began to pace the woods like a lawyer giving an opening address. 'And asked for their accounts of what happened, under the premise that it was research for a piece Lizzie was doing. They were only too happy to talk after an ouzo or four.'

'Wh . . . what did you find out?' asked Kat, unsure if she wanted further confirmation that Andreas had lied.

'Well,' said Lizzie, her eyes flashing in the dappled light. 'As it transpires, Chrístos was kind of the leader of their group. It's over, by the way, between me and him. Anyway, that day in question, he'd got hold of a load of brandy and drunk most of it. He'd suggested they should steal Pétros' car but Andreas tried to stop him. After the car crashed into the wall, the other boys all ran off and Andreas stayed to take the blame. He insisted on saying it was him who was driving and that was the story all the boys stuck to. In the same way that if you tell yourself a lie often enough, you begin to believe it's a fact. But Pétros had seen the whole thing, which is why he took pity on Andreas. Don't you see, Kat? Andreas was just trying to belong and didn't want to betray his friends or be a snitch. As he said himself, Chrístos had protected him once from a bully and he felt like he owed him the same loyalty. This was Andreas repaying the favour. He wasn't the one who drove the car drunk. Andreas was trying to be a good friend and save Chrístos from getting into trouble, but he did nothing wrong. It was Chrístos behind the wheel all along. Andreas is innocent!'

Lizzie and Jamie nodded at each other, obviously delighted with their investigative work. Kat was stunned.

'But . . . but why didn't Andreas say? I don't understand why he'd take the blame for something so awful and why Chrístos would make it all up, saying it was Andreas and not him who was drunk and stole the car?'

'Because apart from the misplaced loyalty on Andreas' part, Christos is jealous,' said Jamie. 'Jealous of a guy who is kind, successful, irritatingly good-looking and talented . . . Need I go on? I was envious of Andreas the second I met him, so those boys would have felt the same, I'm sure. And now he's a star and Christos has been left behind. He's just a teenage brute in a grown man's body who allowed everyone to believe the lie back then and is still repeating it. Maybe he wanted to make himself look good for Lizzie. But it's all been a horrible mix-up.'

'That's the problem with only getting half a story: it never quite adds up to the whole,' said Lizzie putting her phone back in her pocket.

Kat sunk onto the blanket, horrified at her mistake. 'What have I done?' she said, her throat constricting with emotion. 'I've ruined everything with Andreas for nothing. I'm such an idiot, so hung up about drink-driving that I didn't give him the chance to explain. He was the only good thing to happen to me for years – sorry, Jamie, no offence.'

'None taken, as usual. What I said to you yesterday about second chances, what do you reckon?'

Her head shot up to look at him; surely he wasn't talking again about their marriage.

'I . . . Jamie, look, you and I aren't ever going to . . .'

Jamie guffawed so loudly, his skin reddened with the effort. 'Not me and you, Kat, for God's sake! That ship has long since sailed. I wish you'd get the right end of the stick for once. You and Andreas.'

'I don't think I can. He's still in London, I think, and he would never . . .' She stopped speaking as Lizzie suddenly grinned and gestured to a path with a series of steps leading down to Dragonéra beach. She pulled Kat up from the ground and nudged her forwards.

'Never say never, Kat.'

Kat's knees trembled as she stood at the top. The flight of steps curved around into the trees, and she gripped the length of frayed rope acting as a poor excuse for a banister.

As she rounded the final corner, the spectacular view was revealed making her breath catch: it was unspoiled and stunning. The small, secluded bay of golden sand was surrounded by turquoise waters and pines as far as the eye could see. There was nobody around. But still she couldn't work out why her friends made her come here. Until a figure emerged onto the sand from the woods at the far end of the shore, unmistakably dressed from head to toe in linen.

Chapter 44

Kat's legs almost gave way as she stepped down onto the beach. It felt like she was trying to walk across dense layers of cotton wool and could hardly locate her feet as she made painfully slow progress. She had no idea what to say and even if she did, her mouth was as dry as the sand underfoot. Finally, after walking the distance, which seemed to take an age but was surely only a handful of seconds, they met in the middle beside the tideline.

The sight of him connected straight to her heart and the feelings she'd tried to suppress rose to the surface. He seemed taller, that or she'd shrunk from the weight of heartache since they parted over a week ago, which already felt like a decade of misery.

'I . . .' they both began at the same time and laughed nervously, breaking the initial tension. But as their smiles faded, the strain returned.

'You first,' he said, but she didn't know where to begin. She mentally scrolled through all the trials and secrets she'd uncovered since arriving on Agístri, searching for a starting point.

'Pétros is under the patio,' she blurted, and he seemed taken aback.

'What?' he said.

'Yes, under the loose tile where the cat sleeps. That's why nobody knew where he was buried. Mrs Rálli was bound to silence. He's been there all along.'

Andreas shook his head. 'That house has so many secrets and sorrow. But . . .' He paused as he stepped closer until she was painted with his shadow. She was desperate for his touch; her fingers burnt to be this near without contact, but she couldn't read his expression. It had been like that since they'd met. 'We had the chance, Katerína, to make new, happy memories in your home. And then you took it away. You wouldn't listen to me or give me the benefit of the doubt. I took responsibility for someone else's mistake many years ago. And if you'd let me explain, you would have known the truth.'

He was going to end it for good, she thought. It was all her doing for being bloody-minded, so furious at everyone trying to protect her for so long that she'd refused to hear him, allowing her moral compass to condemn without facts.

'Andreas, please. You have no idea how sorry I am.' Her cheeks heated with shame from her mistake. 'It's my biggest trigger, drinking and driving – you know that about me. I saw red and didn't give you a chance, I know.'

Although he was in front of her, it felt like he was miles away, as if he'd already emotionally retreated from what they'd been building. Her father's words from the store on Aegina flashed in her memory: '. . . *something is only yours if you build it, if you didn't build it, it is not yours.*'

But they *had* been building something special together, with magical feelings she'd never thought possible. And Kat wanted to fight for it. She didn't want to lose him, though feared she'd already pushed him too far away. She wouldn't blame Andreas if he left Agístri for Hollywood to become the shining star he seemed destined to become and she'd be a distant memory, barely a whisper.

His voice cut through her thoughts. 'I used to admire the way you'd always say what you think, but this one time at the most important moment, your reasoning was wrong.' Kat couldn't look at him as he spoke. 'Lizzie called me and told me everything, Katerína, about the misunderstanding and what Chrístos had told her.' He muttered the only Greek swear word she knew, and she wholeheartedly agreed. A glimmer of optimism rose in her heart but still she couldn't meet his eyes; it was too painful. 'She felt terrible about telling you what she thought was the truth at the time and orchestrated bringing us together today along with Jamie. But I'm so hurt too. I thought you knew better than to believe a stranger over me.'

Kat was mortified but still an ounce of hope remained. He had gone along with her friends' scheme, so she must mean something to him. Or maybe he wanted a definitive finale; cut, roll credits, the end, with no sequel planned in the future.

'What are you thinking, Katerína? For once I don't know. You say very little or give me any idea about what you feel,' he said steadily. She felt the intensity beneath his words, though still had no clue as to his feelings. He had softened during the time they'd spent together, opening up, even trusting her, but she had forced him to return to the guarded version he used to be; the one she'd first met at the airport. His heart was closed; she was too late to make amends.

She continued to study the beach beneath her feet, the countless minuscule specks of colour that joined to form one golden blanket.

'If you really want to know what I'm thinking then I'll tell you, as corny as it is.' She lifted her head and bravely looked into his beautiful eyes, the same colour of the sea that surrounded them, as her own filled with tears. 'There are ten thousand stars for every grain of sand on earth, but there is only one star that I want.' She longed for him to speak. He put his hands in his pockets and the prolonged silence was torture.

Finally, Andreas found his voice. 'You know, your father's love of philosophy inspired me, and I found this quote that kind of sums us up: *"Opinion is the wilderness between knowledge and ignorance".*' She couldn't help but smile at his words as she searched his eyes for an indication of his perspective, absorbing the weight of his stare. 'You've become so used to secrets that you've forgotten what the truth feels like. I am the most open book you will find when I trust someone. And before all this happened, I believed in you, Katerína, and in us. I thought you'd never hurt me, but you did.' His hand pressed against his heart. 'Ask me anything you want, and I will answer you with complete honesty if only to prove that I don't lie. I haven't and wouldn't, for what it is still worth,' he said shrugging his shoulders.

It was a bullet to the gut. She had nobody to blame but herself for all that had transpired with Andreas. Everything that had happened to her on Agístri had been about uncovering lies and secrets about the past. But she'd foolishly believed the one untruth that affected her future happiness, and it was a crushing lesson to be forced to learn.

Though it seemed like a lost cause, she dug into her strength and asked the question she still needed the answer to. It could help her put this heartbreak behind her once and for all. Or turn out to be an agony she'd have to endure forever. Either way, she had to know.

'What were you going to say to me in the taverna the night I smashed up the kitchen?'

He laughed but looked out towards the water as if he didn't want to respond. But he had promised, and he'd always said he wouldn't break a promise. He eventually returned his eyes to hers. 'First, Katerína, will you allow yourself to follow your heart?'

She nodded, as he matched the sentiment of Nik's words to her before he died. 'Always,' she whispered. She had nothing else to lose, though her pulse accelerated in expectation of his answer.

'What I was going to say is still true, in fact I know it as sure as there are stars in the sky and sand beneath our feet.' His hand reached for her cheek, landing with the sweetest touch she'd ever felt. 'I didn't get to say it in the taverna, but now I will say it to you a thousand times over, Katerína, in every language I can speak. *Agápi mou . . . s'agapó*. My love . . . I love you.'

Artemis & Apollo

The philosophies of the ancients resonated with gods and mortals alike, within reason, as gods chose what morality suited them often without conscience. But ignorance was said to be the greatest of evils and clarity the sole path from misery. As Socrates wrote, it is better to suffer an injustice than to commit one.

Chapter 45

Three days later

Kat placed a cobalt blue bowl piled high with freshly picked lemons on the new pale quartz kitchen island, the centrepiece she'd imagined when she first walked into the house.

Mrs Rálli and Kat's mother had been cooking a feast all morning that could feed several hundred, not just their intimate gathering. The white walls and warm wooden beams overhead created the perfect blank canvas for the navy cabinetry. Splashes of yellow from the linen blinds, artwork and upholstery on the padded seating nook brought the colour scheme together.

Kat wanted to twirl around the kitchen and hug everything, which wasn't just about décor. The past few days had been like the most exquisite recurring dream. She and Andreas had rediscovered each other all over again and Kat wanted to collect each moment with him and make a memory within every second. She couldn't hear him say 'I love you' enough. He'd uttered it between their kisses, amid his touch and with his body. She'd never felt so alive.

The constant toll of grief that had marked her days for so many months, had shifted. It was as if a lead weight had been extracted from the depths of her heart because she had finally made her own choices about the house, her life and her heart.

'Ladies, please! The grill is lit, and I am ready to barbecue, but you three are holding me up,' her father said suddenly appearing in the kitchen brandishing a spatula, which he waved individually at her mother, Mrs Rálli before finally pointing at Kat. 'Keeping a man from his lunch is the very worst crime. As Winston Churchill once said, *"We will not say that Greeks fight like heroes, but that heroes fight like Greeks."* Do not, please, make me go to war with women for lamb chops! You will all lose!'

'Two minutes, *Babá*!' Kat said. For a housewarming present, Andreas had generously bought her a state-of-the-art outdoor grill, which thrilled Giórgios and he'd taken immediate charge. This was her parents', Lizzie's and Jamie's last day on Agístri and there was much to celebrate and commemorate.

Mrs Rálli opened the oven.

'Not yet! Is not ready,' her mother shouted shrilly. Why she needed to speak at full volume as if she was back in Zorba's Kitchen, Kat had no idea. But the two women were fun to watch, the push-pull of their jousting for position over the shiny new stove and double oven was highly amusing.

'Mína, it is ready. I know what I am doing,' said Mrs Rálli defiantly removing the baking tin with a flourish.

'You say this and yet, I cannot smell the sweetness, which is how *I* know when it is done. And my baking is always perfection.'

Mrs Rálli adjusted the steaming tray on the island trivet

and poured the cooled lemony syrup she'd made earlier onto the cake before looking at Mína defiantly.

'I've been making *lemonópita* my whole life. Katerína said it was the best she'd had.'

Mína rounded on Kat with a thunderous look, hands on hips. 'The best? You say is the best you've ever had!? Did you say this, Katerína?'

Kat held her hands up. 'Don't involve me. I'm off to get dressed. It's only a cake.'

She heard their exasperation as she left, catching her mother saying, 'This child says "only a cake". Why would she wish to hurt me so . . .'

Kat went upstairs to her room grinning. The baking wars with Mrs Rálli were one of the things she'd miss when her mother left. But her parents would soon return having promoted Cousin Eléni to run their restaurant. They'd found that being away from work had given them a new zest for their marriage, and also for Greece. Kat was grateful their grief hadn't pulled them apart. It had, in fact, glued them together.

Sitting on her bed, she moved the glossy magazine aside that featured Lizzie's exclusive, in-depth interview with Andreas. The cover was the photograph Nik had taken of him, and it was beautiful to see it out in the world on news-stands. Her twin would have been so proud, and Kat felt it on Nik's behalf. She then reread the printout of the countersigned publishing contract on her bedside table and squealed aloud in delight. She would stay on the island to continue her usual monthly column for *Love Interiors* but more thrillingly she'd begin writing her first book. For the first time, she could refer to herself a writer without feeling like a pretender.

During her time on Agístri, so much had changed. When it had felt like most things were ending, she couldn't have envisaged such a series of beginnings.

Everyone was already dressed in their finery and Kat needed to change – helping out in the kitchen would have ruined what she planned to wear. She slipped the pristine dress over her head and clipped her hair up in a messy bun. Not perfect, but she would have to do.

A knock at the door made her tut, expecting it to be her father harassing her again to lunch.

'Come in!' she said, still checking her appearance in the mirror. Reflected in the glass was Andreas standing in the doorway, his mouth open in shock. She gave him a twirl. 'You like?'

He moved towards her looking her up and down. She could feel how much he desired her, but it was so much more than that.

'You have never looked more beautiful, Katerína *mou*. My Katerína. I don't just like, I love. *Eísai polí ómorfi.* You are beautiful,' he said as he reached around her waist pulling her towards him. 'I love you, I love the dress but I would love to take it off you right now.' He started to kiss her neck, along her exposed collarbone and her resolve began to disperse.

'Andreas, please do try to control yourself. We have guests.' She teased with faux coyness. 'I didn't get to wear this when I was supposed to, and I'd like to try not to ruin it for at least ten minutes.' It was the white dress meant for his film premiere. He'd bought the gown out of sentimentality, never expecting to see it on her following their break-up. She kissed him with tantalising featherlight brushes, and he groaned.

'Later,' she promised, straightening the collar of his white linen shirt. 'I love you, Mr Linen.' She kissed him again. 'Come on, let's eat, then say a proper goodbye to Pétros and to Nik again. All of us, together.'

* * *

Following a blissfully languid lunch with her parents, Mrs Rálli, Andreas, Jamie and Lizzie, Kat wanted a moment alone before their special ceremony. She was full not only from the staggering amount of food, but also from being surrounded by such affection. Her heart brimmed, satiated with love, though Nik would always be missing. She needed to find a way to get used to that, as much as she ever could.

Taking the red evil eye with her down to the beach, Kat stood on the sand looking out at the sunset. She clasped the *máti* in both of her hands almost in offering to the sun, as the collision of pastel hues in the sky blended with the sea like a painting. In the daytime, Greece was so sharp and vibrant, but as it slowly surrendered to night, it became softer around the edges and for her, the most beautiful.

'*Kalispéra*, Katerína,' called Father Serafím from the road. 'What a fine dress. It looks like it's your wedding day. Congratulations!' He'd said what her mother had declared as Kat appeared with Andreas before lunch. Mína had promptly burst into tears at 'the happy couple' and taken several photographs. Kat feared for her old wedding picture with Jamie on the sideboard at her parents' house. It would likely be consigned to the back row for good.

'No wedding,' she said laughing. 'Although my family would love it to be, I'm learning to never say never, Father Serafím.'

The old man hummed in approval at her words. 'When we yield to matters of the heart, there is strength in vulnerability. It is a brave person who finds there is no weakness in admitting they need help. Even the wisest warrior requires an army of support.'

Kat appreciated all he had taught her since she arrived on Agístri. He'd been a guiding light, appearing whenever she needed him, offering the perfect piece of advice at precisely the right time.

'You remember you said to me when we first met that what I might be looking for could be right in front of me.'

'Ah! You recall,' he said stroking his beard.

'Well, you weren't entirely correct.'

He frowned. 'Oh?'

'Yes, some were right under my nose, but I also found something rather important and quite surprising next door.'

He laughed. 'I am old, what can I tell you? Though the directions may be inaccurate, my guidance, perhaps, led you to find more than you bargained for. Remember, the decisions you make in the moment are the ones that will lead you on your path. There is no map for life, only what you know in your heart, Katerína. When you follow it, that is where you are meant to be.'

Kat looked at the water again, now tinted a rich burnished gold, like an endless altar, glinting as far as the eye could see. Squeezing the evil eye in her hand, she was moved by his counsel.

'Father, do you have time to join us . . .' She turned back to him as she spoke, but he had gone. Looking left, then right, there was no sign of him. How strange, it was like he'd evaporated into the air. Perhaps he'd lived in her imagination all along and hadn't ever been here at all. She laughed at her absurd thought. Turning, she headed back to the house to say goodbye to the past, hand in hand with her family, friends and the man she loved.

* * *

Andreas and Jamie held the final patio tile between them. Those gathered surrounded the gaping space in the terrace beneath the lemon tree, which was illuminated with fairy lights. Patch had crept across the lawn to observe, giving a high-pitched mew to announce his presence.

Mrs Rálli knelt down and carefully set the little wooden casket containing Pétros' ashes back into the ground. She crossed herself as she sat back on her heels. Mína then helped her up and embraced her before adding a bunch of white wildflowers, an icon of a saint along with Pétros' novel dedicated to Nik in the earth. Kat in turn placed the red evil eye beside the wooden box.

'*Look after all of us,*' she said silently as the little red disc nestled into the ground.

After their assembled party sprinkled a handful of dirt over the ashes, one at a time, Jamie and Andreas positioned the large missing tile, closing the gap. The new matt grey flagstones spread the length of the patio and circled the ancient trunk of the lemon tree. But this last tile had a handmade mosaic, the one that Kat had sketched during her first morning on Agístri weeks ago. Made from the scores of pink pebbles she'd collected as they'd appeared, it depicted the sun and the moon around a hunter's bow; a blend of her and Nik's tattoos. It was better than she'd imagined, especially tonight, under the full moon that had now risen high in the sky above the garden, illuminating their gathering.

Giórgios took Mína's hand who then reached for Kat's and the chain continued, with Andreas, Mrs Rálli, Jamie then Lizzie. An unbreakable emotional circle to honour the two men that had united them all in grief, dispelled their secrets and ultimately joined them in every kind of love: maternal, paternal, platonic and romantic.

As the moon continued to ascend painting the world a liquid silver, Kat stared upwards feeling the pull of its invisible threads. Just as it rose, so it would set, allowing the tide to recede, preparing the way for a new dawn. The certainty of the sun and moon would endure for the unborn ages yet to come. The opposing twins that lit the hours of both day and night, would outlive them all. Shifting what once was new to old, igniting turmoil that would yield to forgiveness, but ultimately bringing hope and endless possibility.

Kat turned to Andreas. He looked at her with a love that was matched in the deepest part of her soul. She smiled as Patch nuzzled her legs, vying for attention, then he too looked up at the moon, seemingly absorbing its serenity before settling down to stand sentry over the newly positioned tile. Tears clouded her vision and Andreas put his arms around her.

She felt like she was home. But a home wasn't only bricks, or a building, mortar and plaster, it was a feeling that Kat had found in the most unexpected of places. And grief is simply love that is missing its target; heartbreak cannot exist without the richest of unfathomable feelings. What Kat had learnt above all since she'd arrived in Greece was that everybody made mistakes and deserved a second chance.

And she'd found forgiveness. Perhaps the hardest lessons were such because they were the most important. Nik, her darling brother, would always be the unfilled gap in her life and there was no way to avoid that immense sense of loss; she couldn't alter what had happened, she could only try to carry the weight of his death a little lighter each day, though it would never completely disappear. But wherever she was in the world, he'd live forever in her heart, on the air that wrapped around her, existing side by side the way they had when they first came to be in this life. Eternally joined, never to be parted, the sun and the moon, under the lemon tree.

'Night, night, moonlight,' she whispered.

Recipe Page

I adore the messages I receive from readers asking about the recipes for dishes I mention in my novels – I am only too happy to comply! Spreading word about the much underestimated Greek cuisine is a calling and I'm delighted to be an evangelist for food! *Lemonópita* is a key cake in both life and in *Under the Lemon Tree*, so it seems only fair that I enlist the very best to help you recreate a piece of Greece in your own kitchen! Ákis Petretzíkis is the most wonderful Greek chef and he has generously given me his brilliant recipe for this heavenly sweet treat to share with you all! Follow him on social or check out his website – you won't regret it! Bake to your heart's content and don't forget to tag me @emmacowellauthor and @akis_petretzikis in your pictures on Instagram before you tuck in! *Kalí órexi!*

Lemonópita: Greek lemon phyllo pie

Ingredients

For the syrup

700 g granulated sugar
550 g water
50 g lemon juice
Peel of 3 lemons
1 stick of cinnamon

For the lemon pie

200 g strained yoghurt
Juice of 1 lemon
200 g sunflower oil
200 g granulated sugar
½ tsp vanilla powder
4 medium-sized eggs
Zest of 1 lemon
20 g baking powder
1 pinch of salt
450 g phyllo (filo) dough sheets
1 tbsp sunflower oil, to grease the pan

To serve

Vanilla ice cream
Mint leaves

Method

For the syrup

1. In a medium-sized pot add the sugar, water, lemon juice and peels and cinnamon stick, and place it over high heat.
2. Allow the mixture to come to a boil until the sugar is completely dissolved.
3. Remove the pot from the heat and set the syrup aside to cool.

For the lemon pie

1. Preheat the oven to 170°C (340° F) and set to fan.
2. Put the yoghurt and the lemon juice into a large bowl and whisk them well.
3. Add the sunflower oil, sugar, vanilla powder, eggs, lemon zest, baking powder and salt, and whisk them very well.
4. Cut the phyllo sheets into thin strips and spread them out with your hands to prevent them from sticking together.
5. Add ⅓ of the phyllo strips into the bowl with the rest of the ingredients and mix with a serving spoon.
6. Follow the same process for all the phyllo sheets.
7. Grease a 25x32 cm rectangular baking pan, spread the whole mixture in it, and bake the lemon phyllo pie in the oven for 40 minutes.
8. Remove the pan from the oven and pour the cold syrup over the hot pie, using a ladle.
9. Set the pie aside until it cools and absorbs all the syrup, for about 30 minutes.
10. Cut the pie into pieces, serve it with vanilla ice cream, and garnish with mint leaves.

Acknowledgements

When I first went to Agístri, I was writing *The Island Love Song*. It was somewhere new to explore before returning to Hydra where I'd set that third novel. But as with Hydra, Agístri stuck with me along with its neighbour, Aegina, and I knew I had to set a book there. Visiting in early May when it was quiet gave me a glimpse of authentic island life. The people I met and of course the food I tasted inspired me hugely. Our hostess, Maria in Mylí, cooked a barbecue one night under the light of a full moon using the fish she and her husband had caught that day. The scent of grilled food drifted up to the heavens and out to sea. Even the local priest stopped by to take a break from his rounds. You see how everything creeps beneath the skin of a writer and emerges at some point in a story? Although the house, the one next door and the lemon tree are fictional, most of the places in the novel are real and Agístri is yet another corner of Greece that has captured my heart!

Thank you to all my Greek friends for answering my annoying language queries, for sharing your families and culture with me, especially Katerína and Vasilis, a fabulous husband and wife duo who unknowingly gave me so many nuggets of wisdom including the Tupperware line and named Father Serafím and Pétros! And thank you to the brilliantly talented Ákis Petretzíkis for generously allowing me to share his delicious *lemonópita* recipe with you all.

Twins are fascinating and having totted up those I've known there are seven sets encountered so far, which seems a lot! The twins still in my life, thank you: dearest friends Sarah and Emma, my most excellent cousins Rachel and Rebecca, the exquisitely mischievous Cosima and Apollo, and my beautiful godchildren Tristan and Patrick.

I want to say a huge thank you to you, lovely reader, bloggers, fellow authors and the online book gang. I've said it before, but it is worth repeating that it is a great honour to be published, but an even greater honour to be read. And this book wouldn't be possible without you and your continued incredible support.

Which leads me on to Team Avon at HarperCollins. Thank you every single one of you for your unswerving enthusiasm. It has been so much fun working with you, Rachel Hart, my fabulous editor. You've given me so much, yet I've only given you the gift of a limoncello spritz, which seems way out of balance! And thank you, *efharistó polí*, to Sophie Antonellis for Greek checking my miserable attempts at your beautiful language.

Kate Burke, my agent and spirit animal and all the team at Blake Friedmann, thank you for all you do, and for convincing publishers around the world to translate my writing!

To my friends and family, it's not possible to do this without your encouragement, love and cheerleading. Especially my father, Martin, for his wisdom and humour and to my brother, David, I love you so very much. Darling Mama, I wish you were here to celebrate all of this with me.

During the writing of this story, we lost our beautiful fur baby Papoushka Gerald Cowell. She was a magnificent cat who reached the grand age of twenty and used up all of her lives and found a few bonus ones. I wanted to lean into the mad cat lady writer persona and have a four-legged friend in the story, to stand sentry, protecting those around it. That's what Papoushka did for me, guarding my heart in hard times and good, tapping me awake with her paw in the wee small hours to remind me of a deadline, and rewarding me with unsolicited gifts of decapitated animals. I miss you so much, my furry serial killing supermodel.

And finally, my first reader TC; my benchmark for love. Thank you for believing in me and my writing. Here's to many more Grecian odysseys together!

Will walking in her mother's footsteps help Sophie discover who she was meant to be all along . . . ?

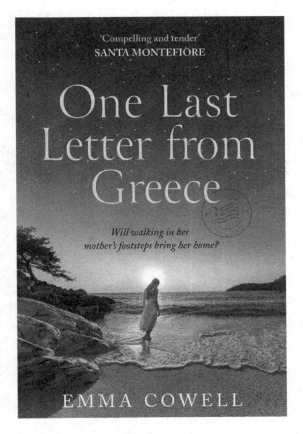

The breathtaking, escapist debut novel from Emma Cowell.

Will one week in Greece change their lives for ever?

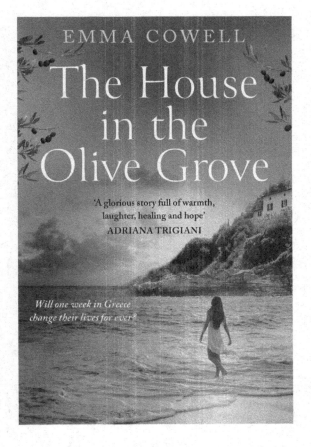

The second sweeping, emotional, romantic escape from Emma Cowell.

**Two sisters. Decades of secrets.
And a love song that changed everything.**

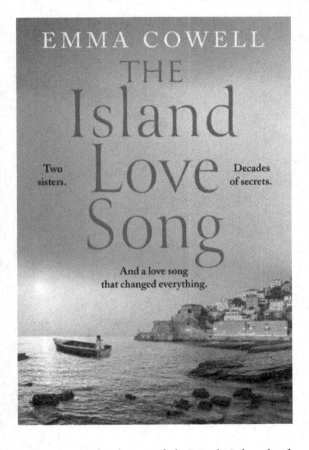

Escape to the beautiful Greek Island of Hydra with this moving novel, filled with family secrets and romance.